PUFF

SWALLOWS
FOR EVER

ARTHUR RANSOME

Ever since their unforgettable holiday with the Swallows and Amazons, Dick and Dorothea had both longed to be able to sail. So when their mother's old friend Mrs Barrable invites them to stay on her yacht, it seems too good a chance to miss. However, when they reach the *Teasel*, they are horrified to discover that Mrs Barrable has no intention of sailing anywhere at all!

The whole holiday seems to be in ruins, until a chance encounter with Tom Dudgeon, a local boy with years of sailing behind him, brings a hope that not all is lost. Tom is a member of the Coot Club, which is dedicated to the preservation of the wildfowl nesting in the Norfolk Broads, and spends a lot of his time, with the other members – the young crew of the *Death and Glory* and the twins, Port and Starboard - watching and marking all the local nests. The day Dick and Dorothea arrive, Tom becomes involved in a nasty incident with some noisy tourists on a motor cruiser, simply by trying to save a nesting coot, and plunges everybody, Dick and Dorothea included, into the most exciting adventure they have ever had.

Arthur Ransome's much-loved adventures on the Norfolk Broads, *Coot Club* and *The Big Six*, have been carefully and sympathetically abridged and appear together for the first time in one volume. They bring the wonderful scenery, the delights of watching birds in their natural habitats, and the pure joy of sailing to a new and appreciative generation of readers.

SWALLOWS
AND
AMAZONS
FOR EVER

ARTHUR RANSOME

PUFFIN BOOKS

Puffin Books, Penguin Books Ltd, Harmondsworth, Middlesex, England
Penguin Books, 40 West 23rd Street, New York, New York 10010, U.S.A.
Penguin Books Australia Ltd, Ringwood, Victoria, Australia
Penguin Books Canada Ltd, 2801 John Street, Markham, Ontario, Canada L3R 1B4
Penguin Books (N.Z.) Ltd, 182–190 Wairau Road, Auckland 10, New Zealand

First published as two books, *Coot Club* and *The Big Six*
Coot Club first published by Jonathan Cape 1934
Published in Puffin Books 1969
Copyright © the Estate of Arthur Ransome, 1934

The Big Six first published by Jonathan Cape 1940
Published in Puffin Books 1970
Copyright © the Estate of Arthur Ransome, 1940

This abridged edition first published in Puffin Books 1983
Copyright © the Estate of Arthur Ransome, 1983
All rights reserved

Made and printed in Great Britain by
Richard Clay (The Chaucer Press) Ltd, Bungay, Suffolk
Filmset in 10/12 Monophoto Baskerville by
Northumberland Press Ltd, Gateshead

CONTENTS

CONTENTS

CHAPTER I

JUST IN TIME

Thorpe Station at Norwich is a terminus. Trains from the middle of England and the south run in there, and if they are going on east and north by way of Wroxham, they run out of the station by the same way they ran in. Dick and Dorothea Callum had never been in Norfolk before, and for ten minutes they had been waiting in that station, sitting in the train, for fear it should go on again at once, as it had at Ipswich and Colchester and the few other stations at which it had stopped. The journey was nearly over. They had only a few more miles to go, but Dorothea, whose mind was always busy with scenes that might do for the books she meant to write, was full of the thought of how dreadful it would be if old Mrs Barrable, with whom they were going to stay, should be waiting on Wroxham Station and the train should arrive without them. So Dick and she had wasted ten whole minutes sitting in the carriage, looking out of the open window at the almost empty platform.

A whistle blew, and the guard waved a green flag.

'Bring your head in now, Dick,' said Dorothea, 'and close the window.'

But before Dick had time to pull the window up, they saw a boy come hurrying along the platform. He was heavily laden, with a paper parcel which he was hugging to himself so as to have that hand free for a large can of paint, while on the other arm he had slung a coil of new rope. He was hurrying along beside the train, looking into the windows of the carriages as if he were searching for someone he knew. And Dorothea noticed that, though it was a fine, dry spring day, he was wearing a pair of rubber knee-boots.

'He'll miss it if he doesn't get in,' said Dick.

'Hurry up, there, if you're going,' a porter shouted and at that moment, just after he had passed their window, the boy stumbled over a rope's end that had fallen from his coil. Down he went. His tin of paint rolled on towards the edge of the platform. His parcel burst its paper. Some blocks and shackles flew out.

The train had begun to move. A porter far down the platform was running towards the boy, who had jumped up again almost as if he had bounced, had grabbed his blocks and crammed them in his pockets, and had stopped the escaping paint-tin with his foot just before it rolled between the platform and the train. In another moment he had the tin in his arms and was running beside the carriage.

'Don't try that now,' shouted a ticket inspector.

'Wait for the next,' shouted the porter, who was running after the boy.

'Heads!' called the boy.

The next moment the paint-can came flying through the open window between Dick and Dorothea. The coil of rope whirled round and shot in after it. The door was opened and the boy flung himself in head-first and landed on all fours.

Dorothea pulled the door to. Dick said: 'They always like it shut,' and reached out and closed the handle.

The porter, left far behind, stopped running.

'Just in time,' said the boy. 'I didn't want to miss it. Lucky for me you had your window open.'

'Haven't you hurt yourself?' said Dorothea.

'Not I,' said the boy, dusting his hands together, hands that looked so capable and hard-worked that Dick, at the sight of them, wanted to hide his own.

The train was running close beside the river, and they saw

a steamer going down from Norwich. They crossed a bridge, and there was a river on both sides of the line, the old river on the left curving round by the village of Thorpe with crowds of yachts and motorboats tied up under the gardens, and, on the right, a straight ugly cutting. In another minute they had crossed the old river again, and the train was slowing up at a station. Close by, across a meadow, they could see a great curve of the river, and three or four houseboats moored to the bank, and a small yacht working her way up.

'Interested in boats?' said the boy, as the others hurried across the carriage.

'Yes, very much,' said Dorothea. 'Last holidays we were in a houseboat frozen in the ice.'

'They're always getting frozen in, houseboats,' said the boy. 'Done much sailing?'

'We haven't done any at all,' said Dick. 'Not yet.'

'Except just once, on the ice, in a sledge,' said Dorothea.

'It wasn't really sailing,' said Dick. 'Just blowing along.'

'You'll get lots of sailing at Wroxham,' said the boy, looking up at the big black and white labels on the two small suitcases.

'We're going to live in a boat,' said Dorothea. 'She isn't at Wroxham. She's somewhere down the river.'

'What's her name?' said the boy, 'I know most of them.'

'We don't know,' said Dorothea.

'Mine's *Titmouse*. She's a very little one, of course. But she's got an awning. I slept in her last night. And she can sail like anything. This rope is for her. Blocks, too. And the paint. Birthday present. That's why I've been into Norwich.'

Dick and Dorothea looked at the blocks and fingered the silky smoothness of the new rope. It certainly did seem that they had come to the right place to learn about sailing.

Dick and Dorothea had set their hearts on learning, but they had given up all hope of getting any sailing before the summer. And then, half-way through the Easter holidays, the letter from Mrs Barrable had come in the very nick of time. Mrs Barrable, long ago, had been their mother's school-mistress, but she painted pictures and was the sister of a very famous portrait painter. And she had written to Mrs Callum to say that her brother and she had chartered a small yacht on the Norfolk Broads, and that her brother had had to go off to London to paint portraits of some important Indians, so that she was all alone in the boat with her pug-dog William, and that if Dick and Dorothea could be spared she would like to have their company. Everything had been arranged in a couple of days, and here they were, and already, before they had got to Wroxham, they had met this boy who seemed to know about sailing. Things were certainly coming out all right.

'Hullo,' said Dick, soon after they passed Salhouse Station. 'There's a heron. What's he doing on that field where there isn't any water?'

'Frogging,' said the strange boy, and then, suddenly, 'Are you interested in birds, too?'

'Yes,' said Dick. 'But there are lots I've never seen, because of living mostly in a town.'

'You don't collect eggs?' said the boy, looking keenly at Dick.

'I never have,' said Dick.

'Don't you ever begin,' said the boy. 'If you don't collect eggs, it's all right ... you see we've got a Bird Protection Society, not to take eggs, but to watch the birds instead. We know thirty-seven nests this year ...'

'Thirty-seven?' said Dick.

'Just along our reaches ... Horning way ...'

'Our boat's near there,' said Dorothea.

'By the way,' said the boy, 'you didn't see two girls in this train   twins? No? They were in Norwich this morning, but I expect they drove back with their father. Otherwise they'd have come this way. We always do. Going by bus, you don't see anything of the river worth counting.'

'There's a hawk,' said Dick.

'Kestrel,' said the boy, looking at the bird hovering above a little wood. 'Hullo! We'll be there in a minute.'

The train was slowing up. It crossed another river, and for a moment they caught a glimpse of moored houseboats with smoke from their chimneys where people were cooking midday meals, an old mill, and a bridge, and a lot of masts beyond it. And then the train had come to a stop at Wroxham station.

The strange boy was looking warily out of the window.

On the platform he saw an old lady looking up at the carriage windows. He also saw the station-master. He chose his moment and, slipping down from the carriage with his paint-can and coil of rope, was hurrying off to give up his ticket to the collector at the gate. But the station-master was too quick for him.

'Hum,' he said, 'I might have guessed it was you, when they rang me up from Norwich about a boy with a ticket for Wroxham jumping on the train after it had fairly got going. Told me to give you a good talking to. Well, don't you do it again. Not broken any bones this time, I suppose?'

The boy grinned. He and the station-master were very good friends, and he knew that the railway officials in Norwich had not meant him to get off so easily.

'I was on the platform in time,' he said. 'Only I was looking for Port and Starboard, and then I slipped, and the train started, and I simply had to catch that train.'

'Port and Starboard?' said the station-master. 'I saw them go over the road-bridge with Mr Farland more than an hour ago. They'll have had their dinners and be on the river by now . . . Yes, madam. Let me give you a hand.' He was talking now to Mrs Barrable, the old lady, who had just found Dick and Dorothea. The station-master reached up to help Dorothea down with her suitcase.

'Well, and here you are,' said Mrs Barrable, kissing Dorothea and shaking hands with Dick.

'And who was that other boy?' she asked.

'We made friends with him in the train,' said Dorothea. 'He knows a lot about boats.'

'And birds,' said Dick.

Mrs Barrable watched him as he hurried through the gate and down the path to the road. 'Haven't I seen him before?' she said. 'And who are the Port and Starboard he was asking about?'

'That's Tom Dudgeon, the doctor's son from Horning,' said the station-master. 'You'll maybe have seen him on the river in his little boat. He's not often away from the water in the holidays. And Port and Starboard, queer names for a couple of girls ...' But there was the guard, just waiting to start the train, and the station-master never finished his sentence.

'Busy man,' said Mrs Barrable. 'Come along, Dick. Written any more books, Dot? You really have done well in keeping your luggage down. We'll easily find room for these. I've got a boy with a hand-cart to take your things to the river. We're going down by water. Longer but more fun. There's a motor-launch going down to Horning, and the young man says he'll put us aboard. The *Teasel*'s lying a good long way below the village. But we must have something to eat first, and I must get you some boots like those that boy was wearing. You'll want them every time you step ashore.'

CHAPTER 2

DISAPPOINTMENT

Never in all their lives had Dick and Dorothea seen so many boats. Mrs Barrable had taken them shopping at a store that seemed to sell every possible thing for the insides and outsides of sailors. She had taken them to lunch at an inn where everybody was talking about boats at the top of his voice. And now they had gone down to the river to look for the Horning boatman with his motor-launch.

Mrs Barrable saw the boatman waving to them. A minute or two later they were off themselves, in a little motor-launch, purring down Wroxham Reach. In the bows of the launch were the two small suitcases, and the parcels that had been sent down to the river by the people at the village store. Dorothea looked happily at one large, awkward, bulging parcel. Mrs Barrable had bought them cheap oilskins and sou'westers as well as sea-boots. There was no excuse for wearing such things on a fine spring day, with bright sunshine pouring down, but just to look at that bulging parcel made Dorothea feel she was something of a sailor already.

The houses came to an end. Here and there, looking through the trees, Dick and Dorothea caught the flash of water. Through a narrow opening they saw a wide lake with boats sailing in a breeze, although, in the shelter of the trees, the few sailing yachts they had passed had been drifting with hardly enough wind to give them steerage way. A little further down the river they caught a glimpse of another bit of open water. Then again they were moving between thickly wooded banks. Suddenly they heard a noise astern of them, and one of the big motor-cruisers that they had seen at Wroxham came roaring past them, leaving a high angry wash that sent the launch tossing.

'Just like real sea,' said Dorothea, holding on to the gunwale and determined not to be startled.

'They got no call to go so fast,' said the boatman. 'Look at that now. Upset his dinner in the bilge likely.'

The boatman pointed ahead at a little white boat tied to a branch of a tree. It was very much smaller than any yacht they had seen, hardly bigger, in fact, than the dinghies most of the yachts were towing. It had a mast, and an awning had been rigged up over part of it, to make a little shelter for cooking. The wash of the big cruiser racing past sent the little boat leaping up against the overhanging boughs, and a great cloud of smoke poured suddenly out.

'It's Tom Dudgeon,' said Dorothea.

'It's the *Titmouse*,' said Dick. 'There's the name.'

The boatman slowed up the launch for a moment as they went by.

Tom Dudgeon, who had been kneeling on the floor to do his cooking, looked out with a very red face. They saw that he had a frying-pan in his hand.

He nodded to the boatman. 'Bacon fat all over everywhere,' he said. 'Oh, hullo!' he added, seeing Dick and Dorothea.

'Shame that is,' said the boatman as he put on speed again. 'Proper young sailor is Tom Dudgeon. Keeps that little *Titmouse* of his like a new pin.'

'Ah,' said Mrs Barrable. 'Now I dare say you can tell us who are the Port and Starboard he was talking about to the Wroxham station-master . . .'

'The station-master said they were queer names for girls,' added Dorothea.

The boatman laughed. 'Port and Starboard,' he said. 'We all call 'em that. Nobody call 'em anything else. Mr Farland's twins. All but sisters to young Tom, they are, what with Mrs Farland dying when they was babies, and Mrs Dudgeon, the doctor's wife, pretty near bring them up with her boy.'

They left the trees. The river was beginning to be wider, flowing between reed-fringed banks with here and there a willow at the water's edge. A fleet of five little yachts was sailing to meet them, tacking to and fro, like a cloud of butterflies.

'Racing,' said Mrs Barrable.

The boatman looked over his shoulder. 'If it's no hurry, ma'am, I'll pull into the side while they go by.'

'Of course.'

He shut off his engine and let the launch slide close along the bank until he caught hold of a willow branch to hold her steady. Dick caught another.

And then, as the first of the little racing boats flew towards them, spun round, and was off for the opposite bank, the boatman turned to Mrs Barrable.

'There's Port and Starboard, ma'am, if you want to see 'em. Fourth boat. Mr Farland gener'lly do better'n that.'

The second boat shot by and the third. The fourth came sweeping across the river. 'Ready about!' they heard the helmsman call, and the little boat shot up into the wind, with flapping sails, so close to the launch that Dorothea could have reached out and shaken hands with one of the two girls who were working the jib-sheets.

'He've good crew, have Mr Farland,' said the boatman, 'though they don't weigh as much as a man, the two of 'em together.'

'I don't believe they're much bigger than us,' said Dorothea delightedly.

'You'll be seeing 'em again,' said the boatman starting up his engine. 'They'll be going down river past your boat and back again before they finish by the Swan at Horning.'

'Your boat,' he had said. How long now before she and

Dick were pulling ropes like those two girls, and listening for the word from Mrs Barrable at the tiller? Dorothea was planning a story. Why, if only she and Dick could sail like that, almost anything might happen. She looked at Dick. But Dick was busy with his pocket-book. In the winter holidays it had been full of stars, but with the year going on and nights getting shorter, birds had taken the place of stars. Heron, kestrel, coot, water-hen, he had already added to his list of birds seen, and just before meeting those racing boats he had seen a bird with two tufts sticking out from the top of its head, and only its slim neck showing above the water. He had known it at once for a crested grebe.

On and on they went down the river. They were coming now to another village. The launch slowed up. They were passing wooden bungalows and a row of houseboats. The river bent sharply round a corner. There was an old inn at the bend, the Swan. Then there was a staithe* with a couple of yachts tied up to it. Beyond the staithe were big boat-sheds, like those they had seen at Wroxham.

'This is Horning,' said Mrs Barrable.

'Our boat's not far now, is it?' said Dick.

'This is where Tom Dudgeon lives,' said Dorothea, 'and those two girls.'

The river went on bending and curling and twisting, and every other moment they thought they would be seeing their boat.

They came in sight of her at last and did not know her, a neat white yacht, moored against the bank, with an awning spread over cabin and well, as if she were all ready for the night.

'Oh, look, look!' cried Dorothea. But it was not at the yacht that she was looking. Working up the river was an old black

* A staithe in Norfolk is a place where boats moor to take in or discharge cargo: much what a quay is elsewhere.

ship's boat, with a stumpy little mast and a black flag at the masthead. Two small boys were rowing, each with one oar. A third, standing by the tiller, was looking through an enormous ancient telescope at something on the bank. The three small boys had bright coloured handkerchiefs round their heads and middles as turbans and belts. The launch was racing down the river to meet them, and in a moment or two, Dick and Dorothea were reading the name of the boat, *Death and Glory*, not very well painted, in big white letters, on her bows.

'You hardly expected to meet pirates on the Bure, did you?' said Mrs Barrable.

The boatman laughed. The steersman of the *Death and Glory* waved his big telescope as the launch went by, and the boatman waved back. 'Horning boys,' he said over his shoulder. 'Boatbuilders' sons, all three of 'em. Friends o' Port and Starboard an' young Tom Dudgeon.'

But what was happening? The noise of the engine had changed. The launch was swinging round in the river towards that moored yacht. The loose flaps of the yacht's white awning stirred. A fat fawn pug clambered out on the counter and ran, barking, up and down the narrow side-deck.

'It's William!' cried Dorothea.

'Hullo, William!' said Dick.

'Here we are,' said Mrs Barrable. 'Poor old William must be tired of taking care of the *Teasel* all by himself.'

'She's ever so much bigger than she looks,' said Dick.

The parcels and suitcases had all been put aboard, the little dinghy had been tied up astern, the launch had gone, and Dick, who had been standing rather unsteadily on the counter of the yacht, had climbed down into the well to find himself in a comfortable sort of tent, full of light which poured through the white canvas of the awning.

Presently Mrs Barrable lit a Primus stove in the cooking locker in the well and put a kettle on to boil. Dick and

Dorothea were watching the kettle, and Mrs Barrable was in the cabin, putting some paint-brushes to soak, when the noise of water creaming under the forefoot of a boat made them look out just in time to get a second view of the yacht race, as the five little racers sailed by. Port and Starboard and their father were now third.

'They've got time to win yet,' said Mrs Barrable.

Twenty minutes later they saw them again, on their way back up the river. The folding table had been moved into the well, tea had been poured out, and Dick had been sent into the cabin to get William's chocolate-box from the little sideboard, when Dorothea, peeping out from the stern, saw the white sails moving above the reeds. In another moment the boats themselves were in sight, and Dorothea, Mrs Barrable and Dick hurried out on deck.

'They've done it,' cried Dorothea.

'Very nearly,' said Mrs Barrable.

'*Flash*, their boat's called,' said Dick, and *Flash* was second, and the steersman of the leading boat kept looking anxiously over his shoulder.

'Go it, go it!' cried Dorothea, and almost fancied that Port ... or was it Starboard? ... one or other of them, anyway ... smiled at her as the *Flash* foamed by. All five boats were out of sight in no time round the bend of the river above where the *Teasel* was moored.

And then, just after Dick and Dorothea had settled down to enjoy their first tea afloat, suddenly and altogether unexpectedly, the blow fell.

'When are we going to start?' said Dick, asking the question that had been for some time in both their minds. 'I suppose it's too late to do anything tonight.'

'Start?' said Mrs Barrable, puzzled. 'Start what?'

'Sailing,' said Dick.

'But, my dears, we aren't going to sail ... Didn't I explain to your mother? We can't sail the *Teasel* with Brother

Richard away ... I can't sail the *Teasel* by myself ... And you can't, either ... We're only going to use her as a houseboat ...'

There was a moment's dreadful silence. Castles in Spain came tumbling down. It was all a mistake. They were not going to learn sailing after all.

Dorothea made a tremendous effort.

'She'll be a very splendid houseboat,' she said.

'And there are lots of birds to look at,' said Dick.

'My dear children,' said Mrs Barrable. 'I am most dreadfully sorry.'

CHAPTER 3

NUMBER 7

Late in the afternoon Tom Dudgeon came sailing home.

Tom lowered his sail, and tied up the *Titmouse*. Then he went round the house towards the river, and in at the garden door, listening carefully. Asleep, or awake? Awake. He heard a chuckle, and his mother's laugh in the room that these holidays had become the nursery once again.

'Hullo, Mother,' he called, racing upstairs from the hall. 'How's our baby?'

'Our baby?' laughed his mother. 'Whose baby is he, I should like to know? The twins were in at lunch-time, and they seemed to think he was theirs. And your father calls him his. And you call him yours. And he's his mother's own baby all the time. Well, and how was it last night? Very cold? Very uncomfortable? You look all right . . .'

'It just couldn't have been better,' said Tom. 'It wasn't cold a bit in that sleeping-bag. And it wasn't uncomfortable really except for one bone.' He gave a bit of a rub to his right hip-bone which still felt rather bruised. 'Anyway,' he said, 'nobody expects floorboards to be like spring mattresses. And there was a snipe bleating long after dark. The awning works splendidly.'

'Where did you sleep?'

'In Wroxham Hall dyke.'

'And you went to Norwich this morning?'

'I got rope and paint and hinges and blocks, and there's about half a crown left, and they gave me the screws for nothing.'

'River pretty crowded coming down? Hardly yet, I suppose, though the visitors do seem to begin coming earlier every year.'

'Not an awful lot,' said Tom. 'There was one beast of a motor-cruiser made me slosh the bacon fat all over the place when I was cooking my dinner.'

'There was one yesterday,' said his mother, 'going up late in the evening, upset half Miss Millett's china in her little houseboat. She was talking of seeing the Bure Commissioners about it.'

'Probably the same beasts coming down again,' said Tom. 'Most of them are pretty decent nowadays, but these beasts swooshed by with a stern wave as if they wanted to wash the banks down. I've got to get some hot water and clean those bottom-boards at once before the twins come.'

'Coot Club meeting?' asked his mother. 'Like a jug of tea in the shed?'

'Very much,' said Tom. 'Hullo! There they are! All in a bunch, too. There's *Flash*.' He had caught a glimpse of the white sails of the racing boats coming up the river.

Tom's mother held the new baby up at the nursery window to see the white sails go by. She and Tom stood listening at the window after the sails had disappeared. Higher up the river they heard two sharp reports, 'Bang! Bang!' almost at the same moment.

'Pretty close finish, anyhow,' said Tom. 'I'll dash down now, if you don't mind. They'll be along in a minute or two.'

Presently he heard them.

'Now then. Hop out, you two, and give her a push off. I'll put her to bed.' That was Uncle Frank (Mr Farland), who must for a moment have brought the *Flash* alongside the foot of the doctor's lawn.

'All right now?'

'All right.'

'Push her off then. And don't be late for supper. Mrs McGinty'll be asking what I've done with you as it is.'

'Eh, mon, dinna tell me ye've droon't the puir wee bairrns.' That was Port's voice, talking Ginty language.

'Tell her we won't be late. Macaroni cheese tonight. Specially for you, A.P.' That was Starboard talking to her Aged Parent.

'Tell her the bairrns'll be hame in a bittock.' That was Port again.

'I'll tell her to lock you both out,' laughed Mr Farland.

Tom heard the running footsteps of the twins, and in another moment the two of them were at the door of the shed.

'Hullo, Tom!'

'Hullo! Who won?'

'We were second,' said Starboard, 'but it wasn't Daddy's fault. We had to go about and give them room just as we were getting level.'

'What about No. 7? Hatched yet?'

'Still sitting. At least I think so. She was when we went down. Coming up we were in the thick of things just there and we'd passed her before I could see.'

No. 7 was for two reasons the nest that mattered most of all those that the Coot Club had under its care. It belonged to a pair of coots, one of which was distinguished from all other coots by having a white feather on its wing in such a place that it could be seen from right across the river. Coots are common enough on the Norfolk Broads, but coots with white feathers where there ought to be none are not common at all, and ever since it had first been seen, this particular coot had been counted the club's sacred bird. Then, too, it had nested unusually early. It had begun sitting on its eggs long before any other coot on the reaches that the Coot Club (when not busy with something else) patrolled. Any day now its chicks might hatch out, and every member of the Coot Club was looking forward to seeing the sacred coot as the successful mother of a family, and to putting down the date of the hatching against nest No. 7 on the map they had made of their reaches of the river.

'The Death and Glories'll have seen all right,' said Port. 'They've been on patrol down there.'

'They do know there's a meeting, don't they?' said Tom. 'It's no good having one with only half the club.'

'We told them, anyhow,' said Starboard. 'They ought to be here by now. They were well past Ranworth when we passed them last.'

'Here they are,' said Port.

There was a splash of oars, a rustling of reeds, and the old black ship's boat came pushing her way into the dyke. Under their gaudy handkerchiefs the faces of her crew looked much more worried than ever pirates' faces ought to be.

'You're jolly late,' said Starboard.

'Look here,' said Tom, 'what's the use of fixing up a Coot Club meeting if you three go off pirating and don't come back till nearly dark?'

'No, but listen,' said Joe, at the tiller. 'It ain't pirating.'

'It's B.P.S. business,' said one of the rowers, Bill. 'It's No. 7 . . . Something got to be done.'

'What?'

'No. 7?'

'What's happened?'

No. 7 nest. The club's own coot. The coot with the white feather.

'Everything was all right when we went by,' said Port.

'It's since then,' said Joe. 'One o' them big motor-cruisers o' Rodley's go an' moor right on top of her.'

Tom ran into the shed for their plan of the river, which hung from a nail on the wall. There was no need of it, for every one of the six members of the Coot Club knew exactly where No. 7 nest was to be found.

'What did you do?' Starboard asked.

'We let Pete do the talking,' said Joe. 'As polite as he know how. "If you please" and "Do you mind" an' all that.'

'Well?'

Pete, a small, black-haired boy, the owner of the enormous telescope, spoke up.

'I tell 'em there's a coot's nest with eggs nigh hatching,' he said. 'I tell 'em the old coots dussen't come back.'

'We see her scuttering about t'other side of the river,' said Bill, forgetting his handkerchief was a turban and taking it off and wiping his hot face with it. 'She'll never go back if that cruiser ain't shifted.'

'And didn't they go?' said Starboard.

'Just laugh. That's what they do,' said Peter. 'Say the river's free to all, and the birds can go nest somewhere else, and then a woman stick her head out o' the cabin and the rest of 'em go in.'

'What beasts!' said Port.

'I try again,' said Joe. 'I knock on the side, and some of 'em come up, and I tell 'em 'twas a beastly shame, just when eggs is going to hatch.'

'And I tell 'em there's a better place for mooring down the river,' said Bill.

'They tell us to clear out,' said Joe.

'And mind our own business,' put in Peter.

'I tell 'em 'twas our business,' said Joe. 'I start telling 'em about the B.P.S.'

'They just slam off down below. Makin' a noise in them cabins fit to wake the dead,' said Bill.

'Let's all go down there,' said Starboard.

'I'll deal with them,' said Tom. 'The fewer of us the better. Much easier for one.' He looked at the *Titmouse* in her neat awning. 'I'll take the punt.'

Already he had untied the old *Dreadnought*, pulled her paddle free and was working her out of the dyke.

'Look here,' he said. 'If it's as bad as you say, I may have to do something pretty tough.'

'We did try talking to 'em,' said Bill.

'Well, if there's a row about it, you'd better be out of it. All Coots off the river. Go and do some weeding for someone in the village. Slip along with them, Twins, and make sure someone sees them doing it.'

The *Dreadnought* slid out from the dyke into the open river. The last of the tide was running down, and Tom, with steady strokes of his paddle, sent the old home-made punt shooting down the middle of the stream to get all the help he could from the current.

CHAPTER 4

THE ONLY THING TO DO

With steady strokes of his paddle, a long reach forward, a pull, and then a turn of the blade at the right moment, Tom drove the old *Dreadnought* down the river. If only it had been any other nest, he told himself, it would not have been quite so bad. Horrible anyway for any bird to be cut off from her nest by a thing like that. He remembered what he had just heard of a cruiser charging through a little fleet of sailing boats instead of keeping out of the way of them as by the rule of the road she ought to do. He remembered little Miss Millett in her houseboat with the china rocked off her shelves. He remembered the smell of burnt fat and the spattering grease as that cruiser roared past the *Titmouse*. And these people had refused to move even when Pete had explained to them what they were doing. Well, move they jolly well should. Even if he had to wait till dark. There was only the one thing to do, and he would have to do it. Lucky that so few people seemed to be about. And then, just as he shot past the Ferry, he saw George Owdon leaning on the white-painted rail of the ferry-raft and looking down at him.

If George had been any other kind of larger boy, Tom might have asked his advice and help. But he knew better than that. George might be Norfolk, like himself, but he was in his way more dangerous even than the cruiser. George was an enemy. He had much more pocket-money than any of the Coots but was known to make more still by taking the eggs of rare birds and selling them to a man in Norwich. He would be ready to go and smash the nest on purpose if he guessed that Tom and his Bird Protection Society were particularly interested. So Tom paddled steadily on.

'You're in a hurry, young Tom.'

Tom, by instinct, paddled rather less fast.

'Not particularly,' he said.

'What's the secret this time?' jeered George Owdon.

Tom did not answer. He was soon round the bend below the inn and out of sight from the Ferry. He could not tell what was going to happen, but he wished George Owdon had not been there.

He paddled faster again, and presently heard a strange jumble of noise from farther down the river. Faint at first, two tunes quietly quarrelling with each other, it grew louder as he came nearer until at last it seemed that the two tunes were having a fight at the top of their voices.

Suddenly he knew that all this noise was coming from one boat, a big motor-cruiser, that same *Margoletta* that had upset his cooking for him in the *Titmouse*. So that was the enemy. There it was (Tom could not think of a thing like that as 'she') moored right across the mouth of the little bay in which the coot with the white feather had built her nest. A narrow drain opened out here into the river. There were reeds in the entry, and among these reeds, just sheltered from the stream, was No. 7. Members of the Coot Club had watched every stage of the building. The Death and Glories had found it almost as soon as the coots had begun to lay one bit of pale dead reed upon another. That was a long time ago now, in term-time, when Port and Starboard were away at school, and Tom could get on the river only at week-ends. Joe, Bill and Pete had each in turn played truant in order to visit it. There had been those days of great rains and Tom had feared that the rising river would have drowned the nest or even swept it away. But the coots had not let the floods disturb them. They had simply added to their nest, and, when the water had fallen again he had come down the river just as he was coming now, to find the coot with the white feather sitting on her eggs on the top of a broad, high, round platform made of woven reeds.

And now was all that to go for nothing? The bows of the big cruiser were moored to the bank above the opening. The stern was moored to the bank below it. 'So that the lazy brutes can go whichever way they like on shore without having to use their dinghy,' said Tom to himself. But he could hardly hear himself speak for noise. There was nobody to be seen on the deck of the *Margoletta*. All the Hullabaloos were down below in the two cabins, and in one cabin there was a wireless set and a loudspeaker, and in the other they were working a gramophone.

Tom let his *Dreadnought* drift down with the stream, close by the *Margoletta*. Should he or should he not try to persuade those Hullabaloos to move? If one of them had been looking out of a porthole he might have had a try. Not that he thought for a moment that persuading would be much good with people who on a quiet spring evening could shut themselves up in their cabins with a noise like that. And anyway the Death and Glories had tried it and had told them about the coots.

The coots made up his mind for him. There they were, desperately swimming up and down under the bank opposite the little bay that the cruiser had closed to them. Up and down they swam, giving small sharp cries of distress quite unlike their usual sturdy honk. They hardly seemed to know what to do, sometimes taking short flights upstream, spattering the water as they rose, flopping into it again, and swimming down. And Tom knew just why they were so upset. Close behind the cruiser and the dreadful deafening noise was the nest that they had built against the floods, and the eggs that must be close on hatching. Something had to be done at once. How long had the coots been kept from their eggs already?

It was no use trying to talk to those Hullabaloos. If he did it would only put them on their guard and make things much more difficult.

Tom paddled quietly in to the bank below the *Margoletta*, landed, tied the *Dreadnought* to a bunch of reeds, and then crept along the bank until he came to the stern mooring rope of the cruiser. He stopped and listened. Those two tunes went on with the battle, each trying to drown the other. He heard loud, unreal laughter. Bending low, Tom pulled up the rond-anchor,* coiled its rope as carefully as if it were his own, and laid anchor and coiled rope silently on the after-deck. A single glance told him that the nest and the eggs were still there. They might so easily have been smashed during the cruiser's mooring.

So far, so good. Bent double, he hurried back along the bank and, in a moment, was afloat in the *Dreadnought*. There was no sign that anybody in the *Margoletta* suspected that anything was happening. He paddled upstream past the cruiser and landed again. Creeping down along the bank he pulled up the bow anchor, coiled its rope, and laid it on the foredeck. There was such a noise going on in both cabins that he need not have been so careful. Then he leant lightly against the *Margoletta*'s bows. Was she going to move, or would the stream itself keep her where she was? She stirred. She was moving. The stream was pushing its way between her and the bank. In a moment Tom was back in the *Dreadnought*, pushed off and with a hard quick stroke or two set himself moving downstream, away from Horning and home and the Coot Club's private stronghold in the dyke below his father's house.

He had made up his mind about that before ever he had touched the *Margoletta*'s anchors. Supposing the Hullabaloos should see him going upstream they would be sure to think

---

* A rond-anchor is a stockless anchor with only one fluke for mooring to the rond or bank.

of the Death and Glories who had gone that way after asking them to move. That would never do. He must lead them downstream instead. With luck he would be round the bend and away before they saw him. He would leave the *Dreadnought* somewhere down the river, and slip back to Horning by road. Lucky it was that it wasn't the *Titmouse* he had taken.

He paddled swiftly and silently downstream. The *Margoletta* was adrift and moving. He could see into the little bay. He glanced across at the troubled coots. Another few minutes and they would be back at the nest. Unless, of course, they had been kept away too long already. He passed the cruiser and settled down to hard paddling. What a row those Hullabaloos were making. They still did not know they were adrift. And then, just as he reached the turn of the river below them, he heard an angry yell, and, looking back over his shoulder, saw the *Margoletta* out in mid-stream, drifting down broadside on, and on the open deck between the two cabins a man pointing at him and shouting, and, worse, watching him through field-glasses.

The thing was done now, and the hunt was up. Tom wished he had oars with outriggers in the *Dreadnought*, to drive her along quicker than he could with his single home-made paddle. He forced her along with tremendous jerks, using all the strength in his body. He had been laughed at for making that paddle so strong, but he was glad of it now. Already he was out of sight of the *Margoletta*, but she would be round the bend in a moment as soon as they got their engine started, and in this next reach there was nowhere to hide. He must go on and on, to make them think that the boy who had cast them loose had nothing to do with Horning, but had come from somewhere down the river. If only a nice bundle of weeds would wrap itself round their propeller. But it was too early in the year to have much hope of that. Yes, there it was. He heard the roar of the engine. They were after him. And then the roar stopped suddenly and there were two or three loud separate pops. Engine trouble. Good! Oh, good! He might even get right down to the dyke by Horning Hall Farm, where he had friends and could hide the old *Dreadnought* and know she would come to no harm.

On and on. He must not stop for a moment. He paddled as if for his life. Whatever happened they must not catch him. For everybody who did not understand about No. 7, he would be entirely in the wrong.

He thought of landing by the boat-house with the ship for a weather vane, startling the black sheep, and leaving the *Dreadnought* in the dyke below the church. But supposing the Hullabaloos were to see her, why, the first person they asked about her would tell them to whom she belonged. No, he must go much farther than that.

He was close to the entry to Ranworth Broad when he heard again the loud drumming of the *Margoletta*'s engine away up the river. Too late to turn in there. The dyke was so straight. They would be at the entry long before he could get hidden. He paddled desperately on and twice passed small dykes in which he could have hidden the punt and then dared not stop her and turn back. Louder and louder sounded the pursuing cruiser. Would he have to abandon ship and take to the marshes on foot? And with every moment the thing he had done seemed somehow worse.

And then he rounded a bend in the river and caught sight of the *Teasel*. That yacht had been lying in that place for over a week. He had noticed her several times when sailing up and down inspecting nests for the Bird Protection Society. There was nearly always a pug-dog looking out from her well or lying in the sunshine on her foredeck. Tom had noticed the pug, but had never seen the people who were sailing the *Teasel*. At least for some time now they had not been sailing. Just living aboard, it seemed. And today it looked as if they had gone away and left her. The dinghy was there, but that meant nothing. There was no pug on the foredeck, and the awning was up over cabin and well. Perhaps the people were away on shore. And, at that moment, Tom had an idea. He could abandon his ship and yet not lose her. He could take to the reeds and yet not leave the *Dreadnought* to be picked up by the enemy. All those yachts were fitted out in the same way. Every one of them had a rond-anchor fore and aft for mooring to the bank. Every one of them had an anchor of another kind, a heavy weight, stowed away in the forepeak, for dropping in the mud when out in open water ...

Tom looked over his shoulder. The cruiser was not yet in sight, but it would be at any moment. Things could not be worse than they were whatever happened. His mind was made up. With two sweeps of the paddle he brought the *Dreadnought* round and close under the bows of the moored yacht. He was on deck in a flash with the painter in his hand. Up with the forehatch. There was the heavy weight he wanted. Tom lay down and reached for it and hoisted it on deck. He made his own painter fast to the rope by which he lowered the clumsy lump of iron into the punt. He wedged his paddle under the seat, and stamped the gunwale under, deeper, deeper, while the water poured in. The *Dreadnought*, full of water, and with that heavy weight to help her, went to the bottom of the river. Tom scrambled to his feet, jammed the hatch down on the anchor rope, and took a flying leap from the *Teasel*'s foredeck into the sheltering reeds.

CHAPTER 5

ABOARD THE *TEASEL*

Mrs Barrable was making little drawings in the margin of her letter and on her blotting-pad. This was a habit of hers and, when she was writing to the mother of Dick and Dorothea, it did not matter. Writing to strangers, she often had to copy her letters out all over again, because of the illustrations that had somehow crept in.

'Very nice children they are, my dear,' Mrs Barrable had written, 'and Dorothea is very like the little girl you used to be, but, you know, I should have been afraid to ask them here if I had known they both had such a passion for sailing ... Of course, they want to learn and I fear they will find it very dull to be cooped up in a yacht that is moored to the bank and really no better than a houseboat with only an old woman like me to keep them company.' (Here she had let her pen run away with itself and there was a picture of a pair of lambs and an old woman in a poke bonnet all frisking together.)

Mrs Barrable drummed on her teeth with the end of her penholder and glanced through the cabin door into the canvas-roofed well, to see Dick earnestly wiping plates, and Dorothea, with a hand luckily small enough to get inside, scooping the tea-leaves out of a little tea-pot. What fun it would have been to take them round the old haunts, away down to Yarmouth and through Breydon Water and up the Waveney to Beccles, where she had been a child herself ... And then she looked out of the opposite portholes, and forward through the children's cabin. There was a porthole right forward, beside the mast, through which she could see a charming circular picture of the bend of the river upstream.

And just then, into that picture seen through the porthole, there came a boy in an old tarred punt, shooting round the bend of the river and paddling as if in a race. Instantly Mrs Barrable forgot everything else.

People in a hurry always interested her. She was always ready to take sides with anybody running to catch a train, and had been known to clap her hands when she saw someone make a really good dash for an omnibus. 'Good boy,' she murmured to herself, and waited to see him again when he should come paddling past the portholes on the opposite side of the cabin.

But he never came past those portholes at all. There was the faintest possible jar as he caught hold of the *Teasel*. There was a sudden, slight list, very slight, for Tom was not heavy, but enough to make Dick and Dorothea in the well wonder what Mrs Barrable could be doing. Mrs Barrable leaned forward again and, through that same round porthole by the mast, caught a glimpse of a rubber sea-boot on the foredeck. There was the faint but unmistakable noise of the opening of the forehatch, a fumbling with ropes, the shifting of a heavy weight, quick steps on the foredeck, a bump, a slow, sucking gurgle, the slam of the forehatch closing, a thud on the bank, the crackle of dry reeds and then, a few moments later, a tremendous salvo of barking from the watchdog, William, leisurely returning to duty.

Mrs Barrable pushed away the folding table and hurried out of the cabin. The washers-up looked at her in astonishment. Both were down on their knees stowing things away.

'What's happened?' asked Dorothea.

'What's the matter with William?' said Dick.

'I don't quite know,' said Mrs Barrable. 'A boy in a punt ...' She worked her way out from under the awning, expecting to see that punt, or whatever it was, lying alongside the *Teasel*. But there was no punt at all. It had vanished, like the boy. And from behind the reeds there came the frenzied barking of the pug.

'William!' called Mrs Barrable. 'William! Come here!'

She went forward along the side-deck, steadying herself with a hand on the awning. There was wet on the foredeck. What could that mean? And a rope led from the forehatch over the side. Mrs Barrable lifted the hatch and looked down into the forepeak. Why in the world, when the *Teasel* was safely moored to the bank, should anybody want to anchor her with the mud-weight as well?

'William!' she called again, and William came out of the reeds, stopping on the gangplank to do a little more barking, over his shoulder, to show people that he was afraid of nobody and that a better watchdog did not exist.

'Quiet, William!'

Dick and Dorothea looked out with wondering faces. They, too, climbed out from the well.

'Quiet, William!' said Mrs Barrable. 'He must have been running away from something. Shut up, William! Listen!'

Yes. They could all hear that something was coming down the river. There was the deep, booming roar of a motor being run at full speed. Another of those motor-cruisers. A very loud loudspeaker was asking all the world never to leave him, always to love him, tinkle, tinkle, tinkle, bang, bang, bang. And beside the loudspeaker there were other voices, loud, angry voices, not singing love songs but shouting at each other. There it was, a big motor-cruiser, coming round the bend.

William was now on the foredeck, but still looking behind him and barking at the reeds on shore. Mrs Barrable, her eyes sparkling, her mind made up, encouraged him, but pointed towards the motor-cruiser that was roaring down towards them. William was puzzled. Quick work, if that boy in the reeds had managed already to be out there on that

noisy thing coming down the river. But he supposed his
mistress knew, and anyhow he hated that kind of noise. So,
with Mrs Barrable whispering 'Cats! William, Bad Cats!' into
his ears, William faced the oncoming cruiser and put into his
barking all he thought about boys who startled honest pugs
by lying hid in reeds so that the honest pugs ran into them
face to face on their own level. There was a good deal of
noise, what with William, and the loudspeaker, and the
quarrel going on among the people aboard the cruiser, who
were all shouting to make themselves heard above the roar
of their engine. Old Mrs Barrable, hiding her excitement,
held William by the fat scruff of his neck, as if she feared he
might leap overboard in his eagerness to tear to pieces the
loudspeaker and its accompanists. Dick and Dorothea worked
their way forward from the counter along the side-decks.
What was happening? Dorothea was trying one story after
another, but none seemed to fit.

Suddenly the quarrel aboard the cruiser seemed to come
to an end. There was a furious shout from the man who was at
the wheel. Everybody was pointing straight at Dick. The big
cruiser swerved towards the *Teasel*. Her engine was put into
reverse and there was a frantic swirl of water as she lost way.

'Whaddo you mean by it?' shouted the steersman of the
cruiser.

But by now another of the Hullabaloos was pointing at
the *Teasel*'s little dinghy lying astern of her.

'That's not the boy,' he shouted, trying to make himself
heard. 'Can't you see the boat, you ass? It wasn't like that.
Bigger boat! LONGER! And that's a white boat. The other
one was dark – a sort of punt.'

'It wasn't you turned us loose?' That was the steersman
again.

'I,' said Dick. 'I ...'

Mrs Barrable spoke. 'He has had nothing to do with you.
He has been with me, moored here, the whole afternoon.'

'Oh. Have you seen a boy go by?'

'In a sort of long black punt.'

'Nobody's gone by since the racing,' said Mrs Barrable.

'Eh?' shouted one of the Hullabaloos.

'Do turn that thing off,' shouted another.

Everybody aboard the cruiser seemed to be shouting at once, and the loudspeaker was still begging all the world never to leave him, nor to deceive him, bang, bang, bang, tinkle, tinkle, tinkle.

'It must have been one of those three guttersnipes this afternoon.' 'Bothering us about a beastly bird's nest.' 'Taking up our anchors and casting us loose.' 'All right. All right. I'll wring the little brute's neck.'

A girl in the gaudiest of beach pyjamas may have thought she was whispering to the man at the wheel of the cruiser, but she had to shout to be heard by him and what she said was just as clearly heard aboard the *Teasel*.

'No good talking to the old woman. He must have gone by.'

Mrs Barrable's eye hardened slightly.

'I shall be obliged to you if you will mind my paint,' she said, as the cruiser was coming dangerously near.

'Paint!' said the girl rudely, and then, shouting into the steersman's ear, 'Don't waste any more time. Let's buzz along. We'll catch him if you only get on. He can't have got very far.'

The engine roared again. The water at the stern of the cruiser was churned into foam. There was a heavy bump as her stern swung in and struck the *Teasel*, and the *Margoletta* went roaring, singing and quarrelling down the reach and out of sight. William, after giving a good imitation of a hungry lion being with difficulty held back from the savaging of helpless victims, turned round towards the reedy bank and barked once more.

Mrs Barrable also faced the reeds.

'They've gone on,' she said, in a very clear voice, though quite low. 'Hadn't you better come out and explain?'

37

There was a rustle and stir among the reeds, and Dick and Dorothea saw the boy they had met in the train come out, looking rather shy and bothered, close by the pug's gangplank.

'Were you lurking all the time?' said Dorothea.

'You?' said Mrs Barrable. 'We've seen you once before today.'

'Twice,' said Dick. 'Once in the train, and once when he was cooking in his boat.'

'That was most awfully decent of you,' said Tom, 'sending them off like that.'

'Well,' said Mrs Barrable, 'it was five to one, wasn't it? But what was it all about? And what have you done with your boat? And why did you put my mud anchor overboard?'

'It was the only thing I could think of that would be heavy enough,' said Tom. 'You see, I had to sink her.'

'Sink her?' Mrs Barrable exclaimed. They all looked down into the brown water. 'Do you mean to say your boat was here right under our feet all the time those people were talking?'

'She went down all right,' said Tom, 'once I got her properly under.'

'But how will you get her up again?'

'She'll come when the mud-weight's lifted. And anyhow I hitched the painter to your rope. She'll come all right. But I'm very sorry. You know I didn't think there was anybody aboard. There was no pug on deck, and there usually is. And I knew I wouldn't be doing any harm to the anchor. Just for half an hour till those Hullabaloos had gone by. There wasn't time to do anything else. I could hear them already . . .'

'Hullabaloos?' said Mrs Barrable. 'What a very good name for them. But what had you done to them? And don't you think they may be coming back any minute? It wouldn't look well for them to find you here. Come inside and wait till we can be sure they are not turning round again. No, William.

No! Friend! Friend! But what had you done to them? What-ever it was, I expect they deserved it ...'

The noise of the *Margoletta* was now far away, but it could still be heard, and it would certainly be awkward if the Hullabaloos came back and found him where he was.

'I can stay hid in the reeds,' said Tom.

'But we want to hear about it,' said Mrs Barrable, 'and I don't want to have to hide in the reeds while I listen. Much better come inside.'

Tom looked anxiously at the anchor rope that disappeared into the water at his feet. It was just as he had left it. The *Dreadnought* was all right down there at the bottom of the river. She could be taking no harm. He followed Mrs Barrable down into the well.

'And now,' said Mrs Barrable, when they were all in the well and under cover, including William, who was slowly changing his mind about Tom, 'do tell us what it was all about. But, of course, you needn't if you don't want to.'

'It was birds,' said Tom.

'Herons?' broke in Dick, who had spent a lot of time watching one on the opposite bank during the afternoon.

'Coots,' said Tom. 'You see, the birds are nesting now, and when people like that go and shove their boat on top of a nest anything may happen. And this is our particular coot. She's got a white feather on one wing. We've been watching the nest from the very beginning. An early one. And the eggs are just on the very edge of hatching. And then those Hullabaloos moored clean across the opening where the nest is, and frightened the coots off. Something simply had to be done.'

'I can quite understand that,' said Mrs Barrable. 'But what was it you did?'

'Well, they wouldn't move when they were asked,' said Tom.

'Who asked them?'

'The Bird Protection Society,' said Tom.

'But how did they come to know about it?'

'They were down this way inspecting, because I was up the river and Port and Starboard had to be racing. You must have seen them, I should think. Three of them, in an old black boat.'

'We saw them,' cried Dorothea delightedly.

'Oh,' said Mrs Barrable. 'The pirates . . . turbans, knives in their belts . . . We all saw them.'

'Well,' said Tom, 'you can't expect them to be Bird Protectors all the time.'

'Of course not,' said Mrs Barrable.

'They asked them to go, and they wouldn't, and then, when they found it was no good being polite to Hullabaloos, they came and reported to the Coot Club, the rest of us, at Horning, I mean, and luckily my old punt was in the water. So I came down. They were making such an awful noise, they never heard me put their anchors aboard and push them off. The coots'll be back by now if they haven't been frightened into deserting altogether.'

'Um,' said Mrs Barrable, 'I'm glad I'm not moored on the top of somebody's nest. I shouldn't at all like to find myself drifting downstream.'

'But it wouldn't ever happen to you,' said Tom. 'You wouldn't be beastly like they were if somebody came and explained that there were eggs just going to hatch.'

'I think it was splendid,' said Dorothea.

'They sounded very unpleasant people,' said Mrs Barrable.

But Tom was looking rather grim. Somehow it sounded awful, casting loose those Hullabaloos, when Mrs Barrable said how much she would dislike finding herself adrift. He told Mrs Barrable that he ought to go. They listened.

'They've gone right down the river,' said Mrs Barrable, 'or we'd be able to hear them whether their engine was running or not.'

Tom hurried along to the *Teasel*'s foredeck. Dick and Dorothea hurried after him. Already he was hauling up the *Teasel*'s mud-weight. Up it came, with the painter fast to the rope above it, and after it, with a tremendous stirring of mud, the *Dreadnought* herself rose slowly through the water, like a great shark. Up she came, and lay waterlogged, now one end of her and now the other lifting an inch above the surface.

CHAPTER 6

PUT YOURSELF IN HIS PLACE

Tom paddled the *Dreadnought* up the river. Considering that she was a flat-bottomed, home-made punt, she really was fairly steady, but, on the whole, he thought it safer not to turn round and wave good-bye. She was very wet and rather slimy after being at the bottom of the river, and Tom was content to be able to keep his balance and to keep her going at the same time. He was still feeling the narrowness of his escape from the Hullabaloos. Things had certainly turned out much better than had seemed likely. How lucky that the *Teasel* had been moored there. How lucky, too, that the little old lady had taken his boarding of her yacht in the way she had. Why, she had played up against those Hullabaloos almost as if she had had a share herself in clearing them away from the coot's nest.

He slowed down as he came near No. 7. One great advantage of paddling a punt is that you face the way you are going. Tom, as he paddled, was searching the side of the river opposite the little opening that the coots had chosen. He was looking for round black shadows stirring on that golden water under the reeds. He saw only the broad bulging ripple of a water-rat. No. At least the coots were no longer scuttering up and down in terror as he had seen them last. Quietly he edged the old punt over towards the other bank so as to be able to look into the opening as he passed it. There was an eddy here or nearly dead water, and Tom never lifted his paddle high enough to drip. He slid by as silently as a ghost.

He knew exactly where to look into the shadows. There was the clump of reeds, and there at the base of them, among them, the raised platform of the nest. Was it deserted? Or not? Tom peered through the twilight. No. It was as if the centre of the nest was capped with a black dome, and on the dome he had just seen the white splash of a coot's forehead. And what was that other shadow working along close under the bank? It was enough. Tom did not want to frighten them again. He paddled quietly on. One thing was all right, anyhow. The coots of No. 7 were at home once more.

It was growing dark now. Nobody but Tom was moving on the river, and the only noise was the loud singing of the birds on both banks and over the marshes, whistling blackbirds, throaty thrushes, starlings copying first one and then the other, a snipe drumming overhead. Everything was all right with everybody. And then a pale barn owl swayed across the river like a great moth, and with her, furiously chattering, a little crowd of small birds, for whom the owl was nothing but an enemy. And suddenly into Tom's head came a picture of the *Margoletta* as a hostile owl, mobbed by a lot of small birds, the Death and Glories and himself.

And Tom, remembering what he had seen and heard while he was lurking in the reeds beside the *Teasel*, knew that the Hullabaloos of the *Margoletta* were very angry indeed. He had made enemies of them. They had not sounded at all as if they were the kind of people who would forget what had happened or forgive it. And what if they found out who he was and went and made a row about it? The doctor's son casting loose a moored boat full of perfect strangers ... His cheeks went hot at the thought. But at least no one who knew him had seen him ... and then, suddenly, Tom remembered George Owdon lounging on the ferry-raft when he had been paddling the *Dreadnought* on his way to the rescue of No. 7. Would George tell? Hardly. George was a beast, but, after all, he was a Norfolk coot, like the rest of them, though, of course, not a member of the Coot Club, which was an affair of Tom and the twins. No, not even George Owdon would do a thing like that.

But, as he paddled on and on up the river, Tom grew more and more bothered about what had happened. It had all come about so quickly. What ought he to have done? Let No. 7 be ruined at the last moment, after all that watching and the careful way in which the coots had fought the floods by building up their nest? Again he saw those anxious scutterings at the far side of the river. He could not have allowed them to be kept off their eggs until it was too late. What else could he have done?

CHAPTER 7

INVITATION

Different people in different places woke next morning thinking of what had happened on the river the day before.

Dick and Dorothea, sleeping their first night in the *Teasel*, were waked by a farm-boy who came alongside with a can of fresh milk. Mrs Barrable was up already, and they heard her tell the boy that she was not quite sure if they would want milk tomorrow, but that they would let him know at the farm if they were still there.

'But I thought she said the *Teasel* wasn't going to move,' whispered Dick.

'I know,' said Dorothea.

And then, after breakfast, Mrs Barrable had taken the dinghy and rowed away upstream with William.

'Can we come, too?' Dick asked, eager to have another try with oars.

'Not this time,' said Mrs Barrable. 'You and Dot can tidy the boat up, and you'll find lots of birds to look at in the marsh and among those swallows. Put your sea-boots on if you go ashore. I'll be back as soon as I can.'

Tom, sleeping in the *Titmouse*, was waked very early by hearing a boat brushing through the reeds at the mouth of the dyke. He bobbed up at once to listen and hit his head against a thwart. Was it the enemy coming to look for him? But, of course, it was only the Death and Glories coming to ask what in the end Tom had done about No. 7. He told them and saw that, as boatbuilders' sons, they were a good deal shocked.

'Cast 'em adrift?' said Joe. 'Did you oughter 'a done that?'

'Couldn't do anything else,' said Tom.

'But how didn't they cotch ye?'

Tom told, briefly, how he had had to make a submarine of the *Dreadnought*. Of that they thoroughly approved.

'Gee whizz!' said Joe.

'That were a real good 'un,' said Bill.

'Prime,' said Pete.

They wanted there and then to go down the river to have another look at No. 7, but Tom thought better not, and they decided to look at a few upstream nests instead.

'And look here,' said Tom, as the *Death and Glory* went off out of the dyke. 'Try to find out, if you can, how long those people are going to have the *Margoletta*. I'll have to keep out of the way till they've gone.'

He went into the house for breakfast. What was the good of cooking in the *Titmouse* if he could not safely take her down the river?

Tom poured out the whole story.

'It's a pity it's happened, of course,' said his father. 'But I don't really see what else you could have done. They'll have forgotten about it themselves this morning, unless their livers are badly out of order.' But Tom thought otherwise. His father had not heard the anger in their voices when they were talking to the old lady of the *Teasel*. The only real hope was that those people would presently be giving up the *Margoletta*. A week was the usual time for which people hired a boat. He would have to keep out of sight until they were gone.

As soon as breakfast was over Tom went back to his ship, and was hard at work in her when he heard two short blasts on a whistle and two longer ones, from among the bushes on the farther side of the dyke.

The twins.

'Hullo!' said Tom gravely.

'What's the matter?' said Port.

'Couldn't you get them to move?' said Starboard. 'Is No. 7 done after all?'

'Is that why you didn't come and tell us last night?'

'No. 7's all right,' said Tom. 'At least, it was when I came home. And it was pretty dark before I got back. But things went wrong a bit. It was the *Margoletta* on the top of No. 7, and I set her adrift . . .'

'Good,' said Starboard.

'I couldn't think of anything else to do,' said Tom. 'And the worst of it is they saw me. One chap had field-glasses. And then although I went down river, they thought I was one of the Death and Glories. So I've got the whole Coot Club in a mess.'

'The Death and Glories'll be all right,' said Starboard.

'Anyway, it isn't your fault,' said Port. 'One of us would have had to do it.'

'But how did you get away?' said Starboard.

'I forgot to tell you about a couple of kids I met in the train. Well, they're in the *Teasel*, you know, where that pug's usually hanging about, and there's an old lady in the *Teasel* with them . . .' And then he told of how he had boarded the *Teasel* and used her mud-weight, and sunk the *Dreadnought*, and hid in the rushes, and how, after the Hullabaloos had been sent off down the river, he had gone back aboard the *Teasel* by invitation.

And at that moment he gave a sudden start and listened. There was the sharp, impatient bark of a small dog, close behind the house. It sounded almost as if it came from the river. Tom had too lately lain in the reeds face to face with William not to know that voice again.

Without another word he crept round the side of the house and peered out through the willows. The others followed him on tiptoe. Yes. Tied to one of the small white mooring posts at the edge of the lawn was a dinghy, and in it, alone, a pug.

'She must be here,' whispered Tom, and they slipped quietly back to the shed.

'Come to complain?' said Starboard.

'She was awfully decent yesterday,' said Tom.

And then Mrs Barrable and Mrs Dudgeon came round the corner of the house together.

'Well, Tom,' said his mother, 'you seem to have made some friends last night as well as some enemies. Mrs Barrable has a plan to suggest.'

'How do you do?' said Tom, dusting the sawdust off before shaking hands.

'And these,' said Mrs Dudgeon, 'are Nell and Bess.'

'Port and Starboard,' said Mrs Barrable. 'We saw you racing yesterday and we all hoped you would win.'

'It wasn't Daddy's fault we didn't,' said Starboard. 'If the river'd been a wee bit wider nothing could have saved them.'

At that moment there was a determined and rather indignant yelp from 'our baby' somewhere upstairs in the house.

'Is he all right?' said Tom.

'Perhaps you'd like to talk it over with them,' said Mrs Dudgeon.

'You run away, my dear,' said Mrs Barrable, just as if Mrs Dudgeon was herself only a little girl.

Tom's mother laughed. She did not seem to mind. She shook hands with Mrs Barrable and was gone.

'And is that the *Titmouse*?' asked Mrs Barrable, looking along the dyke. 'You do keep her smart.'

'She wants another coat of paint, really,' said Tom. 'I've got the paint, but I don't want to put it on till the end of the hols. You see it won't matter her being wet when I have to go to school.'

'Does she sleep two?'

'There's room for two,' said Tom. 'One each side of the centre-board. But I've only had her fitted for sleeping these last two nights. She isn't really finished yet.' He turned back the awning to let Mrs Barrable see inside. 'Those lockers are all going to have doors.'

And then suddenly Mrs Barrable turned to the business that had brought her to the doctor's house. She told them how her brother had been coming to the Broads for some years and how this year he had chartered the *Teasel*, meaning to take his sister for a cruise right through Yarmouth and up to Beccles, where they had been children together, and round to Oulton and up the Norwich river.* She told them how, after a week on the Bure and at Hickling, he had suddenly had to go off, and how she had invited Dick and Dorothea to come and keep her company in the *Teasel*. 'But what I didn't know,' she said, 'was that the two of them had set their hearts on learning to sail. And, of course, they're dreadfully disappointed ... No, no. They don't say so. If they did I shouldn't feel so bad about it. I'm rather disappointed, too. I'd been looking forward to seeing Breydon again, and sailing in to Waveney and the Yare ... Now, how would the three of you care to come and sail the *Teasel* for us? I know Tom knows how to sink a boat.'

'Sail her?' said Tom.

'Take her down to the southern rivers and back,' said Mrs Barrable. 'Just to let those two children feel they'd seen something of the Broads. And you'd have to teach them a little first, so that they wouldn't feel they were only passengers.'

Tom looked down at the *Titmouse*, at the new awning, and the lockers. Black treachery it would be, to leave her for the *Teasel*.

'I've thought it all out,' said Mrs Barrable. 'You'd have to bring the *Titmouse* or we shouldn't have enough sleeping room at night. If you could do with Dick in the *Titmouse*, we four will have the *Teasel* to ourselves ... two cabins, one for the twins, and Dorothea will share the other with me. Two

* The River Yare.

or three days' practice first in the easy waters up here, I thought, and then away for a cruise so as to be back in time to send them home before the end of the holidays.'

'The *Teasel*'s a splendid boat,' said Tom.

For one moment the twins' eyes lit like his at the thought of such a voyage in charge, in actual command, of such a vessel. Then they remembered.

'We'd simply love to,' said Starboard, 'but we can't ... really can't. You see there's a race tomorrow, and then another one, and father's entered *Flash* for five races the last week of the holidays, and he's arranging to get back early each day on purpose.'

'You try to persuade them, Tom,' said Mrs Barrable.

But Tom knew the twins too well. 'It's no use,' he said. 'They won't be able to come ... And I can't either, after last night. At least not so long as those people are about.'

But Mrs Barrable was not to be refused. She had seen the light in Tom's eye and in the eyes of the twins. She knew that all three of them wanted to come.

'They won't know you except in your punt,' she said. 'And we can always hide you, besides, they'll have forgotten about it by now ... Anyhow, come along the three of you this afternoon and see what sort of a crew you think you could make of my visitors. I'll expect you soon after lunch.'

'Dick's pretty keen on birds,' said Tom. 'And he doesn't collect eggs. And I could hop ashore if we heard those people coming.'

It was a queer way of accepting an invitation for the afternoon, but what it meant was clear enough.

'We'd love it,' said the twins, and then Mrs Barrable said that she had a few more things to do, was welcomed into her dinghy by a barking William, and rowed away towards the village.

Mrs Barrable, rowing steadily, with William sitting up in the stern of the dinghy, was almost out of sight beyond the boat-building yards when, suddenly, all three Coots turned and listened.

'The *Margoletta*,' whispered Tom.

In a moment there was no one to be seen on the green lawn in front of the doctor's house. The three Coots, crouching among the willows, were looking out through the tall reeds.

A big motor-cruiser had turned the corner above the Ferry and was thundering up the river with a huge gramophone open and playing on the roof of the forecabin. Two gaudily dressed women were lying beside it, and three men were standing in the well between the cabins. All three were wearing yachting-caps. One was steering and the other two were using binoculars and seemed to be searching the banks as the cruiser came upstream at a tremendous pace.

'They're looking for the *Dreadnought*,' whispered Tom.

CHAPTER 8

THE INNOCENTS

Mrs Barrable had seen the big cruiser coming and had made ready for it, but she was nearly swamped when it swept by her, the people in it turning round to laugh at the sight of the little dinghy tossing like a cork in the swirling water. She comforted William, who had not liked being thrown about, and rowed on to the staithe. The *Margoletta* was already tied up there when Mrs Barrable, looking over her shoulder, saw the *Death and Glory*, the old black ship's boat with its crew of three small boys, coming round the bend by the Swan Inn. There was no chance of warning them. She saw the two rowers turn to look at the *Margoletta*. She saw them hesitate, and then, as if they had nothing whatever to fear, row calmly on and moor at the staithe a little above the cruiser. The three men from the cruiser leapt ashore, and before the small Coots had time to change their minds and bolt for it, were already within reach.

'That's the one. The biggest of them. We'll teach you to come casting off other people's ropes and anchors,' said a big, red-haired man, suddenly shooting out an arm and catching Joe by the collar of his coat.

'That's him.'

Mrs Barrable tied up her dinghy and walked quietly towards them. But Joe seemed well able to look after himself. He flung his arms suddenly upward and, with a single wriggle, left his coat in the hands of the enemy.

'Catch him, one of you,' shouted the red-haired man. 'Don't let him go. Grab him, James!'

'Catch him yourself, Ronald!' said one of the others.

'Look out for my coat,' urged Joe, skipping backwards a few yards out of reach. 'It's got my rat in it.'

The red-haired man dropped the coat and reached again at Joe, who dodged.

'Rat!' shrieked a woman in orange pyjamas who had come ashore to see what was to be done to Joe.

There was a sudden interruption.

'What's all this?' a deep voice asked, pausing between the words. Mr Tedder, the policeman, had been digging in his little garden by the staithe, and hearing the noise had thrust his spade into the ground and hurried out, putting his coat on as he came.

'It's this boy,' said the red-haired man, setting his yachting-cap at a jauntier angle to impress Mr Tedder, who had seen too many yachting-caps to be impressed. 'The biggest of these three. He came along yesterday evening when we were all in our cabins, and unfastened our anchors and set us adrift. Wanton mischief, nothing else.'

'Set you adrift?' said Mr Tedder judicially. 'That won't do.'

'But I didn't,' said Joe. 'I couldn't. Why, last night ...'

Mr Tedder looked at him. 'Why so you was,' he said at last. He turned. 'And what time do you say the offence took place?'

'Ten past five,' said the woman eagerly. 'I know it was, because I was boiling eggs, and looked at the clock just when Ronald shouted that we were floating down the river ...'

'Ten past five,' said Mr Tedder slowly. 'Why from five o'clock all these boys was doin' a bit o' weedin' in my patch, an' gettin' worrams for to make a bab ... for liftin' eels ... Couldn't 'a been this boy cast you adrift. Why, 'twas all but dark when they go home with their worrams ...'

'But I tell you we'd had them round earlier with some tale about a blasted bird.'

'They was in my patch at ten past five,' said Mr Tedder doggedly.

'It must have been some other boy,' said the thin man the other had called 'James'.

'Not these,' said Mr Tedder. 'You skip along, you three. No need to hang about the staithe.'

'And my coat?' said Joe.

He came warily forward and picked it up, put it carefully on and then pulled out of an inner pocket a large white rat, which sat on his arm, sniffed the air contemptuously, and looked about it with its round pink eyes.

'Take that thing away,' screamed the woman.

Mr Tedder pulled out a notebook.

'If you want to make complaint ...' he was beginning, when a quiet voice close beside him said, 'Officer!'

'Ma'am,' said Mr Tedder, straightening his back and turning sharply on his heel, to see a little old lady with a pug. Mrs Barrable had thought it time to intervene.

'Am I mistaken?' she asked, 'or is there a speed limit of five miles an hour through Horning village? I think I have seen the notices.'

'No boats to go above five miles per hour,' said Mr Tedder, 'not between the board t'other side of the Ferry and t'other board at top of Horning Reach.'

'This motor-cruiser,' said Mrs Barrable, 'seems to make a practice of disregarding the speed limit as well as the convenience and safety of other users of the river. I have noticed it before, and today I think I have been fortunate not to have been swamped by it. Do I lay an information with you, or must I see the Bure Commissioners ...?'

Mr Tedder turned again, but he and the old lady and the pug were alone. The people from the cruiser, with their yachting-caps, their berets and their bright pyjamas were hurrying angrily back to their vessel. The three small boys were standing open-mouthed in the *Death and Glory*, wondering at the sudden collapse of the enemy.

'I wouldn't do nothin' about it, ma'am,' said Mr Tedder slowly. 'They hear what you say.'

'Thank you, officer,' said Mrs Barrable, 'I think you're perfectly right. No, William!'

William had felt the quarrel in the air, and, as the *Margoletta*'s engine started up and she swung away from the staithe and upstream, he had allowed himself a single bark.

'Least said, soonest mended,' said Mr Tedder, though not thinking of William. 'Takes all sorts to make a world, but fare to me as we could do without some of 'em. There's been trouble up at Wroxham with that lot, making such a noise by the bridge nobody in the hotels could get their sleep. But where's the use? Here today they are and gone tomorrow. Casting off their moorings? Now who's going to do a thing like that? More likely they forget to make 'em fast.'

CHAPTER 9

THE MAKING OF AN OUTLAW

That afternoon there was not wind enough to stir the flame of a candle when Tom and the twins rowed down the river in the *Titmouse*. 'We'd better all go in one boat,' Tom had said, 'and then I can hop into the reeds if we hear the *Margoletta*, and you can hang about and pick me up again when they've gone by.' That morning's happenings on Horning Staithe had shown the Coots that it was no good thinking that the Hulla-baloos were of the kind that forgive and forget. So the three of them together rowed slowly down the river, looking at the nests as they passed them, and rejoicing to see that the coot with the white feather, on No. 7 nest, was sitting as steadily as if she had never been disturbed.

'Hullo,' said Tom, when at last they came in sight of the *Teasel*, 'they've taken the awning down.'

'Mustn't let them think us quite incapable,' Mrs Barrable had said when she came back from her shopping, and she and Dick and Dorothea between them had folded up the awning and stowed it in the forepeak, and lowered the cabin roof, and washed down the decks with the mop and generally done their best to make the *Teasel* look as if she were ready for a voyage.

'She's a jolly fine boat,' said Starboard. 'It's a pity those kids can't sail.'

'There they are,' said Tom.

Dick and Dorothea had come out of the cabin and were standing in the well. Dorothea was waving. Dick was looking anxiously round the *Teasel*. They had done the best they could, but he felt sure that something or other ought to have been stowed a little differently. Well, it was too late to alter anything now. Dorothea was finding, all of a sudden, that now that these sailing twins were close at hand, she did not know what to say to them. She found it easy enough to make up stories in which everybody talked and talked. Indeed, already, since yesterday, she had gone through half a dozen imaginary scenes in which she and Dick met and made friends with Port and Starboard. And now here they were, and she could not get one single word out of her mouth and was quite glad that William was doing all the talking and doing it very loud.

The *Titmouse* slid alongside.

'How do you do?' said Tom, as Mrs Barrable came out of the cabin, and William stopped barking, remembered that Tom was a friend, and came and licked the hand with which he was keeping the *Titmouse* from bumping the *Teasel*.

'I am so glad you managed to come,' said Mrs Barrable. 'These are Dick and Dorothea. And one of you two is Nell and the other is Bess, and one is Port and the other is Starboard, and the two of you are twins, and I don't know yet which is which.'

'It's quite easy, really,' said Starboard.

'Once you know,' said Port.

'Oh, yes,' said Mrs Barrable. 'I remember now. Nell's the one with curly hair.'

'And the right-handed one,' said Tom. 'That's why she's Starboard, and Bess is left-handed and so she's Port. It comes very handy for sailing.'

'Not much sailing for anybody today,' said Mrs Barrable, looking up the glassy river.

And then, before they had even had time to shake hands, something happened which Dorothea had not imagined in any of her scenes, something which turned them all into old friends working together.

'Why look,' said Mrs Barrable. 'Isn't that those piratical bird-protectors?'

Round the bend of the river above the *Teasel*'s moorings, just where, last night, Mrs Barrable had seen Tom racing down in his old *Dreadnought*, and then the *Margoletta* roaring after him, came the old black ship's boat, Joe standing in the stern and steering, Pete and Bill rowing like galley-slaves so that there was a white ripple of bubbling water under her forefoot.

'They're in a mighty hurry,' said Starboard.

'Something's up,' said Tom.

'It's those Hullabaloos again,' said Port.

'Easy,' shouted Joe, as the *Death and Glory* swept down the river. The sweating galley-slaves bent forward, panting, over their lifted oars.

'It's that cruiser,' called Joe, swinging his vessel round. 'A man from Rodley's come down to see my Dad, and we ask him. He don't know when that lot's giving up the *Margoletta*. But they're coming down river. Changed a battery they have.'

'They must use a lot of electricity,' said Dick, more to himself than to anybody else, 'with a wireless like that going on all the time.'

'The doctor tell us where you was,' said Joe. 'Down here any time they may be.'

Tom looked at the reeds.

'I'll just have to hide again,' he said. 'And you three had better clear off, or we'll be getting the *Teasel* mixed up in it too.'

'Tom mustn't let himself be caught,' explained Port, 'because it would be so awful for the doctor.'

'It's Coot Club business, anyhow,' said Starboard, 'and we're just not going to *have* him caught.'

'If he's going to skipper the *Teasel*, it's our business, too,' said Mrs Barrable, and laughed when she saw Dick and

Dorothea both staring at her. 'We may be going to manage a voyage after all,' she said, 'if the Coot Club can turn you two into sailors ... And this is no place for first sailing lessons, out in the open river. If those Hullabaloos are coming down again, they shan't find any of us. We'll vanish, pirates and all.'

'But how?' said Tom.

'Into Ranworth Broad,' said Mrs Barrable.

'No wind,' said Starboard, looking up the river on which the only ripple was made by a water-hen swimming across.

'We could quant,'* said Tom, 'but don't you think I'd better just hide?'

'They can't search the *Teasel*,' said Mrs Barrable. 'You come aboard and you can always slip into the cabin. Don't let's lose time. Have you three pirates got a rope?'

'We've a good 'un.'

'I'll look after *Titmouse*,' said Port. 'You'll want Starboard to steer while you quant.'

Tom and Starboard climbed aboard the *Teasel*. Bill and Pete brought the *Death and Glory* near enough for Joe to throw Tom the long rope they always carried with them in hope of salvage work. Many a time it had come in useful when they had found beginners who had got themselves aground in their hired boats and did not know how to get off. The rope uncoiled in the air. The end fell across the foredeck. Tom had it as it fell and made it fast round the mast.

'Come on, you,' cried Starboard to Dick, as she jumped ashore to get up the anchors. 'And what about the gang-plank?'

'We'll take it with us,' said Mrs Barrable. 'William would miss it at the next place.'

'The next place ...' Simple words, but glowing with glorious meaning. No mere houseboat after all. Here today and gone tomorrow. Mrs Barrable had gone into the cabin to see that no jampots full of paint-brushes were going to

* To quant is to pole a boat along. A quant is a long pole used for quanting.

upset. Dick and Starboard were both ashore. Tom was getting the quant ready. Dorothea, alone in the well, laid a daring hand upon the tiller. This, indeed, was life.

'That's right,' Starboard was saying to Dick. 'Coil it up so that you bring it aboard all ready to stow. Hang on, half a minute. Hi, you, what's your name, Dorothea, just tell the Admiral we're all ready . . .'

'The Admiral?'

'Well, just look at her fleet.'

Dorothea laughed happily. There certainly was a fleet, what with the *Death and Glory*, and the *Teasel*, and the *Teasel*'s little rowing dinghy, and the *Titmouse* out in the river with a twin at the oars.

'Admiral,' she said, through the low cabin door. 'Port . . . I mean Starboard . . . says they're all ready.'

'Good,' said the Admiral, coming out, 'then we're only waiting for the tug.'

'Cast off forrard!' That was Skipper Tom on the foredeck.

'Quick, you. Give her a bit of a push off. Now's your chance. Hop aboard.' That was Starboard, who was moving along the bank with the stern rope amid a great rustling of bent reeds. Dick jumped, grabbed a shroud and landed on the deck.

'Stern warp aboard,' called Tom, and then, glancing aft to see Starboard leap down into the well, where Dorothea eagerly made room for her at the tiller, he waved a hand forward.

'Half ahead!' called the skipper of the tug-boat, *Death and Glory*.

The tow-rope tightened with a jerk. The *Teasel* answered it. She was moving.

'Full ahead!'

Dick and Dorothea looked at the little dinghy brushing the reeds where only a minute ago they had been able to step ashore. Wider and wider was the strip of water between the

Teasel and the bank. The tow-rope that at first had tautened and sagged, and tautened and sagged again, dripping as it lifted, now hardly sagged at all. With quick short strokes, Bill and Pete, those two engines of the tug, kept up a steady strain. And there was Tom, lifting the long quanting pole, finding bottom with it, and hurrying aft along the side deck, leaning with all his weight against the quant's round wooden head. A jerk as he came to the stern, and back he went on the trot, lifting the quant hand over hand, finding bottom with it and again leaning on it, forcing the *Teasel* along, so hard that if the engines of the tug had eased up for a moment he would have taken the strain off the tow-rope.

'She's moving now all right,' said Starboard. 'If only we can get round the corner in time.'

'Where is the corner?' asked Dorothea.

'You'll see it in a minute,' said Starboard.

'But here they are!' said Dorothea. 'We're too late.'

'That's not the *Margoletta*,' said Starboard. 'That's only a little one.'

A small motor-cruiser, making a good deal of noise for its size, but nothing like the noise of the *Margoletta*, was coming down river to meet them. It slowed up on seeing the fleet, the *Death and Glory* towing the *Teasel* and the little *Titmouse*, rowed by Port, acting as encouragement and convoy.

'Decent of them,' said Tom. 'Keep an eye on the tug,' he added, jerking the quant from the mud and running forward again.

A single, shrill whistle sounded from the *Death and Glory*. It was answered on the instant by a single hoot from a motor-horn on the little cruiser.

'Good for Joe,' said Tom.

'What does it mean?' asked Dick.

'He's telling everybody that he's directing his course to starboard,' said Tom, 'and they're going to do the same.'

The little motor-cruiser passed them, and the people on

61

board waved to them, going full speed again as soon as they could see that their wash would not bother the rowing-boats.

'They're not all like the Hullabaloos,' said Starboard.

'Wouldn't it be awful if they were?' said Dorothea.

'Feathers for Ginty!' called Starboard suddenly. 'Pick them up, Twin!' She was pointing at a little fleet of curled white swan's feathers, some in mid-stream, and some close against the reeds. 'Mrs McGinty looks after us,' she said, seeing Dorothea's puzzled face. 'She always wants swan's feathers. For a cushion or something. She's been collecting them for years.' Port, in the *Titmouse*, dropped astern, rowing from feather to feather.

Port was a long way astern of the fleet when, just as they were turning into the long straight dyke that leads to Ranworth Broad, Dorothea heard again the noise of a motor-cruiser. This time she said nothing, but looked at Starboard. Starboard had heard it too. Mrs Barrable turned round.

Starboard nodded.

The captain of the *Death and Glory* was looking over his shoulder. He, too, had heard.

Tom, for a moment, stopped quanting as they turned the corner.

'They're a long way off,' said Starboard.

'They come at such a lick,' said Tom, racing forward with the quant. 'They'll see us for certain,' he panted as he came aft again. 'We'll never get to the Straits in time.'

Dorothea looked ahead to where the long narrow dyke disappeared among the trees, over which, far away, showed the grey square tower of Ranworth Church. The Straits must be those trees, if the Broad was beyond them.

'*Titmouse* ahoy!' shouted Tom suddenly, but there was no answer, and they could no longer see the river except just where the dyke left it.

'She's all right,' said Mrs Barrable. 'They're looking for you in a punt. They aren't looking for a girl. Or for the *Titmouse*.'

'We'll be all right too, if we can get to the Straits,' said Starboard. 'Let me have a go at the quant.' But no. Tom would have felt even worse if he had not had the quant to push at, to feel he was doing something in driving the *Teasel* along. As for the engines of the *Death and Glory*, their panting could be heard by everybody.

'If only there were two quants,' said Starboard.

'They're simply bound to look down the dyke,' said Tom, 'and they'll see the Death and Glories towing, and if they've got any sense at all they'll come and have a look.'

Nearer and nearer behind the reed-beds came the noise of the *Margoletta*. Everybody except Starboard – and even she glanced over her shoulder every other moment – was looking back towards the river, watching for the *Margoletta* to show in the opening at the mouth of the dyke. Who would show there first, Port or the Hullabaloos? And, oh, how far it seemed to those trees.

'There she is,' said the Admiral.

'But she's rowing quite slowly,' said Dorothea. 'She can't not have heard them. And she's not turning in. She's at the other side of the river, picking feathers ... But there weren't any feathers there ... Or were there?'

'Well done, that Port of yours,' cried the Admiral. 'I should never have thought of it. Dick, where are those glasses? Well done, Port,' said Mrs Barrable again. 'Well done! Well done!'

There was the huge bulk of the *Margoletta* passing the mouth of the dyke. The *Teasel* and the Death and Glories were all in full view of them. But not a single one of the Hullabaloos was looking their way. Mrs Barrable was silently clapping her hands. 'They're wondering what on earth that girl is doing. And they can't look both ways at once.'

The *Margoletta* passed the mouth of the dyke, and went roaring on down the river. And the crews of the *Teasel* and the *Death and Glory* saw Port in the *Titmouse*, taking short lazy strokes with her oars, disappear behind the reeds as if she were going on upstream.

'Dodged them all right this time,' said Tom, 'thanks to Port.'

In another minute or two the *Teasel* was in the Straits, with trees on either side of the narrow dyke. The dyke bent to the left, and divided into two, one branch blocked with posts and chains, the other slowly widening towards a sheet of open water, still as glass, except for birds swimming and stirring the reflections of the reeds.

'Where do you want to stop?' asked Tom. 'The staithe?'

'Much quieter here,' said Mrs Barrable.

'There's a good place for mooring,' said Starboard, pointing to a little bay.

'Easy!' shouted Tom. 'Casting off the tow-rope!'

Splash! The end of the tow-rope fell in the water, and Joe in the *Death and Glory*, was hauling it in, hand over hand. The *Teasel* slid slowly on in dead smooth water. Tom seemed to be everywhere at once, getting ready anchors and warps.

'Will that do?' called Starboard, as the *Teasel* slid alongside a low grassy bank.

Tom jumped from the foredeck. Starboard jumped from the counter. Dick, Dorothea and the Admiral were, for the moment, passengers only. The *Teasel* was moving no longer. A moment later she was moored in her new berth.

'Well done everybody,' said the Admiral.

'Even William,' said Dorothea. 'At least he didn't bark and he easily might have.'

'Narrow squeak that were,' said Joe. Bill and Pete were too much out of breath even to speak. They grinned and wiped their foreheads and blinked the sweat out of their eyes.

And then there was the sound of oars from among the trees, and there was Port with the *Titmouse*.

'Well done, Port!' everybody shouted at once.

Port looked happily over her shoulder, steadied the *Titmouse* with her oars and stopped rowing.

'I knew they'd be looking down the dyke if I turned in,' she said. 'So I dropped a few of Ginty's swan feathers under the other bank and picked them up again one by one. The Hullabaloos nearly swamped me, they came so near to see what it was I was getting. Water-lilies in April I expect they thought.'

'They'd have seen us for certain if they hadn't been looking at you,' said Tom.

'It's the most gorgeous lake,' said Dorothea. 'It's full of good hiding-places. Anybody could be an outlaw hidden in here for weeks and weeks while people were hunting for him outside.'

'You could, you know,' said Starboard. 'Those Hulla-baloos can't be about for ever, and we could bring supplies.'

'It's a good idea,' said Port. 'They're sure to catch you if you just hang about Horning.'

'You'll have disappeared, just like the *Teasel*,' said Dorothea.

Tom looked from one to the other. All this romance was rather puzzling. He had got into trouble with some unpleasant people who had hired the *Margoletta*. He had to keep out of their way because if they caught him it would be hard to prevent his father, the doctor, from being dragged in. It was most unlucky, just when the *Titmouse* was ready for distant voyaging. But somehow this Dorothea, and even Port and Starboard, who were Norfolk Coots and usually as practical as himself, were talking of his misfortune as if it were some kind of exciting story.

'If they did come in here to look for him,' said Dorothea, 'he could hide among the reeds like a water buffalo, with only his nose above water.'

'Jolly cold,' said Tom.

'Tell you what,' said Joe. 'They can't come up this way without they come by Ludham, or by Acle or by Potter

Heigham, and we know chaps in all them places. We'll tell 'em to telephone to Dad's yard, to give us a warning if that lot come through. Then we'll know where they be.'

'But we don't know where they are *now*,' said Tom. 'They may be close to. They may have stopped just round the corner.'

'Um,' said Starboard. 'It wouldn't do to run right into them.'

'I must get home, anyhow, and tell Mother what I'm going to do,' said Tom.

'Look here,' said Starboard. 'We've got to get back early. We'll take a passage with the Death and Glories, and tell Aunty you'll be late. Then you can dodge back home when it's beginning to get dark.'

'Much the best plan,' said Mrs Barrable.

And presently the *Death and Glory*, with Port and Starboard pulling an oar apiece and the three small Coots taking turns in the steering, disappeared behind the trees. Tom waited in the *Titmouse*, tied alongside the *Teasel*, fitting hinges to locker doors, with Dick and Dorothea watching and passing him screws at the right moment.

At the first hoot of an owl over the marshes he said 'Good night' to his new friends. By dusk all yachts and cruisers on the Bure are tied up or hurriedly looking for moorings for the night. But the bye-laws say nothing about little boats, and though there was still no wind, he hoped to get home not too dreadfully late for supper.

'Do you think he'll come back?' asked Dick.

'He simply couldn't find a better place to lurk,' said Dorothea.

'He's got a very nice dyke,' said Mrs Barrable, 'without stirring from his own home. We shan't see him again tonight. I expect he'll try to get here tomorrow before the Hullabaloos wake up in the morning.'

But last thing, when they had done their washing up after

supper, and Mrs Barrable had tired of telling them what the Broads had been like in the wild old days of forty years ago, and it had long been dark, and Dick and Dorothea climbed out on the counter, to stand there and watch the stars, and to listen to the night noises in the reed-beds, they caught sight of a pale glimmer away under the trees where the dyke divided.

'He's back,' said Dick.

'Far away, at the edge of the marshes,' said Dorothea, more to herself than to Dick, 'the watchers saw the glimmer of the outlaw's lonely light.'

CHAPTER 10

LYING LOW

First Day

Dick and Dorothea in the little forecabin of the *Teasel* slept until a Primus stove in the well burst into a sudden roar as Mrs Barrable set it going to boil the breakfast coffee. They hurried out to feel the side-decks wet with dew and cold to their bare feet, but their first glance across the water towards the other side of the Straits showed them that Tom in the *Titmouse* had long ago begun his day. The awning of the little boat had been turned back at the stern, and they could see the outlaw himself leaning out and washing up a plate.

'Won't he be coming here for breakfast?' asked Dorothea.

'He must have had his ages ago,' said Mrs Barrable. 'He was scrubbing his face when I first looked out. Hurry up and scrub yours and then, as soon as you've had something to eat, you can row across and ask him where we get fresh milk. I've opened a tin for now.'

Half an hour later, when they had stowed the *Teasel*'s awning, and Mrs Barrable was setting up her easel in the well to paint a picture of the Broad, Dick and Dorothea began their first lesson in sailing. There could not have been a better day for it. Sunshine, a crisp air, and a wind not strong enough to be dangerous, but quite strong enough to send the *Titmouse* flying through the water so that any mistake in the steering showed at once. They beat up to the staithe, took the milk-can to the farm, brought it back filled, went to the little shop and post office and sent off postcards to Mr and Mrs Callum. One sentence was the same on both cards: 'We have begun to learn to sail.'

Up and down they sailed in the sunshine, first one and then the other at the tiller, while Tom held the mainsheet so that nothing could really go wrong. They very soon stopped catching their breaths every time a harder puff of wind sent the *Titmouse* heeling over, and Tom said they would do all right as soon as they had learnt that when you are steering you must think of nothing else. He said this after Dick had had a long turn at the tiller. Dick was careful enough when there was nothing to look at, but keen as he was on being able to sail, the sight of a bird was too much for him, and as Ranworth is full of birds of all kinds, the *Titmouse*, with Dick at the tiller, had sailed a very wriggly course.

But it was not much better with Dorothea. Her mind, too, kept slipping away. She was sailing, yes, and all of a tremble lest she should do something wrong, but she could not help thinking of the outlaw and the *Margoletta*, and of the Admiral quietly painting in the well of the *Teasel*, but at the same time ready to give warning of approaching Hullabaloos. How would it be to make a real sentinel's post in one of the taller trees at the outer end of the Straits? What would happen if suddenly, now, this minute, the *Margoletta*, full of enemies, were to come roaring out into the Broad? 'The boy outlaw leapt overboard and swam for the reeds, bullet after bullet splashing in the water round his head ...'

'Look out, Dot, we'll be aground.'

And there was the boy outlaw close beside her, grabbing at the tiller. The *Titmouse* spun round only just in time, and they felt the centre-board move stickily in the mud and then break free again.

Half-way through the morning Port and Starboard came rowing out of the Straits with two bits of urgent news, one that the first of No. 7's eggs had hatched, and the other that while Tom had been busy teaching Dick and Dorothea how to sail, other people had been doing their best for Tom. Far and wide, it seemed, the alarm had been given, and all over the Broads the outlaw's friends were alert and on the watch.

'It's all fixed up,' said Starboard. 'Joe's taken Bill's bike and gone down to Acle to fix up with a boy there to keep a look-out. Bill's gone up to Potter Heigham on the bus (Coot Club funds, of course), and Pete's got a lift into Wroxham to see what he can find out at Rodley's about how long that lot are going to have the *Margoletta*.'

Second Day

Dick wrote in his notebook, 'Found two coots' nests in a reed-bed close to Ranworth Staithe. Watched crested grebes fishing. What I thought was a foghorn last night and the night before was a bittern. There was no fog, and Tom heard it, too, and told me.'

Port and Starboard came in their rowing-boat to spend the whole day. Dick and Dorothea were taken out by turns first in *Titmouse* and then in the rowing-boat, and made to sail and row by themselves, with the elder Coots as mere passengers to tell them what they did wrong. William went hunting, ashore. Mrs Barrable painted a picture. Port and Starboard and Dorothea did the day's cooking.

In the afternoon the *Death and Glory* came rowing through the Straits with the news that the *Margoletta* had been seen going through Yarmouth to the south the day before. That made everybody feel a good deal more comfortable. All six Coots came to tea in the *Teasel*. Joe brought his white rat, and Dorothea made herself stroke it. They had tea in the *Teasel*, William and the white rat as far from each other as possible, William at the forward end of the cabin and the white rat with Joe at the after end of the well. The *Death and*

Glory hoisted her patched and ragged old sail, and Dick and Dorothea went sailing in her, while the Admiral and the three elder Coots held a conference. It was decided that next day, while the twins could be there to help, they should set sail on the *Teasel* and try her on the Broad before venturing out into the river.

Third Day

This plan came to nothing, because in the morning they woke to the steady drumming of rain-drops on stretched canvas. It was no day for a trial trip. Neither Tom nor the Admiral wanted to get sails wet at the very start. Awnings were left up all day. Dick and Dorothea wore their oilskins and sea-boots and got some rowing practice in the rain. Dorothea planned a story, 'The Outlaw of the Broads'. Dick helped Tom in the *Titmouse*, and between them they finished up the lockerdoors. William, for fear of chills, was given a spoonful of cod-liver oil.

In the afternoon, when the rain was at its worst, Port and Starboard, in oilskins and sou'westers, came rowing into the Broad.

'What are you doing tomorrow?' said Mrs Barrable.

'We've got to hang about at home tomorrow. The A.P.'s got people coming to tea, and we have to be there to pour out.'

'Next day, then?' said Mrs Barrable. 'What about coming with us for a day or so just to help Tom to put us all in the way of handling the *Teasel*?'

'We'll have to be back the night before the first of the championship races,' said Starboard.

'We could do a tremendous lot in three days,' said Tom.

'Potter Heigham, I thought,' said the Admiral.

'Bridge to go through. Two bridges. Just what's wanted,' said Tom.

'And then through Kendal Dyke and up to Horsey. It used to be a wonderful place for birds.'

'It still is,' said Tom.

'Good,' said Dick.

That night, in the cabin of the *Teasel*, the Admiral, Tom, Dick, and Dorothea pored over the map together. The Admiral, with the wrong end of a paint-brush, was tracing the curling blue line that marked the River Bure past the mouth of the Ant and on to the place where it was joined by the Thurne, and the blue line thickened and curled away down the map towards Acle and Yarmouth. Tom's eye followed it down there, thinking of tides and the other dangers of Yarmouth and Breydon which make a cruise on the rivers of the south as exciting an adventure for the children of Horning or Wroxham as a cruise on the rivers of the north is for the children who live down at Oulton or Beccles.

But Mrs Barrable's paint-brush was moving up that other river, the Thurne ... Potter Heigham ... 'such a pretty little place it used to be' ... two bridges, road and railway ... on and on and then sharp to the north-west through the narrow line that marked Kendal Dyke, and into a largish blue blot that meant the widening waters of Heigham Sound, and on again through a narrow wriggling line into another blue blot that was Horsey Mere. At one side of this blot was a short line marking a dyke, and at the end of it the sign for a windmill. 'That's where we'll spend the night,' said the Admiral, 'in the little cut close by that windmill ...'

The others leant over the cabin table. Closer and closer they put their heads to the paper. It was very hard to see, all of a sudden. Dimmer and dimmer.

'What's happened to the light?' said the Admiral.

They looked up at the two little glass bulbs that usually lit the whole cabin. They dazzled no longer. A curly red wire was slowly fading in each bulb.

'The battery must be run down,' said Dick at once. He switched off one light, and, for a moment, got a rather brighter glow out of the other.

'Well,' said the Admiral, 'we've been looking at the wrong end of the map. We can't set out on a voyage with no light. Candles are all right in the well, but I don't like them in the cabin. We'll have to sail up to Wroxham to get the battery renewed.'

Dorothea felt a pang of disappointment as she went into the well for the candlestick. They had come from Wroxham that first day and so had seen that part of the river already. Sailing to Horsey would have been sailing into the unknown.

Help came, unexpectedly, from Tom.

Dorothea lit her candle, and brought it into the cabin, setting it on the table where it threw its queer flickering light over the faces round the map. She saw at once that Tom had something to say.

'Wroxham's a bad place for sailing. Specially now that the leaves are beginning to come. Get blanketed altogether in some reaches. It's no good going up there for a trial trip. Much better get it done tomorrow. It's safe enough with the *Margoletta* away through Yarmouth. I'll take the battery up to Wroxham first thing in the morning. I'll be back by tea-time.'

The Admiral looked at him in the candlelight, and laughed.

'Tired of lying low?' she asked.

'I'd like to give *Titmouse* a run,' said Tom. 'And it's perfectly safe now with somebody watching at Acle.'

'It certainly would be rather waste of Port and Starboard not to have some real sailing while we've got them,' said the Admiral. 'And there are no bridges on the way to Wroxham.'

'It's stopped raining,' said Tom, putting his hand out through a porthole to feel.

A few minutes later he was baling out the *Teasel*'s dinghy

for the third time that day. Dick ferried him across to the *Titmouse*. Tom lit his lantern and looked about him. 'Bone dry,' he said, 'in spite of all that rain. That's the first time the awning's had a proper wetting.'

He watched Dick vanish into the darkness, listened for his safe arrival aboard the *Teasel*, and turned in for the night, feeling extraordinarily happy. Jolly good that the twins were coming in the *Teasel*, at least to Horsey and back. It was all very well, but he really did not much like the idea of handling a boat as big as the *Teasel* for the first time, with only Dick and Dorothea to help. And jolly good, too, to think that tomorrow, Hullabaloos or no Hullabaloos, the little *Titmouse* would herself be voyaging once more.

TOM IN DANGER

It was a fine clear morning with a north-westerly breeze. Tom was up early, and long before breakfast was ready in the *Teasel* he had come alongside. He and Dick made a double sling with the end of the *Teasel*'s mainsheet, and lowered the heavy battery carefully into the *Titmouse*.

'Do you really think it's safe?' said Dorothea. 'They may be just waiting to pounce.'

'Not they,' said Tom. 'And we'd know if they were. Joe's got a friend watching at Acle. And, anyway, I'll be back in no time. No tacking. I'm going to row every yard I can't either run or reach.'

It was a dullish morning without him. They washed up. They swabbed the decks. They took William with them as a passenger to Ranworth Staithe when they went to get some fresh water. On the way back they looked in on two coots' nests, and met a pair of crested grebes out fishing, but, with William aboard, they found it harder to come near the grebes than when they were alone. William sat up on a thwart, put his paws on the gunwale and looked out as keenly as Dick, but he could not see a bird on the water without barking. They went back to the *Teasel* at last and found the Admiral busy preparing a canvas. Dick settled down in the cabin, making a fair copy of his roughly scribbled list of birds he had seen in Norfolk. Dorothea tried to write some of the new book that had seemed almost half done when she had put down a list of its chapter headings ... The Secret Broad, The Outlaw in the Reeds, The Black Coot's Feather, The Bittern's Warning, and so on. What a book it was to be, and yet, somehow, the first chapter had ended after a paragraph or two, and the second would not go beyond the first gorgeous sentence: 'Parting the reeds with stealthy, silent hand, the outlaw peered into the gathering dusk. Away, across the dark water ...' Well, what was it that he saw? Dorothea found herself wondering instead what Tom was seeing on his voyage up to Wroxham to change the *Teasel*'s battery. Had he managed to see Port and Starboard on his way through Horning? The morning slipped away, and still the outlaw in the book was peering out of the reeds across the dark water. Dorothea had to leave him there, for suddenly it was too late to do any more writing. The Admiral wanted to get dinner over, to have a long afternoon for painting.

After the meal, Dorothea hurried Dick into the dinghy to give the Admiral a fair chance, and asked if it would be all right if they rowed up to the main river.

'Don't fall in,' said the Admiral. 'Better leave William with me. Where *did* I put that turpentine?'

Rowing side by side, with an oar apiece, they paddled away from the *Teasel*. The Admiral absent-mindedly waved a paintbrush at them. They waved back. The trees closed in on either side of them. They were in the Straits and the *Teasel* and the open Broad were hidden behind a curtain of young spring leaves. They paddled steadily on, out of the shelter of the trees into the long straight dyke leading to the river.

'There's a sail!' said Dorothea, looking over her shoulder at a white triangle shining in the sunlight, moving along above a distant line of willow bushes.

'One, two,' said Dick. 'One, two ... You must keep time. Look out! we'll be into the reeds. Not so hard. One, two. One, two. That sail's going down the river. They'll have met Tom, I should think.'

'I wonder how far he's got,' said Dorothea. 'Probably started back. All right, Dick. It's really you forgetting to pull ... And they're only water-hens ...'

Dick said nothing. He knew he had all but let his oar wait in the air while he watched two water-hens disappear into a shady hole among the reeds.

'Upstream or down?' said Dorothea as they came at last to the mouth of the dyke. 'Do you realize we're in a boat by ourselves? Let's go upstream. We might meet Port and Starboard.'

'Upstream,' said Dick. 'Let's try and find No. 7.'

'Let's,' said Dorothea. 'Starboard said the little ones are out of the eggs.'

'We'll keep a look-out for a coot with a white feather.'

But long before they had come as far as that little reedy drain where the coot with the white feather was looking after her family of sooty chicks, they had other things than birds of which to think.

They paddled slowly along, keeping near the bank, past the water-works and as far as the church reach, where they saw two coots, but without white feathers, and dozens of water-hens scurrying to and fro between the rough bushy bank on one side of the river and the green grass that was being clipped short by the black sheep on the other. Dick had a good look at the water-hens, noting their flashing tails, and the bright scarlet of their beaks when they lurked close under the overhanging bank while he and Dorothea paddled by. A yacht came sailing down the reach with the water bubbling under her forefoot. Tomorrow, thought Dorothea, they, too, would be sailing just like that. How very much better things had turned out than had seemed likely when first they came aboard the *Teasel* and Mrs Barrable broke the news to them that they were not going to sail at all. 'And we owe it all to No. 7,' said Dorothea. 'And the Coot Club, of course.'

'What?' said Dick.

Dorothea had spoken aloud without meaning to. But Dick never got his answer. Dorothea had lifted her oar from the water and was listening to a loud drumming from somewhere down the river.

'Another of them,' said Dick. 'I hope it doesn't make an awful wash like the Hullabaloos. I wonder if we ought to land till it's gone by?'

'It's just as noisy,' said Dorothea, and the next moment the cruiser swung into sight round the bend by the water-works. 'Dick,' she cried. 'It's them. The *Margoletta*. They've come back. No, don't look at them. Go on looking at the black sheep . . .'

With a roaring engine and a tremendous blare of band music from the gramophone on its foredeck, the big cruiser passed them. Its high wash, racing after it, lifted the tiny dinghy so suddenly that Dorothea clutched the gunwale and lost her oar. By the time she had got it again, the *Margoletta* was already out of sight, though the waves were still tearing angrily at the banks.

'They'll get him. He doesn't know they're here. He can't possibly escape. Dick, Dick! What ought we to do?'

Dick's mind could be counted on to work fast as soon as it was interested. The difficulty was to get it interested when it happened to be thinking about something else. The *Margoletta* had done that, and Dick had already come to a decision while the little dinghy was still tossing on that brutal wash.

'Come on, Dot,' he said. 'We've got to find the others. They'll know what to do.' He gave a hard pull. The dinghy swung round. 'Come on, Dot, pull for all you're worth.'

'And Mrs B.?'

'No time to go back there. Come on, Dot. Pull! One, two. One, two.'

But it was no good. Paddling easily together, when in no hurry, they could keep the dinghy more or less on its course.

But, when the two of them were pulling as hard as they could, first one and then the other got into the stronger stroke, and the little dinghy seemed to be trying to head all ways at once.

'Let me have the other oar.'

Dorothea gave it up to him and sat in the stern.

'I'm not going to bother about that feathering,' said Dick. He clenched his teeth and pulled, lifted his oars probably rather higher than the Death and Glories would have approved, shot them back, gripped the water with them and pulled again. There was a good deal of splashing, but those days of hard work on Ranworth Broad had not gone for nothing, and the little dinghy pushed through the water at a good pace. By giving a harder tug now and then on one or other oar, he managed to keep her heading up the river most of the time. Not always.

'Look out!' said Dorothea. 'You'll be into the reeds again.'

'Do like they told us they used to do,' he panted back. 'Keep pointing always bang up the river. With a hand. Human compass. Then I can just watch your hand without having to turn round to know where I'm going.'

Dorothea sat still with her right hand just above her knees pointing straight up the river, so that when Dick's bad rowing made the dinghy swerve, he could see at once what had happened by looking at her pointing fingers. On and on he rowed.

'That coot's got a white feather,' said Dorothea.

Dick looked round with eyes that hardly saw. He did not stop rowing. He was breathing hard. He could no longer keep his teeth together. As for looking at coots, he could hardly see Dorothea's pointing hand only a foot or two before his face.

'Swop places,' said Dorothea. 'Let me row for a bit.'

Dick pulled desperately on.

'Scientific way,' said Dorothea. 'Relay. First you then me, so that we can keep going at full speed.'

It was the word 'scientific' that persuaded him. With

shaking knees he changed places with Dorothea. Try as he would, his hand trembled as he held it out for a compass-needle, pointing the way up the river. Dorothea, with fresh arms, sent the dinghy along faster, but even more splashily than before.

'It's a good thing the Death and Glories can't see us,' she said, after a worse splash than usual.

'Don't talk,' said Dick. 'It makes it worse later if you do.'

Dorothea said no more. He was right. In a very few minutes she was far past talking. She felt as if her arms would come loose at the shoulder, as if her back would break, as if something in her chest was growing bigger and bigger until presently there would be no room for any breath. And, after all, what was the good? It was too late now. Nothing could save the outlaw from his fate. And then, suddenly, she saw Dick's face change. What had happened? What was it he was saying? 'Easy! Dot, go slow! Don't go so fast. They mustn't think we're hurrying. Look here, let me row.'

She glanced over her shoulder. They had passed the little windmill. Horning Ferry and the Ferry Inn were in sight. There, tied up to the quay-heading in front of the inn, lay the *Margoletta*. Three men and a couple of women were talking to a boy who was pointing up the river. They were just walking across the grass towards the inn. The cruiser had stopped. There was a chance yet, if only they could slip past and up into Horning, and tell Port and Starboard or the Death and Glories. The Coots would surely find some way of getting a warning to Tom.

They changed places again. Dorothea sat in the stern trying not to pant so dreadfully, and not to look as hot as she felt. Dick, carefully feathering as Port had taught him, rowing as if he had nothing to think of but style, pulled steadily on, past the *Margoletta*, past the Ferry, past the neat little hut of the Bure Commissioners and the lawn and garden seat where the Commissioners can sit and watch the river that is in their charge.

'Did you see that boy,' asked Dorothea, 'talking to the Hullabaloos?'

'No,' said Dick shortly.

'Sorry! Sorry!' said Dorothea. She had forgotten for a moment that she was being a human compass, and Dick, who was pulling away again as hard as he could, had had a narrow shave of ramming the bank through watching a hand that was pointing at nothing in particular.

A hard pull set him right, but he had no breath to waste on talk.

Dick rowed on up the village, past the willow-pattern harbours, and the big boat-sheds.

'There's the *Death and Glory*, anyhow,' cried Dorothea. The old tarred boat lay against the staithe. A moment later they caught sight of Joe and the twins, all three looking at the notice-board, where people are told not to moor their boats for too long a time.

'Hi!' shouted Dorothea.

'Hullo!' shouted Joe. He ran to the edge of the staithe to catch the nose of the dinghy as they came in. Putting his hand to his mouth, as if that would make a shout more like a whisper, he asked excitedly, 'Have you seed that?'

'What?'

'They've papered him,' said Joe. 'Reward.'

'The *Margoletta*'s coming up the river,' said Dorothea.

'Come and look at this,' cried Starboard.

'But there's no time to lose,' said Dorothea.

Dick could not speak and the others did not seem to hear her.

'Read what it say,' said Joe.

'But Tom's alone up the river,' said Dorothea.

'Just look at it,' said Port.

'Quick, quick!' said Dorothea.

'Read what it say,' said Joe. 'It weren't there yesterday, but I see it just now as soon's I tie up.'

Dick climbed out on the staithe and hurried across to the notice-board. Dorothea was almost run across the gravel by Port and Starboard, who helped her ashore together.

This was the notice they read:

REWARD

A reward will be paid to any person who can give information concerning the boy who on the night of April the twenty-second cast off the mooring ropes of the motor-cruiser Margoletta *then moored to the north bank below Horning Ferry.*

Apply to.............................

(There followed a name and an address, that of Rodley's, the boat-letting firm who owned the cruiser.)

'Well,' said Starboard, 'nobody'll give them any information, anyway.'

'George Owdon might,' said Port.

'If he could talk to them,' said Starboard, 'but even he wouldn't like people knowing he'd done it.'

'Anyway, Tom'll have to look out. It's a good thing the Hullabaloos are away the other side of Yarmouth . . .'

'But they aren't,' Dorothea almost screamed. 'We've been telling you. They're here.'

'Coming up the river,' said Dick. 'Stopped at the Ferry.'

'And Tom's up at Wroxham,' said Dorothea. 'They can't help catching him if they go on. And there was a boy talking to them.'

She described the boy.

'That's George Owdon,' said Port.

Joe made half a move towards the *Death and Glory*.

'Pete and Bill away to Ludham,' he said. Not with the best of wills could he by himself get much speed out of the old ship's boat.

'We'll go up the river,' said Starboard.

'Where's Bill's bicycle?' asked Port.

'I can get it,' said Joe.

'You may catch Tom at Wroxham before he starts back.'

Joe was gone.

'You two'd better wait here. You can't go really fast in that dinghy. And we've got two pairs of oars. Besides we must have someone on the look-out here to know what they do. Come on, Port!'

CHAPTER 12

UNDER THE ENEMY'S NOSE

It is a long way to row or sail in a small boat from Horning to Wroxham, but it is not much more than a couple of miles by road. In about half an hour from the time he left them, Dick and Dorothea heard the shrill 'Brrr ... brrr' of Joe's bell as he came flying round the corner by the Swan, jammed his brakes on so that his wheels skidded on the gravel, and flung himself off beside them.

'Missed him,' he panted. 'By a lot. Tom'd been gone long before. Must be half-way down by now. Has that cruiser gone up?'

'Not yet,' said Dorothea ...

'Here she come now,' said Joe, looking down the river.

With a big spirting bow wave, the noise of some huge orchestra turned on as loud as possible through the loudspeaker, and a wash that was tossing all the yachts and houseboats moored along the banks, the *Margoletta* was roaring up from the Ferry.

Long after she had disappeared the three stood listening to the noise of her. Somewhere up there were Port and Starboard racing against time. Somewhere up there was Tom in the *Titmouse* sailing down from Wroxham, knowing nothing of the danger that was thundering to meet him.

Port and Starboard had no need to talk. For years they had rowed that boat together. Port rowed stroke and Starboard bow, each with two oars. Port set a steady rate after the first minute or two. She remembered that they might have to keep it up for a long way. On and on they rowed, past the notice that tells you to go slow through Horning, past the eelman's little houseboat, up the long reach to the windmill and the houseboat moored beside it, on and on and on. And all the time they were listening for the unmistakable roar of the *Margoletta*, and at every bend of the river Starboard looked upstream hoping each time to see the *Titmouse*'s little, high-peaked sail. They passed the private broad with the house reflected in the water. They passed the entrance to Salhouse where, on any other day, they would have looked in to see the swan's nest and the crested grebe's. And then they heard it. No other boat on all the river would try to deafen everybody else with a loudspeaker. No other had an engine with that peculiar droning roar.

'Too late!' said Port.

'But here he is!' cried Starboard.

There, close ahead of them was the little *Titmouse*, sailing merrily down the middle of the river.

'Look out, Tom!' they shouted. 'Look out! Hullabaloos! The *Margoletta*! They'll be here in two minutes ... And nowhere to hide!'

Tom, in the *Titmouse*, was very much enjoying himself. He had seen the twins, when he stopped at Horning on the way up. Everything was settled and they were to join the *Teasel* early tomorrow morning and come for a two-day voyage. They would have to be home on the third day for the first of the championship races, but by that time, Tom thought, he and those two strangers ought to be able to manage the *Teasel*, with the Admiral to lend a hand if need be. He had made a fast passage of it, from Horning to Wroxham, by rowing wherever he had not got a fair wind. At Wroxham, the first man he had seen was the man whose business it was to look after the batteries in the boats belonging to the firm that owned the *Teasel*. Not a moment had been wasted, and while the man went off in a punt with the old battery, Tom had hurried to the enormous village store and worked through the Admiral's shopping list, and then ate the sandwiches his mother had given him for his dinner while sitting on the cabin roof of a business wherry, *Sir Garnet*, and talking to Jim Wooddall, her skipper. He had forgotten all about outlawry and Hullabaloos. He was thinking of the voyage to the south, and Jim Wooddall was telling him how to make the passage through Yarmouth easy even for a little boat by waiting for dead low water before trying to go down through the bridges. Several times while they were talking, Jim Wooddall looked up at a notice that had been nailed that morning on the wall of the old granary where the wherry was lying. Tom never saw it, and Jim Wooddall said nothing about it, though he stepped ashore and read it again, after the man had come back with the new battery, and Tom had said 'Good-bye' and was sailing away down Wroxham Reach. If Tom wasn't going to speak of it, Jim Wooddall wasn't. He could put two and two together as well as any man. He had heard of questions asked by that young Bill from Horning about the people in the *Margoletta*. He had just come back from a voyage to Potter Heigham, where another small boy had asked him if he had seen the *Margoletta* anywhere about. He read that notice again, and looked at the disappearing *Titmouse*. Well, of one thing Jim was certain, and that was that if Tom had had anything to do with it, the other people were probably to blame. Foreigners anyway and not pleasant folk. Jim had been in Wroxham when there was that trouble about the *Margoletta* keeping the people in the inns awake all night. And if they were not to blame? Well, Jim Wooddall was Norfolk too. 'If a Norfolk boy done it,' he said to himself, 'those chaps can cover the place with paper before anybody give him away.' He was not in the least surprised, some time later, when Joe came panting down to the riverside on a bicycle, and asked anxiously for Tom, to find, after Joe had hurried off again, that the notice had vanished from the wall.

By that time Tom was far down the river. He had used his oars through the reaches most sheltered by the trees, had slipped out into Wroxham Broad and found a grand wind there, had slipped into the river again by the southern entry, and was sailing merrily along, thinking only of his little ship, when, suddenly, just as he was coming to a sharp bend in the river, a rowing-boat shot into sight, and he recognized Port and Starboard, whom he had left at home in Horning, pulling at their oars as if they were rowing in a race.

'Hullo!' he called.

The next moment they were both shouting at him. 'Look out! ... Hullabaloos! ... Here in two minutes ... Nowhere to hide! ...' Whatever was the matter with them? And then he heard it, too, the droning roar of an engine, and some tremendous voice shouting a comic song along the quiet river.

He knew now. He looked quickly up and down the river. No. They were right. There was nowhere he could stow the *Titmouse*. Too late. The noise was close upon them. And that thing could move at such a pace.

'Turn round!' he shouted to the twins.

He leapt forward and loosed his halyard. Yard and sail came toppling down.

'Quick! Catch my painter.'

He coiled it and threw it aboard. Port made it fast in a moment. Backing water and pulling, they had the rowing-boat heading downstream.

'Don't row fast,' he said, unshipping his tiller and lugging his rudder aboard. 'Nearly forgot that,' he said to himself. 'Slowly now. Not in a hurry. And don't look at them!' He threw himself down and burrowed in under the untidy sail. The next moment the big cruiser was round the bend, bearing down on them, towering above them ... That man with field-glasses, standing like a figurehead above her bows, saw nobody but two small girls, paddling slowly downstream, towing an empty sailing boat. It was amusing to see how violently the mast of the little empty boat swung from side to side, as the big cruiser roared past and left those two small girls splashing and tossing in its wash.

CHAPTER 13

THE *TITMOUSE* DISGUISED

The new battery was in its place and Dick had spent happy minutes carefully connecting up the wires. It was almost dazzling to look into the cabin of the *Teasel*. Nobody would have guessed that under those bright and cheerful lamps there was talk of giving up the voyage to the south altogether.

'It's like this,' said Tom. 'That beast George must have told the Hullabaloos to look for me in the *Titmouse*. It's no good my coming with you. The only thing to do is to slip home and stay hid in the dyke.'

'Rubbish,' said the Admiral. 'Why, in another ten days you'll be back at school and not be able to sail at all. Now listen to me. First of all, you've promised to skipper the *Teasel*...'

'But the moment they see the *Titmouse* ...'

'Listen. Have those people ever seen the *Titmouse* ... really seen her, so as to know her again? No. What can your George Owdon (horrid name) have told them about her? ... a small sailing-boat called *Titmouse*. But supposing she doesn't exist ... Supposing there *is* no *Titmouse* on the river ...'

Breakfast was over. Washing up was done. The *Teasel*, stripped of her awning, was ready to sail. But William, of all her crew, was the only one aboard. Dick and Dorothea were in the bows of the *Titmouse* cocking her stern up out of the water. Admiral Barrable was kneeling in the stern of the *Teasel*'s dinghy, with her palette on one hand and a paint-brush in the other. Tom was in the dinghy with her, holding it as steady as he could. The black E of 'Titmouse' was vanishing under fresh white paint, as the *Death and Glory*, with the twins at the oars, Joe in the bows and Bill and Pete in the stern, came out from among the trees.

'Got that rope?' shouted Tom.

'We got him,' shouted Joe.

'Whatever do you want it for?' asked Starboard, and at that moment everybody in the *Death and Glory* saw what had happened to the name on the *Titmouse*'s transom.

'Gee whizz!' said Joe. 'If that don't puzzle 'em.'

'You won't know her when we've done with her,' said Tom. 'Just wait till we've got that rope rigged all round her for a fender.'

'Well, Joe,' said Mrs Barrable. 'What about that watcher of yours at Acle? He doesn't seem to have been of much use yesterday.'

The twins laughed.

'Him?' said Joe indignantly. 'I been down to Acle last night. Bill's bike. That Robin never see 'em go through the bridge. And for why? Fourpence I leave him for the telephone. His mam keep him in bed with a stomach-ache. You wouldn' think a chap *could* get a stomache-ache for fourpence. But he done it. He go and buy a lot of dud bananas cheap and eat the lot.'

'Disgraceful,' said the Admiral.

'I'll stomach-ache him when I get him,' said Joe.

In a very few minutes the rope had been fixed all round the *Titmouse*, outside, tied to the rings that had been screwed in there for lacing down the awning. The rope was an old warp that Tom had saved when one of the wherrymen was thinking of throwing it away. It was very thick and dark with age, and when it was fastened on, it made the *Titmouse*, with her mast stowed, look like a rather neglected yacht's dinghy. Only those who knew her well could have recognized Tom's smart little sailing-boat.

'Poor old *Titmouse*,' said Tom, as he made her painter fast on the *Teasel*'s counter.

Dick, in sea-boots, jumped ashore and pulled up the anchor.

'That's right,' said Starboard. 'Coil the warp. Pull her along. Push her out. Jump! ...'

'She's sailing,' cried Dorothea.

Dick, kneeling on the foredeck, was hooking the fluke of the rond-anchor through a ring-bolt. The bushes on the bank were slipping away. Tom, hauling in the mainsheet, headed out into the Broad, went about and brought her racing back for the Straits with the water singing under her bows. In the *Death and Glory* they were hauling up their own old sail as the *Teasel* flew by.

'You're in charge while we're away,' Tom called out.

'Back the day after tomorrow,' shouted Starboard.

'Right O,' Joe called back to them.

'We shan't see Ranworth again,' said the Admiral, and Dick and Dorothea looked for the last time at the little Broad where the lurking outlaw had given them their first sailing lessons. In another moment the *Teasel* was slipping along on an even keel in the shelter of the trees. Then she was clear of the Straits and foaming down the narrow dyke. The dyke had seemed long when they were quanting and towing through it in a calm. It seemed very short today, as they swept through it, and turned into the wind to beat down the river.

There was not really much to see at Potter Heigham, and all the serious shopping had been done by Tom at Wroxham the day before. But they had come there by water, under sail, in the *Teasel*, and that made all the difference. They went to the Bridge Stores and bought picture postcards of the old bridge, and the ancient thatched hut beside it, and one of a boat like the *Teasel* actually towing through under the low archway. 'This is our first port of call,' wrote Dorothea on the card she sent to her mother, 'like Malta was when you and Father went to Egypt.'

'Come along now,' said the Admiral, 'or those three skippers will be thinking their crew have run away.'

As usual, two or three people were looking down from the top of the bridge watching the boats at the staithe. Among them was a biggish boy, leaning on a bicycle. He was keeping a little way back from the wall of the bridge, as if he wanted to see without being seen. Just as Dorothea noticed him, he turned away with a smile on his face, jumped on his bicycle and rode off.

'Dick,' cried Dorothea. 'Dick, did you see him?'

'See what?' said Dick.

'I'm sure that's George Owdon. That boy. There. On the bicycle. The one we saw talking to the Hullabaloos at Horning . . .'

But the boy was already riding away along the road, and Dick could not be sure.

'He'll have seen Tom with the *Teasel*, and he'll go and tell the Hullabaloos where to look for her,' said Dorothea. 'Just when everything was going all right.'

'He may not have seen Tom at all,' said the Admiral.

But, as they themselves came to the bridge and looked down, there was the *Teasel* with her mast lowered, all ready to go through, and there were the twins sitting on the cabin roof, and there was Tom himself in full view, never thinking of who might be watching, busy with a long-handled mop cleaning a splash of mud off her top-sides.

'He'll have gone to tell the Hullabaloos already,' said Dorothea, looking up the road, where the bicycling boy was already disappearing in the distance. She ran down on the staithe with the dreadful news.

'Let's get out of sight of that bridge,' said Tom.

They sailed on. The sun still shone, and the wind blew,

the very best of winds for working through the long dyke into Horsey Mere. But, for Tom, life had somehow gone out of the day. If George Owdon had seen him with the *Teasel*, and told the Hullabaloos, the worst might happen almost any time.

This way and that they sailed about the Mere, and, at last, followed another sailing yacht into the little winding dyke, with a windmill at the end of it, just as the map had showed. Here they tied up the *Teasel* and made her ready for the night.

After a latish supper Tom and Dick went off to the *Titmouse*, to sleep one each side of the centre-board. The others settled down in the *Teasel*.

'You comfortable?' said Tom when lights were out.

'Very,' said Dick.

'Bet you aren't,' said Tom. 'It's just that one bone that's always a bother. Work round till that one's comfortable and you'll find nothing else matters.'

But for a long time after lights were out, people were awake in both boats, listening to at least three bitterns booming at each other, and the chattering of the warblers in the reed-beds, the startling honks of the coots, and the plops of diving water-rats.

It was very late when the Admiral, listening to the steady breathing of the twins in the forecabin, leant across to Dorothea. 'Why are you not asleep?' she whispered.

'Supposing the Hullabaloos came and found us,' whispered Dorothea.

'It's all right, Dot. You needn't worry. An Admiral's boat is her castle, and they'd have to sink us before we'd give him up.'

CHAPTER 14

NEIGHBOURS AT
POTTER HEIGHAM

A night's sleep seemed to have sponged the Hullabaloos from everybody's mind. Even Dorothea was thinking less of the dangers threatening the outlaw than of the coming voyage of the exiled Admiral home to her native Beccles. Today and tomorrow with the twins to help, and then she and Dick would have to take their places. The *Teasel* that morning was training ship and nothing else. Sails were set and furled three times over, just for practice. And then, hour after hour, the *Teasel* flew to and fro on Horsey Mere, beating, running, reaching, jibing, one thing after another, with the apprentices taking turns at tiller and mainsheet, each with a lecturing skipper.

But they were not allowed to forget the Hullabaloos altogether. Tom and Dorothea, when they tied up that night at Potter Heigham, looked to see if George Owdon was among the idlers by the bridge. He was not, but, as time went on, they noticed that, though other people came and went, a small, tow-haired, scrubby little boy seemed unable to tear himself away.

The funny thing was that he seemed to take no interest in sailing yachts. But every time a cruiser came to the staithe the small boy left the bridge and came strolling along the bank, whistling and looking in all directions except at the cruiser, until he was near enough to be able to read her name.

'I wonder if that's Bill's friend,' said Dorothea. 'He said he had one here, watching, and that boy was here yesterday when we went through.'

'Soon find out,' said Starboard. 'Hullo, you. Looking for someone?'

'Only for a cruiser . . . Leastways not exactly . . .'

'*Margoletta?*'

The small boy goggled at her.

'You lookin' for her, too? Don't say as I tell ye,' he whispered.

'That's all right,' said Starboard. 'Your friend's name is Bill.'

Not until dusk did the small boy leave his post.

'She won't come now,' he said, as he passed them, pretending to look the other way, and presently disappeared behind the first of the bungalows, along the bank of the river.

'A much better sentinel than Joe's stomach-ache boy down at Acle,' said the Admiral.

It was perhaps an hour and a half after that, or even more, when Tom, in the bottom of the *Titmouse*, snug in his sleeping-bag, first heard the distant throbbing of a motor-boat.

It was quite dark, long after the time at which all hired cruisers are supposed to be moored for the night. For a moment, Tom thought that worry about the *Margoletta* had made him dream of her. But there it was, a steady, thrumming noise, and it seemed to be coming nearer. Yes. There was no doubt about it. A motor-cruiser was coming up the river. Tom lay listening.

'Tom!'

That was Dick's voice, very low, from the other side of the centre-board case.

'Yes.'

'Do you hear anything?'

'Yes.'

The noise was coming nearer and nearer.

Dick whispered, 'Is it them?'

94

'It's the noise they make.' Nobody could mistake that loud rhythmic thrumming.

'No wireless this time.'

'They oughtn't to be moving after dark, anyway. That's why they aren't using it. Unless . . .'

'What?'

'Perhaps they want people to think it isn't them.'

'What can we do?'

'Don't talk.'

The noise came nearer and nearer, and suddenly lessened. An engine had been throttled down. Whatever it was, it did not want to rouse all Potter Heigham in the dark. Tom and Dick lay, silent. The awning above their heads paled for a moment as the beam of a searchlight swept across it. Tom held his breath. If they had spotted him that light would come again. It did not. Yet he could hear the cruiser close at hand. The noise of the engine changed again. Stopping. Reversing. Swinging round. Waves from the wash lifted the little *Titmouse* and slapped up under the counter of the *Teasel*. Were any of the others awake? At any moment William might start telling those people they had no right to be about. The cruiser was going ahead again. No. Again they heard her put into reverse. There was a bump against the wooden quay-heading. Someone landed heavily on the grass. Orders were being given in a low voice.

For a long time Tom and Dick listened. If it was indeed the Hullabaloos, they had tied up somewhere very near them. There was a faint murmur of talk, but not louder than might have come from any other boat. There was not a sound from the *Teasel*. The Admiral, the twins, Dorothea and William were all tired out and solidly asleep.

Time went on and on. The murmur ceased. There was no noise at all but the gentle tap tap of a rope against the *Teasel*'s mast, and the quiet lapping of the water against the quays on the other side of the river. The inn had closed long before and it had been an hour at least since the last motor car had crossed the bridge.

A breath of cold air touched Dick's face. He woke suddenly to find that Tom was no longer lying beside him, but had got up and turned back a flap of the awning.

'Tom.'

'Keep quiet.'

'What are you doing?'

'Going to see if it's them or not.'

Dick felt the *Titmouse* sway as Tom leaned out and took hold of the wooden piling along the edge of the staithe. He felt her lurch as Tom scrambled silently ashore. He fumbled for his spectacles, found them, and put them on. There wasn't much go left in that torch of his, but it might come in useful. He wriggled himself out from under the thwart. Whatever happened he must make no noise. Ouch! That was his hand between the *Titmouse* and the quay. Everything was pitch black out there. Just beyond the *Teasel* was a huge mass, and something pale creeping towards it in the grass. Dick stood up and the next moment stumbled over a mooring rope.

There was a long silence.

Dick lay still, and so did the other creeping thing that was now close to the bows of the *Teasel*. In that strange moment, Dick heard the boom of a bittern far away over the marshes, but hardly noticed it. He felt his way forward, found the next mooring rope by hand instead of by tripping over it, and, at last, was close beside Tom, looking up at the dim high wall of a big cruiser's stern.

Tom whispered, 'I can't read the name.'

Dick said nothing, but found Tom's hand and pressed his torch into it.

Tom pointed the torch down towards the black water at their feet, covering the bulb with his hand so that when he switched it on, it gave out nothing but a faint red glow. He let a little more light out between his fingers. That was no good. He held the torch close against the dark stern of the cruiser and lifted it inch by inch, until it showed them the name. One half second was enough to let them know the worst:

Margoletta

And there was Tom, as near to the cruiser and its sleeping Hullabaloos as he had been on the evening when for the sake of No. 7 he had turned himself into a hunted creature.

There was the *Margoletta* within a few yards of the *Teasel*'s bows. Their mooring warps crossed each other. There was hardly room between them for the *Margoletta*'s dinghy. Aboard the *Teasel*, everybody was asleep. It was the same aboard the *Margoletta*. Even Hullabaloos must sleep sometimes, and there they slept while Tom and Dick crept home along the bank and shut themselves in once more under the *Titmouse*'s awning.

'But what are you going to do?' whispered Dick.

Tom was thinking.

'There's only one thing to be done,' he said at last. 'But we've got to do it without waking the others ... If William wakes he'll wake everybody ... And it's no good trying to do it until it's light enough to see.'

And so, keeping awake as best they could, Tom and Dick waited for the dawn. In the end, of course, they slept, and woke in panic remembering who were their neighbours. Silently they stowed the *Titmouse*'s awning, unstepped her mast and made her a dinghy once more. It was already light, but everybody slept about them. The little wooden houses slept, and the boat-yards, and the moored yachts, and the great threatening bulk of the *Margoletta*. Only the morning chorus of birds sang as if impatient to stir the sleepers.

'They'll go and wake William,' whispered Dick. It was not at all the way in which he usually thought of the songs of the birds.

The worst moment was when Tom had to unlace a bit

of the *Teasel*'s awning, so as to lift a leg of its framework and get the tiller amidships. Then, in spite of all his care, he heard someone stir in the cabin. But there was no barking.

'Look here, Dick,' he whispered. 'You never *have* steered with a foot. But it's quite easy. You've got to steer standing on the counter, so as to see over the top of the awning.'

Silently the mooring ropes were taken aboard. Silently Tom pulled the *Titmouse* out into the river. The tow-rope tightened. The *Teasel* was moving. Dick, steadying himself with a hand on the boom, steered as well as he was able.

''Sh! 'Sh!' he whispered, as the flap of the awning was flung back, and Dorothea, like Dick, in pyjamas, looked sleepily out in time to read the dreaded name on the sleeping cruiser's bows, as the *Teasel* slipped downstream, only a yard or two away.

CHAPTER 15

PORT AND STARBOARD
SAY GOOD-BYE

Port and Starboard, sleeping in the forecabin of the *Teasel*, missed the excitements of the night. All was over, and Tom and Dick had moored the *Teasel* at a staithe three-quarters of a mile down the river, when Port, hearing their voices, leaned across from her bunk, tugged at Starboard's blankets and began, in the best Ginty manner, 'Time for the bairrns to be stirrin'. It's a braw an' bonny mornin' ... What? ... What's happened? Where are we?' She had caught sight through a porthole of a bungalow that had certainly not been there the night before.

''Sh!' whispered Dorothea. 'Don't wake the Admiral. She's been awake and gone to sleep again, and so's William.'

She squeezed through into the little forecabin and told them how the *Margoletta* had come up in the dark and moored just below them, almost touching the *Teasel*'s bow, and how Tom and Dick had slipped out early, and, towing and steering, had taken the *Teasel* into safety, out of sight and hearing of the enemy.

'But that was in a dream,' said Port. 'I dreamt I heard their beastly engine.'

'I don't believe it,' said Starboard.

'It wasn't a dream,' said Dorothea. 'I saw the *Margoletta* myself. And the Admiral says we're all to get to sleep again. She and William are asleep already.'

But nobody could sleep for very long. Even Tom and Dick, who had lain awake half the night, could not settle down.

In the end even the Admiral gave up hope of sleep, and, long before the usual time, was about in the well, stirring the Primus stove to action.

'Well,' said the Admiral, when they had crowded into their places on the bunks at either side of the cabin table and she was passing Tom his mug. 'Are you going to make a habit of casting off people's moorings without telling them anything about it? And *we* weren't moored over a coot's nest.'

'It was the only thing to do,' said Tom.

'Like last time,' said the Admiral, laughing at him.

'But he didn't send you adrift,' said Dick. 'He just towed you into a safe place.'

'I do think you might have waked us,' said Starboard.

'I didn't want to wake anybody,' said Tom. 'They were almost touching us. One bark from William and we'd have been done.'

'Let's slip back along the bank and have a look at them,' said Port.

'What for?' said Tom, who wanted never to see them again. 'Let's get on. They may wake any minute and come charging down the river.'

'I wonder,' said the Admiral. 'Now, supposing somebody happened to know we'd gone up through Potter Heigham, and supposing the somebody told your Hullabaloos, they may very well have come along just to wait at the bridge and make sure of Tom when he came back.'

'If the twins hadn't been in such a hurry to get back, we'd have been coming down this morning,' said Tom. 'I'd have come rowing out from under the bridge towing the *Teasel*. They couldn't have helped seeing me, and I wouldn't have had a chance of getting away.'

'And now,' said the Admiral, 'they'll be sitting there all day, watching the bridge and waiting for the criminal to come through.'

That was a very pleasant thought and lent an extra relish to the eggs and bacon.

It was turning out another fine spring day. The south-easterly wind was freshening up again. 'Just the wind,' Starboard said, 'to take us back to Horning. And we needn't be there till afternoon.'

The twins wanted to make the very most of the *Teasel*'s last day as a training ship. Tomorrow she would be sailing south without them, and they were determined that she should sail with as good a crew as could be trained in the time. 'Train them?' Port had said. 'We're simply going to cram them.' And on this last day, the moment breakfast was done with, they got Dorothea so muddled with questions first from one side and then from the other about the rule of the road that, when asked what she would do if, running before the wind, she met two boats beating on opposite tacks, she said, 'I should ask the captain,' which the Admiral said was a very good answer indeed. The twins simply had to keep themselves busy, so as not to feel too sad to think that they were not coming too, to help in sailing the *Teasel* in the big rivers of the south. It could not be helped. Their A.P. was counting on them. But the good wind, and the brisk spring day made staying at home and sleeping in beds instead of in bunks a very gloomy prospect.

There was no doubt that the *Teasel*, as a training ship, had been a great success. Neither Dick nor Dorothea hesitated for a moment now when asked to touch their port cheeks or starboard shoulders, though the mischievous Port had them both muddled when suddenly she ordered them: 'Now, quick; no waiting! Touch your starboard noses.' They knew the names of all the ropes and could find the right one if not too desperately hurried.

On this last day of their training, Tom and the twins made Dick and Dorothea sail the *Teasel* almost by themselves, of course, after lending weight on halyards to get the sails properly set. They left the last of the Potter Heigham bungalows, and reached past the Womack Entry, and beat down to Thurne Mouth, and ran before the wind when they turned by the signpost into the Bure, while the Coots stood by, giving a word of advice sometimes, and easing out or hauling in the mainsheet. Nothing went wrong, except that just once a pair of reed buntings very nearly made Dick steer into the bank.

In the main river they had a grand wind to help them, and they sailed home at a great pace, past Ant Mouth, and Horning Hall Farm, and the *Teasel*'s old moorings and the entry to Ranworth where the outlaw had lain low. They swept by too fast to see much of No. 7, but they all saw the coot with the white feather, and Dick, who had the glasses, thought he could see the sooty young ones in the nest. As soon as they passed the Ferry, Tom hauled the *Titmouse* close up to the counter.

'I can't take her up to the staithe,' he said. 'Anybody who knows her would be sure to see her name's been painted out. I'll hide her in our dyke, and come along at once.'

The wind was already not so strong, and Tom slipped easily down into her, and the *Teasel* sailed on up the village without a dinghy towing astern of her while the disguised *Titmouse* with the rope fender round her and Mrs Barrable's oil paint over the letters on her transom, disappeared behind the reeds, and was tied up once more beside the ancient *Dreadnought*.

'Well, and how did you get on?' asked his mother, when Tom ran in just to have a look at our baby before running up the lane to join the others at the staithe. 'I hear dreadful stories about you and the twins up the river.'

'Oh, that was all right,' said Tom, 'but we had a narrow squeak last night. Those people moored next door to us at Potter in the dark, but we got away before they woke this morning.'

'Trust you,' said his mother. 'But what about your crew?

Do you think you and Mrs Barrable will really be able to sail her yacht with only those two children to help?'

'They're coming on like anything,' said Tom. 'We'll manage all right. But I wish the twins were coming too.'

The twins meanwhile had brought the *Teasel* up to the staithe in style, and swung her round and laid her alongside so tenderly that if Dick and Dorothea had been holding fenders packed with valuable eggs instead of with scraps of old cork, not an eggshell would have been broken. Then, teaching to the very last, they put their apprentices through the whole routine of stowing jib and mainsail.

And then Mr Farland, back from the office in Norwich, strolled along the staithe to fetch his daughters.

Port and Starboard stepped ashore with their knapsacks and rugs. They were ready to say good-bye now. It would be more than they could bear, to come in the morning, and wave handkerchiefs, and see the *Teasel* sail away without them.

'Good-bye! Good-bye! And thank you ever so much, Admiral.'

'Good-bye, and good luck to your racing.'

'And thanks most awfully for showing us how to do things,' said Dorothea.

'Touching starboard noses for instance,' said Port.

At the last minute it was hard to go. The twins stood there on the staithe, as if there was still something they wanted to say if only they could remember what it was.

'Come along,' said their A.P., picking up both their knapsacks. 'You must get a good sleep tonight. Remember you've a championship race tomorrow.'

CHAPTER 16

SOUTHWARD BOUND

Early next morning, the *Teasel* set out. The water was creaming under her forefoot. The wind exactly suited her. Tom said nothing, but that noise was a song in his ears. If only Port and Starboard had been with them! The boat-sheds were astern of them, the willow-pattern harbour, and now his own home, still asleep in the early morning sunshine. There was the entrance to his dyke, between willows and brown reeds. There, behind bushes, farther back from the river front, was the twins' house. He looked at the windows ... No ... There was not a sign of them. Everybody was still asleep.

'It's an awful pity they couldn't come,' said Dorothea, and Tom started, at hearing his own thought spoken aloud. But it was no good thinking it. He set himself again to the business in hand. There must be no mistakes. He knew that the success of the voyage and the safety of the *Teasel*, and of the little *Titmouse*, too, towing astern, depended on him. Mrs Barrable was very good in a boat, but, talking it over among themselves, the three elder Coots had decided that the Admiral, though a good sailor, was inclined to be a little rash. And then there were the new A.B.s. Well, they were certainly shaping like good ones. As soon as they were in a reach where there was less chance of an unexpected jibe, he would have them at the tiller, standing by, of course, in case of accident. They had managed very well with the hoisting of the sails. And there had been nothing to be ashamed of in the actual start. He wished the twins had been there to see how well their pupils had remembered what they had been taught. And now the *Teasel* was sweeping past the Ferry. The next bit would be easy sailing.

'Come on, Dick. Take over for a minute or two.'

Dick was ready, clutched the tiller as if he thought it might get away, watched the burgee fluttering out, and glanced astern to see how badly the *Teasel*'s wake betrayed the unsteadiness of his anxious steering.

'Never mind about the wake,' said Tom. 'You're doing jolly well.'

He looked into the cabin, to see what had become of the Admiral. She was sitting on her bunk with William beside her. William had decided that it was still too early for pugs to be out-of-doors. Seeing Tom, the Admiral held up some sheets of paper she had folded so that they made a little book. On the outside page she had drawn a little sailing yacht, and under that picture she had written, in very gorgeous printed letters:

LOG OF THE TEASEL

'I forgot all about the log,' said Tom.

'Sailed 6.45 a.m.,' said the Admiral. 'Within a minute or two. Anyhow, I've put it down.'

'Thank you very much,' said Tom.

At first the *Teasel* seemed to be the only vessel moving on the river. The few yachts and motor-cruisers they passed were all moored to the banks, covered with their awnings, still asleep. But not far from Horning Hall they came round a bend in the river to find an eelman in his shallow, tarred boat, going the rounds of his nightlines. He was a friend of Tom's, and lifted a hand like a bit of old tree root as they swept past him, calling out their 'Good mornings'. Then they met a wherry quanting up with the last of the flood.

'Hullo, young Tom,' called the skipper of the wherry, seeing Tom at the mainsheet of the *Teasel*. 'Have you seed Jim Wooddall?'

'He's lying above Horning,' shouted Tom. 'I saw old Simon on the staithe last night.'

'Do you know everybody on the river?' asked the Admiral.

'I know all the wherrymen,' said Tom. 'You see, they all come past our house.'

Already there were sails moving far away over the fields towards Potter Heigham, and they were coming to the mouth of the Thurne and the sharp turn of the Bure down towards Yarmouth, where the signpost on the bank points the way along the river roads.

Tom hauled in on the mainsheet.

'Round with her,' he said. 'Steadily, right round.'

Dick pulled the tiller up. The jib flew across. There was a flap and a violent tug as the mainsail followed it. Tom paid out the sheet hand-over-hand. It was a beautiful jibe. The *Teasel* was in waters where Dick and Dorothea had never been. The outlaw, the exile and the new A.B.s were southward bound at last.

CHAPTER 17

PORT AND STARBOARD
MISS THEIR SHIP

At the moment when the *Teasel* was sailing down the river past their house, and Tom was looking at the windows and thinking they were still asleep, Port and Starboard were lying awake in bed. They were both thinking of the voyage of the *Teasel*, and had been awake for some time.

'They're sure not to get off as early as they meant to,' said Starboard.

'Nobody ever does,' said Port.

'It'd be awful hanging about to see them go,' said Starboard.

'We've said good-bye once,' said Port.

There was a long silence, except for the birds and for a growing rustling noise in the trees.

'I wish they'd gone straight on yesterday,' said Starboard. There was another long silence. It was broken by Mrs McGinty coming in with a big can of hot water. The twins after lying awake so long had got to sleep again just before she came to call them. They pushed their noses into their pillows. The hot water stood there cooling. The next thing they heard was the banging of the breakfast gong, when they shot out of their beds, one to port and the other to starboard, tubbed and dressed without more than half drying, and raced downstairs.

'Good morning. Sorry we're late.'

But the A.P. was not there.

'An' well you may be sorry,' said Mrs McGinty. 'Mr Farland's had a letter the noo and I'll be keepin' his buttered eggs warm ... So help yoursel's while ye can.'

'Good old Ginty,' said Starboard. They both knew that Mrs McGinty was never as cross as she sounded.

'A letter?' said Port, looking at the pile by her father's plate. 'But he's had lots.'

'Well, he's ta'en this yin to the telephone,' said Mrs McGinty, and then they heard their father's voice through the open door of the study.

'Hullo! Is that you, Walters? Thank goodness for that. Nip round to the office and get me all the papers in that Bollington business. Consultations on it this week. Yes ... All in the folder. And the deeds ... Yes, yes. Bring the whole lot down to the station. Coming in by car. You'll get it garaged after I've gone. I've got to catch the nine-one. Right. Good man. Everything on the case ...' He hung up the receiver, took another mouthful of buttered egg from Starboard, washed it down with a drink of coffee offered him by Port, and hurried back to the dining-room.

'You aren't going away?' said Port.

'These things will happen,' said Mr Farland. 'I didn't expect this business to come on for another two months at least ...'

'But what about *Flash* and the championship? Couldn't you put it off for a week?'

'Impossible,' said Mr Farland, scooping the last of the buttered egg off his plate.

'But the first race is tomorrow.'

'I've got to scratch for it,' said their father. 'I've got to scratch for the lot. And with old *Flash* properly tuned up she'd have shown them her heels in every race.'

'Oh, A.P. How awful! And when you'd got everything ready.'

'I'll have to telephone to the secretary right away, and get him to explain to the others. Never mind, *Flash* shall challenge the winner as soon as I get back. I'll tell him so at once.'

'Are you going today?'

'Didn't you hear me say so? Going this very minute. Pass that toast-rack, will you ... and the marmalade.'

In the hurry and bustle of getting him off, it was not until the very last moment that the thought came to Starboard that the A.P.'s going changed everything, and that now there was nothing to keep them at home.

'I say, A.P.,' she said. 'If you're going away, and *Flash* won't be racing, what about us sailing in the *Teasel* with Tom and Mrs Barrable and those two children?'

'But you haven't been asked, have you?'

'Oh yes,' said Port.

'We said "No",' said Starboard.

'But if *Flash* isn't racing we'd like to.'

'Consolation prize, eh?' said Mr Farland, stowing his suit-case in the back of his car.

Nothing was said by either twin in reply to that.

'I don't see why you shouldn't, if Mrs Barrable'll have you,' he went on, throwing himself into the driver's seat, and starting the engine.

'Good-bye.' 'Good-bye.'

Mr Farland waved with his left hand, steered with his right, swung out of the gate and was gone.

'Come on,' said Starboard.

The two raced for the house and upstairs again into their bedroom. The knapsacks, unpacked with such melancholy last night, were taken once more from the hook behind the door. The twins' packing was less orderly than Mrs McGinty's. Drawers were pulled out and left out. Shoes were tossed under the bed and rubber sea-boots put on. Sweaters, sand-shoes, washing things and night clothes were crammed into the knap-sacks, rugs rolled up, and, by the time Mrs McGinty had climbed upstairs, the twins were already rushing down.

'But look at yon room,' said Mrs McGinty.

'Fair awfu',' said Port. Starboard was already leaping down the last flight of stairs. 'Leave it till we come back, Ginty.

We'll tidy up then. There simply isn't time now. We're in a worse hurry than father.'

'Ye're aye that,' said Mrs McGinty.

They kept up a steady trot all through the long lower street of Horning.

'We'll be in time to help them up with the sails,' said Starboard jerkily. 'Those two . . . not very strong.'

'Shan't have any breath,' panted Port.

'Keep it up,' said Starboard.

At last they swung round the corner at the end of the boat-yards and came out on the staithe where, last night, they had said good-bye to the *Teasel*.

The *Teasel* was there no longer.

'They've shifted her,' said Starboard.

'They've gone,' said Port.

The staithe was deserted. Even the old *Death and Glory* that had been tied up close by the Swan had disappeared. The twins ran to the water's edge, and looked down the river. Not a boat was stirring.

'Too late,' said Starboard.

'And with this wind there was no need,' said Port. 'They'll be at Stokesby with hours to spare before the tide turns against them.'

'Of course, they didn't think we were coming,' said Starboard.

An old wherryman, Simon Fastgate, came to the end of the staithe with his arms full of parcels, and a big bottle of milk. He untied an old boat that was lying at the end of the boat-sheds, dumped his parcels into it, pushed himself off, and paddled away upstream.

'Ask Simon,' said Port.

'Hullo, Simon. Do you know when the *Teasel* sailed?'

'Been gone before I come ashore,' said Simon. 'And that's an hour and more.' He pulled away as hard as he could.

An hour already. Perhaps more. If only Tom had not been in such a hurry. The twins looked miserably at each other. It was one thing to give up a voyage to Beccles in order to help the A.P. to win his races. It was a different thing altogether to miss it for no reason at all. A whole week's voyaging lost for nothing. And after the A.P. had himself given them permission to go.

'We can't do anything,' said Starboard.

'Go back to Ginty,' said Port.

And just then, they heard the splash of a quant, and looked up the river. A wherry with mast up and sail ready for hoisting was coming into sight round the bend. They knew the wherry *Sir Garnet*, and they knew the skipper Jim Wooddall, when they heard him shout at his mate, who was already scrambling aboard and making fast his boat to a bollard in the stern.

'Simon, ye gartless old fool. Ye've missed us this tide. We should'a been gone two hour since.'

There was no reply. Simon was already hurrying to the winch and the big black sail of the wherry began to lift. Jim Wooddall had indeed been in a hurry, to start quanting his wherry round to the staithe to look for his mate, and old Simon knew that hoisting sail was better than excuses.

Suddenly Starboard dropped her knapsack and her rug and shouted at the top of her voice.

'Jim! Jim Wooddall. *Sir Garnet*! Ahoy! Jim. JIM!'

The wherryman waved a hand to her. He was already laying his quant down, and going aft to the tiller. *Sir Garnet* would be sailing in a moment.

'Jim!' shouted Port.

They both waved their arms at him, until Jim Wooddall, in a hurry as he was, saw that there was something urgently needed.

'Half a minute, Simon!' he called. The clanking of the winch pawl stopped. The gaff had been lifted not more than a couple of feet. *Sir Garnet* was hardly moving, except with the stream. But she had steerage way, and Jim brought her round close by the staithe. The twins, picking up their knapsacks, ran along the staithe to meet him, and then walked with the wherry, explaining as she drifted down.

'Can't wait,' said Jim. 'Simon's lost us a tide down to Gorleston.'

'But we want to get to Stokesby,' said Starboard. 'Tom's taken the *Teasel* down there, and they're going on tomorrow.'

'We're going too,' said Port. 'Only we missed them.'

'You see, we didn't know till this morning we could go.'

All this time the wherry was moving. Another few yards and they would be at the end of the staithe, so that they could walk no farther.

'Ah,' said Jim. 'So Tom don't know he left you.'

'That's just it,' said Port.

'Ain't supposed to take passengers,' said Jim Wooddall. 'Let's have them bags . . .' The knapsacks and rugs were swung aboard. 'Now then!' Port and Starboard leapt from the staithe after their knapsacks. 'Pierhead jump,' said Jim Wooddall. 'I'll take you down to Stokesby. But you'll have to work your passages. Peelin' potatoes. Now then, Sim!'

The winch clanked again. The huge black sail climbed up and spread above them, and the wherry, *Sir Garnet*, late with her tide, gathered speed and stood away down the middle of the river.

CHAPTER 18

THROUGH YARMOUTH

A little brown heron flew low over the reeds on the Upton side of the river.

'Isn't it a bittern?' asked Dick. Dorothea was steering and Dick was free to look at birds.

'It's a bittern all right,' said Tom, but just then he was not interested in bitterns. As he himself had once said of the Death and Glories, 'You can't expect them to be bird protecting all the time.' The *Teasel* was sweeping down towards Acle, and at Acle, he knew, would come the first real test of her crew. Never before had they lowered the mast and raised it again without the help of Port and Starboard. And at Acle Bridge there are always lookers-on, waiting to enjoy the misfortunes of the unskilled. Tom could give none of his mind to birds. But Admiral Barrable pleased Dick a good deal, by reaching into the cabin for the log of the *Teasel* and writing in it: 'Sighted bittern over Upton Marshes.' The Admiral, after that one nervous moment at Horning, seemed to have no worries at all. It seemed to Tom that she must have forgotten that every minute's sailing was bringing them nearer not only to Acle but to Yarmouth and Breydon, racing tides and every kind of possible disaster. Tom felt like the newly appointed captain of a liner on his first voyage in a new ship approaching a coast long noted for its dangerous shoals.

But the passing of Acle Bridge was a most comforting success. True, in rounding up to the northern bank, to lower sail, the *Teasel* hit the bank a little harder than Tom intended, but the bank is soft mud, and a great many people hit it harder still. And Dick, on the foredeck, was not flurried by the bump, but jumped ashore and stamped the rond-anchor well in, as if he had been doing it for years.

Tom, with his eye always on the time and the tide, felt better now. He was steering because, alone of his crew, he could manage the tiller with one hand and a pork pie in the other without danger of running the *Teasel* into the reeds. Sitting on the coaming that ran round the well, he could even manage to hold a bottle of lemonade between his knees. Acle Bridge was left astern. The tide had still a couple of hours to run down, and already they were nearing Stokesby where, at first, they had planned to spend the night. They were going to be able to do much better than that.

The Admiral, however, would have been content to stop.

'What about it, Tom?' she asked, as Stokesby windmill came in sight, and then the houses of the little village. 'Have we done enough for the first day?'

'We'll be down at Yarmouth in time for low water,' said Tom, 'with the wind holding like this. We could get right through Breydon ...'

'Wouldn't it be lovely if we got to Beccles,' said Dorothea.

'It would certainly be very pleasant,' said the Admiral, 'to know that we were through Yarmouth.'

'Well,' said Tom, 'of course it *is* much the worst bit. It'd be jolly nice to get it over.'

And just then they saw something that made them decide at once that wherever they might stop for the night it would certainly not be at Stokesby.

Dorothea went suddenly quite white. She stammered. 'L-l-look! ... T-t-tom! ...'

'What's the matter, Dot?' asked the Admiral.

'We must turn back,' gasped Dorothea.

'I can steer her,' said Dick quickly.

'Take the tiller somebody,' said Tom, and dived head first into the cabin.

A big motor-cruiser was lying moored to the quay by the inn at the lower end of the village.

'You'd better let me have her,' said the Admiral. 'But are you sure that's the one? There are lots of them about, and they are very much alike.'

'I can read the name,' said Dick, who was looking at it through the glasses.

All three of them could read it now, and Tom, lurking in the cabin, could read it, too, looking through a porthole. There it was, 'MARGOLETTA', in big brass letters on the cruiser's bows.

'Well, we can't possibly stop here,' said Tom, coming back into the well.

'All right, skipper,' said the Admiral, 'but I do count on being able to make some tea before very much longer.'

'I wonder if they're coming down, too,' said Tom. 'Oh well, we'll hear them coming. But I shan't be able to hide while we're going through Yarmouth bridges.'

He took the tiller again, and soon forgot the Hullabaloos in the excitement of steering the *Teasel*. With this good wind, and the tide under her, she seemed to be going faster every minute, and he could almost see the river narrowing as the tide ebbed. This was not at all like steering in the gentle streams and easy tides that run above Acle Bridge.

'Deepest water round the outer side of the bends,' Tom murmured to himself, after cutting a corner too fine, and feeling the *Teasel* suddenly hesitate and then leap forward again as her keel cut through the top of a mudbank.

Mile after mile the *Teasel* and the *Titmouse* flew down those dreary lower reaches of the Bure. Windmills slipped by one after another, and the rare houses called by their distance out of Yarmouth, 'Six-Mile House', 'Five-Mile House', and so on. And still the ebb was pouring down, and the mud was widening on either side of the channel. Were they going to reach Yarmouth too soon? Tom knew well enough that many a boat had been carried down and smashed against the bridges after getting there too soon and not being able to stop in the rush of the outflowing tide.

On the left bank now was a low wall of cement shutting in the river.

'It wouldn't do to bump into that,' said Dick, remembering the harmless reeds and mud of the upper waters.

Tom did not answer. The *Teasel* was sweeping round the bend, heading down for Yarmouth and its bridges, and he could see by the way the flecks of foam were being swept along that there was a lot of the ebb to run out yet before low water. 'A dolphin on the right bank going down ...' Jim Wooddall had told him exactly what to look for, and he had been down here before with Mr Farland and the twins. Tom looked anxiously down the river for the group of heavy piles standing out into the channel, so that boats can tie up to them and wait in safety. With wind and tide together, the *Teasel* was moving dreadfully fast.

'Too early,' he said quietly to the Admiral. 'We'll have to turn round and hang about a bit ... if we can. We're going too fast to make sure of catching the dolphin. Ready about!'

There was sudden bustle in the well of the *Teasel*. Nobody had expected this, and even Dick could feel that Tom was worried. Dick and Dorothea fumbled together at the jib-sheet.

'No. No,' said Tom, 'just be ready to harden in when she's round.'

The *Teasel*, still being carried down by the tide, swung round into the wind.

'Mainsheet,' said Tom.

Hand over hand the Admiral hauled it in. The *Teasel* was sailing again, but heading up the river the way she had come. She could point her course and was moving fast through the water, but Tom was looking not at the water but at a little stump on the bank. Would she do it or not?

'She's going backwards,' said Dorothea, almost in panic.

'Give her a little more mainsheet,' said Tom.

Slowly, slowly, inch by inch, though the water was foaming under her bows, she began to move up the river. The stump on the bank was level with her mast, was level with Tom at her tiller, was left astern.

'She can do it,' said Tom exultantly. As long as the wind held like that they were safe.

And then a man appeared on the bank.

'Take you through Yarmouth, sir?' he said.

Tom glanced at him.

'Fetch her in here and I'll come aboard,' said the man.

But Tom was no visiting stranger but a Norfolk Coot. He had heard about the wreckers of Yarmouth who are always ready to lend a hand and, a little later, to do a bit of salvage work. He knew that the Yarmouth Corporation itself warns visitors to apply for help at the Yacht Station and nowhere else. And the Admiral had not forgotten the tales of years ago, when she had been a little girl. She gave one look at Tom.

'No thank you,' said Tom, 'we're in no hurry.'

'You just throw me a warp then,' said the man, 'I'll make you fast.'

'We don't mind sailing till the ebb slackens,' said Tom.

All this time the *Teasel* was slowly creeping up the river again, and the man was keeping pace with her, moving foot by foot along the cement wall.

'Bit o' soft mud just here,' said the man. 'You head her in for me, and you'll be all right.'

'I'll try it next year,' said Tom.

The man threw out his hands as if to signal that he had failed. Instantly three other men bobbed up from behind the wall and joined him, and all four of them settled down to play cards while waiting for an easier victim.

'Those were the ones who were going to save us when he had got us into a mess,' said Tom.

'Real wreckers,' said Dorothea. 'How lovely.'

'Not for us,' said Tom, 'if we'd let them get a foot aboard.'

At last the tide began to slacken and the *Teasel* moved faster past the stumps and stones Tom noticed on the banks.

'We can do it now,' he said. 'Ready about!'

Once more the *Teasel* swung round and a moment later was flying downstream again towards the bridge.

'Phew,' said Tom. 'Sorry. I ought to have thought of it before. We'll want the anchors off their ropes. The anchors will be in the way for tying up.'

'Don't tumble off, Dick,' cried Dorothea. Dick was again sailor and nothing else, and had darted forward. It was an easy job, slipping the loop at the end of the rope clean over the anchor and then pulling it out through the ring on the shank. Dick was back in a moment with an anchor in his hand. Dorothea was unfastening the stern anchor in the same way.

'Shove them anywhere,' said Tom.

'Now,' said Mrs Barrable quietly, watching the dolphin as they swept down towards it.

'I'll go forrard to make fast,' said Tom. 'Could you steer? I'll bring her round, and then you just edge her over and I'll grab the dolphin and hang on . . .'

The *Teasel* swung round in the stream.

'She'll do it,' said Tom, and ran forward. 'A wee bit nearer,' he called. There was the dolphin, huge, above him, a great framework of black piles, with a platform. He got hold of the platform, and with the other hand flung the warp round a pile. He caught the end of it again. Safe. 'Hi! Look out. Fend her off.' The *Teasel* was swinging hard in against the piles. 'All right now.' He made the warp fast and lowered the peak. In another moment he had the jib in his arms, brought it down on deck, pulled a tyer from his pocket, and made sure that it would not blow loose. And now, comfortably, without hurry, the mainsail was lowered, and Tom looked happily at the brown water still pouring past them, and at the bridge below them, and at a few small boys who were critically watching.

'All right now,' said Tom. 'We've just got to get the mast down ready to go through as soon as it's dead low water.'

'Let's have the mast down now,' said the Admiral, 'and then we'll be ready when the tide's ready for us, and we can have our tea while we're waiting for it.'

Tea was ready and the whole crew of the *Teasel* were enjoying it in the well, when they were hailed from the shore. They looked up to see a little old sailor man with a white beard standing on the bank.

'Wanting a tow through the bridges?' he said. 'They know me at the Yacht Station,' he added, but there was no need. Anybody could see in a moment that he was not one of the wreckers.

The Admiral looked at Tom.

Tom, just for a moment, thought how pleasant it would be to take a tow and have no more to worry about. And then he thought of Port and Starboard. He would like to be able to tell them that the *Teasel* had got through alone.

'It's just as you like,' said the Admiral.

'No thanks,' said Tom. 'We're going to wait for slack water.'

'You'll be all right,' said the old man cheerfully. 'Tide be setting up Breydon already.* But you'll be coming back another day. If you want a tug then to pull you through Yarmouth, you ring up the Yacht Station from Reedham or St Olave's and say you want the *Come Along* to meet you on Breydon. They'll give me the word.'

'The *Come Along*,' repeated Mrs Barrable.

* The flood tide begins to run up the Yare while the ebb is still pouring out of the Bure.

'What a lovely name for a tug,' said Dorothea.

'She's a lovely tug,' said the old man. 'Motor-boat, she is. Take you up no matter how the tide run. When she say come along, they have to come.'

Mrs Barrable scribbled down the name in the log of the *Teasel*.

'You wait for slack water and you'll come to no harm,' said the old man, and went off along the bank.

'We're in for it now,' said Tom, 'but I know it's easy enough if you don't start down too soon.'

'All right, Skipper,' said the Admiral. 'We've done very well so far.'

'Hang on with the stern warp,' said Tom. Standing in the *Titmouse* he cast off the *Teasel*'s bow warp. There was still enough current to swing her slowly round.

'Cast off stern warp!' They were doing jolly well, those two, but at a moment like this he could not help wishing for the twins.

'Everything's loose,' said Dick.

'Everything's loose . . .' Port and Starboard would hardly have put it like that. But Tom knew what Dick meant. Slowly, easily, he settled to his oars. The dolphin was slipping away astern. The *Teasel* tugged at her tow-rope, tugged half-heartedly once again, but presently came more willingly.

'Is she steering all right?' Tom asked.

'Beautifully,' said the Admiral.

'There's one bridge gone already,' said Dorothea.

The *Teasel* slipped down between the high quays, and the little houses that seemed to rise out of the river mud. There was a dreadful smell of dead fish. Moored to ring-bolts in the walls of the houses and lying on the mud beneath them were little fishing-boats, some with brown nets spread to dry.

But Tom, steadily rowing in the *Titmouse*, had no eyes for this. It had seemed to be nearly dead water up above the bridges, but the further he got the faster the stream was pour-

ing out between the mud-banks. Had he, after all, made the
mistake he had been warned against, and in spite of all that
waiting, started down too soon? There could be no going back
now. It would be all right if only he did not miss the dolphin
when they came out from under the third bridge where the
rivers meet at the top of Yarmouth Haven. The second bridge
was gone. A motor-bus roared across the third close behind
him. Now was the time. Keep close to the right bank. He
edged nearer, and began to wonder if he had better make
fast to the dolphin with his own painter or with the tow-rope
itself. Better with the tow-rope if he could. The shadow of
the bridge fell across him. He was through. He glanced over
his shoulder. There was a steamer coming up out of the lower
harbour. A schooner was moored against the quay on the left
bank. There were the dolphins, black and white, and beyond
them open water, miles of it, and the long white railway bridge
over Breydon, with the swing bridge in it open for the passing
of the steamer. And the Admiral and Dick and Dorothea,
looking at all these things, were steering gaily down the middle
of the river.

Tom yelled: 'Starboard! Head her to starboard! This side!'
Oh, if only the twins had been aboard.

He pulled as hard as he could across the stream and towards
the dolphins. There was one that would do if only he could
get to it and make fast in time. Over his shoulder he saw the
iron bar flecked with green weed, fixed upright on the pile
for people to pass their warps round. But it was more than
he could do with the *Teasel* heading straight downstream.

'This side!' he shouted again. At last they understood. The
Teasel headed after him towards the dolphin. The tow-rope
slackened. Another stroke, another, and his hands were clutch-
ing at the slippery pile. 'Go through, you beast!' he muttered
to the spare end of the tow-rope as he pushed it in behind
the iron bar. It was through at last. He freed the rope from
the thwart of the *Titmouse* and hung on. The *Teasel* drifting

down with the stream tautened it, stretched it, stopped and swung. A moment later he was alongside her bows, and had given the end of the rope to Dick to make fast. They were safe.

'Well done, Tom,' said the Admiral as Tom came aboard and tied the little *Titmouse* to the *Teasel*'s counter. 'Sorry about our steering.'

'The steering was all right,' said Tom. 'Only that last bit. I was afraid there wouldn't be time to make sure of the dolphin. But it was all right. Come on, Dick, let's have the mast up and get away.'

The mast went slowly up, and the jib, and Tom and Dick and Dorothea were being very particular about the set of the mainsail. Tom wanted it exactly right for sailing up Breydon.

'That man's shouting at us,' said Dorothea.

A sailor on the schooner away by the quay was giving them a friendly warning. 'Ahoy there. Best stir yourselves. They'll be closing the bridge.'

'Cast off,' cried Tom, and Dick let go one end of the tow-rope, and began hauling in hand over hand on the other as it came slipping round the bar on the dolphin. The fore-deck was all a clutter of tow-rope and halyards, but no matter.

The *Teasel* was sailing.

'Close-hauled,' called Tom to the Admiral. 'We've got to tack up through the bridge.'

'You'd better come and take her, Tom.'

'You deal with these ropes, Dick. Sit on the roof when she goes about. But tidy up as well as you can.' Tom ran aft and jumped into the well.

The Admiral seemed glad to let him have the tiller. Dorothea was anxiously watching Dick, who was busy on the fore-deck, trying to coil down the ropes exactly as he had seen them coiled by the Coots.

'The tide'll take us through,' said Tom. 'We've just got to keep her moving and head her in between the piers. And once we're through and round the corner we'll have a free wind up Breydon.'

'They seem in a bit of a hurry on the bridge,' said the Admiral. High on the bridge, someone was leaning from a signal cabin and waving.

'Ready about!' sang out Tom. 'Sit down and hang on, Dick!' The *Teasel* had gone almost as far as the opposite shore of the Yare. She swung round now on the port tack, but not for long. 'Ready about!' Tom sang out again. Again Dick sat down on the end of the cabin roof and took a firm grip of the mast.

'She'll do it now,' said Tom, and headed in between the piers. Railwaymen up on the bridge looked down on the little *Teasel*. The crew of the *Teasel* looked up at great iron girders above them on either side. The sails flapped. Tom was heading straight into the wind, counting on the tide to carry him through. Another ten yards. Another five. There was the clang of a changing signal, and the noise of levers slipping into place. They were through and already the huge swinging span of the bridge was closing astern of them. Presently a train roared across.

Dick finished tidying up the foredeck and joined the others in the well. William barked at the train. Tom gave a little flourish with his hand, without really meaning to do anything of the sort. 'We've done it,' he said. 'Got through Yarmouth, anyway.'

'Chocolate all round,' said the Admiral. 'We've done it without letting the *Teasel* get a single scratch.'

'I do wish Port and Starboard were here to see,' said Dorothea.

'They'll be just finishing their race,' said the Admiral.

CHAPTER 19

SIR GARNET OBLIGES FRIENDS

The twins had missed their ship, but what of that? They were aboard the fastest wherry on the river, and would catch the *Teasel* at Stokesby if they did not catch her before. They were extremely cheerful. Everything had been saved at the very last minute, and after all, they too would share in the voyage to the south, for which they had been training the Admiral's eager crew.

All the time, Port and Starboard were looking eagerly down each reach of the river as it opened before them, until, at last, Jim Wooddall noticed it and laughed.

'He've a long start of us, Tom have.'

Old Simon was steadily working away, making beautiful flat coils of the warps on the top of *Sir Garnet*'s closed hatches. He came aft now, and went into the little cabin, and came out with a bucket of potatoes and a saucepan half full of water.

'Better give him a hand,' said Jim Wooddall. 'Workin' yer passage, you are.' And old Simon sitting on the hatch with the bucket between his knees made them laugh by opening an enormous clasp knife and offering it to Starboard.

But they had knives of their own, of a handier size and were soon hard at work, though old Simon peeled four potatoes to every one of theirs, and did not think much of them as cooks.

'Look ye here, Miss Bess,' he said, 'if you takes the topsides off that thick, what sort of a spud'll ye have left for puttin' in the pan?'

They were close to the mouth of the Ant when they heard and saw the *Margoletta*. She was coming up the river against the tide, and the wherry with wind and tide to help her was sweeping down. They were close to each other when the *Margoletta* swung round and into the Fleet Dyke, where, only yesterday, the *Teasel* had been.

'Lookin' for him in South Walsham, likely,' said Jim Wooddall with a grin.

The assistant cooks of *Sir Garnet* stared at him.

'But how do you know about it?' said Starboard.

'Easy,' said Jim Wooddall, puffing at his pipe. 'Them cruisers talk enough. There's only one boy down Horning way what have a black punt and paddle her from the stern. Tom Dudgeon and his old *Dreadnought*. Tom say nothin' about it to me that day he come to Wroxham, and there was me, readin' that notice over his head. And after he go, up come that lot in *Margoletta* asking for a boy in a sail-boat ... Tom Dudgeon and his *Titmouse* for certain sure. And you missies know somethin' about how they didn't cotch him that day.' And he grinned again.

'Look here, Jim,' said Port. 'Nobody but George Owdon would have told them Tom was gone up the river in a sailing boat. And the night before last they came up to Potter Heigham, and we think George must have told them Tom was gone up the Thurne.'

'They as good as said someone tell 'em, that day Tom come to Wroxham.'

'But what we don't understand is this,' said Starboard. 'If George wants them to catch Tom, why doesn't he send them straight to Doctor Dudgeon?'

'Simple,' said Jim Wooddall. 'Fare to me that George he want 'em to cotch young Tom, but he nat'rally don't want to be in it himself. So he send 'em where he think they can't fail for to meet him. If they meet young Tom and know him, how be George Owdon to blame? But if them cruisers go to the doctor and ask for his son, why, how do they know the name of a boy they seen once in their life? Somebody must 'a told 'em. And everybody in Horning'd know who 'twas.'

'Phew!' said Port. 'I wonder if they met Tom sailing the *Teasel* today.'

'They didn't cotch him,' said Jim Wooddall. 'They'd be going to Horning or Wroxham to raise a bobbery else. Eh, Simon,' he broke off, looking at his huge old watch, 'we'll never get to Gorleston on this tide. They'll be laughin' at us when we go through Acle Bridge.'

Jim Wooddall, late with his tide, was as much in a hurry as the twins, and he was sailing *Sir Garnet* as if in a race, trimming her huge black sail, keeping always in the fastest water. Presently they came to Thurne Mouth, where the two rivers join, and had to jibe round the corner just as Tom had jibed in the *Teasel*, as they turned south for Acle. The huge black sail swung across with a clap and a creak of the gaff jaws, and a clang as the big blocks of the mainsheet shifted. Port and Starboard, themselves accustomed to racing in the little *Flash*, knew just how well their friend the wherryman was handling *Sir Garnet*.

Once through the bridge, Jim let the twins have the tiller. The mast was lifting the moment they had cleared the bridge. The big black sail rose bellying in the wind. *Sir Garnet* had left Acle Bridge astern of her, and was sailing once more. And never a sign of the *Teasel*.

'He'll have gone right through to Stokesby,' said Starboard, and went on steering the wherry, while the wherrymen finished their dinner, and old Simon made some very strong tea. Then the twins had all the bacon and potatoes they could eat. 'I would'n have Mr Farland think we starved ye,' Jim said.

Almost sooner than they expected, the windmill and the roofs of Stokesby showed above the reedy banks.

'What about putting us ashore?' asked Starboard.

Port dived down into the cabin and handed up the rugs and knapsacks that had been stowed there out of harm's way.

'Anything to break in these?' asked Jim.

'No.'

'That's lucky,' said Jim. 'We'll heave 'em ashore, an' give you an easy jump an' a soft landin'. Can't stop now.'

'But where are they?' said Port. 'Tom said he was going to moor at this end, by the windmill if he could. The wind's just right for it, but he's not there.'

'By Stokesby Ferry, likely,' said Jim.

But *Sir Garnet* swept on round the long Stokesby bend, past the windmill, and the farm, past the village, past the inn, past the ferry. Stokesby was astern of them, and one thing was clear to both of them. It was no use going ashore at Stokesby, for the *Teasel* was not there.

And now, for the first time, it came into the heads of the twins that nobody but themselves and the wherrymen knew where they were. Ginty and the A.P. thought they were aboard the *Teasel*. Aboard the *Teasel* everybody thought they were at Horning. It was one thing just to take a lift on a friendly wherry as far as Acle, or even as far as Stokesby, but here they were sailing on farther and farther from home with every minute and not knowing what was before them. What if the Admiral had changed her mind and put off going south, and Tom and the *Teasel* had gone up the Ant to Barton and Stalham, or made another trip to Potter Heigham? Some word might have reached Tom about the *Margoletta* and given him a reason for a change of plan.

The wherrymen were troubled, too. The one thing on which a wherryman prides himself is making the best use of the tides. There is no sense in sailing against the tide when an hour or two earlier or later you might be sailing with it. A wherryman sailing with the tide is always ready to laugh when he meets another struggling against it. Bad seamanship is what it seems to him. And now here was *Sir Garnet* leaving Stokesby with ten miles to go to Yarmouth, and Jim and his mate knew that if they had been an hour earlier they would not have been a minute too soon. Jim kept taking a look at his big watch, and at the mud that was showing below the green at the sides of the river. Once the tide turned it would be a long time before they could get down to Gorleston against it. And besides all this, Jim was thinking that perhaps he had been a bit hasty in taking Mr Farland's twins aboard. 'If Tom Dudgeon hadn't knowed they was coming, why should he stay waitin' for 'em? That boy'd use his tides right, and not go foolin' 'em away like some folk, darn it.'

'We can't go no further,' said Jim Wooddall at last, as he brought *Sir Garnet* quietly alongside some mooring-posts. 'This'll do for us.' For a few minutes Simon and he were busy stowing the big sail. Then he stood, rubbing his chin and looking at the worried faces of the twins.

'Tom may be down by the Yacht Quay,' said Starboard.

'Sure he come this way?' said Jim.

'They said last night they were going down to Stokesby.'

'If he come this far, he'd be taking the flood up Breydon,' said Jim. 'You can't catch him ... Best be takin' a bus to Horning if ye can get one.'

What would Mrs McGinty say if they came home with a tale like that, or even Mrs Dudgeon ... sailing off on a wherry to Yarmouth to look for a boat that might be anywhere?

'We've simply *got* to find them,' said Port.

'Ye'll be gettin' me into trouble with Mr Farland.'

And then, suddenly, Starboard saw that old Simon was pointing down river towards the bridge. A yacht with lowered mast was coming through, towed by a little motor-boat with a big red-and-white flag.

'Ye're right,' said Jim suddenly. 'If young Tom go down here, Old Bob see him. Comin' and goin', Old Bob see all.'

The *Come Along*, with the tide to help her noisy little engine, was soon passing close by the wherry. Port and Starboard saw a little old sailor in a blue jersey, by himself in the little tug, looking back every now and then over his shoulder because the people in the yacht he was towing were not steering very well. It needs practice to steer well standing on the counter of a yacht and reaching the tiller with a foot through a lot of shrouds and halyards draped about the lowered mast.

'Ahoy!' shouted Starboard. 'Have you seen the *Teasel*?'

'Hi!' shouted Jim. 'Half a mo', Bob.'

'Eh? What's that?' The little old sailor was trying to quiet his engine without stopping it altogether.

'Friends of ours,' Jim was explaining. 'Joinin' a little yacht, the *Teasel*, with Tom Dudgeon from Hornin' aboard. Seen her go through?'

'Boat full o' children with an old lady an' a dog? I see 'em. Went through at low water, they did. Wouldn't take help from no one. Last I see of 'em they was away through Breydon Bridge.'

Jim bent lower. The old man shut his engine off.

'They *got* to do it,' Port heard Jim say. 'Can't send 'em back now.'

The old man looked at the twins.

'Hop in,' he said suddenly. 'I got to go up Breydon to fetch a yacht down what's missed her tide. Hop in. We'll catch that *Teasel* for you if she've not gone too far. Easy now.'

In another two seconds the twins and their knapsacks and their rugs were aboard the *Come Along*. Jim and Simon were wishing them good luck. The twins were thanking the wherrymen. The old man had started his engine again and they were off once more, chug, chug, chug, chug, against the muddy tide that was pouring up under the town bridges.

CHAPTER 20

WHILE THE WIND HOLDS

A strange peace filled the well of the *Teasel*. There was a good wind, and they felt it more on the open water of Breydon than sheltered between the banks of the river. But that was pleasure only, and the good wind was helping them on their way. The thing that Tom had been worrying about for a week was safely over. They had got through Yarmouth. Everybody felt the same. It was as if by passing Breydon railway bridge they had passed from a turbulent day to one of settled weather. They began looking at things afresh, with the eyes of people who have no longer a care in the world.

'The Hullabaloos would have come through by now if they were coming,' said Tom.

Dorothea looked back towards Breydon. There was not another boat to be seen.

'Of course, they may come tomorrow,' said Tom, 'whatever they do today. Those beasts can get about so fast. But we're all right for now. What I was afraid of was their coming down while I was towing in the *Titmouse*.'

'It seems to me,' said the Admiral, 'that we get about pretty fast ourselves.' She shaded her eyes to look over the water ahead of them towards the evening sun. 'What do you think, skipper? Where shall we tie up for the night?'

'Let's go on sailing for ever,' said Dorothea. 'We could take turns in being awake.'

'Let's go on as far as ever we can,' said Tom. We've got a grand tide with us, and the wind's holding, and it won't be dark for a long time yet.'

'We'll see what we can do,' said Mrs Barrable.

'You'll be at Beccles tomorrow, Admiral,' said Dorothea. 'Won't she, Tom?'

'Depends on the wind,' said Tom. 'Look here, Dot, keep away from the red posts. We don't want to have to tack if we can help it.'

'I say,' cried Dick suddenly. 'Isn't that a spoonbill, there, with hunched-up shoulders, and another, dipping in the mud where that trickle is? . . . White, like storks.'

'They must be,' said Tom. 'Let's have the glasses a minute. I've only seen them once before. This goes down in the Coot Club book.'

'And in the log,' said the Admiral.

On and on they sailed.

The sun had set, the wind was dropping, but the *Teasel* was still gliding on, so smoothly, so easily, that it seemed impossible to stop. A sunset glow spread over the sky, and the reeds stood out black against it. On and on. They could hardly see where the reflections ended and the banks began. Nothing else was moving. Windmills, dark against the darkening sky, seemed twice their proper size. At last, peering forward, they could see that the river was dividing in two.

'Oulton Dyke,' said Tom, hardly above a whisper. For some time now he had been at the tiller.

There was hardly enough wind to give the *Teasel* steerage way as she bore round up the Waveney River. It died altogether. The boom swung in. The mainsheet dipped in the water.

'Have you got a torch?' said Tom. 'Mine's in the *Titmouse*.'

Dick was into the cabin and out again with his torch.

'Will you take her, Admiral?' Tom hurried forward and stood waiting with the rond-anchor in his hand, flashing the light of the torch along the bank.

'We'll try here,' he said. 'Bring her in. She's hardly moving. Will she steer?'

Gently the *Teasel* pushed her nose towards the bank. There was a thud and a squelch as Tom jumped ashore. He had the anchor fixed in a moment and was back aboard again as the dying tide swung the *Teasel* slowly round. Aft, in the well, they heard the faint rattle of the block as the jib came down. The peak of the mainsail came slowly, and with difficulty, for the halyard had swollen with the evening dew. By the light of their torches they stowed the sails. By the light of their torches they rigged the awnings, first over the *Teasel* and then over the *Titmouse*.

'Well, it isn't the furthest anybody's ever done in a day,' said Tom, 'but she really has come a jolly long way.'

'It seems a pity,' said the Admiral, 'but I suppose we must try to keep awake, just until we've had our supper.'

CHAPTER 21

COME ALONG AND *WELCOME*

The twins had been very near despair when the wherry had tied up above Yarmouth and the wherryman had told them that the best they could do was to go home. Suddenly, Old Bob and his *Come Along* had filled them with hope once more. With a motor-boat like the *Come Along* they felt sure they would be overhauling the *Teasel* in a minute or two.

'She's a splendid little tug,' said Starboard. 'SPLENDID TUG,' she shouted, seeing that the old man had not heard her.

Old Bob, sitting snugly in the stern with his arm over his tiller, agreed with a smile.

'She's a good 'un,' he shouted back. 'When she say "Come along", they have to come, and no mistake about it. Many a hundred she've pulled off Breydon mud.'

Both Starboard and the old man had been shouting to make themselves heard, but now, perhaps just to show what she could do, Old Bob opened the throttle and let her out. It was no use even shouting. Port and Starboard looked astern at the following wave racing along the quays. Somehow it seemed quite different from the wash of a motor-cruiser. It simply gave them a pleasant feeling that they were really moving through the water. It was a cheerful promise of catching up the *Teasel*. They settled down to enjoy the chase.

Old Bob pulled a pair of binoculars from under a thwart and looked into the distance ahead of them.

'Where was they bound?' he shouted into Starboard's ear.

'Beccles,' shouted Starboard.

The old man looked back over his shoulder and seemed to settle himself closer to his tiller.

They came to the top of Breydon Water and the long wall of black piling that guards the Reedham marshes. They passed the point of the spit that divides the Norwich river from the Waveney. Ahead of them, moored against the bank, was the old white hulk of the Breydon pilot.

'He'll have seed 'em,' shouted Old Bob, above the chug, chug of his motor. He leaned forward and shut down his throttle. The *Come Along* seemed almost quiet.

The pilot, hands in pockets, was walking up and down the deck of his hulk, and stopped, and stood at the rail and waited for them, when he saw that Old Bob meant to have a word with him.

'Evenin', Bob,' he said.

'Evenin',' said the old man. 'Ha' you seed a little yacht, with some children aboard, an' a dog an' an old lady?'

'The *Teasel*?' said the pilot. 'They'll be through St Olave's by now, the way they was going. Aimin' for Beccles, they said.'

'I got two first-class passengers what missed the tender,' said Old Bob, and then, suddenly, 'Is that a sail beatin' down river?'

For one moment Port and Starboard were full of hope, but the pilot said, 'Yes. Tide's too strong for her. She've been beatin' there these last twenty minutes and makin' nothin' of it.'

'That'll be my tow,' said Old Bob, opened the throttle and sent the *Come Along* racing up the river to meet her.

'But what are we to *do*?' shouted Starboard.

'I reckon we've missed 'em,' the old man shouted back. 'Gone too *far*. I got to take that *tow* ... You'd best give up and come back to Yarmouth wi' me .. If there's no bus I reckon my missus'd ...' And then, seeing Starboard's face, he stopped short. He looked back over his shoulder at the Thames barge coming up Breydon. He looked forward at the white triangle of sail showing above the banks far up the river. 'My tow won't have seed me yet,' he shouted with a grin, swung the *Come Along* round and headed back the way they had come.

'He isn't taking us back to Yarmouth now?' said Port. But nobody heard her.

Back they went, past the place where the two rivers join and there by the Reedham marshes at the top of Breydon they met the barge, forging grandly along with a curl of white water under her bows. They could see a big old man standing at the wheel, a woman busy with some knitting close beside him, and another man sitting on a hatch and playing a mouth organ. They could see his hand move to and fro across his mouth, but could hear nothing at all but the chug, chug of Old Bob's engine. Just as they met, Old Bob swung the *Come Along* round, came alongside, and closing the throttle of his engine reduced speed until the *Come Along* was keeping pace with the barge.

'*Welcome* of Rochester,' said Starboard, reading the name on a lifebuoy.

With the engine quietening, they could hear the noise of the barge rushing through the water, and the creaking of blocks and gear. The old skipper of the *Welcome* had turned over the wheel to his mate and came to the side.

'Hullo, Bob,' he said.

'Hullo, Jack. Bound for Beccles?'

'Beccles Mills,' called the skipper.

'Friends o' mine,' said Old Bob, 'joinin' a boat gone up just ahead o' ye. Will ye give 'em a lift?'

The skipper of the *Welcome* hesitated a moment, looking down with a puzzled face at the two small girls in the little tow-boat, but before he could speak the woman who was knitting was standing beside him.

'Don't you be so slow, Jack,' she said. 'Of course we will, and welcome.'

'But . . .' began Port.

Old Bob was edging his little boat nearer to the barge. The two were touching now, with only the tow-boat's fenders between them.

'Can you make it?' he shouted.

'Give me a 'and, missie.'

'Up she goes. And the next . . .'

The two boats, the little tow-boat and the big barge were moving fast through the water. But there was no time to think. There were strong arms to help them. Somehow or other, both twins found themselves aboard the barge. Their knapsacks and rugs came flying aboard after them. Old Bob's engine roared again, and the *Come Along* had sheered off and was racing up the river.

'I say,' said Port. 'We've never thanked him.'

'And what about a nice cup o' tea?' asked the woman with the knitting. 'I was just going to make tea for my 'usband, that's Mr Whittle. I'm Mrs Whittle. And the mate's name is Mr 'Awkins.'

'Our name's Farland,' said Starboard. 'I'm Nell and this is Bess.'

'Well, you 'ave 'ad a day of it,' said Mrs Whittle, when they had told about finding the *Teasel* gone from the staithe, and how Jim Woodall had given them a lift down to Yarmouth, and how Old Bob had taken them up Breydon in the *Come Along*.

On and on they sailed down that straight narrow cut, feeling all the time as if there was scarcely room between the banks for the barge and her own bow wave, which rushed along the piling on either side of her. Beyond the little bridge they would be coming into the Waveney again, and

COME ALONG AND WELCOME

the twins were doing their best to catch sight of the *Teasel*'s sail.

They were close to the bridge before there was any sign of its opening. The twins looked at Mr Whittle. He seemed at ease though the big barge was racing down the narrow cut, and there was certainly no room to turn her.

"'Ere y'are, 'Awk,' said Mr Whittle, putting his hand in his trouser pocket. "'Ere's the money for the butterfly net.'

Almost as he spoke, the bridge seemed to split in half, and both halves cocked up in the air. Two men appeared, one of them with a little bag at the end of a long pole. Mr Hawkins went to the side. The barge swept through, and as she passed the bag was held out and Mr Hawkins, holding his hand high above it, dropped two shillings in it.

'Keep the change,' he said. 'There ain't none,' he added, turning with a wink to the twins.

The barge was through.

'P'raps they haven't got so far,' said Starboard to Mr Whittle.

Mr Whittle shouted out to a man in a blue jersey and sea-boots who was digging in a potato patch just where the New Cut joins the Waveney River.

'Say, mate, you seen a little white yacht, wiv a white tender to 'er? Lot o' kids aboard.'

'They was by here half-hour ago. From Hornin' they tell me. Pushing on to see how far they could get afore dark.'

Half an hour ahead. Only half an hour. It almost seemed to the twins that they were in touch with the *Teasel* at last. Evening was closing in, too. The Admiral would soon be moor-ing for the night. Any time now they might see the *Teasel* tied up to the bank, with the *Titmouse* astern of her, and Tom and Dick and Dorothea hard at work getting the awnings up.

The twins went forward to the bows of the barge, and stood there, looking out. Mrs Whittle and Mr Hawkins came forward to join them.

'She's the finest ship we've ever been in,' said Starboard to Mr Hawkins.

'There ain't many barges afloat to touch 'er,' said Mr Hawkins. 'Carries 'er way, and 'andy, too. You should see 'er in the London River.'

'She's been foreign many a time,' said Mrs Whittle. 'Gives you quite a turn, coming up out of that companion after a night at sea to find yourself in a foreign 'arbour and everybody talking Dutch.'

But the twins were really thinking less of the *Welcome* than of the *Teasel*. They had remembered that half an hour ahead at the end of a day might be a very long time.

'They will be 'appy when they sees you,' said Mrs Whittle. 'Getting almost too dark to knit,' she added. 'Cold, too.'

And then, suddenly, the wind failed them. It had been weakening for some time. Now it died utterly away. Flat shining patches showed on the river astern. A windmill was reflected as if in glass. The skipper's eye noted some old mooring posts standing up above the reeds.

'Topsail, 'Awk! Foresail! Brails!'

As if by magic the foresail came down and the other sails shrank away against the mast. The great sprit towered bare into the sky.

'Dead water,' said the skipper. 'Tide's turning.'

The *Welcome*, hardly moving, slid nearer to the reeds.

'Couldn't 'ave let us down 'andier.'

The next moment he had left the wheel and he and Mr Hawkins were busy with creaking warps, mooring the *Welcome* for the night.

'But they aren't going to stop here?' said Starboard in despair.

'No wind,' said Mrs Whittle. 'Getting dark, too.'

'Won't he use the engine?' suggested Port.

'Not 'im,' said Mrs Whittle. 'We ain't due in Beccles till tomorrow, and you won't catch 'im wasting owner's petrol.'

'What's sails for?' said the skipper. 'Dark coming, too. We've a good berth 'ere, and we'll be in Beccles tomorrow before they want us.'

'But what about Tom and the *Teasel*?' said Starboard.

''E ain't expecting you,' said Mr Whittle. 'So 'e won't worry. And you'll give 'im a 'ail in the morning and startle 'im out of 'is skin.'

CHAPTER 22

THE RETURN OF THE NATIVE

William had waked the *Teasel* early. He had gone ashore by his private gangplank and met a terrier. He had not exactly run away, but he had waited to bark until he was safely back aboard, and after that nobody had been able to sleep another minute. Tom, still thinking of record passages, had called out from the *Titmouse* that the wind was just right and the tide running up. They had moored in the dusk quite close to a little ancient church, with a tower built in steps, like a pyramid. 'Burgh St Peter,' the Admiral had said. As soon as they were dressed she had sent Dick and Dorothea off along the bank to the Waveney Inn near by to get the milk for breakfast. Tom had stowed both awnings by the time they had got back. They had sailed on after a hurried breakfast. Trees on the banks had bothered them a little, but Dick had been allowed to do some quanting. And now, for a long time, the tower of Beccles Church had been in sight, and Dorothea had been expecting the Admiral to make some memorable remark.

· 'At last. At last. The town of his birth lay before him in the evening sunshine. The exile tottered, leaning on his stick. For a moment towers and houses and long-memoried trees vanished in a mist of tears.' Something like that, Dorothea thought, the return of a native ought to be. 'Long-memoried' pleased her a good deal. It was better than 'well-remembered', and did not mean the same thing either. Of course, really, it was going to be morning, not evening, and the returning native was Mrs Barrable, and not an aged man. But for Dorothea the main thing was that there would be a good deal of feeling about it. And somehow the Admiral seemed hardly to realize that she was coming home at last. She was making studies of trees in her sketch-book. 'In spring,' she said, 'one has a chance of seeing their bones.'

And then, sweeping slowly round a bend, they came in sight of the tall Beccles mills, and the public staithe, and a dyke full of boats still at their winter moorings, and a road bridge, with a railway bridge beyond it. Under the bridges they could see the curving river, houses almost standing in the water, rowing-boats tied to the walls, and a flock of white ducks swimming from one back door to the next.

The next moment they were rounding up by the staithe. Dick jumped ashore. Tom turned to the Admiral with a grin.

'We've got to Beccles,' he said. 'Now for Oulton. And then we may have time to get right up to Norwich before we start back.'

'Oh, but Tom,' said Dorothea. 'It's the Admiral's old home. She won't want to start again at once.'

'I want to do a little shopping first,' said the Admiral.

'And we must send off postcards to the twins,' said Tom. 'Just to let them know how far the *Teasel*'s got.'

Sails were lowered. The *Teasel* was moored fore and aft. Tom looked her over critically and decided that she was neat enough, and all five of them made ready to leave her and go up into the town.

'What's that big boat?' asked Dick, looking at a brown topsail moving above the trees far away over the meadows.

'Thames barge,' said Tom. 'You can see her sprit. She'll be here by the time we get back, the way she's moving.'

'I expect I shall hardly know the little place again,' said Mrs Barrable. Dorothea looked at her hopefully, but romance died as Mrs Barrable went on, 'Better bring both shopping baskets, Dot. I don't know what your mother would say if she knew how badly I've been feeding you. Fresh vegetables we want, and something not out of a tin. The butcher's name used to be Hanger, but I suppose he's gone long ago. What do you think about fried chops if we can get them?'

They found the post office, with the mail van waiting outside it, so, to Tom's delight, they were able to get their postcards off by the early post. They sent pictures of Beccles to the twins, to Mrs Dudgeon, and to the three small Coots of the *Death and Glory*. 'Burgh St Peter last night. Beccles this morning, 8.45 a.m.,' wrote Tom triumphantly, on his postcards to the twins. 'Wish you were here,' he added, finding there was a little room left on each card.

'And I must send one to Brother Richard,' said the Admiral.

Dorothea chose one for her, showing the river flowing close under the old houses.

The Admiral wrote her postcard and held it out for Tom to see what she had written. 'Left Horning yesterday. Beccles today. Look at the postmark. *And not one scratch on her paint.*'

'Where shall we sail for next?' the Admiral was saying, as they turned the corner and came out on the green grass.

'But we've only just got here,' said Dorothea. 'There must be heaps more things in Beccles that you want to see again.'

'That barge has got here all right,' said Tom, 'and tied up at the mill just opposite the *Teasel*. Come on, Dick, let's get a good look at her. You never see one of them in the North River. What a beauty ...' His face suddenly changed ... 'Why! ... There can't be ... There is ... There's somebody aboard the *Teasel*. Hi! You!' And he set off at a run to turn out the invader.

'Wait a minute,' called the Admiral, but he did not hear her.

They saw him take a flying leap into the *Teasel's* well from the edge of the staithe.

'He didn't wipe his shoes,' said Dick, who was always being reminded by Tom to wipe his before coming aboard.

'Something must really be wrong,' said Dorothea. 'Hulla-baloos, perhaps, lurking in the cabin. Come on, Dick ...'

All three of them hurried to the rescue as fast as they could, with William galloping among them and nearly sending them headlong by getting mixed up with their feet.

'Tom,' called Dorothea.

Just as they came to the edge of the staithe there was a burst of laughter from the *Teasel*'s cabin, and Port and Starboard and Tom came tumbling out together.

'But however did you get here?'

Port and Starboard, bursting with pride, pointed across the river at the *Welcome* of Rochester moored by the mill.

Everybody was talking at once. 'But that's a Thames barge.' 'Not at Horning.' 'Jim Wooddall took us in *Sir Garnet*.' 'But the championship races ...' 'The A.P. going off in a rush and Ginty packing.' 'Awful when you weren't at Stokesby or Yarmouth.' 'Hullabaloos?' 'Nosing into Fleet Dyke looking for you.' 'Needn't be back for a week.' 'Yes. In a cupboard bunk.' 'Oh, three million cheers!'

And then the twins wanted to know all about the voyage of the *Teasel*.

'Those apprentices must have done jolly well.' 'Should think they did.' 'How was it at Yarmouth? Did you take a tug?' 'Came through by ourselves.' 'Good for you.' 'And the bridges?' 'Lowering the mast?' 'Nobody could have done better.' 'You won't really want us as well.' 'What rot!' 'Of course we do.' 'Ten times the fun with all of us together.' 'And we were jolly lucky with the weather.' 'We couldn't have managed without you if it had come properly blowy.'

'Well,' said the Admiral when the hubbub had subsided a little and not more than three people and William were talking at once, 'with two spare skippers we can go almost anywhere. But we must at least have dinner. And somebody must go back into the town and buy another couple of good big chops.'

'We'll all go,' said Starboard.

'I'll stay in the *Teasel*,' said the Admiral, 'and get the cooking started. I want to feed you properly for once. Specially if we're sailing for Oulton this afternoon . . .'

'The Admiral's an explorer by nature,' Dorothea explained to Port as they went off with the others to see the butcher again. 'She isn't like a returning native, not really . . . Coming home means nothing to her at all.'

CHAPTER 23

STORM OVER OULTON

The twins had joined the *Teasel* none too soon. All the way from Horning to Beccles there had been nothing too difficult to be managed by Tom with no one to help him but the Admiral and a most inexperienced crew. But when they were waked in Beccles by a milkman bringing the morning milk down to the staithe, they saw, as soon as they put their heads out, that the weather did not look so kind as it had been. There was a sulky feeling in the air, and the sky was dark in the east.

'Thunder coming,' said Tom, when he and Dick went aboard the *Teasel* for breakfast.

'Looks as if it's going to blow,' said Starboard.

'Rain, too,' said Port.

'Let's get away quick,' said the hopeful Admiral, 'and we'll be in Oulton before it starts.'

The moment breakfast was over they were off. With a full crew once more, two to a halyard and one to spare, not counting the Admiral and William, the *Teasel* set sail in record time, while Mr Whittle and Mr Hawkins, smoking their pipes, watched from the deck of the *Welcome* at the other side of the river.

'You've got a smart ship, you 'ave,' said Mr Whittle as the *Teasel* headed towards the big barge, swung round close by her and was off, racing down the river with the wind abeam.

Mrs Whittle came up the companion to shake a duster just in time to use it to wave farewell.

*

They were just moving with the stream, while the rain poured down on them, dripping off the sail on the cabin roof and off the cabin roof on the side-decks. Already there were lakes in the valleys of the *Titmouse*'s awning. Then, gently at first, the wind came again, and they worked round the bends by Black Mill and Castle Mill, and were able to reach the rest of the way down the Waveney to Burgh St Peter and the mouth of Oulton Dyke. Here the wind headed them.

It was really hard work sailing, and in a wind like this that found its way through everything, not even oilskins seemed able to keep the rain out.

'I can feel it trickling down my collar,' said Dick. 'And, oh, my beastly spectacles!'

'It's gone right up my sleeves,' said Port, who had been looking after the mainsheet.

Tom said nothing. His were old oilskins, and the proofing had cracked across the shoulders, and all the top part of him was wet. While steering he had not noticed until it was too late that water was running off the oilskins straight into one of his sea-boots. Every time he moved his right foot he could feel the water seeping round it. But this was no time to think of things like that. The wind was growing harder and harder, and backing to the east. If it was as bad as this between the banks of sheltering reeds, what would it be like when they came out into Oulton Broad?

'It isn't very much farther,' said the Admiral, 'and it really does look rather fine.'

'Thunder,' said Dorothea.

'I thought it must be coming,' said Starboard.

There was a distant rumbling, and then a sudden crash, followed by a clattering as if an iron tea-tray ten miles wide was tumbling down a stone staircase big enough to match it.

'Look!'

'And over there!'

Threads of bright fire shot down the purple curtain of cloud into which they were beating their way. There was a tremendous roll of thunder. And then, just as they were coming out of the Dyke into the Broad, the rain turned to hail, stinging their hands and faces, bouncing off the cabin roof, splashing down into the water. In a few moments the decks were white with hailstones. The noise of the hail was so loud that no one tried to speak. It stopped suddenly, and a moment later the wind was upon them again. The *Teasel* heeled over and yet further over, till the water was sluicing the hailstones off her lee deck.

'Ease away mainsheet,' shouted Tom. 'Quick!'

There was a crash somewhere close to them, in the *Teasel* herself. They looked at each other.

'Water-jar gone over,' said Port.

'Ready about!'

Crash.

'There goes the other jar.'

'Ease out. In again. Must keep her sailing.'

'Look *out*, Tom, you'll have her over.'

'Sit down, you two. On the floor,' said the Admiral. 'My word,' she murmured.

It was a gorgeous sight. There was that purple wall of cloud, with a bright line along the foot of it, and against this startling background, white yachts and cruisers afloat at their moorings in the Broad shone as if they had been lit up by some strange artificial light. The green of the trees and gardens looked too vivid to be real, wherever it was not veiled by a rain-squall. It was a gorgeous sight, but not for the Coots, who were finding it all they could do to keep the yacht sailing and yet not lying over on her beam ends. It was a gorgeous sight, but not for Dick and Dorothea, who began to think that they had not yet learnt much about sailing after all. And it was not at all a gorgeous sight for poor William, who was thrown from one side to the other whenever the *Teasel* went about, and was shivering miserably on the floor of the cabin, sliding this way and that with the sand-shoes that had been thrown in to keep dry.

They were half-way down the Broad now, looking at the Lowestoft chimneys, and the Wherry Inn, and a great crowd of yachts at their moorings. Tom kept telling himself to think only of keeping the *Teasel* sailing, and not to bother about the yacht harbour until they came to it. But he could not help wondering all the time what he would find. He knew it had been changed since he had been there with the twins and their father. He would soon have to be making up his mind where to tie up. With the wind that was blowing he did not think the *Teasel's* mud-weight would hold her if they were to try to anchor in the open Broad. And all the time they were getting nearer. The *Teasel* was crashing to and fro, beating up in short tacks nearer and nearer to all those boats, and the road beyond them, where motor-buses were driving through the rain. Suddenly to starboard he saw a wooden pier with a tall flagstaff at the farther end of it, where the opening must be. Behind it was clear water ... a stone quay ... little grey buildings ... a moored houseboat. And there was a man in oilskins running out on the quay and waving. To the *Teasel*? It must be to her. There was no other boat sailing.

Tom headed for the flagstaff. The *Teasel* flew past it, round the end of the wooden pier, and was in the yacht harbour. The harbour seemed much too small, as a squall sent her flying along between the pier and the quay. Tom swung her round, judging his distance from the beckoning man. How far would she shoot, going like this? He had never before had to moor her in such a wind, and against a stone quay, too.

'Let fly jib-sheet! Slack away main! Fenders out!'

'Not you, Dick!' But Dick was already out of the well, and hanging the fenders over the sides.

'Look, out of the way, Dick.' Port was hurrying forward.

Nearer and nearer. Tom looked up at the high stone quay. Would she fail to get so far? Would he have to bring her round and get her sailing again? Nearer and nearer. And then, close alongside the quay, the *Teasel* stopped, without even touching. That man in oilskins was holding her by the forestay. Port was already on the foredeck, handing him up the mooring warp, rond-anchor and all. The rain was stopping. The wind had suddenly dropped now that the *Teasel* had escaped it. Tom, rather shaky in the knees, went forward to help in lowering the sails. The man was talking.

'Good bit of work you did then,' he was saying. 'Didn't think you'd make it as neat as that with the wind blowing as it was. She had all she wanted coming up the Broad. The *Teasel*, is she? Are you Mr Tom Dudgeon? I've a telegram for you sent on from Beccles.'

'A telegram?'

'I've got it in the office. I'm the harbour-master.'

He ran across the quay and was back in a moment with a red envelope. Tom tore it open. He had never had a telegram in his life. But there it was, plain on the envelope, and again on the telegram form:

TOM DUDGEON YACHT TEASEL BECCLES
ARE TWINS WITH YOU TELEPHONE IMMEDIATELY
MOTHER

In the harbour-master's little office, all three Coots wanted to use the telephone at once. Tom was talking to his mother.

'But they're here ... They caught us up at Beccles just after we'd sent off those postcards ... Jim Wooddall gave them a lift ... and then a barge ... They're here now.' He turned to speak to the twins. 'It's those postcards we sent to you first thing in the morning. They got the early post. And Ginty went flying round to Mother ...'

Starboard grabbed the receiver. 'Good morning, Aunty ...

Oh, no ... We're as good as gold, really ... We always are ... Rather wet ... Come on, Port ... Your turn ...'

Tom got the telephone again. 'Hullo, Mother. No. I've shut them both up. Oh, Ginty wants to talk to them. All right. What did Joe say? ... I can't hear ... Sorry ... Beasts ... Stuck in Wroxham? Three cheers ... Awning for the *Death and Glory* ... Good ... I thought they would ... I'll telephone from Norwich. Somewhere, anyhow. Everything's going fine. The *Teasel*'s a beauty. Oh, no. The storm wasn't so awfully bad. We got through it quite all right. What? Ginty waiting? Oh, all right. Good-bye, Mother. Love to our baby and Dad. Come on, Port, Ginty's coming to the telephone to give you what for ...'

Port took the telephone and waited. There was a short pause. She frowned and signalled to Tom and Starboard to keep quiet. Tom was bursting with good news.

Then: 'Yes. Hullo. It's a braw mornin', Ginty, and we're all well the noo, and hoping your ainsel's the same.'

'Oh, Port, you idiot,' said Tom. 'What did Ginty say?'

'Ye young limb ... All right, Ginty ... I'm only trying to tell them what you said to me ...'

The anxious watchers in the *Teasel* knew the moment the Coots came out of the office that the telegram had not brought bad news.

'It was only those postcards,' Tom explained to Mrs Barrable from the edge of the quay. 'Ginty couldn't think what had happened when those postcards came for the twins saying how much we wished they were with us. So she shot round to Mother, and wanted to send telegrams all over the place. It's lucky Mother didn't let her send one to Uncle Frank. And the Hullabaloos are stuck at Wroxham for repairs. They bust someone's bowsprit, and got a hole in old *Margoletta* at the same time, charging across the bows of a sailing yacht ... big one, luckily. And Joe's been making an awning for the *Death and Glory.* I thought he would when he'd seen *Titmouse*'s. I've promised to telephone again from wherever we go to next.'

'Stupid of me,' said the Admiral. 'I ought to have thought of telephoning myself.'

'It would have been much worse if you'd telephoned before we arrived,' said Starboard.

'It's all right now, anyhow,' said Port.

'Everything's going righter and righter,' said Dorothea. 'First, Port and Starboard coming, so we're all together. And now no more Hullabaloos.'

CHAPTER 24

RECALL

The *Teasel* carried a light-hearted crew next day when she sailed from Oulton for the Norwich river. No need now to think of Hullabaloos. If the *Margoletta* was safely out of the way being patched up in a Wroxham boat-yard Tom, for the time, was outlaw no longer.

They sailed from Oulton in the afternoon, to catch the last of the ebb though the New Cut. The harbour-master stood by to give them a hand, but there was no need. Everything went well, and their voyage out of Oulton with a light south-westerly wind was very different from that mad crashing to and fro in the storm as they were beating their way in.

'Yo ho for Norwich,' said Port. 'There's nowhere else left to go to.'

But they never got to Norwich.

No one can count on the wind, and that afternoon, when they had passed Somerleyton and Herringfleet, and Dorothea had dropped the money into the butterfly net for the men who open the road-bridge on the New Cut, the wind was dying away to nothing. They drifted out of the New Cut into the Norwich river, but there was not wind enough to carry them up through Reedham Bridge against the stream, and Tom had to jump into the *Titmouse* and do some hard towing. They tied up for tea above the bridge, and sailed again later in the evening, past Hardley Cross and the mouth of the Loddon past Cantley, where a foreign-going steamship was loading at the wharf, and moored for the night a mile or so higher up. Next day the wind was not much better, and they cruised slowly on, coming to Brundall in the afternoon. There was so little wind that no one minded when the Admiral suggested tying up while she made a sketch of that lovely bend of the river. They found a good mooring-place at the mouth of a dyke, close to an old sailing ship that was being dismantled and turned into a houseboat. The Admiral settled down in the well of the *Teasel* to make her sketch, and the others went ashore, and climbed a ladder to the deck of the dismantled ship, and watched a man who was cutting through the old iron-work with a jet of hissing, white-hot flame.

Tom had watched this for some time when he remembered his promise about telephoning home.

'Now's your chance,' said Starboard. 'They're sure to have a telephone at the inn here, and we'll never get up to Norwich tonight.'

'We'll come, too,' said Port, and the three Coots left Dick and Dorothea watching the flame-cutter, and strolled slowly along the dyke and so to the Yare Hotel.

Mrs Dudgeon had hardly answered the telephone before the twins, watching Tom's face, saw that he was getting serious news.

'I'm so glad you rang up,' Mrs Dudgeon was saying. 'I've an urgent message for the twins, and for you, too. Which day were you meaning to start back?'

'Day after tomorrow.'

'Uncle Frank's written to say he's coming back by the early train the day after tomorrow, and the twins must be here by then, because he's racing *Flash* at eleven. You'll have to come through Yarmouth tomorrow if the twins are to be in time. Do you think you can manage it? ... If not they'd better come by train or bus. Brundall, you said, didn't you?'

'We were going on to Norwich tomorrow.'

'Better not. We've had a call from a friend of yours, one of the wherrymen.'

'Jim Wooddall?'

'Yes. He thought we ought to know that those people in the *Margoletta* have been boasting that they knew the boy they were after had gone south. This was in some inn, up at Wroxham. They even knew the name of the *Teasel*. You were right about George. Someone's seen him talking to them. And Bill's here, waiting for a word with you. He says the *Margoletta* will be only two more days at Wroxham getting mended. So come through Yarmouth tomorrow if you can. Your father doesn't want you to leave the *Teasel* in the lurch, specially with the twins having to leave too, but he thinks the sooner you're safe home the better ... Hang on now while I call Bill in. He's been weeding all day just outside, so as to be able to talk to you if you rang up. Mischief of some sort, I've no doubt. *Bill!*'

Tom passed on the news.

'I say,' said Starboard. 'There's a jolly little wind. Do you think we can get down to Yarmouth in time?'

'If we can't,' said Tom, 'you'll just have to take the train at Cantley or somewhere.'

'Tide's all right tomorrow,' said Port, 'if we do get down. And if we get up to Acle before dark, we can easily get to Horning next day, before breakfast if somebody wakes us up.'

'If those beasts know about the *Teasel* being down south,' said Tom, 'it's no good waiting to be caught by them. Once they leave Wroxham they can get anywhere in no time. And they'd only have to hang about Breydon to make sure of catching us on our way through.'

'Come on,' said Port. 'We'll just slip home and diddle them again.'

'Yes ... Yes ... Hullo!' Tom had the telephone receiver at his ear, and waved at the others to keep quiet.

'That you, Bill?'

'Hullo ... That Tom Dudgeon? ...' Tom could hear Bill's anxious puffing and blowing at the other end. 'The grebe's

nest in Salhouse Entry been robbed. Rest all right. We thought
No. 7 had lost a chick but it was only Pete counted wrong
... Er ... See here ...' There was a long pause. Tom heard,
more faintly, his mother's voice. 'All right, Bill, if it's a secret
I'll go out of the room.' There was more anxious puffing.
Then Bill's voice came again. 'Say, Tom. Which day you
comin' through? ... Ter-morrer? ... Afternoon tide? ... Can
ye hear? Joe's mended our sail, and made a crutch, and we
got a tarpaulin, so's we can sleep under like you ... see? ...
Joe an' Pete's took her down-river ... down to Acle ... I'm
bikin' down now ... An' a boy at Rodley's is going to telephone about the *Margoletta* ... So we'll have the news for
ye ...'

'Will you pay for another three minutes?' the indifferent
voice of a telephone operator broke in from the Exchange.

'No, no,' said Tom hurriedly. What was the good of throwing money away like that when it could be spent on ropes
and other really useful things? 'Good-bye, Bill. See you at
Acle tomorrow night ...'

'At Acle?' said Port and Starboard together.

'They've fixed up their awning for the *Death and Glory*,' said
Tom. 'Those three kids are going down to Acle, and someone's going to let them know when the Hullabaloos are going
to leave Wroxham.'

'Jolly good,' said Starboard.

'Let's get away at once,' said Port. 'We ought to get as
far down the river as we can before dark. Buck up.'

They ran along the dyke to the *Teasel*.

Tom stopped just before they reached her. 'I say,' he said,
'the others'll be awfully sick at having to start back.'

'Well,' said Starboard, 'it can't be helped. We've got to
get home for the A.P.'s race. You've got to get home because
of the Hullaballoos. It'd be much worse if they came down
here and caught you in the *Teasel*. And anyway we can't leave
the Admiral and those two to get home by themselves.'

But, for various reasons, Dick, Dorothea and the Admiral were as ready to start as the Coots.

The Admiral was for sailing at once. 'We've done so well,' she said, 'we don't want anything to go wrong now and spoil it.'

'Good,' said Dick. 'We'll be seeing Breydon again tomorrow. Those spoonbills may still be there. And Norwich is only a town anyhow.'

'Let's start now,' said Dorothea. 'The warning came and the outlaw bolted for his lair. It would be too dreadful if he got caught after all. We've had a splendid voyage ... And the Admiral's done her sketch ... Or haven't you?'

The Admiral laughed. 'Luckily, I've done it,' she said.

'And the man who was using that flame-cutter has stopped work for the day,' said Dick.

Ten minutes later, sails were set, and the *Teasel* drifted out of Brundall, homeward bound, with hardly wind enough to stir her. They sailed her as long as they could, and tied up at dusk not far from Buckenham Ferry.

CHAPTER 25

THE RASHNESS OF THE ADMIRAL

'That wretched curlew must have been whistling the wrong tune,' said Port.

The morning had brought them an easterly wind.

'Fine for going up the Bure,' said Starboard.

'But we've got to get down to Yarmouth against it first,' said Port.

Tom and the twins began their calculations over again. How long must they allow to get down to Yarmouth against the wind so as to be at Breydon Bridge exactly at low water?

Meanwhile the Admiral and Dorothea were looking through the larder and calculating how to make four eggs (all that were left) do for six people. There was fortunately plenty of butter to scramble them, but when breakfast was over, nobody would have said 'No' to a second helping.

'We don't know what time we're going to get down to Reedham,' said the Admiral, 'but we'll get all we want there.'

'We'd better keep the tongue to eat on the voyage,' said Dorothea. 'It's only a very little one anyway.'

In the end the navigators gave up all hope of making their figures agree. There were too many things to think of, the speed of the current, the speed of the *Teasel* when tacking, the speed of the *Teasel* when reaching, how much of the river would be tacking, and how much of it would let them sail with the wind free, and, on the top of all that, the wind itself seemed very uncertain.

'There's only one thing to do,' said Tom. 'We'll sail right

down to Reedham straight away. People will know there what the tide's doing.'

'So long as we're not too late, nothing else matters,' said Starboard.

All down those long reaches by Langley and Cantley they sailed the *Teasel* as if she were a China clipper racing for home. Tom and the Coots were for ever hauling in or letting out the sheets to get the very best out of the wind. Dick and Dorothea took turns with the steering whenever the wind was free, but gave up the tiller to a Coot whenever it was a case of sailing close-hauled and stealing a yard or two when going about. The little tongue was eaten while they were under way, cut by the Admiral into seven equal bits, for William was as hungry as everybody else. Indeed, he did not think his bit was big enough, and the Admiral promised him that as soon as the *Teasel* came to Reedham he should have some more.

But as the *Teasel* turned the corner into the Reedham reach, and Tom was looking at the quay in front of the Lord Nelson, thinking where best he could tie up, above or below a couple of yachts that were lying there, they saw that the railway bridge was open, and that the signalman was leaning out of his window.

'He's beckoning to us to come on,' said Dorothea.

'He's probably going to shut it for a long time,' said Starboard.

'Two trains, perhaps, or shunting,' said Dick.

'Well, I'm going through now, to make sure of it,' said Tom. 'It'd be awful to be held up.'

'What about our stores?' said the Admiral.

'Let's hang on till Yarmouth,' said Tom. 'We'll have to stop there anyway.'

It was no use arguing. Tom had other things to think of. Beating against the wind, and carried down with the tide, he had to work the *Teasel* through Reedham bridge. Just as he came to it he had to go about and the tide swept the *Titmouse* round quicker than he thought it would. The *Titmouse* bumped hard against one of the piers. Tom glanced wretchedly over his shoulder, and winced as if he had been bumped himself.

'She's got that rope all round her,' said Dorothea. 'The bridge won't have touched her really.'

'Bad steering,' said Tom. 'My own fault.'

The bridge closed behind them. The red flag climbed up, and they knew that they might have had to wait a long time before it would be opened again. They were beating on towards the New Cut. Just for a moment they could see right down it, a long narrow lane of water, and, in the distance, the little road bridge, where the porters who open it catch their two shillings in a long-handled net.

'Couldn't we have stopped below the railway bridge?' said Dorothea.

'We can't turn back,' said Tom.

On and on they went, beating down the Yare against the wind but helped by the outflowing tide. And then, after being afraid of being too late, they began to be afraid of being too early for the tide.

'We'll have to stop somewhere,' said Tom.

'The banks look unco' dour,' said Port.

'Fare main bad to me,' said Starboard, who talked broad Norfolk because of her sister's talking Ginty language.

'I'll tell you what,' said Tom. 'We'll go round into the Waveney and tie up by the Breydon pilot. He'll tell us when to start again ...'

'All right,' said the Admiral. 'But what about stores? William and I are starving. There isn't an egg in the ship. And no bread. And both water-jars are empty ...'

Dorothea was looking at the map. 'There are two houses marked near the mouth of the river,' she said.

'We could get milk and eggs at the Berney Arms,' said Tom. 'Water, too, probably.'

On and on they sailed. Already the wind seemed colder coming over Breydon, and they could hear the calling of the gulls. A red brick house came into sight on the bank, close above them.

'That looks like a farm,' said the Admiral. 'Let's tie up and ask here.'

'I daren't,' said Tom. 'Not with the *Teasel*, and the tide going out. No good getting stuck. Come on, Starboard. You take over. I'll slip ashore in *Titmouse*. You sail round the corner. The pilot'll tell you the best place to moor. I'll be along with the stores by the time you get the sails down.'

He hauled *Titmouse* alongside, and dropped carefully into her, while Starboard took the speed off the *Teasel* by heading her into the wind. Port and Dick between them gave him the big earthenware water-jar. Dorothea handed down milk-can and egg-basket. The Admiral gave him the ship's purse and told him to take what was wanted out of it.

Tom let go, and, as the *Teasel* sailed on, was left astern, fitting his rowlocks and getting out his oars. As they turned the bend, they saw him already rowing in towards the bank.

'My word,' said Starboard, 'she sails a lot better without *Titmouse* to tow.'

'*Titmouse* is very useful,' said Dorothea.

'All right,' laughed Starboard. 'We couldn't do without her, but the *Teasel* does like kicking up her heels without a dinghy at her tail.'

'There's the Berney Arms,' said the Admiral, and then, as they began beating down the last reach of the river, 'And there are the Breydon posts.'

Ahead of them was black piling and a tall post marking the place where the two rivers met. Beyond it they could see where open water stretched far into the distance, with beacon posts marking the channel. They were at the mouth of the river. There, round the corner, was the old hulk of the Breydon pilot's houseboat.

'We've never seen Breydon with the water all over everywhere,' said Dorothea.

'Just look at the birds,' said Dick.

'Can't we just go down a little way to have a look at it?' said Dorothea.

Port looked back up the river. There was no sign of Tom.

'It'll take Tom a long time to come round in *Titmouse*,' said Dorothea, 'and the *Teasel* sails awfully fast.'

Starboard was already bringing the *Teasel* round the end of the piling, and heading her up towards the Breydon pilot's moored hulk.

'What do the Coots think?' said the Admiral.

'We'd be able to get back all right with the wind as it is,' said Starboard. 'You can see by the way she's going now.'

'Do let's,' said Dorothea.

'I don't think we could possibly get into trouble if we went down as far as the end of the piling,' said the Admiral.

'Hurrah,' said Dorothea.

'Good,' said Dick, who had the binoculars all ready in his hands in hopes of seeing spoonbills.

'All right,' said Starboard. 'In with the mainsheet. Ready about.'

The *Teasel* swung round into the wind, went about, and, with the tide helping her once more, beat down into Breydon Water.

'Tom'll see us all right,' said Dorothea.

'We'll turn back in plenty of time,' said the Admiral.

On they sailed, beating slowly to and fro, against the north-east wind, but hardly noticing how fast the ebb was carrying them with it.

'She can jolly well sail,' said Starboard. Even the twins, though doubtful about what Tom would think of it, could not help enjoying themselves, sailing in this wide channel, leaving a red post on one side, and turning again when they came near a black post on the other, although, with the tide as it was, the water on both sides stretched far away beyond the posts.

'Fog at sea,' said Starboard, as they heard the foghorn of a lightship off the coast.

'It really *is* just like the bittern,' said Dick.

'We'd better turn back now,' said Port.

'Just a wee bit farther,' said Dorothea.

'It's getting foggy over there,' said Port.

'It's rather foggy here,' said Dick. 'It *is* like a bittern, that horn.'

And suddenly, almost before they knew it was coming, the fog was upon them. Yarmouth had disappeared, and the long line of those huge posts seemed to end nearer than it had. They could see only about a dozen ... only six ... and some of those were going ... had gone ...

'Turn her round,' said the Admiral sharply. 'We must get back to the river as quick as we can.'

But it was too late. The fog bank had reached them and rolled over them. The *Teasel* turned in her own length, and began driving slowly back over the tide, with the boom well out and the wind astern. But, already, her crew could not see the mouth of the river. They could see nothing at all except a black post close ahead of them.

'Leave the post to starboard,' said Port.

'Teach your grandmother,' said her sister.

'Don't lose sight of it until you see the next one,' said the Admiral.

'Not going to.'

'We'll just have to sail from post to post.'

There was something terrifying in sailing quite fast through the water with nothing in sight but a dim, phantom post that seemed hardly to move at all. That was the tide, of course, carrying them down almost as fast as they sailed up against it. It was quite natural, and nobody would have minded if only it had been possible to see a little farther. But now, alone, in this cold, wet fog, with everything vanished except that ghostly post, it was as if they had lost the rest of the world. The long deep hoots from the lightship out at sea and the sirens of the trawlers down in the harbour made things worse, not better. The fog played tricks with these distant noises, making them sound now close at hand and now so far away that they could hardly be heard. Dorothea knew that the Admiral was worried, and she listened anxiously for the note of fear in the voices of the others. She could tell nothing from their faces as they stared out into the fog.

'I'm going forward,' said Dick. 'Even a few yards may make a difference in looking through the fog for that next post.'

He was gone, clambering carefully along the side-deck with a hand on the cabin roof. On the foredeck, holding on by the mast, it was as if he were a boy made of fog, only of fog a little darker than the rest.

'Keep your eye on that post,' said the Admiral again.

'It's going.'

'I can see it.'

'Can't see anything at all.' Dick's voice came from the fore-deck.

Starboard was not accustomed to steering in the dark. And this pale fog was worse than darkness. Dimly, away to her right, she could see that post, but she had a lot of other things to remember. There was the tide trying to take the *Teasel* down to Yarmouth, and the wind blowing her the other way. What if the wind were dropping? She glanced over the side at the brown water sweeping by. The little ship was moving well, but oh how slowly she was leaving that post. She must not lose sight of it, until she had another to steer for. Was the wind changing? If it did change, why, anything might happen. Funny. There it was on her right cheek. She could

feel it on her nose. A moment ago it was not like that ...
Why, it wasn't dead aft any more ...

'Haul in on the sheet, Twin. She isn't going like she was.'

'The post's moving,' said Dorothea. 'It's going. Dick, Dick,
can't you see the next? We've passed this one. It's gone ...
No ... I can still see it ...'

'Something's wrong with the wind,' said Starboard in a
puzzled voice.

'The post's gone,' said Port.

'It was over there a moment ago,' said Dorothea, pointing.

'It can't have been there,' said Starboard. 'More sheet in,
Twin.'

'We're bound to see the next post in a moment,' said the
Admiral.

And then, suddenly, all five of them in the well, and
William, tumbled against each other. It was as if someone
lying under water had reached up and caught the *Teasel* by
the keel. She pushed on a yard or two, stickily, heeling over
more and more. She came to a standstill.

'Ready about,' said Starboard. Instantly Port let fly the
jib-sheet. But the rudder was useless. The *Teasel* did not stir.
Starboard looked despairingly at the Admiral. 'I've done it,'
she said. 'I've gone and put her aground.'

'It's my fault,' said the Admiral. 'If you'd been alone you'd
never have come down here.'

'We might try backing the jib,' said Starboard. 'Or the
quant.'

'We'll stay where we are,' said the Admiral. 'Nobody'll run
into us here. And anything's better than drifting about in the
fog.'

'But what about Tom?' said Dorothea.

CHAPTER 26

THE *TITMOUSE* IN THE FOG

Tom pulled in towards some quay-heading, tied up the *Titmouse*, and went up the bank to the house. There was no one about. He wandered round to the back, but there was no answer to his knocking, the windows were all closed, no smoke was coming from the chimneys and he soon made up his mind that everybody was away from home. He hurried down the bank again to the *Titmouse*, saw that the river had fallen several inches in those few minutes, and was presently drifting downstream with the tide.

He stepped her mast, hoisted her sail, lowered her centreboard and tacked down-river to the Berney Arms. Here he chose his moment, dropped the sail again, pulled up the centreboard, and brought the *Titmouse* alongside what seemed to him the best landing-place. He made fast her painter round the top of an old pile, and went up the bank to the inn, taking with him basket, milk-can and stone water-jar.

A cheerful young man met him at the door.

'Two dozen of eggs? And a quart of milk? And I daresay we can find you a loaf. But where's your ship? You won't be eating all this in that little boat.'

'She's gone round to the Breydon pilot's,' said Tom, looking away towards Burgh over the strip of land between the two rivers, and wondering why he could see nothing of the *Teasel*. Afloat in the *Titmouse* he had not been able to see beyond the banks.

'Not that little yacht gone down Breydon?'

'Gone down Breydon?'

That certainly did look very like the *Teasel*'s sail, tacking away down there towards the open water. But what were they doing? Could they have made a mistake about the plan? Port and Starboard knew what they were about, surely.

'You'll have a job to catch her.'

'They'll be turning back in a minute,' said Tom, but kept his eyes on that white sail, growing smaller and smaller, while a girl was sent off to collect eggs, and, after she had brought his basket back full of eggs, had to go off again to fill his milk-can. The young man took the big water-jar and filled it with fresh water at the pump.

So Tom, in the *Titmouse*, wedging the water-jar between his knees and remembering that he would have to be careful not to spill it in going about, beat down to Breydon Water in pursuit of his runaway ship. A long way down they had taken her already. And the tide was pouring down. Bother those twins. He had been counting on having a word with the pilot in the hulk just up the Waveney river, so as to make sure of getting to Breydon Bridge exactly at slack water. He did not like the look of the weather either. It was very misty down towards Yarmouth. And then, suddenly, he saw that bank of fog rolling up Breydon from the North Sea. Just before the fog reached the *Teasel*, he saw her swing round, too late now, close by one of the black beacon posts on the northern side of the channel. Then the fog rolled over her, and only a few minutes after that, he was himself unable to see more than a yard or two from the *Titmouse*.

'They'll be pitching the mud-weight over,' said Tom to himself. 'They'll be all right, anchoring where they are.' He never guessed for a moment that this was the one thing they had not thought of doing.

His first idea was to do the same for the *Titmouse*. These sudden fog banks that on a day of easterly wind sometimes sweep up from the sea over the lower reaches of the tidal rivers seldom last long. He had only to take the *Titmouse* to the side of the channel, anchor her and wait till the fog rolled away. He could see nothing, but, at the moment, he knew where he was, and feeling the cold wind on his right cheek-bone he kept the *Titmouse* close-hauled, until the black tarred piling by Reedham marshes loomed suddenly close ahead. He headed into the wind and lowered his sail. The black piling, dim in the fog, was sweeping by as he drifted down with the tide. He would anchor, light his oil-stove in the bottom of the boat, and do a little cooking.

He was just going to throw his mud-weight over, a lump of iron, painted green to keep the *Titmouse* clear of rust, when his own hunger reminded him of the *Teasel*'s empty larder. It was all very well for him to sit comfortably in the *Titmouse* and make himself a pot of tea and boil an egg or two, but the crew of the *Teasel*, anchored away in the middle of Breydon, with nothing to do, would have to go on starving until the fog had passed.

Standing in the drifting *Titmouse*, looking into pale fog and at the ghostly piling at the edge of the marshes, Tom changed his mind. Somehow or other he had to bring food and water to the *Teasel*. Could it be done? Why not? The *Teasel*, he had seen, was on the northern side of the deep-water channel down Breydon. He, too, drifting past the piling, was on the northern side of the channel. If he could manage to keep close along that side of the channel as he drifted down, the tide itself would take him within hailing distance of the *Teasel*. Suddenly the piling ended. He was out on Breydon now, with nothing to look for but the big black beacon posts which seem near enough together in clear weather but ever so far apart in a fog. Yes, only the posts to look for above water, but what he had to follow was the bottom, where the shallow Breydon mudflats drop steeply into the deep dredged channel. He pulled up his centre-board. *Titmouse* with centre-board down was no joke to row. What was that? A huge black post loomed suddenly beside him, and was gone. Phew! Wouldn't have done to go bumping into that. He got out his oars, and spun the *Titmouse* round, and began paddling her stern first, the better to keep a look out for the next post.

But the next post seemed long in coming. Tom paddled harder. Then he stopped paddling altogether, and did a little thinking. He prodded down over the side with an oar, and could not touch the bottom. His mud-weight had only a short rope, but longer than the oar. He lowered it over the side, using it as a sounding lead. It touched nothing. He must be well out in the dredged channel. He could see nothing but fog and a yard or two of brown water all round the boat. But all that water, though it looked still, was sweeping down to the sea, with the *Titmouse* upon it. Which way? Unless he could see something, or touch the bottom, he could not tell. The cold wind gave him some idea of the direction in which he was moving. But the wind might have changed. Tom looked blindly round him in the fog.

Suddenly he jumped to his feet. What an idiot not to remember his compass. He opened the after-locker of the *Titmouse* where the compass lived in a little box of its own, hooked under the stern-sheets so that it could not get thrown about. Uncle Frank had laughed at him for taking a compass with him when sailing in the Bure. It was going to be useful now. As a general rule a compass is not much use for navigation unless you have a chart. But Tom's trouble was a simple one. All he wanted to do was to get back to the north side of the channel. The compass would make that easy enough. He laid it carefully on the floor of the *Titmouse*, in front of the water-jar, which, now that he was no longer sailing, was standing in the stern. North? What? Over there? He paddled the *Titmouse* stern first, due north as the compass showed him. Good. There was another of those posts, dim in the fog, with the water swirling round it.

He found bottom with his mud-weight. The *Titmouse* swung

round, giving him, roughly, the direction of the tide. He hauled up the weight again and paddled on. Every now and then he saw the ghost of a beacon. Every now and then he dipped over the side with an oar, and, sounding and paddling, with the tide to help him made his way along the edge of the channel. He grew a little over-confident, and paddled for a long time without sounding at all. Then, when he sounded, he found deep water again. He paddled northwards. Another of those posts showed for a moment and was gone. Worse than blind man's buff, thought Tom. How far had he come by now? The *Teasel* could not be very far away. No harm in hailing. He rested on his oars, drifting silently and listening. Gulls chattering. Foghorn. A steamer's siren. He gathered his breath and shouted, '*Teasel!* Ahoy . . . oy!'

There was no answer. Probably the fog made it hard to hear. He hailed again, '*Teasel!* Ahoy . . . oy . . . oy!'

That did sound almost like an answering hail, faint, far away. He glanced at the compass. Yes. East-north-east. Tom paddled away, straining his eyes into the fog and listening. He was almost sure he had heard them.

He hailed again, and listened.

'Ahoy . . . Ahoy . . . Ahoy!'

There they were. No doubt about it. But still far away.

He paddled on.

Suddenly he heard the barking of a dog. He pulled his oars in and stood up, letting the *Titmouse* drift.

'*Teasel!* Ahoy . . . oy!'

The barking broke out again, and a chorus of shouts. There they were. He had done it. Come down Breydon in a fog and found them. No need to worry about compass now, or mud-weight. They would be anchored at the side of the channel, and he had only to join them.

'Ahoy!' he shouted, settling to his oars, spinning the *Titmouse* round and heading directly towards William's welcome barking.

'*Titmouse*, ahoy!' That was Dorothea. Too shrill for either of the twins.

'All together,' he heard Starboard's voice. And then there was a really splendid yell from the whole of the *Teasel*'s crew, '*Titmouse! Ahoy!*'

Tom rowed as if in a race, quick strokes and as hard as he could, fairly lifting the *Titmouse* along. 'Good old William,' he said to himself. William seemed almost to have guessed how useful it would be, and kept up excited barking all the time.

'Ahoy!' panted Tom, and the next moment his oars were scraping on mud, the *Titmouse* had come to a standstill, and he had tumbled backwards.

He was up in an instant and frantically digging at the mud with an oar. The oar sank in as he pushed. He felt the *Titmouse* stir beneath him, and then settle again as he pulled to get the oar unstuck.

And then, too late, the fog began to clear. Twenty yards away over the wet grey mud he saw a ghostly *Teasel* heeled over on her side, with her ghostly crew crowded together in her well. The *Titmouse*, drawing only her inch or two, was stuck fast. The muddy water was already creeping away from her.

'I say,' he gasped. 'I'm aground.'

'So are we,' said Starboard.

'And some of us are very hungry,' said the Admiral.

'I've got the water,' said Tom, 'and the eggs and the milk, and they gave me two loaves of bread.'

And then, prodding into the mud with his oar, he realized that with only twenty yards of it between them, the *Titmouse* and the *Teasel*, until the tide rose once more, might just as well be twenty miles apart.

CHAPTER 27

WILLIAM'S HEROIC MOMENT

'Idiots we are, idiots,' said Starboard. 'We ought to have shouted to him to keep away.'

'Can't shift her,' he shouted to them.

'We're done until the tide comes up again,' said Starboard.

'I say,' said Tom. 'We shan't be able to get down to Yarmouth even then. Wind and tide'll both be against us. It comes up at a terrific pace.'

'If only we'd stopped at Reedham we could have telephoned for the *Come Along* to meet us,' said Mrs Barrable. 'But it's no good saying that. And it's my fault. Disobeying the skipper. If we'd gone straight to the pilot's everything would have been perfectly easy. No, William, it's no good asking. There simply isn't any food. Not even for you.'

'I'd better try to get across the mud with some of the grub,' called Tom.

'No,' said the Admiral. 'You're not to try ... If you did sink in we couldn't do a thing to save you ... And we wouldn't be any nearer having anything to eat.'

'You couldn't chuck a rope?' shouted Tom.

'Too far.'

'Is the tow-rope long enough?' asked Dick. 'The big coil in the forepeak. The one we used at Yarmouth.'

'It's long enough,' said Starboard, 'or jolly nearly. But we can't get it across.'

'There *is* one way we could do it,' said Dick. 'If William

helped. But he wouldn't like it. And I don't suppose you'd let him, really.'

'William?'

And then Dick explained his idea, and, as they listened, even the twins cheered up a little, wretched though they were at having to wait on the mud. Would it work, or wouldn't it?

'Of course he doesn't weigh much, and if only he keeps going pretty fast.'

'He'd feel the string pulling him back.'

'It needn't be string. It doesn't matter how light the first thing is. We could start with cotton, and then string. There's a huge ball of string in the stores.'

'I've got a reel of cotton,' said Dorothea. 'Mother put it in, in case buttons came off Dick.'

'And if it unrolls on one of the Admiral's pencils,' said Dick, 'William wouldn't feel it at all. Is the hole through the middle big enough?'

Dorothea slipped into the cabin sideways and worked herself along it to get at her little suitcase. The cabin was on such a slant that walking through it was impossible.

'Poor old William,' she said, looking at him. Disliking the fog, he had made himself comfortable on the lee bunk.

'Get his harness,' said the Admiral. 'In the cupboard under the looking-glass.'

The Admiral poked a pencil through the cotton reel, and made the reel spin by patting it.

'He'll never feel the pull of that,' said Dick.

'William,' said the Admiral.

William snuggled down on the port bunk. The next moment he felt his mistress take a firm grip of the scruff of his neck. He was plucked forth, out of the cabin into the cold fog and dumped in the well, which, like the cabin, seemed to have taken a permanent slant. William made a half-hearted attempt to get back into the cabin, but found people's legs in the way.

Mrs Barrable was putting his harness on him.

'Hullo, William,' called Tom, and William barked back.

'He'll do it,' said Dorothea. 'He always does do what Tom tells him.'

'Have you got the cotton ready?' said the Admiral over her shoulder.

'Here's the end of it,' said Dick. 'I'm going to hold the pencil at each end so that the reel won't slip off. If only he'll go ...'

'Now, William,' said the Admiral, tying the end of the cotton to the ring in the harness to which the leather lead was clipped. 'This is your moment. It comes to everybody, just once, the moment when he has to be a hero or not think much of himself for the rest of his life. Are you ready, Dick? Luckily it's good stout cotton ... Good little dog. Clean, tidy little dog ... Never gets his feet muddy ...'

'You be ready to call him, Tom,' shouted Starboard.

'Call who?' said Tom, his voice coming queerly from the shadowy little boat away over the mud. Tom had been busy stowing his sail. It would be needed no longer, and he was making a neat job of it.

'William,' called Dorothea. 'He's bringing a cotton across.'

'A life-line,' called Port. 'He's a pug-rocket.'

And then, suddenly, William's own mistress lifted him up and lowered him over the side of the *Teasel* down to the Breydon mud, keeping firm hold of his lead for fear the mud should be too soft even for pugs. The next moment she was wiping the mud from her eyes. William made a desperate, splashing effort to get back aboard the *Teasel*. But he could get no hold for his forepaws. In half a minute he was more like a little grey, muddy hippopotamus than a dignified and self-respecting pug.

'Quick,' said the Admiral, reaching down again to unclip the lead from the harness. 'The mud'll bear him.' William was free on the mud, held by nothing but the thread of cotton.

'Now!' everybody shouted at once. 'Call him, Tom. Call him.'

'Good boy,' called Tom. 'Come on, William! William! Come on, boy! Come on! Chocolate, William ...'

'Is there any chocolate?' asked Dorothea.

'There's a scrap in his box,' said Dick. 'I left a bit when I gave him his breakfast.'

'Go on, William,' said the Admiral. 'I can't help it. You've just *got* to be a hero. Go on! Go to Tom!'

'William!' Tom's voice came again. 'Good old William!'

William stopped struggling to get back aboard the *Teasel*. He looked over his shoulder. Never in all his life had he been so badly treated. Dumped into sticky grey mud. Green slime, too. And after all this talk about wiping paws on the mat. William barked. His bulging black eyes looked as puzzled as he felt.

'Go away, William. Get out, we don't want you. Go to Tom! Tom! Go to Tom! Fetch him!'

William gave a last disgusted look at the crew of the *Teasel* and waddled off across the mud.

'The reel's unrolling perfectly,' said Dick.

The others watched it spinning on the pencil that he held by both ends.

'It's stopped. Tom! Tom! Do make him go on!'

But William had hesitated only for a moment. He had gone more than half-way. The reel spun once more as the cotton unrolled.

'He's got there.'

'Tom's yanked him aboard.'

Tom's voice suddenly changed its tone. He had been calling to William, begging him to come on, but now in the *Titmouse* William was shaking himself, and Tom was doing his best to save his sail. 'Shut up, William! Keep still! I'll wipe it off for you! *Do* keep still.'

'Have you got the cotton?' called Dick.

'I've got it! Steady, William!'

'Haul it in gently. Very gently!'

'Sure you've made the string fast to it?'

The ball of string leapt from side to side in the well as they paid it out over the side, and Tom hauling in the cotton dragged the end of it across the mud.

'Got it,' shouted Tom. 'Well done, whoever thought of that! Do keep still, William.'

'Now for the rope,' said Dick, 'and then we can get the things across. The string won't bear anything . . .'

'Haul in again, Tom,' called Starboard, who without cutting the string had made it fast to the end of the big coil of rope that had not been used since they came through Yarmouth. A snake of rope crept away over the mud as the twins paid it out from the foredeck, while the string went on unrolling in the well.

'Got it,' shouted Tom. 'Now what?'

'We must haul our half of the string back,' shouted Dick. 'Hang on to your end of it. Then we can use it for pulling things each way along the rope.'

'You'll want a shackle to run on the rope,' shouted Tom. 'There's a spare one in the forepeak. Right in the bows.'

'I've got it,' said Port.

'Splendid,' said the Admiral. 'But, oh, I do hope poor William won't have caught his death of cold.'

'We'll send across his bit of chocolate.'

'Cod-liver oil,' said the Admiral, 'is what he ought to have.'

'We'll send that across, too,' said Dorothea, wriggling into the slanting cabin. 'Tom'll have a spoon, won't he?'

'William always likes to have his own,' said the Admiral.

So the first parcel ready to travel by the rope railway that now stretched between the *Teasel* and the *Titmouse* was a scrap of chocolate, a bottle of cod-liver oil, and his own spoon for William, the pioneer, who had crossed the mud and made the railway possible.

'It'll get awfully muddy going across,' said Dorothea.

'Couldn't we hoist it up at both ends?' said Dick.

'Of course we could,' said Starboard. 'Hi! Tom! Hoist your end of the rope up ... Top of the mast ... Keep things out of the mud ...'

That was easy. Tom fastened *Titmouse*'s halyard to his end of the rope and hauled it up as if he were hoisting a sail. The twins, aboard the *Teasel*, did the same. A moment later the rope was no longer lying on the mud, but stretched from masthead to masthead. The shackle, loose on the rope, had already been made fast to the string, and William's parcel had been tied to the shackle.

'All ready now,' called Starboard.

Tom hauled in on the string. The parcel, amid cheers, left the masthead of the *Teasel* and moved slowly out. The rope sagged a bit in the middle, but the parcel was well above the mud. When it had reached the masthead of the *Titmouse*, Tom slacked away his halyard and a moment later had the parcel in his hands.

'Send us across a drop of water,' called the Admiral, 'and we can pour it into our kettle and put it on to boil. Don't try to send too much at once.'

'Does William have his oil after chocolate or before it?' asked Tom, as the *Titmouse*'s kettle went on its way, slopping a little from the spout in spite of Dick's trying not to jerk it as he hauled in on the string.

'Chocolate always comes afterwards,' called William's mistress.

'Now, William,' said Tom, carefully balancing the brimming spoon, as he gathered the muddy William in one arm and made him sit as he had seen him sit on the Admiral's knee that wet day at Ranworth and again at Oulton Broad. And William, glad of anything to which he was accustomed, sat on Tom's knee in the *Titmouse*, aground on the Breydon mud, and lapped up his cod-liver oil as if he had been at home.

Soon in both ships everybody was settling down to the first good meal that day. They were aground on the mud. They had missed their tide. They had lost their chance of getting through Yarmouth that day. Everything was going wrong. But, at least, thanks to Tom, to Dick, and to the heroic William, no one was any longer in danger of starvation.

CHAPTER 28

WRECK AND SALVAGE

'Tide's begun coming up again,' called Tom at last. 'It'll be turning in the Bure in another hour, and boats going south'll be coming through.'

Tom's plans were made. As soon as the *Teasel* floated he would tow her out into the deep water, and then they would sail back to the pilot's moorings to wait for the morning tide.

'Anything else to go across?' he shouted.

'Couldn't you send William back by the railway before you take it down?' suggested Dorothea.

'Too heavy,' said Tom. 'He'd drag in the mud and make the *Teasel* as dirty as poor old *Titmouse*. He's fairly clean now.'

'You keep him,' said the Admiral.

'The water's right up to me,' called Tom. 'I'll be afloat in another ten minutes.'

'It's all round us already,' Dorothea shouted back.

The water spread slowly over the mud between the *Titmouse* and the *Teasel*. Anyone who did not know that it was mostly only an inch deep might have thought they were afloat, except that the *Teasel* was leaning over on one side.

'There's the first boat through,' called Dorothea.

'Motor-cruiser,' said Port, glancing over her shoulder.

'It's a jolly big one,' said Starboard.

All work stopped aboard the *Teasel*.

'But it can't be,' said Starboard. 'Bill said yesterday they wouldn't be able to leave Wroxham for another two days.'

'He must have got it a day wrong,' said Port. 'I'm sure it's them. Tom! Tom! Hullabaloos!'

'Oh, hide! hide!' cried Dorothea.

Tom turned round and stopped wrestling with the *Titmouse*'s mast. There could be no doubt about it. The cruiser had passed the rowing-boat now, and came racing up Breydon, foam flying from her bows, a 'V' of wash spreading astern of her across the channel and sending long bustling waves chasing one another over the mudflats. Even in the dark Tom had known the noise of the *Margoletta*'s engine. He knew it now, and the tremendous volume of sound sent out by her loudspeaker.

He looked this way and that. If those people had glasses or a telescope they might have seen him already. Anyhow, there could be no getting away. He felt like a fly caught in a spider's web, seeing the spider hurrying towards it. There they were, *Teasel* and *Titmouse*, stuck on the mud in shallow water, plain for anyone to see. If only the water had risen another few inches and set them afloat. But even if it had, where could they have gone? There was only one thing to be done. It was a poor chance, but the only one. Tom made one desperate signal to the others to disappear, and, himself, slipped down out of sight on the muddy bottom-boards of the *Titmouse*, and, holding William firmly in his arms, told him what a good dog he was and begged him to keep still.

Aboard the *Teasel* no one saw that signal. Their eyes were all on the *Margoletta*. It was not till several minutes later that Dorothea whispered, 'Tom's gone, anyway.'

The little *Titmouse*, now that the water had spread all round her over the mud, looked like a deserted boat, afloat and anchored.

On came the *Margoletta*, sweeping up with the tide, and filling the quiet evening with a loud treacly voice:

I want to be a darling, a doodle-um, a duckle-um,
I want to be a ducky, doodle darling, yes, I do.

'Indeed,' muttered Port, with a good deal of bitterness.

'Try next door,' said Starboard.

They spoke almost in whispers, as the big motor-cruiser came nearer and nearer, though no one aboard it could possibly have heard them.

'We ought to have done like Tom and hidden,' said Dorothea. 'Let's.'

'Keep still,' said the Admiral. 'It's too late now. They're bound to notice if we start disappearing all of a sudden.'

'Good,' whispered Starboard. 'They're going right past.'

And then the worst happened.

William, still slippery with mud in spite of Tom's pocket handkerchief, indignant at being held a prisoner while this great noise came nearer and nearer, gave a sturdy wriggle, escaped from Tom's arms, bounded up on a thwart and barked at the top of his voice.

'Oh! William! Traitor! Traitor!' almost sobbed Dorothea.

'They've seen!' said Port.

The man at the wheel of the cruiser was looking straight at the *Titmouse* and at the *Teasel* beyond her.

'Here they are,' he suddenly shouted, to be heard even above the loudspeaker and the engine. He spun his wheel, swung the *Margoletta* round so sharply that she nearly capsized, and headed directly for the *Titmouse* . . .

'Ow! Look out!' cried Starboard, almost as if she were aboard the cruiser and saw the danger ahead.

'They've forgotten the tide,' said Port.

The next moment the crash came. Just as the rest of the Hullabaloos poured out of the cabins, startled by the sudden way in which the steersman had swung her round, the *Margoletta*, moving at full speed towards the *Titmouse*, and swept up sideways by the tide, hit the big beacon post with her port bow. There was the cracking of timbers and the rending of wood as the planking was crushed in. Then the tide swung her stern round and she drifted on.

The noise became deafening. The loudspeaker went on pouring out its horrible song. All the people aboard the *Margoletta* were either shouting or shrieking and something extraordinary had happened to the engine which, after stopping dead, was racing like the engine of an aeroplane. Nobody knew till afterwards that the steersman had switched straight from 'full ahead' to 'full astern', had wrenched the propeller right off its shaft, stalled his engine, started it again and was letting it rip at full throttle, pushing his lever to and fro trying to make his engine turn a propeller that was no longer there.

Everything had changed in a moment. That crash of the *Margoletta* against the huge old post on which Tom had been watching the falling and the rising of the tide brought him up from the bottom-boards of the *Titmouse* in time to see the wreck go drifting up the channel with a gaping wound in her bows and the water lapping in. No longer was he hiding from the Hullabaloos. They were shouting at him to come and save them, shouting at Tom, whom only a few moments before they had thought was a prisoner almost in their hands. And Tom was desperately rocking the *Titmouse* in an inch or two of water, trying to get her afloat so that he could dash to their rescue.

The three Coots, Tom, Port and Starboard, knew at once how serious was the danger of the Hullabaloos. Just for a moment or two the others were ready to rejoice that Tom had escaped them. But soon they, too, saw how badly damaged the *Margoletta* was. They saw, too, that the Hullabaloos, instead of doing the best that could be done for themselves, were making things far worse. The *Margoletta* had been towing a dinghy. Two of the men rushed aft and tried to loose the painter and bring the dinghy alongside. They hampered each other. One pulled out a knife and cut the rope, thinking the other had hold of it. The rope dropped. They grabbed at it and missed. The dinghy drifted with every moment farther out of reach. They seized a boat-hook, tried to catch the dinghy and lost the boat-hook at the first attempt.

'She's down by the head already,' said Starboard. 'Oh can't they stop that awful song?'

The crew of the *Teasel* watched what was happening, hardly able to breathe. There was the cruiser drifting away with the tide up the deep channel. With every moment it was clearer that she had not long to float. Were the whole lot of the Hullabaloos to be drowned before their eyes? Would no one come to the rescue?

They looked despairingly towards Yarmouth. A rowing-boat was coming along. But so slowly, and so far away. Too late. They would be bound to be too late, with nothing but oars to help them. But something was happening in that boat. They could see the flash of oars, but surely that was a mast tottering up and into place in the bows. And then, in short jerks, a grey, ragged, patched old lugsail, far too small for the boat, rose cockeye to the masthead. The sail filled, and the oars stopped for a moment while the sheet was taken aft.

'Hurrah!' shouted Port as loud as she could shout. 'Hurrah! It's the Death and Glories!'

Nobody else in all Norfolk had a ragged sail of quite that shape and colour. How they had got down to Breydon nobody asked at that moment. It was enough that they were there, while the *Teasel* and the *Titmouse*, still fast aground, could do nothing but watch that race between life and death. The wind was still blowing from the east, and the old *Death and Glory*, her oars still flashing although she was under sail, was coming along as fast as ever in her life. She might do it yet. And then the watchers turned the other way to see the drifting cruiser, her bows much lower in the water, the Hullabaloos crowded together on the roof of her after-cabin.

'She'll go all of a rush when she does go,' said Starboard under her breath.

'Deep water, too,' said Port.

Minute after minute went by, and then the *Death and Glory* swept past them up the channel, her tattered and patched old sail swelling in the wind, Bill and Pete, each with two hands to an oar, taking stroke after stroke as fast as they could to help her along, while Joe stood in the stern, hand on tiller, eyes fixed on the enemy ahead who had suddenly become a wreck to be salved.

'Go it, the Death and Glories!' shouted Starboard.

'Stick to it!' 'You'll do it!' 'Hurrah!' 'Keep it up!' shouted the others. And William, not in the least knowing what it was all about, jumped up first on one thwart of the *Titmouse* and then on another and nearly burst his throat with barking.

The noise of the engine had stopped. The shouting of the Hullabaloos was growing fainter as the *Margoletta* drifted up the channel with the tide.

'It's going to be a jolly near thing,' said Starboard, who was looking through the glasses at the sinking cruiser already far away.

Far away up the channel the *Death and Glory* had drawn level with the *Margoletta*. Her ragged old sail was coming down. From the *Teasel* nothing could be heard of what was being said, but it was clear that some sort of argument was going on. They could see Joe pointing at the *Margoletta*'s bows. They could see the five Hullabaloos, crowded together on the roof of the *Margoletta*'s after-cabin, waving their arms, and, so Starboard said, shaking their fists. The two boats were close together, drew apart and closed again. A rope was thrown and missed and coiled and thrown once more.

'But why don't they take those poor wretches off?' said Mrs Barrable.

Starboard laughed.

'Boatbuilders' children,' she said. 'They won't be thinking about people when there's a boat in danger. All they're worrying about is not letting the *Margoletta* go down in the fairway. You'll see. They'll tow her out of the channel before they do anything else.'

She was right. The *Death and Glory* moved towards one of the red beacon posts on the south side of the channel, towards which the cruiser had drifted. The cruiser, at the end of the tow-rope, was following her, stern first, her bows nearly underwater. The *Death and Glory* left the channel, passing between one red post and the next. The *Margoletta* followed her. She stopped.

'Aground,' said Port.

'Safe enough now,' said Starboard. 'Well done, Joe.'

They saw Joe jump aboard the wreck, moving on the foredeck almost as if he were walking in the water. They saw him lower the *Margoletta*'s mud-weight into the *Death and Glory*. They saw the *Death and Glory* pulling off again, to drop the weight into the mud at the full length of its rope. Then, and then only, when the *Margoletta* was aground on the mud in shallow water and safe from further damage, were Joe and his fellow salvage men ready to clutter up their ship with passengers. 'Idiots!' said Starboard, watching through the glasses. 'All trying to jump at once.'

'Well,' said Mrs Barrable, as the distance widened between the salvage vessel and the wreck, and she saw that all the Hullabaloos were aboard the *Death and Glory*, 'I'm very glad that's over.'

'Of course,' said Dorothea, 'in a story one or two of them ought to have been drowned. In a story you can't have everybody being a survivor.'

'If it hadn't been for the Death and Glories,' said Port, 'there wouldn't have been any survivors at all. The *Margoletta* would have gone down in the deep water and the whole lot of them would have been drowned. What's Joe going to do with them now? It looks as if he's putting up his sail.'

'He can't do anything against the wind,' said Starboard. 'The *Death and Glory* never could. And with the tide pouring up ... Hullo! Tom's afloat!'

'Get the tow-rope ready on the counter,' shouted Tom.

All this time the water had been rising. Just as the last of the Hullabaloos had left the wreck of the *Margoletta* Tom had felt the *Titmouse* stir beneath his feet. He had her mast down in a moment. Her sail had been stowed long ago. Tom got out his oars and paddled her round to the stern of the *Teasel*. William, welcome in spite of his muddiness, scrambled back aboard his ship. Tom made the tow-rope fast.

'Try shifting from one side to the other,' he said.

The *Teasel*'s keel stirred in the mud. The creek by which she had left the channel in the fog had filled, and Tom with short sharp tugs at his oars made the tow-rope leap, dripping, from the water.

'She's moving,' said Dick.

'She will be,' said Starboard, pushing on the quant, while Port hung herself out as far as she could, holding the shrouds, first on one side of the ship and then on the other, and Mrs Barrable, Dick and Dorothea shifted first to one side and then to the other of the well.

'She's off.'

The *Teasel* slid into the creek. A moment later the tow-rope had been shifted to her bows and Tom was towing her back towards the channel. In a few minutes she was once more on the right side of the black beacons, drifting up with the tide, while Port and Starboard were hoisting her mainsail. The tow-rope, now more or less clean, was hauled in, hand over hand. Tom came aboard, and the little *Titmouse* became once more a dinghy towing astern.

'Let's just see if she'll do it,' said Starboard, looking away down Breydon to the long railway bridge. If only they could get through that bridge they might, after all, be home in time for tomorrow's race.

Port was busy with a mop. 'Foredeck's clear of mud,' she said. 'What about that jib?'

Dick and Dorothea were already bringing it carefully from the cabin, while the Admiral was keeping a firm hold of the muddy William, for fear he might print a paw upon it.

Up went the jib, and the *Teasel* went a good deal faster through the water, away across the channel to a red post on the farther side. Round she came and back again. She had not gained an inch. Once more Tom took her across the channel. Once more he brought her back. No, there was no doubt about it. This time she had lost ground. The wind was dropping, and the tide pouring up was sweeping her farther and farther from Breydon Bridge.

'It's no good,' said Tom. 'We'll just have to go back to the pilot's and have another shot at getting through Yarmouth tomorrow.'

'We're done,' said Port. 'It's too late now. We'll never get home by land tonight.'

'And the A.P.'ll have no crew,' said Starboard.

The *Teasel*, a melancholy ship, swung round and drove up with the tide to meet the *Death and Glory*.

The *Death and Glory* was desperately tacking to and fro across the channel, losing ground with every tack, even though Bill and Pete were rowing to help her sail. On the southern side of the channel, beyond the red posts, the tide was rising round the after-cabin of the *Margoletta*. A black speck in the distance, the *Margoletta*'s dinghy was drifting towards the Reedham marshes.

'Joe,' shouted Tom, when within hailing distance of the *Death and Glory*, 'you can't get down to Yarmouth against this tide. We can't, either. Going back to the pilot's?'

And at that moment Dorothea looking sadly back towards Yarmouth saw something moving on the water far away.

'There's another motor-boat,' she said.

'Hullo,' said Starboard, 'I do believe it's the *Come Along*. Where are those glasses?'

Well above Breydon railway bridge a yacht was hoisting the peak of her mainsail. The *Come Along* must have brought her through from the Bure, for there, already more than half-way between that yacht and the *Teasel*, there was the little tow-boat with the red and white flag, coming up Breydon at a tremendous pace. Old Bob had seen that something was amiss.

Joe saw the motor-boat, too, and was afraid his salvage job would be snatched from him when all the work was done.

'Them Yarmouth sharks,' he said, and looked at the wreck. But the tide had carried him too far away already. Even with the help of those stout engines, Bill and Pete, he could not get back to stand by the wreck before this boat from Yarmouth reached it.

The *Come Along* seemed to be close to them almost as soon as they had sighted her. She circled once round the wreck, and then made for the *Death and Glory*, probably because Old Bob saw that the old black boat was carrying the shipwrecked crew.

'You leave her alone,' Joe was shouting at the top of his voice. 'She ain't derelict. Don't you touch her. You leave her alone!'

'Take us into Yarmouth,' yelled the Hullabaloos.

'She ain't derelict,' shouted Joe. 'She's out o' the fairway. We've put her in shallow water, an' laid her anchor out. She belongs to Rodley's o' Wroxham, an' you leave her alone.'

Old Bob shut down his engine to listen. He laughed. 'All right, Bor,' he called. 'She'll take no harm there. I'm not robbing you. Good bit o' salvage work you done. And where're ye bound for now?'

'Down to Yarmouth,' shouted the man who had been at the wheel of the *Margoletta*. 'We want to get ashore.'

The *Come Along* swung alongside the *Teasel*.

'Good day to you, ma'am,' said Old Bob to the Admiral. 'Was you going down to Yarmouth, too? And so you found your ship all right?' he added, seeing Port and Starboard smiling down at him.

'I suppose there's no chance now of getting through Yarmouth until tomorrow morning,' said the Admiral. 'The tide seems to be running very hard.'

Old Bob laughed again. 'Take ye through now,' he said. 'Tide or no tide. When the *Come Along* say "Come along", they *got* to come along. I'll be taking this party down to Yarmouth and I'll be taking you at the same time. If you'll be ready to have your mast down for the bridges. You'll have the tide with you up the North River.'

'They'll be in time,' cried Dorothea.

'We'll do it yet,' said Starboard.

'Never say dee till ye're deid,' said Port.

'Perhaps we ought to pick up that dinghy for them,' said Tom, pointing it out in the distance.

'You be getting ready,' said Old Bob. He was off again, chug, chug, chug, chug, to catch the *Margoletta*'s dinghy before it had drifted ashore.

'Oh, can't you let the blasted dinghy go?' shouted one of the Hullabaloos. But Old Bob did not hear him.

All was bustle aboard the *Teasel*. Tom sailed her to and fro close-hauled, waiting for Old Bob to come back. Port and Starboard were ready on the foredeck to lower the mainsail. Dick and Dorothea were stowing the jib once more in the cabin. Presently the *Come Along* came chugging back, bringing the *Margoletta*'s dinghy. Old Bob brought the *Death and Glory*'s long tow-rope and threw it to Tom aboard the *Teasel*. Then he threw the end of *Come Along*'s tow-rope across the *Teasel*'s foredeck. Starboard caught it and made it fast.

'All ready?' shouted Old Bob. 'Mind your steering.'

Slowly he went ahead. First the *Teasel* and the *Titmouse* felt the pull of the little tug. Then the *Death and Glory* swung into line astern of them. They were off.

CHAPTER 29

FACE TO FACE

'Come on and take the tiller, Tom,' called Port.

Tom heard her. He was standing on the foredeck, with an arm over the foot of the lowered mast, looking at the *Come Along*, at old Bob hunched up in the stern of her hugging his tiller, at the dinghy of the wrecked *Margoletta*, and ahead at the long iron railway bridge and Yarmouth town. But he hardly saw the things he was looking at. He had failed after all, and the others did not seem to know it. All this time he had kept out of the way of those foreigners and now, in the end, there could be no escape for him. The others aboard the *Teasel* were thinking of wreck and rescue and getting through Yarmouth and up the river in time for tomorrow's race. But he could think of one thing only. With every yard they made down Breydon they were nearer to the moment when the Hullabaloos would have to know whose son it was that had cast off their moorings and sent them drifting down the river. His father had told him to keep out of their way, and now there they were, all being towed down Breydon together. He could not bring himself to look at them. But, through the back of his head, as it were, he could see them, towing astern, in the *Death and Glory*, too, after all that those three young bird preservers, pirates and salvage men had done to help him to keep clear. Well, he could not exactly wish the Hullabaloos had all been drowned. He himself would have gone to help them if he had been able to get *Titmouse* off the mud.

'Come on, Tom,' said Port.

He went aft, and stood there, steering with a foot on the tiller. He could not help glancing down into the little *Titmouse*, spattered all over with the mud poor William had brought with him after heroically taking the life-line from ship to ship. Close astern of the *Titmouse* was the *Death and Glory*. He wondered if the Hullabaloos, crowded together in the old black boat, could see the name that had been painted out on the *Titmouse*'s stern. It seemed now that he might just as well have left it as it was.

'Look! Look!' cried Dorothea. 'Joe's got his white rat on his shoulder.'

In spite of himself, Tom had to look round.

Right in the bows of the *Death and Glory* were Bill and Pete, looking over at the flurry of foam from her fast towing. In the middle of the boat were the Hullabaloos, and in the stern, steering, with a face of simple happiness and pride, was Joe. His white rat crawled slowly from one shoulder to the other round his neck, but Joe's eyes never shifted from the stern of the *Teasel*, and his steering was as steady as Tom's own.

The Hullabaloos were far past minding being in a boat with a white rat. Men and women, looking all the more wretched for their gaudy clothes, they huddled together in the *Death and Glory*, miserable, angry, and silent after all that frantic shouting. Far away up Breydon a speck on the silver water at the side of the channel was all that could be seen of the *Margoletta*.

After all, even if while they had her they had used her to make things uncomfortable for other people, upsetting old ladies in their houseboats, throwing dinghies against quays and tearing down the banks with their wash, even if they had carried their horrible hullabaloo into the quietest corners of the Broads, they now were shipwrecked sailors. They had lost their ship. And, in a way, Tom felt it was his fault. If only he had not been there in the *Titmouse*, if he had not let William get loose and bark, indeed, if only he had not managed to dodge them for so long, they never would have sent their vessel crashing into a Breydon beacon.

Tom began to think how awful he would have felt if he had wrecked the *Teasel* in such a way ... or the little *Titmouse*. The thought was so upsetting that he gave the *Teasel* a sudden sheer that surprised young Joe in the *Death and Glory*, and made Old Bob in the *Come Along* look reprovingly over his shoulder.

Through Breydon Bridge the *Come Along* towed them, and round the dolphins and into the mouth of the North River, where the tide was running up. Old Bob signalled with his arm. He was swinging round to bring them head to tide alongside the quay. The moment was very near now when Tom would have to meet his enemies face to face.

'It's all right,' said Dorothea, who seemed, alone, to guess what was in his mind. 'The outlaws rescued their pursuers and everything was all right.'

But was it? There was only one thing to be done, as far as Tom could see. As soon as they were tied up to the quay he went and did it.

The Hullabaloos had come ashore from the *Death and Glory*. They were standing on the quay, explaining. Old Bob was explaining, too, to some fishermen, and telling a friend to telephone up to Rodley's at Wroxham, to say what had happened to the *Margoletta*. A lot of people seemed to be there, which made it rather worse for Tom.

He went straight up to the Hullabaloos, to the red-haired man who had been steering when the *Margoletta* crashed into the post.

'I've come to say I'm very sorry. I'm very sorry about the wreck, of course. Anybody would be. But I mean I'm very sorry about casting off your moorings that time. I wouldn't have done it if only the nest hadn't belonged to a rather special bird. But I oughtn't to have done it at all ...'

The man stared at him, turned as red as his hair, and suddenly shouted at him, 'Blast your special bird ... and that friend of yours at Horning who sent us wild-goose chasing up and down ... the two of you laughing in your blasted sleeves ... You may think it a joke ...'

Tom did not think it a joke, and he could not understand what the man meant about a friend of his at Horning. Surely not George Owdon? But, before he could answer, while the man was still raging on, one of the older fishermen cut him short.

'Stow that now,' he said. 'What ye shoutin' about? Fare, to me that if it hadn't a been for these young folk ye'd be too full o' Breydon water to be talkin' to 'em like that. Let be say I, and be thankful for a dry skin ...'

'Shut up, Ronald,' said one of the other Hullabaloos. 'You've made a mess of things, and the less said the better.'

'Isn't there a hotel in this beastly place?' said one of the two women, the one who had been rude to Mrs Barrable that first day. 'Need you keep us waiting here to be stared at by everybody?'

A boy on the quayside led them off, a melancholy, cross procession, in their white-topped yachting caps and gaudy shirts, and berets and beach pyjamas. 'Rammed a post on Breydon, they did,' the boy explained again and again to the people they passed, as he piloted them off the quay and along the crowded streets.

Not one of them had thought of saying 'Thank you' to the Death and Glories.

Not that that mattered to the Death and Glories. Fishermen and sailors who had listened to Old Bob were looking down at them from the quay and saying what a good job they had done. Presently news came that somebody had got through to Wroxham on the telephone, and that Rodley's were sending a man down to see what could be done with the *Margoletta* when the tide went down.

'They'll float her again easy,' said Old Bob. 'Couldn't have beached her in a better place myself.'

'You'll have saved someone a pretty penny,' said a sailor on the quay to the three small boys fending off their old black boat below him. 'It'll be worth a new mast and sail to you, likely, if you're wantin' 'em in that *Death and Glory* o' yours.'

At that moment salvage was the thing, and Joe, Bill and Pete decided there and then to give up piracy for good and all.

The *Margoletta*'s dinghy was left in charge of a friend of Old Bob's until Rodley's man should arrive. Then the Admiral and the skipper of the *Come Along* had a word or two together, and the Admiral told the others something of what she meant to do. 'It'll take those three far too long to get up the river in that old boat. We'd better give them a tow.'

Once more Old Bob settled down over his tiller and the *Come Along* said 'Come Along' to the *Teasel* and the *Titmouse* and the *Death and Glory*. The whole fleet went up the river together, with cheers for the three small boys from all the people on the quayside and in the moored boats. News like that of the wreck and salvage of the *Margoletta* is very quick in getting about.

'What about yanking our mast up?' said Starboard, as they left the last of the three Yarmouth bridges astern.

'Better wait till we get through Acle,' said the Admiral.

'Acle?' said Starboard.

'Acle?' said Tom.

'It won't take long with the tide and the *Come Along*,' said the Admiral. 'And I should never forgive myself if Port and Starboard were to miss tomorrow's race after all.'

As for the Death and Glories, their faces looked more and more surprised as they were towed up the river, past Three-Mile House, past Scare Gap, and Runham Swim, and Six-Mile House, and the Stracey Arms, and Stokesby Ferry. Was it never going to end?

At last they were through Acle Bridge, and there moored for the night. The Admiral settled up with Old Bob, and Port and Starboard thanked him again for taking them up Breydon from *Sir Garnet* and putting them aboard the barge.

'We'd have missed everything if you hadn't,' said Port.

'Good night to ye,' called the old man, and set off, chug, chug, down the river, back again to Yarmouth. He left the Death and Glories with bursting hearts, for, just as he was going, he had said, 'I'll see ye're not put upon. I'll tell Rodley's myself about that salvage job o' yours.'

Then, free from all fears of Hullabaloos (and after all he had not had to give his name), Tom and the others heard how it was that the Death and Glories had come sailing up Breydon in time to save the *Margoletta*. They heard how, at Acle, Joe and Pete had learnt that Bill had made a mistake about the day, and that the *Margoletta* was coming down to Yarmouth at low water on the very day that the *Teasel* had planned to come through. There was only one thing to be done if they were to save the elder Coots. They set out at once, and with the tide to help them and a lucky tow from a friendly wherry going down under power they came to Yarmouth just as the ebb ended. There was no sign yet of the *Margoletta*, held up, perhaps, by the fog. Tom and the *Teasel*, they were sure, must be waiting at the dolphins at the mouth of the river for the tide to turn up the Bure. There was still time to warn Tom to slip ashore. They rowed down through the Bure bridges. It was dead low water and quite easy. Then, finding no *Teasel*, they thought they might as well go on through Breydon Bridge to see if she were in sight. That they found easier still, for the tide was already sweeping up the Yare. They were just thinking of turning back for fear it would be too strong for them, when they caught sight of the *Teasel* on the mud, far away in the distance. And, at that very moment, the *Margoletta* had come roaring past them and they had known they were too late. They had watched the big cruiser racing up Breydon towards the helpless outlaw and then, suddenly, they had seen her swing round, ram the post, bring up short and drift away. Pete's long telescope had shown them that they had a real wreck to salve at last. The rest everybody knew.

'And now,' said the Admiral, 'those poor Hullabaloos have lost their ship, and are having to explain at the hotel how they had to leave her in such a hurry that they haven't even got their toothbrushes. And all because they moored on the top of a coot's nest, poor things . . .'

'They wouldn't go when they was asked,' said Joe.

'I tell 'em it was our coot,' said Pete.

'They only got themselves to thank,' said Bill. 'Yes, please, I'd like another bit of that chocolate.'

*   *   *   *   *   *

A few months later

CHAPTER 30

OUT OF THE DENTIST'S WINDOW

Pete had a loose tooth, and could not keep his tongue from jiggling it.

The day had been warm and sunny, one of those pleasant days that so often come towards the end of the summer holidays. The season for hiring boats on the Norfolk Broads was nearly over and there were only two vessels moored beside the staithe. One of them was a motor-cruiser that had done its season's work and was waiting to be hauled up into Jonnatt's shed for the winter. The other was the *Death and Glory*.

The *Death and Glory* was unlike any other boat on the river. In the spring she had been no more than an old ship's boat. Then she had been given a new mast and sail and an awning, so that Joe, Bill and Pete and Joe's white rat could camp in her at night. But now they had built a cabin-top on her, and decked her forrard, and Joe's father had made a tabernacle for their mast so that they could lower it for going under bridges. They had made three bunks for themselves inside. They had even got hold of a rusty old stove and cleaned it up and fixed it inside the cabin with a pipe coming out through a hole in the roof. They had had trouble over getting the stove to draw but had got over it in the end by fitting a tall earthen-ware chimney pot over the pipe. Even then they had found the smoke blowing back into the cabin, so Joe had made a conical tin cap with three legs to it to hold it off the top of the chimney. This worked very well, and if the *Death and Glory* was the only ship on the river with an earthenware chimney with a mushroom top to it, her owners did not care. They would be able to sit over a fire in their snug cabin even in the winter, and all through this warm day they had been looking forward to lighting up in the cool of the evening. In old days at the masthead there had been a black flag, but this summer they had given up piracy, and they now flew a white flag with a coot on it to show that they were members of the Coot Club.

On the cabin-top was a narrow board fixed up on edge with 'SALVAGE COMPANY' painted on each side of it. There was a small flagstaff at her bows with a white three-cornered flag with the letters 'B.P.S.' to show that the *Death and Glory* was a patrol boat of the Bird Protection Society, which was really the most important part of the Coot Club. They had spent most of the holidays at work on her, and now she was almost ready for anything. Down in the cabin Joe was busy fixing up a cupboard for stores. On the cabin-top Bill was screwing down a pair of wooden chocks to keep the chimney pot in place. They were expecting Tom Dudgeon to come along with some paint for the chimney. Pete was keeping a look out for Tom, handing screws one by one to Bill, and doing his best to persuade his tongue to keep away from that tooth.

The only passers by who did not have a friendly word for the Death and Glories were a couple of larger boys who strolled along the staithe, stood for a moment in front of Mrs Barrable's easel so that she had to stop her painting till they moved on, and raised their voices so that Bill and Pete, busy on the cabin-top, could not help hearing them.

'Interfering young pups,' said one of the two larger boys.

'What business is it of theirs?' said the other.

Pete, sitting on the cabin-top, looked over his shoulder.

'Hear that George Owdon?' he whispered.

'I hear him,' said Bill.

'What's that other?' said Pete.

'Same sort,' said Bill. 'He's visiting at George's uncle's.'

'Lucky it's not the nesting season,' said Pete and gently jiggled his loose tooth with the tip of his tongue.

'If you jiggle that tooth again I'll put you overboard,' said Bill fiercely.

'Sorry,' said Pete.

'George Owdon won't have much of a chance at beardies' eggs next year, nor yet at buttles','* said Bill. 'Now we've got her so we can sleep in her, come nesting, we'll be watching all the time.'

Late in the afternoon, when the sun had swung round and the shadows were lengthening, Mrs Barrable packed up her painting things and stopped a moment by the *Death and Glory* to say 'Good-bye'.

'Dick and Dot won't know her when they see her,' she said.

'When are they coming?' asked Bill.

'Four days from now.'

'We'll be ready before that,' said Pete. 'There's only them cupboard doors to do and the chimbley to paint.'

'If you were to give that tooth a little bit of a jerk,' said Mrs Barrable, 'I don't believe you'd really feel it coming out.'

'We been telling him all day,' said Bill. He banged on the cabin-top, leaned over and shouted, 'Come up, Joe, the Admiral's just off.'

The noise of hammering stopped and Joe crawled out into the cockpit.

'D's here in another four days,' said Bill.

'Good luck,' said Joe. 'That bring the Coot Club here in Horning up to six. We been short with Port and Starboard away.'

William, the pug-dog, was sniffing noisily along the boat, and put his forepaws on the gunwale as if to come aboard.

'How's Ratty?' said Mrs Barrable.

---

* Bearded tits and bitterns.

'He's all right,' said Joe. 'PETE!'

'Sorry,' said Peter, closing his lips in a hurry.

'Well, good night,' said Mrs Barrable. 'I hope that tooth falls out before you swallow it, Pete.'

'It's not all that loose.'

'It doesn't look to me very solid,' said Mrs Barrable. 'But I expect you know best. Good night. Come along, William.'

They watched her out of sight, with the stout William walking beside her.

'That Tom's later'n he said,' said Bill. 'If he don't look out, it fare to be too late for paint. Rightly it's too late already. No use putting good paint to be dewed.'

'What about grub?' said Joe. 'It's that dark below you can't hit a nail more'n once in three and get your thumb the other two.'

'I'm going to light up that stove,' said Bill. 'We'll do no painting now.'

They tidied up on deck and went into the cabin. Bill lit a fire in the stove, Joe put a kettle on, and, after admiring the way the chimney drew and the fire roared up with a single match, they went out again to admire the smoke blowing away from the top of the chimney.

It was slow work boiling a kettle on the stove, but it saved paraffin, and when the stove was burning it was better sense to use it instead of lighting a Primus in the ordinary way. They sat on the cabin roof watching the sun go down and taking turns to go below to see what was happening to the kettle. When at last the singing of the kettle turned to a brisk bubbling and then quietened while a steady jet of steam poured from the spout they went down into the cabin, made tea, lit their hurricane lantern, hung it from a hook in the roof, and settled down to a solid supper of bread, cheese, butter, marmalade (a present from Mrs Barrable, who had taken a bungalow in the village) and apples. Joe let his white rat out of its box and it sat on his knee on its hind legs, eating bread soaked in milk and nibbling at a nut which it held in its forepaws like a squirrel.

'She's snugger'n a wherry,' said Joe, sitting on his bunk by the stove and looking into the forepart of the old boat at the cupboard on which he had been working.

'Fit to cruise anywheres,' said Bill. 'Pete! Do leave that tooth alone.'

'That fare to drive anybody mad,' said Joe, 'seeing you sitting there goggling at us and jiggling that tooth like it were on a hinge. Bill, we're short of screws for that cupboard door. Can't make do with nails for that.'

Pete sucked his tooth into place. 'I got some,' he said. 'Three. And I'll get some more tomorrow. My Mum promise me threepence when I out that tooth.'

The others turned on him. 'If you'd have said that before,' said Joe, 'we'd have had it out in two twos. Too late now with the shops shut. But if it ain't out before morning we'll take pincers to it.'

'It's getting looser all the time,' said Pete.

'Well, you out it,' said Bill.

The sun had gone down and it was nearly dark outside before running steps sounded on the staithe and there was a tap on the roof of the cabin.

'Who go?' said Joe.

'Coots for ever,' said Tom Dudgeon coming aboard.

'And ever,' answered Joe, Bill and, after a moment's pause, Pete.

'Mind your head,' said Joe, as Tom stooped in the cockpit to come in through the cabin door. He was too late. Tom was several inches taller than the tallest of the Death and Glories.

'I'll never get in without bumping if I live to be a hundred,' said Tom, dropping down on Bill's bunk and feeling carefully to make sure there was room to spare between his head and the beams. 'Sorry I'm so awfully late. Too late for painting, but I've brought the paint. I've shoved it under the after-deck. Hullo! What's the matter with Pete?'

'Loose tooth,' said Pete.

'He's been jiggling, jiggling it all day till we want to knock it down his throat,' said Bill.

'And threepence coming to him when he out it, the young turmot,' said Joe.

'I'm going to out it,' said Pete warily.

'Well, you out it now,' said Joe. 'We won't look.'

Pete turned his back to the others and there was a long silence.

'Outed?' said Joe at last.

'It won't come,' said Pete.

'Let's have a look at it,' said Tom. 'Why, it's as loose as anything. Just give it a pull.'

'Don't touch it,' said Pete.

'Pull it out or stop jiggling,' said Joe.

All three of them looked at the unlucky Pete who hurriedly withdrew his tongue and let the tooth drop back into its place.

Tom laughed. 'I say, Pete, I know a way of getting it out so that you'll never feel it go.'

'I'll out it myself,' said Pete.

'Oh come on, Pete,' said Bill.

'It won't hurt him at all,' said Tom. He spoke privately to Joe.

'We got some fishing line,' said Joe.

'That'll do,' said Tom.

'No that won't,' said Pete. He turned his back on them and fingered his tooth again.

'Come on,' said Tom. 'You get that line and we'll want … I say, Bill …'

'Easy,' said Bill. 'I'll slip across and get one. Come on, old Pete.'

They went out into the cockpit and Tom bumped his head again in getting through the door. It was very dark outside, but the short stumpy mast of the *Death and Glory* showed against the sky.

'It's not high enough,' said Tom.

'She wouldn't carry more sail,' said Joe.

'Even if he climbed to the top it wouldn't be high enough,' said Tom.

'I don't want to do no climbing,' said Pete.

'What we really want's a house,' said Tom. 'Come on. Have you got torches?'

'Gone pretty dim,' said Joe.

'Mine's all right,' said Tom. 'I'll go first. The loft over Jonnatt's boat-shed'll do. Where's Bill?'

Bill came hurrying out of the darkness. 'I got it,' he whispered to Tom.

'I'm going home,' said Pete.

'And you a Coot,' said Joe. 'Tom won't hurt you.'

They went along the staithe and in at the open doors of the big boat-shed, moving carefully because of the rails that ran down from the shed into the river. Tom went first, lighting the way with his torch. They climbed up the ladder into the sail loft. Pete was still jiggling his tooth in the hope that it would come out of itself. The others knew he was jiggling it because every time they spoke to him there was a pause before he answered.

Tom, avoiding piles of boat gear, stored spars, and spread-out sails, went to the window which looked out over the slipway and river. Joe gave him a coil of fine fishing line. Bill gave him a brick which he had taken from the loose top of the wall between the staithe and the road. Pete sat by himself on a bundle of sail close by the top of the ladder, jiggling his tooth in the dark.

It was very dark in the loft. By the light of Tom's torch Joe and Bill made one end of the fishing line fast to the brick. At the other end of the line Tom made a small slip-noose.

'Come along, Pete,' said Joe, and Pete came, wondering why he didn't bolt for it.

'You hold the torch, Bill,' said Tom, and Bill lit up Pete's mouth and that dangling upper tooth while Tom carefully fitted the noose round it and pulled it tight, with a finger against the tooth so as not to jerk it.

Pete squeaked.

'That didn't hurt, did it?' said Tom. 'I'm awfully sorry.'

'No, not bad,' said Pete.

'Come along now and lean out of the window and look down.'

Pete knelt by the low window and put his head out.

'Can't hardly see the ground,' he said. 'It's too dark.'

'Have another look,' said Tom. 'And mind you keep your mouth open. Just as wide as you can ... Wider ...' And then he just reached over Pete's head and dropped the brick out of the window.

'Oo,' squeaked Pete. 'You're hurting my tooth.'

'What tooth?' said Tom. 'It's gone.'

'Why that's a rum 'un,' said Pete. 'It's outed.'

'Hullo! What's that down below?' said Tom suddenly.

The next second there was a crash of breaking glass. Something heavy fell on the floor of the loft and Tom put his hand to his cheek where a splinter of glass had hit it. He felt wet blood on a finger.

Bill switched the torch about.

'It's that brick,' he said, and there it was, with the line still fast to it, and Pete's tooth still at the end of the line.

'Gosh!' said Tom. 'There must have been someone down there on the slip. Hi! Hullo!'

There was no answer.

'There's nobody there,' said Joe. 'They all gone home long since.'

'Well, that brick didn't bounce,' said Tom. 'Somebody threw it back. Lucky I didn't kill him, dropping it on his head.'

CHAPTER 31

FIRST SIGN OF TROUBLE

'Somebody's been up early,' said Bill, sputtering and blowing after dipping his head in a bucket of water. 'Never heard 'em shift that cruiser.'

Joe and Pete crawled out into the cockpit, and rubbed the sleep from their eyes. The *Death and Glory* was alone at the staithe. The motor-cruiser, their neighbour of the night before, that had been tied up ready to be dismantled and taken into Jonnatt's shed, was gone.

'Quiet about it, they was,' said Joe. 'Getting her into the shed too. Why, that old capstan squeak like billyo. Somebody must have given her a drop of oil, or we'd have heard her. Come on, Bill. You done with that bucket?'

'Can I light the stove?' said Pete.

'We don't want that,' said Bill, who was sitting on the top of the cabin rubbing his head with a towel. 'Keep the chimney cool for painting. We'll use the Primus. You slip across and fill the kettle at the pump ... And keep your tongue out of where that tooth was.'

Pete ran across the staithe and filled the kettle, passed it below to Bill who was lighting the Primus and took his turn at the bucket when Joe had done with it and gone into the cabin to make sandwiches of bread and dripping. Then, when he had tied the towel in the rigging to dry, he went ashore once more but came running back to the ship when Joe shouted that breakfast was ready.

For some minutes they were too busy to talk. Pete found

that the gap left by his tooth could be used for blowing on his tea to make it cool enough to drink. He was the first to speak.

'Wonder where they've shifted that cruiser,' he said. 'She's not in the shed. I just see.'

'You haven't looked,' said Bill with a full mouth. 'They'll have haul her up inside.'

'There's nothing in the shed more than was there last night,' said Pete.

'Put that tooth away or you'll lose it,' said Joe.

Pete hurriedly put his tooth back in his pocket.

'Worth threepence, that tooth,' he said.

'Don't you lose it,' said Bill.

'I'll take it home as soon as we done washing up,' said Pete.

But the mugs and spoons were still being joggled overboard in a bucket when the *Death and Glory* was hailed by Tom Dudgeon.

'Letter from the D's this morning,' he called. 'I'll be back in a minute, as soon as I've been into Jonnatt's to tell them about that pane of glass.'

Tom had scarcely gone into the shed before Pete sighted a motor-cruiser coming slowly up the river.

'There you are,' he said. 'I tell you she weren't in the shed. Trying her engines, likely.'

The others turned to look at her.

'We was sleeping hard not to hear 'em start up,' said Bill.

The cruiser came up the river, stopped just below the *Death and Glory* and turned in towards the boat-shed to come to rest on a wooden cradle that was waiting for her on the slip. Two of Mr Jonnatt's boatmen were aboard her and a rowing dinghy was towing astern. One of the men shook his fist at the Death and Glories.

'Don't you boys know enough to leave boats alone?' he shouted.

'We haven't touched her,' said Bill.

'Fiddling about with other boats' ropes,' shouted the man. 'Nice time we've had looking for her. Right down by the Ferry she bring up. Might have done herself a power of damage. Not your fault she haven't. And I know she were moored proper. I tie her up myself.'

'She were here last night,' said Joe.

'I know that,' said the man. 'What I want to know is why did you cast her off?'

The next moment he had jumped ashore from her fore-deck and he and his mate were busy, making ready to haul her up into the shed.

The crew of the *Death and Glory* looked at each other and then at the empty space beside the staithe where the cruiser had lain the night before. The same thought was in all their minds.

'Tom'd never cast her off for nothing,' said Joe.

'With them Hullabaloos there was a reason,' said Bill. 'Mooring on the top of No. 7 nest.'

'But there's no nests on the staithe,' said Pete.

'Nor likely this time of year,' said Bill. 'Birds don't nest in September.'

They waited for Tom to come back from seeing Mr Jonnatt. Tom would explain. Whatever Tom did was right. But when it came to casting off moored boats Bill, Joe and Pete, all sons of boatbuilders, felt that whatever the reason might be it must be a very good one.

They waited, minute after minute. It seemed as if Tom was never coming back.

He came at last, not on the run, but slowly, with a serious face.

'I say,' he said, as he stood beside the *Death and Glory*, 'What on earth made you do it? I couldn't help doing it to the *Margoletta* when there was no other way of saving our coot's chicks. But that boat wasn't doing anybody any harm.'

'Well, we never touch her,' said Joe. 'We was thinking it must have been you.'

'It jolly well wasn't,' said Tom. 'Mr Jonnatt thought it was me. He was quite beastly when I went in and told him about the broken window. He said, "So you *were* here last night. There's other things to talk about besides broken windows." I said I didn't think we'd done anything else, and we didn't break the window really, only it got broken because we were there. Then I said there might be a drop of blood on one of the sails but I didn't think there was, and if there was much on the floor I'd clean it up. And he looked hard at me and asked if I was telling him I didn't do it. And I asked what. And he said, "If it wasn't you it must have been those young friends of yours," meaning you. And then he told me you'd cast loose the cruiser that was lying at the staithe and his men had gone down the river to find her. And he said "This sort of thing has got to stop. I'll have to say a word to their fathers . . ."'

'But we never touch her,' said Bill.

'We never would,' said Pete.

'We thought it was you,' said Joe. 'And we know you must have had a reason for it.'

Tom looked at them. 'Well,' he said, 'I didn't and you didn't, but everybody'll think we did because of what I had to do to those Hullabaloos at nesting time. Mr Jonnatt said there was nobody else who could have done it. He said there wasn't anybody else about here after dark.'

'But there were,' said Pete. 'There were someone who bung that brick back with my tooth.'

'I told him about that,' said Tom, 'but he only laughed. He was very decent about the pane of glass. He said he had a spare bit handy and there was no need to pay for it, and then he said there was no need for fairy stories about bricks with wings either. He said it was an accident, and let it go at that.'

'But that were no fairy story,' said Pete. 'Somebody bung back that brick.' Once more he took the tooth out of his pocket and not without pride let his tongue feel the place where it had been.

'I told him so,' said Tom, 'but he just went on talking about not being able to leave a boat alone.'

Yesterday, and for many days before, everybody who came to the staithe had had a kindly word for them and a friendly question to ask about how they were getting on with the work of turning their old boat into something better. Today all talk was on the same subject.

George Owdon and his friend strolled past, smoking cigarettes. They did not talk to the Death and Glories but talked at them.

'At their old tricks again,' said George loudly. 'Casting off boats.'

'Is that the sort they are?' asked his friend, and stared at them as if they were some ugly sort of animals behind bars in a zoo.

'You've heard of Yarmouth sharks?' said George. 'They wreck boats and then get the credit for salving them. No better than common thieves.'

Tom got hot about the collar. Joe clenched his fists. Pete was on the point of saying 'We didn't,' but caught Bill's eye in time. The four members of the Coot Club said not a word and pretended they had not heard. But, out of the corners of their eyes, they saw George and his friend stroll up the staithe, look at the mooring rings to which the cruiser had been tied and look back at the *Death and Glory*.

'Talking about us,' said Joe between his teeth.

It was bad enough to be suspected by their enemies, but it was much worse to find that even their best friends were ready to think they had had a hand in that kind of mischief.

Mrs Barrable, taking William for his morning walk, stopped by the *Death and Glory*. Pete offered her a humbug and she took it and thanked him. He offered one to William, but she said that William did not really care for humbugs but could do with a lump of sugar if they had one to spare. Then she asked if she might come aboard and Tom sat on the cabin roof to make room for her in the cockpit. And then, sitting in the cockpit in the friendliest way, she said, 'What's this I hear?'

'It's all lies,' said Joe.

She looked at him. 'Well I'm glad to hear that,' she said. 'You people must remember Dick and Dorothea are coming and I don't want them mixed up in any trouble. I don't want them to be turned into outlaws and hunted all over the Broads. Not that I don't think you were right that time, Tom. Those Hullabaloos were most unpleasant people. William thought so too.'

'I didn't cast this boat off,' said Tom. 'And the Death and Glories didn't either.'

'Good,' said Mrs Barrable. 'I was a bit afraid you might have done. Your ship's nearly finished, isn't she?'

'Cupboard doors to do,' said Joe.

'Another coat on the chimbley when that dry,' said Bill.

'We'll be going a voyage in a day or two,' said Pete.

'What are you looking at, Tom?' said Mrs Barrable.

'Watching for the eelman,' said Tom. 'I've got leave to go and see him lift the nets.'

'Think he'll let us come too?' said Pete.

And for a few moments, talking of eels, they forgot what people were thinking of them.

But Mrs Barrable had hardly been gone ten minutes before Mr Tedder, the policeman, came along and stood beside the boat, looking severely at her crew.

'Casting off boats again?' he said.

'No,' said Tom. 'And they didn't cast the *Margoletta* off either.'

'I know that,' said Mr Tedder. 'Weeding in my garden

they was when you put her adrift. But weeding that time's no sort of evidence now.'

'We didn't do it,' said Bill.

'Your Dad won't be too pleased if it was you,' said Mr Tedder, looking at Tom.

'But it wasn't,' said Tom.

'Well, don't you go casting off no more,' said Mr Tedder and walked away.

'They all think we done it,' said Joe angrily.

Not all, however. Twelve o'clock came, and the three boat-builders, fathers of Joe, Bill and Pete, walked by the staithe as usual with a group of their friends, on the way to have their midday pints at the inn. They too stopped by the *Death and Glory*.

'You cast off that boat?' said Bill's father to his son.

'No,' said Bill. 'We didn't. None of us.'

'You hear that,' said Bill's father, turning to his friends. 'Bill never tell me a lie in his life.'

'What about young Tom Dudgeon?' said one of the other men.

'I didn't,' said Tom.

'You was here last night.'

'I went home as soon as we'd got Pete's tooth out,' said Tom.

'Pete's tooth?' said Pete's father.

Pete told the story of how his tooth had been pulled out by dropping a brick out of the window of the sail loft. The men laughed.

'Mum say it was worth an extra threepence but she hadn't the money,' said Pete.

'Up to you, Peter,' laughed one of the men.

'I'll be going short of beer,' said Pete's father, digging in his trouser pocket. 'But here you are. He's a good plucked lad is my Pete and know too much to cast a boat adrift. Didn't I tell you?'

'Well, if none of 'em did it, who did? We tie her up all right. The boat couldn't have cast herself adrift . . .'

The men moved off towards the inn.

George Owdon and his friend came sauntering back and sat on the wall by the pump as if they had nothing better to do than to stare at the Death and Glories. But, now that they knew that their fathers at least did not think they had had anything to do with the loosing of that cruiser, the members of the Coot Club did not care what George Owdon and his friend might be thinking or saying.

'That make sixpence for one tooth,' said Pete.

'Better loosen another,' said Joe.

'What about getting at that pie?' said Bill. 'Come on in, Tom. We've enough for four.'

'I've got to be home by one o'clock,' said Tom, looking anxiously up the river. 'Good. Here he is, coming down now.'

A small black tarred boat, wide in the beam and pointed at both ends, was rounding the bend by the inn, rowed by an old man with a mane of grey hair that hung down on his shoulders from under an old black hat.

The old man came rowing up to the staithe and brought his old boat in close astern of the *Death and Glory*.

Tom took a flying leap to the staithe to meet him.

'How go?' said the old man.

'Fine,' said Tom. 'What about tonight?'

'Bit late for you,' said the old man. 'Tide'll be working up till after twelve and eels won't be running till tide turn.'

'That's all right,' said Tom. 'I've got leave. Can we all come?'

'We'll lend a hand,' said Joe.

The old eelman laughed. 'Come if you like,' he said. 'But come quiet. Midnight. Not after. But who's to wake you? Sleeping you'll be when old Harry draw his setts.'

'We won't,' said Tom.

'Not us,' said Bill.

'Midnight then,' said the old man, 'for them as wakes.'

He stumped off across the staithe to do his bit of shopping.

'Who'll come and dig me out?' said Tom.

'I'll do that,' said Joe.

'I'll put the string out,' said Tom. 'But you'll have to be jolly quiet. We've our baby sleeping in the next room.'

'Bat quiet,' said Joe. 'And you can't beat bats for that.'

'And now I've simply got to bolt,' said Tom, and was gone.

They forgot about the bother over the cruiser until late in the afternoon when a stranger, coming from somewhere down the river, sailed up to the staithe and moored his boat, a tall white-sailed cutter, just where the cruiser had been. The first coat of paint on the chimney had dried and Joe and Bill were standing by while Pete put on the second. All three of them turned to watch. The stranger tied up his yacht, stowed her sails, called out to ask when was the next bus to Wroxham, and was strolling off the staithe when he met George Owdon and his friend who just then rode up on their bicycles. The stranger half turned and looked back at his yacht and then at the Death and Glories. They could not hear what he said.

'Well, don't say we haven't warned you.' George Owdon's rather high voice sounded across the staithe.

The stranger nodded and walked off.

George Owdon and his friend came nearer.

'You're to leave that boat alone,' said George.

'We haven't touched her, have we?' said Joe.

'You'd better not,' said George.

'Patching everything on us,' said Bill.

George and his friend got on their bicycles and rode away.

A little later, the old eelman came back to the staithe laden with his parcels. He got into his boat and pushed off. Beside the *Death and Glory* he rested on his oars.

'Who's been pushing off boats?' he said.

'Don't know,' said Pete. 'But it weren't us.'

'I tell 'em so,' said the old man. 'I tell 'em so. Well, see you midnight if so be you ain't sleeping. Mind you come quiet. When eels run they're like other folk, want to have the river to theirselves. You can fright eels easy, same as other fish.'

After an early supper they turned into their bunks. Joe wound up the old alarm clock that was still working as a clock though not as an alarm. 'Anybody who wake after eleven wake the ship,' he said.

'Better leave the lantern burning,' said Pete.

CHAPTER 32

EEL SETT AT NIGHT

The *Death and Glory* swung slowly round the bend of the river. A distant glimmering light, reflected from the water, showed where the old eelman had his houseboat and his nets.

'Don't go too near,' said Tom.

'I know that,' said Joe, straining his eyes. 'But we got to hit the right place ... Easy both ...' The *Death and Glory* slid silently on. 'Half speed ... Easy ...' Joe stood on the foredeck holding to the mast and peering at the wall of reeds that showed a little darker than the sky. 'Port engine ahead ... Easy ...'

There was a brushing sound as the *Death and Glory* nosed her way into the reeds. She stopped as her stem cut gently into the soft mud, and there was a sudden loud squelch as Joe jumped ashore with rond-anchor and mooring rope.

'Gone in?' asked Tom.

'Not over my boots,' came Joe's voice out of the darkness. 'She'll be all right here.' The dim glow of a torch showed where he was stamping the rond-anchor into the mud.

'Bring our lantern,' called Joe. 'We'll dowse it before we get too near.'

'I'm going to put some more on the fire,' said Pete.

'Buck up,' said Tom.

The four of them, one behind the other, led by Bill with the lantern, squelched their way through the reeds. The ground quivered as they put their feet down. Every now and then a splash told where a foot had gone into the water.

Suddenly the eelman's light showed close ahead of them.

'Dowse that lantern,' said Joe, and Bill blew it out.

'Who go?' A hoarse deep voice spoke out of the dark.

'Us,' called Tom.

'Made sure you'd be sleeping,' said the voice. 'But tide's not turned. You're on your time. We'll not be lifting yet awhile. Mind your step now. Give me your hand . . .'

They were on slippery mud almost touching the black tarred side of the eelman's old hulk. Once upon a time it had been a boat, but it would never swim again unless in a flood. It had been turned into a hut years ago, with a couple of windows, and a stove and a chimney almost as simple as those of the *Death and Glory*. In this old ark the eelman lived and mended his nets and watched the river, and baited his eel lines, and made his babs, when the weather was right for that kind of fishing. But the eel sett, a net stretching from one side of the river to the other, lowered to the bottom when boats were going by and lifted when the eels were running, was his serious business, and the members of the Coot Club had long been waiting for a chance to watch him at it.

'There's a step on the side,' he said. 'Come in now, and better bump heads than stamp feet. Eels don't fare to run with elephants stamping round.'

The four Coots stowed themselves where they could, Tom and Joe on the bench, Bill and Pete on the eelman's bunk. The old man himself poured water from the kettle into a huge enamel teapot. He stirred it with a spoon and put it on the stove beside the kettle.

'How soon will you be lifting the pod?' said Tom.

'Lifting?' said the old man. 'Tide's only turning now. Got to raise the sett first. Give the ebb time to run and eels with it and we'll see.' He took three mugs from nails on the wall of the cabin, filled each mug nearly up with tea as black as stout, slopped some milk in and added a big spoonful of sugar. 'Two to a mug now, and one for me,' he said. 'Take a drink of that now. Why young Pete's gaping. Take a drink of that and keep awake and I'll nip out and haul up.'

The hot, bitter tea scalded their throats, but after a drink of it, even Pete no longer wanted to yawn or rub his eyes. The old man looked out into the dark. 'I'll haul now,' he said. 'Tide's going down. No. You stay here. Don't want you slipping all over.'

He was gone. The four Coots came out of the cabin. At first they could see nothing. But they heard the creak of an old windlass. Then, dimly, they saw that the eelman was crossing the river in his boat. They heard creaking from the other side. Then they saw that he was coming back, though they could not hear the noise of oars. Presently, he was with them again, went into the cabin, told them to shut the door behind them, poured himself out another mug of tea, blew the steam from it and drank.

'You ain't never seen pods lifted?' he said. 'Seventy year tomorrow I see 'em first.'

'Seventy years,' said Tom.

'My birthday tomorrow,' said the old man.

'Today or tomorrow?' said Tom.

'You're right. Gone midnight. Seventy year today.'

'Many happy returns,' said Tom.

'Many of 'em,' said Joe, Bill and Pete.

The old man chuckled. 'Live to ninety we do,' he said. 'Another twelve year anyways. On my birthday seventy year gone my old uncle let me sit along of him by the eel sett same as you're sitting along of me. Above Potter was his old setts ... Drink up. There's plenty more.' He filled up the teapot from the kettle. 'You know Potter, you do? But there been changes since then. There weren't no houses at Potter then, saving the wind pumps. And there weren't no yachts, hardly. Reed-boats and such, and the wherries loading by the bridge. And there were plenty of netting then, and liggering for pike, and plenty of fowl ...'

'Did anybody look after the birds?' said Tom, thinking of the Coot Club.

The old man laughed. 'Gunners,' he said.

'What about buttles?' said Pete.

'Shot many a score of 'em I have,' said the old man.

'Oh I say . . . Not bitterns,' said Tom.

'Many a score. There was plenty of 'em then, and then they get fewer till there ain't none. Coming back, they tell me, they are now. If I was up Hickling way with my old gun . . .'

'But you can't shoot bitterns,' said Pete, horrified.

'And why not?' asked the old man. 'In old days we shoot a plenty and there were a plenty for all to shoot.'

'But that's why they disappeared,' said Tom.

'Don't you believe it,' said the old man. 'They go what with the reed cutting and all they pleasure boats . . .'

Tom looked at the faces of the other Coots, to see how they were taking these awful heresies.

'But they're coming back,' said Joe. 'And no one's allowed to shoot 'em. And there'll be more every year. We found two nests last spring.'

'Who buy the eggs?' asked the old man.

'Nobody,' said Joe. 'We didn't sell 'em. We didn't take 'em. But they would have been taken if we hadn't have watched.'

'Some folk are rare fools,' said the old man. 'Now if I'd have knowed where them nests was, it'd have been money in my pocket and tobacco in my old pipe.'

The Coots looked at each other. It was no good arguing with old Harry, but, after all, it was one thing for an old Broadsman to talk about taking bitterns' eggs and quite another for somebody like George Owdon who had plenty of pocket money already without robbing birds.

The old man caught the look on Pete's face.

'Old thief. Old Harry Bangate,' he said. 'That's what you

think. And I say, No. What was them birds put there for? Why, for shooting.'

'But if you shoot 'em, they won't be there,' said Joe.

'When we was shooting there were always a plenty.'

It was clear that the old man would never understand why the members of the Coot Club spent their days and nights in the spring guarding nests and watching birds, and Tom was wise enough to change the subject.

No one noticed how the time went till at last, looking at a huge old watch hung on a nail, the old man got to his feet, opened the door of his cabin and let in a great rush of cool, night air.

'We'll have a look at them old eels,' he said.

He lit their lantern for them, and took his own from its hook. 'You'll want that in here,' he said. 'Two'll stop here and two with me. Can't have more in the boat.'

'Who'll go first?' said Tom.

But there was no argument about it. The eelman's boat was afloat close by the stern of his old hulk, and he just took hold in the dark of the two nearest to him, who happened to be Tom and Bill, and told them to hop in and hop in quiet. A moment later he had pushed off.

The boat stopped, and the old man reached down with a pole that had a hook on the end of it.

'Here that come,' he said. 'One of you hold the light and t'other give me a hand.'

Up it came, a long tube of netting, keeping its shape because of rings of osier fastened inside it.

Bill and the old eelman lifted the end of it aboard. Tom thought it was empty, but then, suddenly he saw that the narrow tip of it was swollen and shining and white, and he knew that the light of the lantern was reflected from the glistening bellies of the eels.

'Ope the keep,' said the old man and Tom, holding the

lantern in one hand, pulled open the lid of the flat box in the middle of the boat. The old man brought the pointed end of the net over the box, untied a knot and let loose a shining stream of eels. Then he pulled tight the lacing that closed the narrow end, retied it, and dropped the net over the side.

'Tremendous lot,' said Tom.

'They're working. They're working,' said the old man.

'My turn next time,' said Pete as they climbed back into the hulk.

'If you ain't asleep,' said the old man.

An hour and more went by, and again the old man looked at the big watch hung on its nail. Again he opened the door to the night air, but this time Pete and Joe went with him in the boat and Tom and Bill watched from the hulk as the boat moved slowly out along the net, the lantern glowing in the dark.

'They've stop now,' said Bill.

The lantern was lifted up and they saw its reflections dancing in the stirred water as the eelman brought up the pod.

They heard Pete's voice, 'Whoppers.'

They heard the splash of the eels pouring from the end of the pod into the keep. 'Gosh! He's got a lot that time,' said Tom.

Presently the lantern was coming nearer. They were coming back.

'Hundreds,' said Joe, shaking the water from his hands.

'Working nicely, the warmints!' said the old man.

'He's going to give us some of 'em,' said Pete.

And again there was tea to drink, and the door of the cabin shut out the night and the lantern hanging from the roof shone more and more dimly in the steam from wet clothes and the smoke from the old man's pipe.

'How are we going to cook 'em?' said Bill. 'Stew 'em?'

'There's stewing,' said the old man, 'and souping, and frying and smoking. But you won't try smoking. You want a close fire for that and to hang 'em in the chimney.'

'We got a stove,' said Joe.

'And what about our chimney?' said Bill.

'Let's smoke 'em,' said Pete. 'We ain't never tried smoking. And with our stove . . .'

'What do you have to do?' asked Bill.

'Skin 'em and clean 'em and hang 'em in the smoke,' said the old man.

It sounded simple enough, and since the *Death and Glory* had a stove and a chimney it seemed a pity not to try it.

'We'll smoke 'em,' said Bill.

'And you take a couple to your Mum,' said the old man, turning to Tom. 'Don't you go smoking 'em. Mrs Dudgeon she like 'em stewed.'

'I'd like to try smoked,' said Tom.

'You come and share ours,' said Joe, and so it was agreed.

CHAPTER 33

MISLEADING APPEARANCES

Bill woke first. The eelman's lantern was burning palely. A window of the cabin was a bright square in the dark wall. Pete had slipped sideways against Tom as he fell asleep, and Tom had let him lie and had fallen asleep himself. Joe, with his mouth open, was snoring, not loudly, but evenly, as if for ever. Old Harry the eelman was gone, and gone without a lantern. There was the lantern of the *Death and Glory* on the floor in the corner. Bill moved to that brighter window and looked out. There was a glow in the eastern sky. Down river the water shone silver with splashes of green. The dawn was climbing, putting out the last of the stars.

The door opened and the eelman came in.

'Time you was in your beds,' said he. 'And I'm for mine. Eels won't work no more.'

Joe stopped snoring and sat up suddenly, with blinking eyes.

'Gosh!' said Tom. 'Have I been asleep?'

'I haven't,' said Pete. 'The last thing you was saying was ...'

'More'n a hour since,' laughed the old man. 'Fare to be a fine morning, but I don't reckon to see much of it. Fish by night. Sleep by day.' He poured himself out a mug of tea, sloshed some milk in, emptied some sugar after the milk, cut himself a round of bread, put a thick slice of bacon on the bread, and settled to his breakfast. 'Cold bacon afore you goes to sleep and you won't wake with empty belly. Go on, now. Help yourselves.'

222

But not one of the Coots felt like eating. What they wanted was sleep.

'Come on,' said Tom. 'It's daylight already.'

'Wake up, Pete,' said Bill. 'Sleep in your bunk. Joe and me'll work her down to the staithe.'

'No wind,' said Joe. 'Engines.'

'Tom'll steer,' said Bill. 'Hi, Pete! Don't you drop off again.'

The old man came out with them, munching his bread and bacon. 'How are you going to carry them old eels?' he said.

'I'll run for our bucket,' said Bill.

'I'll lend you a bucket,' said the old man. 'I'll be coming down for a pint later on, and pick it up.' He went down to his boat. 'When are you going to cook 'em?' he said.

'When we've had a bit of sleep,' said Bill.

'I'll fix 'em for you,' said the old man. He opened the keep and looked in. His gnarled old hand darted down among the eels like a heron's beak. Up it came again with a wriggling eel. Bang. He had stunned the eel with a blow on its tail. The next moment he had picked up his knife, jabbed it into the eel's backbone close behind its head and dropped it into a bucket. Again his hand shot down into the keep. One after another he brought up half a dozen good eels, stunned them and killed them and dropped them in the bucket as easily and quietly as if he were thinking of something else. The Coots, remembering gory struggles with eels they had caught themselves, cut fingers, tangled fishing tackle thick with slime, watched with awe.

'However do you do it?' said Tom.

The old man looked up. 'Scotching the warmints?' he asked. 'Practice,' he said. 'Practice. Seventy year of it.'

He gave them the bucket, said they could come again some time if they would like another night, and climbed back into his hulk. They thanked him, and splashed off along the reedy bank to get back to the *Death and Glory*. The cool fresh air of the September morning made their cheeks tingle after coming out of that hot cabin, and by the time they got aboard the *Death and Glory* and pushed off into the smooth river, even Pete was thoroughly awake.

The affair of the cast off boat of the day before had gone clean out of their minds. Someone had cast off a boat. People had for a moment thought they were to blame. But they were not and after their night at the eel sett they were thinking of quite other things. They rowed steadily down the river, rounded the bend below old Harry's and were half-way down the short reach above the staithe when Pete gave a sudden shout.

'What boat's that?' he said.

'Funny place to lie,' said Bill.

'Must be a foreigner,' said Tom.

There is just one place in that short reach, just before the river bends round under the inn, where the trees hang out over the water. It is a place that skippers of yachts, even if strangers, usually have the sense to avoid. And just here, close to the trees, was a yacht.

'Starboard your hellum,' said Joe. 'We'll go and have a look at her.'

'Something wrong with that yacht,' said Bill. 'Look how she lie.'

As they came nearer, they saw that things were very wrong indeed. The yacht was neither anchored in the river, nor yet made fast fore and aft along the bank, but lay askew to the stream, held where she was by the top of her mast and by nothing else.

'Hullo,' said Bill. 'She's that yacht was tied up ahead of us.'

'Salvage job,' said Joe. 'Get that rope ready, Pete.'

'How on earth did she get there?' said Tom.

'Drift up with the flood and catch in them trees. Didn't, she'd be away down river. Must have come adrift just before high water.'

'Tide were still flooding when we come up, and it turn soon after,' said Bill.

'She were all right when we leave,' said Joe. 'I see her. Remember, I stand by for fear we touch.'

They were close to her now, and, looking up at the mast-head of the yacht, the salvage company could see that a bough had worked itself in between the mast and the forestay.

'What are you going to do?' said Tom.

'Take her back to the staithe and make her fast,' said Joe. 'Can't leave her like that.'

'Look at her warps hanging,' said Pete.

'That chap must have moored her pretty careless,' said Joe. 'Gently now. Fenders out. Now then, Pete. Don't let her touch there forrard. Unship your oar, Bill.' He unshipped his own as he spoke, leaving the *Death and Glory* with just enough way on her for Tom to turn her and bring her alongside. He was aboard her before the two boats touched. Pete followed.

'You haul in that bow warp,' said Joe, hauling in the rope that hung over the yacht's stern. Both ropes came up with rond-anchors on their ends.

'That's a rum 'un,' said Bill. 'However'd she get away?'

'Got to shift her sideways, same as she come on,' said Joe, squinting up at the leafy twigs between the mast and the stay. 'Let's have that tow-rope, Tom. Under where you're sitting. Keep a hold of one end.'

He made the other end of the rope fast to the yacht's mast and told Bill to take the *Death and Glory* to the middle of the river. 'We don't want to bump her if she come sudden. Never mind the rudder, Tom. Better with the oars.' The Death and Glories, boatbuilders' sons all three of them, were in their element. This was work for the salvage company. Tom, older though he was, waited for orders and did what he was told. There was no argument. Joe was in command.

The *Death and Glory* moved away. The tow-rope tautened. A flutter of leaves dropped from the masthead. Joe, watching, lifted a hand. Bill and Tom let the salvage tug drop back, and then took her forward again, as Joe pointed in a new direction. There was a scraping noise overhead. Twigs and leaves fell on deck and in the water, and the yacht shook herself free.

'Good work,' said Tom.

'Tiller, Pete,' said Joe. 'Half ahead there, in the tug. Go steady.'

The salvage tug moved slowly on towards the staithe, followed by the rescued yacht with Pete steering, while Joe coiled the mooring ropes at bow and stern, with anchors on the top of the coils, ready to take ashore.

'Slow ahead,' he called as they swung round the bend under the inn.

A window was suddenly flung up in the inn, and a maid leaned out of it, shaking a duster. Horning was waking up.

'I'm casting off now,' called Joe. 'Stand by to haul in the tow-rope. All gone!' he ran aft. 'Now then, young Pete. You go forrard ready to hop ashore. I'll bring her in.'

The yacht slid slowly alongside the staithe. Tom and Bill were bringing the *Death and Glory* back to her old berth a few yards lower down. Pete and Joe hopped ashore from the yacht, each with an anchor and warp. They were just making her fast to the rings on the staithe when two larger boys, on bicycles, came round the corner of the boat-shed, rode along the staithe, jumped off and stood watching them.

'At it again,' said one of them. 'Well. There are two witnesses this time. Now then. Just you leave those warps alone. Lucky we were passing. You leave those warps alone. ... Casting boats off and then telling people you didn't.'

'Well, we didn't,' said Pete. 'So there. You can see we didn't. We're tying her up, not casting her off.'

'Likely story. Why, we caught you at it, with the warps already loose. Come on, George, let's go and report them to that policeman right away.'

'When we get back from Norwich,' said George Owdon. 'No time to waste now. Caught them in the act. And young Tom Dudgeon in it too.'

Tom jumped furiously ashore.

'We didn't cast her off. We found her adrift, with her warps hanging loose. Her mast was caught in a tree. Look at the leaves on the deck. Anything might have happened if we hadn't come along.'

'Salvage job,' said Joe.

'Casting off the *Margoletta* was salvage, too, I suppose,' said George Owdon. 'You make those ropes fast again at once, and don't think you can cast her off after we've gone. We've seen you at it.'

'We're making 'em fast anyway,' said Joe. 'You see we was.'

'We saw you with the warps loose, casting her off,' said George Owdon. 'And I suppose you'll say you had nothing to do with all the others. I suppose you'll say you didn't touch the Towzers' rowing-boat, or the green houseboat, or the *Shooting Star*?'

'What?' exclaimed Tom. 'Nobody's gone and touched the *Shooting Star*?'

'Haven't they? You ought to know. I suppose she got away by herself, and the rowing-boat, and the houseboat. Likely, isn't it? And this time you're caught with the warps in your hands. Come on, Ralph. You others'll be hearing about this.'

CHAPTER 34

DARKENING CLOUDS

'Asleep. Don't disturb.' Someone was reading Bill's notice.

'What cheek!' said someone else.

'I'll disturb 'em,' said a third voice.

For some time Joe, Bill and Pete, lying on their bunks in the *Death and Glory* feeling better after a few hours' sleep but in no hurry to get up, had heard people talking close by. Now a hearty bang on the roof of the cabin brought them to their feet. They came out into the cockpit to find the staithe crowded. The stranger whose boat they had rescued was looking at her mooring ropes and talking to George Owdon. The owner of the green houseboat was telling people how he had waked in the night to find himself drifting down the river. The two Towzer boys were telling how they had found their rowing skiff caught in the chains of the ferry. The owners of the *Shooting Star* were explaining that only luck had saved their little racing cutter from being wrecked against some piling, though they had tied her up themselves after sailing in her the day before. Mr Tedder, the policeman, who had banged on the roof of the cabin, was looking at his note-book and sucking the end of his pencil. Everybody seemed to be talking at once but, as the Death and Glories came out into their cockpit, the angry chatter died to a sudden silence.

'So you're at it again,' said Mr Tedder. 'What are you doing it for? Up late last night you were. I see a light in your windows. And now this morning you were seen casting off that yacht . . .'

'Tying it up,' said Joe.

'Why did you want to send my houseboat adrift?'

'What about our rowing-boat?'

'You might have done fifty pounds' worth of damage sending *Shooting Star* down the river.'

'We ain't touched any of 'em,' said Joe. 'Ask Tom Dudgeon.'

'Tom Dudgeon,' somebody laughed. ' "Ask Tom Dudgeon" they say. Why, it was Tom started this game.'

'Where were you last night after twelve o'clock?' said Mr Tedder. 'Where were you? Casting off moorings and sending boats adrift all down the reach. That's what you were doing.'

'We wasn't,' said Joe.

'There'll be no peace on the river till they're off it,' said a voice.

'What's ado here?'

'Dad,' called Pete, as his father pushed his way through the crowd.

Mr Tedder turned round. 'Your Pete'll be in trouble over this,' he said. 'And it'll be you to pay the fine. Why don't you look after him?'

'What you been up to, Pete?' said his father.

'Nothing,' said Pete.

'Haven't they?' Again half a dozen people began talking at once.

Pete's father listened.

'Shurrup,' he said suddenly. 'Pete. You tell me. Have you touch any of them boats?'

'No,' said Pete.

'Hear that,' said Pete's father.

Mr Tedder silenced everybody. 'I'm making this inquiry,' he said. 'Where was this boat last night after twelve o'clock?'

'Up river,' said Joe.

'Down river, you mean,' said somebody.

'Up river,' said Joe.

'What were you doing in her?'

'We wasn't in her.'

'Ar.' Mr Tedder wrote busily in his book.

'They were ashore casting loose my houseboat.'

Mr Tedder waved his pencil to quiet the old man.

'What were you doing?'

'Catching eels.'

'Eels! A likely story. Let's see 'em.'

Bill said not a word but held out the bucket. Mr Tedder looked solemnly at the eels in the bottom of it.

'We was with Harry Bangate at the eel sett,' said Joe.

'I bet that's a lie,' said George Owdon.

'Soon settle that,' said Pete's father. 'Here's old Harry now coming down the river.'

The eelman was rowing steadily downstream. Everybody knew him, with his grey mane hanging over his shoulders from under his tattered black hat. They shouted. He looked round as if to see what they were shouting at, and rowed on silently till he brought his old boat in beside the stern of the *Death and Glory*.

'Done with that bucket?' he said.

Bill emptied eels, blood and slime from the eelman's bucket into their own and began sluicing the borrowed bucket over the side.

'Harry Bangate,' said Mr Tedder. 'These boys say they was with you at the eel sett last night.'

'And so they was,' said the old man. 'Eels run well, the warmints.'

'How long was these boys with you?'

'They come before turn of tide,' said the old man. 'Twelve o'clock, likely, and they stay with me till daylight when the warmints stop running. Anything amiss?'

'I tell you so,' said Pete's father. 'They never touch your boats.'

The crowd drifted away, the owners of the boats that had

been cast loose, George Owdon and his friend, still talking to Mr Tedder and telling him what ought to be done as he walked slowly off the staithe.

'Tom was right,' said Joe. 'they. couldn't prove nothing.'

'Drat 'em,' said Bill. 'What about smoking them eels?'

'What about breakfast?' said Pete.

'Breakfast!' exclaimed Joe. 'We oversleep breakfast. What about dinner?'

'Shove that kettle on the Primus,' said Bill. 'No need for anybody to go home. We got bread. We got cheese. We got apples. We got a tin of milk. And we got tea. Where are them sacks? Joe and me'll be getting wood for the stove and we'll be back, come that kettle on the boil.'

Twenty minutes later they had breakfast and dinner all in one. Two sacks full of waste scraps of wood and shavings lay in the cockpit. Joe and Bill had taken the empty sacks to Jonnatt's boat-shed as usual, but had been angrily told to clear out by the boatmen who were still sure they were to blame for the trouble of the day before. They had been luckier at the boat-sheds down the river and had got a good lot of pitchpine, which always burns well, cedar which burns still better and mahogany shavings which they thought ought to make plenty of smoke.

'Chimbley's good and wide, that's one thing,' said Joe. 'We'll take the cap off. That's easy. Put a stick across and they'll hang beautiful.'

'I'll bend up some wire hooks,' said Bill. 'there's that bit of telephone wire I save. I know that'd come handy for something.'

Then came the skinning of the eels. This was done by Joe and Bill together. Joe cut the skin round the neck of an eel. Bill held its head in a bit of cloth to stop it from slipping through his fingers. Joe worked round with his knife till he had loosened half an inch of skin. Then, with another bit of cloth, he got hold of that and pulled. After a few slips, pull devil, pull baker, pull Bill, pull Joe, the skin peeled off inside out like a glove. Then the skinned eel was handed over to Pete, who did the cleaning, getting rid of the insides of the eel and the black blood along the backbone, while Joe and Bill were getting the skin off another.

'Mucketty truck,' said Pete, scraping away with his knife.

'You get it all out,' said Bill. 'Poison a chap, that would, if you left it in.'

The next job was to get the eels into the chimney. They took off the tin smoke cap they had made to prevent the smoke blowing down their chimney instead of drawing up it. Bill bent four bits of wire into **S**-shaped hooks. Joe held a stout stick while he hung the eels on it, and then, carefully, they lowered the eels down the chimney till the ends of the stick rested on the edges of the chimney pot. Meanwhile, Pete had lit the fire and come up on the cabin-top again to see how things were going.

'There's not much smoke coming up,' said Joe. 'You go down and stoke a bit.'

Pete went below and came out again in a hurry.

'It smoke into the cabin something awful,' he said.

'Bound to,' said Joe.

'Can't help that,' said Bill.

'What about putting the cap back?' said Joe.

'Could do,' said Pete. 'That'd stop it blowing back.'

'That don't want to draw too well,' said Bill. 'There's plenty smoke coming out atop.'

'There's plenty more in the cabin,' said Pete.

All three went below.

Pete choked. Joe coughed. Bill wiped his smarting eyes

'That'll smoke us right out,' said Pete.

'You can't smoke eels without smoke,' said Bill.

'They ain't half bad stewed,' said Pete.

'We'll smoke 'em now we've started,' said Joe.

'Try shutting the door,' said Bill.

'Put the cap on the chimbley quick,' said Joe. 'We'll have the fire out if that go on blowing back.'

Bill fixed the tin cap on the chimney. That helped a little but not much. At least as much smoke found its way out into the cabin as found its way up past the eels. But, as Bill pointed out, if the fire drew too well the eels would be broiled instead of being smoked.

Pete started choking and could not stop.

'You better get out, young Pete,' said Bill, and Pete struggled out into the cockpit.

'I'm going to fish,' said Pete.

'Fish away,' said Bill. 'We could do with some perch. Joe and me's going to smoke them eels or bust.'

'Shut that door,' shouted Joe out of the smoke in the cabin, and Bill took one more breath, and shut the door behind him.

An hour went by and then another. Pete sat fishing on the cabin roof. The eel-smokers coughed and choked below, putting their heads out now and again to save their lives. They had long stopped saying anything. First one head showed in the smoke that poured from the door the moment it was opened, and then the other, and then for as long as they could bear it, they shut themselves in with the smoke.

There is always a chance of a perch by the staithe, and Pete was fishing with small red worms that had spent a week in moss and were at their very best. They were grand worms, red, bright and lively, but for some reason the perch that usually hang about the wooden piling and camp-shedding were not on the feed. One after another Pete kept catching small roach. Big roach are not bad when you have nothing better, but little ones are no good to a cook, and Pete put them back in the water as fast as he caught them, hoping every moment to see the two dips and the steady plunge of the float that would mean that a perch had taken his worm.

But none of the bites were like that. Now the float would slip sideways, now it would sink a quarter of an inch deeper in the water, now it would do no more than steady itself in the stream. At each of these signals, Pete struck. Each one of them meant, if he was quick enough, another roach to be unhooked and dropped back into the river. It was disappointing, but anything was better than being smoked like the eels.

'Forty-seven,' he said to himself. 'Or is it fifty-seven? Come on old perch!' But no perch took his worm. He began to fish not quite so keenly, and presently missed a bite because instead of watching his float he was looking at a small motor-cruiser coming up the reach.

He knew at once that she was not a local boat. Like all the motor-cruisers she carried her official number, and the letter in front of the figures was not B, meaning Bure, but W, meaning Waveney. She must have come up through Yarmouth from the south.

The cruiser was coming very slowly and the man at the wheel slowed her down still more when he saw that Pete was fishing. He even put his engine out of gear and the little cruiser slipped along almost silently. Pete had a good look at her, and saw that she was not an ordinary cruiser but a boat specially built for fishing. He saw rods lying in rests along the cabin-top, and other rod-rests fixed to the cockpit coamings.

'Wonder if he's had any luck,' thought Pete.

He read the name on her bows, *Cachalot*, and remembered that was some kind of whale. He looked at his float just in time to catch a roach. He unhooked it, dropped it back, and almost instantly caught another.

'Hi!' called the man in the cruiser.

Pete looked up and down, saw nobody about, and realized that the man was calling to him. He lifted a hand as the wherry-men do, to show that he had heard. The cruiser was turning slowly round.

'Like to catch me some bait for tomorrow?' called the man.

'Could do,' said Pete.

'Have you got a keep-net to put them in?'

'No,' said Pete. 'But we got a bucket.'

'Best put them in a keep-net. I'll come round and leave you mine. I want a dozen or so good pike baits about the size of that one you just put back.'

Pete took in his rod and laid it along the cabin-top. The *Cachalot* swung round, went downstream and came up again even slower than before and slid close by the *Death and Glory*. The fisherman reached out and swung a keep-net to Pete.

'Penny a bait,' he said. 'Twopence for really good ones. No tiddlers. You be here tomorrow afternoon. I'm going up to Wroxham for the night and I'll call for them on the way down.'

'Waveney boat?' asked Pete, looking with interest at the little cruiser.

'Built in Beccles,' said her owner. 'This is her first season.'

'Fine for fishing,' said Pete.

'That's what she's for,' said her owner.

He put the engine into gear and the slight wash stirred up by the propeller moved the *Death and Glory* where she lay. The cabin door flew open, and Bill's face appeared. He was very red, his eyes were streaming and smoke poured past him out of the cabin.

'What's up?' he said.

'Money for nothing,' said Pete, and pointed to the *Cachalot* which was moving off round the bend. 'He want bait for pike-fishing and I'm to catch 'em. Penny each, and twopence for big 'uns. And there's a shoal right handy. I been putting 'em back one after another.'

'You get him a dozen big 'uns,' said Bill. 'That's two bob. We could stock up well with that.'

Now that roach were wanted, they were not so willing to

be caught. The bites were further and further apart and towards evening stopped altogether. Only four were swimming in the keep-net, hung over the side of the *Death and Glory* and Pete was thinking regretfully of the dozens he had put back before he had known they would be wanted.

At last Tom Dudgeon, who had had his sleep out, came rowing up to the staithe in his little *Titmouse*. On the way up he had been stopped by the Towzer boys who had asked him what the Coot Club was playing at, sending their rowing-boat adrift. Bill and Joe decided that the eels must be pretty well done and that they need stoke no more, but let the smoke blow out of the cabin. They came up and joined Tom and Pete on the cabin roof. They told him how Mr Tedder and all the others had been at them about what had happened in the night.

'But you told them you were at the eel sett?' said Tom.

'We tell 'em so, and Harry Bangate come along himself and tell 'em too.'

'They was still saying it was us,' said Bill.

'They're going to watch the staithe and all this reach,' said Joe.

'We're going down river a bit tomorrow,' said Bill. 'And if we get a bit of money we'll go voyaging, so if anything more happen they can't patch it where it don't belong.'

Just then, the old eelman came down to the staithe, un-fastened his boat, and made ready to row away. He looked gravely at the four sitting on the roof of the *Death and Glory*.

'You didn't play havoc with them boats *before* you come up to mine?' he asked cunningly.

'Of course we didn't,' said Tom.

'There's some of 'em think you did,' said the old man. 'Now that sort of thing you didn't ought to do.'

'But we didn't,' said Tom.

The old man said not a word, but dipped his oars and rowed steadily away up the river.

'You hear that,' said Bill. 'If everybody think that, we'd best be somewheres else.'

'But Dick and Dorothea'll be here the day after tomorrow,' said Tom.

'We won't go all that far,' said Bill.

'What about those eels?' said Tom.

'Ought to be done by now,' said Joe.

'Smoke's well blowed away,' said Bill. 'Let's have supper.'

'They smell jolly good,' said Tom.

Joe, not without burning his fingers, got the cap off the chimney while Bill lifted the stick with the four eels shining black with grease and soot.

'I got a handkerchief,' said Pete.

'We better wash that before you take it back to your Mum,' said Bill a few minutes later.

'They look all right now,' said Tom.

'One apiece,' said Joe. 'You cut the bread, Pete.' He held up his hands to show why. 'Bill, look what you done to that kettle.'

'That'll come off after,' said Bill.

They settled down in the cabin to eat their eel supper.

'It's been an awful job,' said Joe.

'Worth it,' said Bill, smacking his lips, before taking his first mouthful.

For some minutes there was silence.

'Not bad,' said Bill hopefully.

'Bit sooty,' said Joe.

'Try with plenty of salt,' said Tom.

'Go on, Pete,' said Bill. 'Ain't you hungry?'

'Not clammed,' said Pete.

'It's their not being hot and not exactly cold,' said Tom.

'Some eels ain't as good as others,' said Bill. 'This ain't a very good one, that's all.'

237

Presently they gave up and emptied their plates into the river.

'I say, Tom,' said Bill as Tom rowed away, 'you tell your Mum not to try smoking them eels.'

'Stew 'em,' said Joe. 'Less work and better eating.'

CHAPTER 35

TOW OUT OF TROUBLE

All day Pete fished. When at last he saw the little fishing cruiser round the bend above the staithe, he shouted, 'We got 'em.'

The owner of the *Cachalot* waved his hand. He took his little cruiser below the *Death and Glory*, turned her and brought her creeping up alongside with his engine ticking over. Bill took his bow warp, Joe hauled in on a rope the fisherman threw him from the stern, while Pete, lifting the keep-net in the water, showed it half full of silver, splashing roach.

'Well done you,' said the owner of the *Cachalot*. 'How many have you got?'

'Seventeen,' said Pete, 'but there ain't but twelve big 'uns.'

'They look just what I wanted. Let's have the net and I'll empty them into the bait-can.'

In another moment a stream of fish was pouring into an enormous bait-can in the *Cachalot*'s cockpit.

'Seventeen, you said?'

'Only twelve big 'uns,' said Pete.

'Twopence each for the big ones. That's two shillings. And five at a penny ... I'll take them too. Call it half a crown. All right?'

'Rather,' said Pete.

The fisherman of the *Cachalot* handed over a sixpence and two shillings to the fisherman of the *Death and Glory*.

'All ready to slip?' said Joe. 'We'll be off right away.'

'Hullo,' said the owner of the *Cachalot*. 'Are you off on a voyage too?'

'We was only waiting till you come,' said Joe. 'No wind, worse luck, we got to get going.'

'Where do you want to go?'

'Down river.'

'I'm going to Potter Heigham. I'll give you a tow if you want one.'

'All the way to Potter?' said Pete.

'Why not?' said the fisherman. 'It'll be too late for me to fish tonight. So there's no hurry. Have you got a tow-rope? No. Better use mine. Here you are. Don't make fast till she's taken the pull . . .'

'We know about towing,' said Joe.

'Pete,' said Bill, who was holding the bow warp of the *Cachalot*. 'There's your Mum by the Post Office. Tell her where we're going and she can tell ours. We say we was only going a little way down . . .'

Pete leapt ashore and raced from the staithe to the street. He ran full tilt into somebody coming round the corner of Jonnatt's boat-shed.

'Sorry,' he said, and dashed across the road.

'You look where you're going,' said George Owdon.

Pete took no notice, but shouted to his mother, 'Mum! We're off to Potter. Tell Joe's Mum and Bill's.'

'Potter?' said his mother. 'You'll never get there today.'

'Got a tow,' said Pete.

'You'll go to bed in proper time,' said his mother. 'Bill and Joe promised me that. Have you got plenty of food?'

'It's only for one night,' said Pete, who saw himself being stopped and loaded up with stores while the *Death and Glory* went off without him. 'We got lots enough for that. We got to be back tomorrow. Coot Club meeting. That Dot and Dick are coming.'

'Don't you do nothing foolish,' said his mother.

'Hi! PETE!'

The shout came from the *Death and Glory*, and Pete raced

back and jumped aboard just as the *Cachalot* moved out into the stream. Bill was easing the tow-rope round the little bollard on the foredeck of the *Death and Glory*. Joe was at the tiller. The *Death and Glory* stirred and slipped away from the staithe. Bill made fast. In the wide bend by the inn the *Cachalot* swung round with her tow. The *Death and Glory* was on her way, water rippling under her bows, the tow-rope taut, chug, chug, chug sounding from the *Cachalot*'s engine, and the well-known banks of the home reach slipping by on either side.

There was no wind.

'Lot of hard work tomorrow if there don't come an easterly,' said Bill.

'Got an easterly in my pockut,' said Joe.

'Don't you go saying tomorrow you've let it get away,' said Bill.

Joe patted his pocket. 'Never you fear. I'll keep him. Let him out just when we want him. You see if I don't.'

It was as if in leaving Horning they were leaving their troubles behind them.

'Remember when the *Come Along* tow us up to Acle from Breydon Water?' said Pete, and stopped suddenly. He remembered very well that long and glorious tow, but that had been after the salvaging of the *Margoletta*, and it was just because of that old story of the *Margoletta* that people were so ready to think that if a boat was cast adrift the Coot Club must have something to do with it.

No need now to remember things like that.

Dusk was falling as they came to the first of the Potter Heigham bungalows. The master of the *Cachalot* reduced speed. Just for a second or two he shut off his engine altogether, to be able to hear what they said, and shouted back to them to ask where they wanted to stop.

'This side the bridge,' shouted Joe.

They went slowly on, the fisherman of the *Cachalot* putting his engine out of gear every time they passed other fishermen sitting on the bank in front of their bungalows, watching their floats in the quiet water. They came round the last bend and saw the low arch of the bridge ahead of them, and the big boat-sheds, and on both sides of the river a line of moored yachts, one or two with awnings up, but most of them with bare masts and no sails on their booms, waiting to be laid up. One look at the crowded staithe was enough for Joe.

'We'll never get a place along there,' he said. 'We better go through. Hey!' he shouted.

The master of the *Cachalot* may have heard him or may not, because of the noise of the engine. Anyhow, he looked back and pointed at the row of moored boats.

'Through the bridges,' shouted Joe, pointing upstream. 'Give us time to lower. You take her Pete. Bill and I'll have the mast down in two ticks.'

The fisherman waved a hand to show he understood, and kept the *Cachalot* hardly moving while Bill and Joe ran forward over the cabin-top, cast off the forestay and slowly let the stumpy mast fall aft, Joe keeping his weight on the stay while Bill, moving along the cabin-top, eased the mast gently down.

The fisherman was watching, and when Joe signalled 'Ready,' headed the *Cachalot* for the low, narrow stone arch of the bridge.

'You take her, Joe,' said Pete.

But there was no time to change helmsman. The *Cachalot* was already nosing in under the arch. The *Death and Glory* followed her.

'Keep her straight,' said Joe. 'She'll clear.'

'Look out for the chimbley,' yelled Pete.

'If the mast clear, that do,' said Bill.

Joe, crouching on the foredeck and Bill, back in the cockpit, were ready to fend off. They put out their hands and touched the old stones of the arch as they went through.

'Phew!' said Pete with relief when they were out again, and he glanced back over his shoulder. 'It never do look as if there'd be room.'

A minute later they had passed under the railway bridge. They were looking for a place to moor. The *Cachalot* began to work towards the bank. They passed one possible place and then another. The fisherman pointed ahead. Joe, who was standing on the foredeck with rond anchor ready in his hand, pointed to the right. The two boats were hardly moving. Just before they touched, Joe and the fisherman jumped ashore.

'All right here?' asked the fisherman.

'Thank you very much,' said the Death and Glories.

'Going to fish here?' asked Pete.

'Higher up,' said the fisherman. 'A bit below that dyke that goes to the Roaring Donkey. I was up there last week and lost a good one. Come along in the morning and see what your baits are worth.'

'We'll come,' said Joe.

'Well, good night to you,' said the fisherman, pushed the *Cachalot*'s nose from the bank, stepped aboard and went slowly up the river.

They watched him out of sight.

'Wonder if he catch anything,' said Pete.

'Have to get up early if we're going to see,' said Joe.

They lit the stove and made the cabin as hot as they could bear it. Joe let his white rat out for a run, and played tunes on his mouth organ while the others were watching the kettle and cutting bread and cheese. They had supper and, last thing before going to bed, went out into the cockpit for a breath of cool air.

'No wind yet,' said Bill.

'In my pockut for tomorrow,' said Joe.

CHAPTER 36

THE WORLD'S WHOPPER

The morning mist was heavy on the river and on the sodden
fields that lay on either side of it. The fields were below the
level of the river and the Death and Glories, marching along
the rond that kept the river from overflowing, looked down
on feeding cattle and horses whose thick coats were pale with
moisture.

Up at dawn, they had made a hurried breakfast, left the
sleeping bungalows of Potter Heigham behind them and were
getting near Kendal Dyke, hoping every minute to see the
moored *Cachalot* and their friend of the day before.

'There she is,' cried Joe. 'He's got her moored snug.'

The squat, lumpy little *Cachalot* showed through the mist
ahead of them. They broke into a run.

'Hullo, you! Steady on with that galloping.'

A little farther along the bank they saw the fisherman, who
had turned and was standing there in the mist, with a milk-
can in one hand and an empty sack in the other. He beckoned
to them and came back to meet them, and they went on,
trying to walk like cats instead of like elephants.

'I've got one of your baits out now,' he said. 'There'll be
nothing much doing till this fog lifts off the water, but there's
no point in scaring the fish. I'm just going along to the Roaring
Donkey. They promised last night to keep some milk for me
in the morning. You keep an eye on the ship for me. Keep
quiet if you go aboard. See that nobody touches the rod. I'll
be back in a minute or two.'

'Right O,' said Joe.

'If anyone else comes monkeying along, don't drown them right here. It would put the pike off. If anybody comes stamping round, like you did, take him upstream a bit and kill him quietly.'

'Drop him dead,' said Pete.

The fisherman waved his empty sack at them and went off into the mist along the reedy bank.

The *Cachalot* was moored against a bit of firm bank, so that it was easy to step ashore from her or go aboard. They stood, admiring her. A thin cloud of blue smoke hung about a glittering plated cowl on the top of a short chimney that came through the cabin-top.

'See that?' said Bill. 'He's got a stove.'

'Built for fishing,' said Pete. 'He tell me so. She'll be out all winter same as us.'

Ropes were out ahead and astern, and they had a critical look at the rond-anchors.

'Got 'em in proper,' said Joe. 'Not like some.'

'Look at his rod,' said Pete. 'Not that one.' (Joe, by the bows of the *Cachalot*, was looking at a roach rod on the roof.) 'The one he's fishing with.'

They looked at the big pike rod, lying in a rest on the cockpit coaming. They looked at its big porcelain rings, its dark varnish, its enormous reel. Six feet of the rod were poking out over the river and from the end of it a thin green line was pulled out straight by the tug of the stream.

'Where's his float?'

'Gone,' said Joe. 'No. There it is. Away down by them reeds. That's a likely holt for a big 'un.'

'He say we could go aboard,' said Pete.

Joe climbed aboard and stood in the cockpit. Bill followed. 'Aa, you,' said Joe. 'Step easy. You'd scare every fish in the river.' He pointed to the ripples running across the water after Bill had got into the cockpit. 'Now then, Pete.'

'Wonder if the bait's died on him,' said Bill.

Twenty yards downstream, two small pilot floats and a big white-topped pike float swung gently on the top of the moving water, tethered by the thin green line that ran from the tip of the rod. They lay so still that it was hard to believe that anything but a dead bait hung beneath them. Pete watched them as keenly as if he were fishing himself.

Joe was fingering the reel. He gave a gentle tug at the line above it and heard the reel click as it turned. He looked at the back of the reel and touched the brass catch.

'That makes it run free,' he said.

'It's not like the ones on our reels,' said Bill.

Joe pressed the catch, gently at first and then harder. Suddenly it slid back and the reel began to turn, faster and faster as the line ran out.

'He say not to touch the rod,' said Pete.

'He'll have the liver and lungs out of you,' said Bill.

For a moment Joe could not get the catch to move back. He managed it and the tip of the rod dipped and straightened. Far away down the river the floats that had been moving with the current stopped dead.

'Gosh!' said Joe. 'I thought that were going to run right out.'

'Don't you touch it again,' said Bill.

'The bait's waked up,' said Pete suddenly.

The big white-topped float bobbed sideways, twice, and then swung back into line with the pilots above it.

'Will it be an old pike after him?' said Bill.

'Fare to be,' said Joe. 'See if that bob again.'

For some minutes they stood silent in the cockpit, looking away downstream at the two little floats and the big one rippling the water a yard or two out from the reeds.

'Float bobbed again,' said Peter.

'What do we do if an old pike take him under?' said Bill.

'Yell like billyo,' said Joe. 'Nothing else we can do.' He

stopped short. 'He'll have a horn, being a motor cruiser. Here you are. Press that button and it'll wake the dead.'

'That's the starter,' said Bill.

'It might be,' said Joe. 'Well, he's bound to have a foghorn. You keep your eye on them floats, Pete.'

Doubtfully, he opened the cabin door that the fisherman had shut to keep the mist out of the cabin. He saw the glow in the neat enamelled stove. He saw a comfortable bunk, not yet made up after the night, and breakfast things ready on the table. Then he saw what he wanted. There it hung, just inside the door, so as to be within easy reach of the steersman, a smallish brass foghorn. Joe took it from its hook and put it to his mouth.

'Don't you do that,' said Bill anxiously. 'He'll think something's up.'

Joe blew gently into the horn. Nothing happened. He blew a little harder and a sudden 'yawp' startled them all.

'Float's bobbed,' said Pete.

'Don't jump like that,' said Joe. 'Look at the wave you make.' He put the horn carefully back on its hook and closed the cabin door.

For some minutes he stood still, looking now at the floats and now upstream along the reedy bank, half expecting to see the fisherman coming on the run. But the floats did not stir again. It was as if they had gone to sleep. And the fisherman did not come. Joe decided that it was all right. It had sounded pretty loud in the cockpit but, after all, it had been the very shortest of 'yawps'.

'Who's coming scouting?' he said at last.

'I'm coming,' said Bill.

They stepped ashore as quietly as they could.

Pete, his eyes still on the distant floats, said, 'I'm coming too.'

'Come on then,' said Joe.

Pete had one more look. Was that float stirring? No. The

others were already moving off along the rond. Pete had another last look at the floats and joined them.

'Knives in your teeth,' said Joe.

'We needn't open them,' said Bill.

Scout knives are awkward things to hold in the teeth on a cool misty morning and it was as well that these had been well warmed in their owners' pockets. Stooping low, and muzzled by their knives, the three set off along the bank. The reeds already hid the boat from them when Joe, the leader, stopped short and took his knife from his mouth.

'Password's "Death and Glory",' he whispered, and then, startled, 'What's that?'

A harsh 'Krrrrrrrrrrrrr', like the cry of a corncrake, sounded from behind them. Pete's knife dropped from his teeth. He fumbled for it on the ground. Bill, his knife in his hand, listened, gaping.

'Krrrrrrr ... Krrrrrrrrrrrr ... Krrrrrrrrrrrr ...'

'Out of the way, Pete,' shouted Joe. 'Look out, Bill. It's that reel ... It's a pike ...' He rushed back the way they had come, followed by the others.

'Krrrrrrrr ... Krrrrrrr ... Krrrrrrrrrrrr ...'

The rod was jerking. The reel spun ... stopped ... and spun again.

'Krrrrrrrrrr ... Krrrrrrrrrr ...'

The rod straightened. The reel stopped spinning, as Joe climbed aboard.

'Quiet,' he whispered as the others dropped into the cockpit beside him.

'Floats have gone,' said Peter.

'All three of 'em,' said Bill.

'He's off with the lot,' said Joe.

'Look where the line is,' said Pete.

The line no longer stretched straight down the river. It disappeared into the water a little above the *Cachalot* and about half-way across. There could be no doubt that a pike had taken the bait, gone downstream pulling at the rod and had then turned and swum up.

'He's weeded it,' said Joe. 'Weeded it and gone.'

'No, he ain't,' said Pete. 'Line's moving.'

The line, though still slack, was pointing further and further upstream.

'He's still on,' said Bill.

'There's a pilot,' cried Pete.

One of the small pilot floats showed well above the *Cachalot*, moving slowly along the surface of the water. Another showed ahead of it. The big white-topped pike float came to the surface.

'He's thrown it out,' groaned Joe.

'We ought to have struck him,' said Pete.

'Better wind in, I reckon,' said Joe.

Joe wound and wound. The curve of the line slowly straightened. It was cutting the water almost opposite the *Cachalot*. Suddenly the rod dipped, the reel screamed, and the spinning handles nearly broke Joe's fingers. He let them spin and held the rod up.

'He's on,' shouted Joe, getting the point of the rod up. 'He's on. Hi! ... Hey! ... Let go with that foghorn, somebody. Go on. Quick ... Keep at it ... Hey!'

Twenty yards down the river it was as if there had been an explosion under water. Just for a moment they saw an enormous head, a broad dark back and a wide threshing tail, as the big fish broke the surface and dived again.

'Hang on to him,' said Pete.

'Ain't I?' panted Joe. 'Why don't that chap come. Hey! Hey! Hey!'

The reel stopped spinning. Joe began winding in again, getting a few yards, and then having to get his fingers out of the way of the spinning handles when the pike made another rush. And then again the great fish came downstream, this time deep in the water, so that they did not see the floats as he passed. The line tautened again. There was another sudden, long rush, on and on, as if the pike were making for Yarmouth. It stopped. The floats showed on the surface far downstream opposite a big clump of reeds, in the place where they had been lying before the pike had taken the bait. They rested there a moment, bobbed, and came up again close to the reeds.

'He's going back to his holt,' shouted Pete. 'Stop him! Stop him! There he go . . .' The floats shot suddenly sideways into the reeds.

Joe pulled. It was as if he were pulling at a haystack. He wound at the reel till the rod top was on the water. He tried to lift. The line rose, quivering and dripping. Joe let the reel spin to ease it. It was no good. Deep in the reeds the pike lay still and, for the moment, the battle was at an end.

'Lemme have a go,' said Bill.

'You can't shift him,' said Joe. 'No good breaking the line. We'll lose him if you do. Gosh, I wish that chap'd come.'

Bill tried to wind in, while Joe blew frantically on the horn. Suddenly he stopped. 'We can't let him lie there chewing and chewing till he throw the hooks. We got to get him out of that. Where's Pete?'

From behind the reeds, far downstream, came Pete's voice. 'Where is he? This the place?'

The tops of the reeds waved violently.

'Further down,' shouted Joe. 'That's it. Hang on there whiles I bring the boat-hook. Here, Bill. No good winding till he come out. You keep blowing. I'll be back as soon as we shift him.'

Joe took the long boat-hook from the *Cachalot* and ran to join Pete behind the reeds. Just there the reeds were very thick and they could see little of the water. Joe poked this way and that with the boat-hook. The foghorn from the *Cachalot* sounded in long gasps. Suddenly there was a clang as it dropped on the floor of the cockpit.

'He's moved,' shouted Bill. 'He give a tug just now . . . No. He's stopped again.'

Once more the foghorn sounded its desperate call for help.

'May be right in under the bank,' said Joe. 'Come on, Pete. We got to drive him out. Make all the row you can.'

He stabbed away with the boathook, while Pete, standing on the very edge of the solid bank, kicked at the water sending wild splashes through the reeds.

'Touched him?' shouted Joe. 'Gosh, he is a whopper.' There was a tremendous flurry in the water. Waves ran through the stems of the reeds.

'He's close in,' shouted Joe. 'Go on, Pete. Splash! Splash!'

Pete, in his sea-boots, took a further step, stamped in the water, slipped, tried to recover himself and fell headlong. His struggles made a bigger splash than ever he had made with his boots. Reeds swayed this way and that as he fought for foothold in the soft mud, for handhold among the slimy roots.

'You all right?' said Joe. 'Take a grip of the boat-hook.'

'All right,' spluttered Pete, spitting river water from his mouth. 'Ouch!' he yelled suddenly, and came splashing out of the water on all fours. 'Joe,' he said. 'I trod on him.'

'He's out. Joe! Joe!' Bill yelled from the boat. Joe raced back with Pete after him.

'What's all this row about?'

The fisherman, hurrying not at all, with a full milk-can in one hand and a full sack in the other, was coming back along the path. He saw Pete, muddy and dripping, on the bank beside the *Cachalot*.

'Hullo,' said the fisherman. 'Fallen in?'

The foghorn sounded again. 'Hey! Hey!' shouted Joe.

'They've a pike on,' yelled Pete. 'We just chase him out of the reeds.'

The fisherman darted forward.

Joe, in the cockpit, had grabbed the rod from Bill's trembling hands. Far away, out in the middle of the river, a great tuft of reeds showed above the surface, moving slowly across the stream. Joe wound in, and the reeds came upstream, jerking now and then, as if something were tugging angrily at their roots. Bill blew and blew.

The fisherman spoke from the bank behind them.

'Ever caught a pike before?'

'No,' said Bill.

'You take him,' said Joe, looking over his shoulder.

'How long have you had him on?' asked the fisherman.

'Year or two,' said Joe shortly.

'Carry on for another month then,' said the fisherman. 'You're doing very well.'

'He's a big 'un,' said Joe.

'Been all over the place,' said Bill. 'Most up to Kendal Dyke and back and then he go into the reeds.'

'How did you get him out? He seems to have taken a good bunch with him.'

'Chase him out,' said Joe. 'Pete tread on him.'

The fisherman turned to look at Pete, who was standing dripping on the bank, thinking of nothing but the fish. 'Look here, you,' he said. 'We don't want to have you dying. Kick those boots off and get out of your clothes. Go into the cabin and ... don't let that line go slack! Wind in, man! Wind in!'

The pike had turned and was coming back towards the *Cachalot*. Joe was winding for all he was worth. 'You take it,' he said. 'You take it.'

The fisherman, who had come quietly aboard, put out his hand to take the rod, but changed his mind. 'Not I,' he said. 'You've hooked him. You've held him. You've played him. I'm not going to take the rod now. Hullo. He's a beauty ... Go on, Pete, get into the cabin. Never mind the wet. It'll drain into the bilge.'

'Lemme see him caught,' said Pete.

'He's coming now,' said the fisherman and reached for the long gaff that lay on the top of the cabin. 'Wind in a bit more, you with the rod. Now, lift him ... Gently ...'

For the first time, they could see how big the pike was. A huge fish, mottled light green and olive, rose slowly to the top of the water. He had shaken free of the reeds, which were drifting away. He opened a wide, white mouth, shook a head as big as a man's and plunged again to the bottom of the river, making the reel whizz.

'He's all of twenty pounds,' said the fisherman quietly. 'I was sure there was a good one about. Don't lose him now. Bring him in again. That's the way ...'

'There's the float,' said Pete. 'He's coming. There he is.'

'Keep still.'

The fisherman leaned from the cockpit with the long gaff deep in the water. The big fish was coming to the top once more. The fisherman suddenly lifted.

'Look out now,' he shouted, and in another moment the big fish was in the cockpit, threshing its great tail among their feet.

'How are you going to kill him?' said Bill.

The fisherman lifted a seat in the cockpit, took a short weighted club from the locker beneath it and brought it down heavily, once, twice, on the pike's head. The great fish lay still.

'He's swallowed his last roach,' he said. 'By gum, he must have been the terror of the river, that fish. Twenty pounds? He's twenty-five if he's an ounce.'

Joe stood, holding the rod and feeling shaky at the knees.

'Going to weigh him?' said Bill.

The fisherman took a spring balance from the locker. 'I doubt if this is much good,' he said. 'It only weighs up to twenty-four.'

He put the hook of the balance carefully under the pike's

jaw and lifted it. 'Twenty-four anyhow,' he said. 'The balance can't go down any further. We shan't know what he weighs till I take him to the Roaring Donkey.' He laid the fish down again on the cockpit floor. 'Best fish I've ever seen,' he said.

CHAPTER 37

AT THE ROARING DONKEY

Pete's clothes took a long time drying. The fisherman turned them inside out and all but cooked them and hung his boots close under the roof beside the hot chimney. The crew of the *Death and Glory* settled down in the *Cachalot* and heard all about her building, and how her owner meant to use her all through the winter season when the pike fishing was at its best. They heard how he had been trying again and again for the big fish, coming all the way round from Norwich because of the better fishing in the northern waters. He gave them an enormous meal of pea soup and cold roast beef and chip potatoes and jam tart. At last soon after midday he let Pete get into his clothes again, though patches of mud on his knickerbockers were still too damp to brush. They washed up, after the meal, while the fisherman sat smoking, looking at the huge pike.

'And now for the Roaring Donkey,' he said at last.

The mist had been lifted and driven away by a light easterly wind that was shivering the willow leaves and rustling the tall reeds, to Bill's great relief, for he had been afraid they would have a row all the way home. 'Didn't I say I had it in my pockut?' said Joe.

'Ain't you going to do no more fishing?' asked Pete.

'Never get another fish like that,' said the fisherman. 'No. We must get him weighed at the Donkey, and then, if we're quick about it, I'll go down through Yarmouth. That fish is too big to post, and I'll have to take him up to Norwich to have him stuffed. I'll give you a tow as far as Thurne Mouth and you'll blow home all right if this wind keeps up.'

He disappeared into the *Cachalot*'s fo'c'sle and came back with a long plank taken from the fo'c'sle floor. 'How's this for a stretcher?' he said.

Bill and Joe laid the plank on the path beside the *Cachalot*. The fisherman brought the big fish ashore and laid it on the plank.

'Better cover him up,' he said. 'I don't want anybody to see him at the Donkey till I've had a word with the landlord.' He went back into the *Cachalot* and brought ashore a couple of empty coke sacks, with which he reverently draped the corpse.

Joe took one end of the plank. Bill and Pete, one each side, took the other.

'Ready?' said the fisherman.

'Right,' said Joe.

'On with the funeral,' said the fisherman, and the procession set out along the path beside the river until they turned off to the right along the narrow dyke that led to the Roaring Donkey.

The little inn did not look prosperous. The dyke that led to it from the river was only big enough for rowing-boats, so most of the yachts and cruisers passed it by. Even at the height of summer there were seldom more than one or two odd visitors sitting on the benches outside its latticed windows. Today there was nobody. The roof looked as if it badly needed some new thatching. The flagstaff from which hung a tattered green flag with the letters 'ALL ARE WELCOME' was needing new paint, and so was the signboard where a white donkey stood roaring its heart out on a field the green of which had blistered away in patches.

'He'll be crowded out,' said the fisherman, 'when he has that fish on his mantelshelf. They'll be coming all the season through to try to catch another like him.'

'There's one in the Swan,' said Joe.

'This is bigger,' said the fisherman. 'Now look here, you three. Licensed premises. Can't take you in. Round you go into the yard and wait there. Don't let anybody see what you've got.' He waved a cheerful hand towards the big gate into the yard behind the inn and himself went in at the low doorway, stooping so as not to bump his head.

The stretcher-bearers went round into the yard.

'Best go under the shed,' said Joe. 'Don't want anybody coming out and asking questions.'

They went into an open shed at one side of the yard and rested the bier between a pile of faggots and a chopping block. Pete lifted a sack to have another look at the corpse.

'Wouldn't like to have my hand in his mouth,' said Bill. 'He's got teeth in him big as a harrow's.'

'Someone coming,' said Joe, and Pete let the sacking fall back. A girl came out of the back door of the inn, crossed the yard with a bucket, filled it at a pump and went away again, never knowing that three watchers were wondering what to say to her if she should happen to ask what they were doing.

Something moved in a box at the back of the shed. A pale, long, arched body stirred in some straw and put up a clawed foot against the wire netting that covered the front of the box.

'Ferrets,' said Joe.

They went nearer to have a look.

'Now then, Pete, you keep your fingers out of that wire,' said Bill. 'Remember the old keeper that time he show his. Old bitch ferret he had and four young ones. "Don't be afeard of 'em," he say. "They'll never touch you if you show 'em the back of your hand," and he shove his hand in, closed fist, and next minute he were yelling blue murder with all them ferrets fanging his knuckles and the blood spawling out.'

The back door of the inn opened again, and they heard the fisherman's voice.

'A shilling a pound for any fish over twenty pounds, you said?'

'That's right, Jemmy, we hear you say it,' laughed someone else.

'That's all right. If he's a real big 'un he's well worth it. But, see here, Mister, this isn't the first of April.' The landlord, a stout, red-faced man in corduroy breeches, was looking rather as if he thought that someone was playing a trick on him. Two or three labourers came out behind him to see if it was indeed true that the fisherman had caught a monster.

'The corpse is somewhere here,' said the fisherman. 'I told the bearers to carry it into the yard. Hi, you! Oh, there you are.'

Pete, Bill and Joe lifted the bier and carried it out of the shed.

'What do you think of that?' said the fisherman, whisking the sacks off, and showing the great pike with the tackle still hanging from the corner of his jaw.

The men stared at the fish.

'Biggest I've seen in twenty year,' said one.

'Fork out, Jemmy,' said another.

'He's a big 'un all right,' said the landlord, pressing his thumb against the firm, shiny body. 'He's put away some fish in his time.'

'Water-fowl too,' said one of the men, whom the boys knew as a reed-cutter. 'A fish like that make nothing of a young coot or a duckling.'

The landlord went into the shed, took a steelyard from the wall and hung it from a beam.

'Put it at twenty-four pounds to begin with,' said the fisherman. 'We know he weighs that.' He had lifted the pike from the stretcher and brought it into the shed.

With the help of one of the men he hung it from the hook at one end of the steelyard and held it up to keep its tail from the dust and chaff on the floor while the landlord put a stone weight and half a stone and a four-pound weight into the scale. The tail of the fish dropped nearly to the ground.

'Twenty-five pound,' said the landlord and added another pound. It seemed to make no difference.

'Twenty-six pound,' said someone in a tone full of awe.

The landlord added another pound. Then he took off all the smaller weights and added another stone weight to the first.

'Twenty-eight,' he murmured, and added a pound.

'Twenty-nine.'

He added another pound and the fish rose slowly and dipped again.

'He'll go more than thirty pounds,' said the fisherman.

Another pound put the balance on the wrong side. The landlord took it off and slid a smaller weight along the steel-yard. The fish on one side and the weights on the other swayed slightly up and down, and came to rest.

'Thirty pound and a half,' said the landlord, almost as if he were in church. 'Thirty pound and a half ...' and then he slapped his knee. 'Pay!' he almost shouted. 'I'll pay and wel-come. And it'll cost me the best part of a fiver to have him set up and I'll pay that too. If that fish don't make the fortune of the Roaring Donkey I'll give up innkeeping and take to poultry farming. Once they know about that they'll be coming from London and Manchester, and where not. We'll have the spare beds full from June to March.'

The landlord chuckled. 'Come on, chaps. Drinks on the house ... Pop for the young 'uns.'

They had only just finished an enormous dinner aboard the *Cachalot*, but when the landlord's wife came out with three glasses of ginger beer and three hunks of fruit cake, they found a little more room and filled it. They had hardly done when they saw the landlord and the fisherman coming out again into the yard.

'All the same to you,' the fisherman was saying, 'if you let me have two ten shilling notes for this pound?'

The landlord pulled out his wallet, put away the pound note and gave the fisherman two ten shillings notes in exchange.

'Come on now, you stretcher-bearers,' said the fisherman. 'We've got to hurry. Pick him up and away. I want to get down through Yarmouth as quick as I can.' He turned to the landlord. 'All right. I'll give him full instructions and you shall have the fish as soon as he's ready.'

They carried the great fish, laid out once more on the plank, back along the dyke and down the river bank to the *Cachalot*, while the fisherman was telling them what the man in Norwich would be doing, taking a mould of the fish, skinning him, letting the skin dry on the mould, varnishing and painting and setting him up with sand on the bottom of the glass case and a blue back to it and weeds arranged here and there so that the great pike would look as if he were resting in the water ready any moment to dart out at a passing roach.

'Are you all ready to start?' he asked, as he went aboard the *Cachalot* and took the fish from them.

'Have to lower the mast,' said Joe. 'That don't take a minute.'

'Skip along then as fast as you can. I'll be coming down right away, and I'll give you a tow if you're ready for it ... And now ... Just half a minute ...' He pulled three ten shilling notes from his pocket. 'Thirty and a half pounds your fish weighed and the landlord paid up like an honest man. Thirty shillings and sixpence. That's ten and twopence apiece. No need to go telling everybody you've got it, or you'll be snowed under with begging letters. And don't go putting it in the savings bank. There it is. Money to spend and well earned.'

They stared.

'For us?' said Joe.

'Ten bob,' said Joe. 'Ten blessed blooming bob!'

'And twopence,' said the fisherman.

'There's not a boy in Horning as rich as that,' said Joe.

'There's not a boy in Horning who's caught such a fish,'

said the fisherman. 'And there'll never be another. It's quite all right. Your fish. Your money . . .'

'But it were your rod,' said Joe, 'and your bait, and you put the bait out and the old pike hook himself. We didn't do nothing, only hang on till you come and pull him out.'

'I saw what you did,' said the fisherman. 'He'd be in the river yet, but for you, and I'd have lost line and tackle and maybe my best rod as well. Why, no matter who had the rod, no one could have caught him if Pete hadn't gone into the water after him like a spaniel, chasing him out of the reeds. Go on. Put the money in your pockets and keep your mouths shut till the fish comes back from Norwich. Then we'll all go over to the Roaring Donkey and everybody'll get a bit of a surprise. And now, skip along and be ready before I come.'

He went into the cabin, leaving the Death and Glories staring at each other and at the notes in their hands.

'Come on,' said Bill, and they set off at a run to get back to the *Death and Glory*.

'Ten bob apiece . . . Gee whizz!' said Joe as they ran. 'New ropes . . . A proper iron chimney . . .'

'And stock up,' panted Bill. 'We can go cruising for a month . . .'

'Gee whillikins!' said Pete. 'That's something to tell Tom Dudgeon.'

'Can't tell him yet,' said Bill. 'How long do it take to stuff a fish the way he said? Gosh! I'd like Tom to see when we go to the Roaring Donkey to look at that old pike in a glass case.'

They climbed aboard the *Death and Glory* and had her mast down just as they heard a quiet rumble from up the river. The *Cachalot* was coming down.

'Put the forrard anchor aboard Bill,' shouted Joe. 'Pete and I'll hang on to the stern warp and let her swing round. We'll have her heading the right way . . . That's right . . . Push her head out . . . Round she go.'

There was a short toot from the horn they had blown so furiously during the fight with the pike. A moment later, the *Cachalot* was in sight. Her skipper put his engine into reverse and stopped her. She drifted slowly past them. A coiled rope flew to Bill. He caught it and took a turn round the bollard on the foredeck.

'Get aboard, Pete,' cried Joe, hurriedly coiling the stern warp, putting it aboard with its anchor and clambering aboard to take the tiller as the tow-rope began to tauten.

'All clear,' he shouted.

The fisherman threw up his hand to show that he had understood. In another moment there was a flurry of water round the bows of the *Death and Glory*, and they were off.

Just above the railway bridge they passed an old man sitting on a chair on the bank, watching a pike float a few yards below him. The *Cachalot*'s skipper put his engine out of gear to slip by quietly. The old man lifted a hand by way of saying thank you, and called out, 'Nothing doing today. Not a touch since breakfast.'

'We've had one,' said the *Cachalot*'s skipper.

'Any size?'

'Not bad.'

He put on speed again.

'Like to know what he'd call good,' said Joe.

'If you keep looking at that note you'll lose it,' said Bill.

Pete pushed his note deep into his pocket.

They passed under the railway bridge. They shot the stone bridge with care, but there was plenty of room though, as before, there was a moment when they felt sure they were going to touch. They were already well below the bridge when they saw a small boy run out on the staithe.

'There's young Bob,' said Bill. 'What's up with him?'

The small boy was waving wildly.

'Something he want to tell us,' said Pete.

'Well, he can't,' said Joe shortly, busy with his steering as the *Cachalot* swerved to the right to avoid a yacht that was being towed up to the staithe by a couple of men in a dinghy.

Bill and Pete waved cheerfully to the small outpost of the Coot Club, who was still signalling when a bend of the river below the staithe shut him out of sight behind a bungalow.

'Semaphore,' said Pete. 'That stuff Dick and Dorothea show us at Easter.'

'Did you read it?'

'Couldn't,' said Pete. 'I've forgot it. But that's what he were doing.'

'Probably he want to come too,' said Joe. 'But the *Cachalot*'s in a hurry and we can't make him stop.'

'Course we can't,' said Bill. 'We're in a hurry same as he is. Wonder if that Dick and Dorothea get to Horning yet.' He pulled his ten shilling note from his pocket to make sure it was there. He caught Pete's eye and pushed it back again.

'Thirty bob,' he said. 'There's almost nothing we couldn't do.'

They left the bungalows behind and the hum of the *Cachalot*'s engine changed its note. It was higher, more urgent.

'Moving now,' said Pete, looking at the banks flying by. It seemed almost no time before the entrance to Womack was in sight and Thurne Dyke beyond it.

'Gosh!' said Joe. 'We got that mast to get up. You take her, Pete.'

Pete steered. Joe and Bill got the mast up, and made all ready for hoisting sail. They were nearing the mouth of the Thurne. The fisherman aboard the *Cachalot* slackened speed, and waved to the right.

'All ready,' shouted Joe from the foredeck of the *Death and Glory*.

The *Cachalot* swung out into the wide meeting place of the Bure and the Thurne. She swung for a moment up the Bure, so that the *Death and Glory* was heading for home.

'Now then, Bill,' said Joe.

'Up she go,' said Bill.

The little lugsail on its yard staggered up the mast, steadied and filled. Bill joined Pete in the cockpit.

'Ready to cast off?' shouted the fisherman.

'Ready.'

'Cast off!' shouted the fisherman and, as Joe let the tow-rope slip, they saw him hauling it in hand over hand and coiling it at his feet. Already the *Death and Glory* was sailing. The *Cachalot* circled round her. The fisherman lifted the huge pike. The Death and Glories gave a cheer.

'See you again,' shouted the fisherman. 'And keep your mouths shut.' He headed away down river. Just before he went out of sight at the corner they saw him turn and face them, standing in his cockpit, and stretching out his arms as wide as he possibly could.

CHAPTER 38

MONEY TO BURN

Joe's easterly wind filled the sail of the *Death and Glory* and drove her fast up the river, with a pleasant bubbling of water under her bows. But it was late in the afternoon before they drove round the bend by the ferry and came roaring up the home reach.

'Wonder if they've come,' said Pete as they were nearing the doctor's house, with the golden bream high above its thatched roof.

'There's Tom anyways,' said Joe. 'Hullo!'

Tom was waving from the lawn. 'Pull in and tie up,' he shouted. 'They're here.'

A smallish boy with large black-rimmed spectacles and a girl with straw-coloured plaits flying in the wind raced across the lawn to join Tom at the water's edge.

Joe steered to pass close by.

'Meeting in the Coot Club shed,' said Tom.

'Can't stop,' said Joe. 'Got to get up to the staithe before the shop shut.' Such is the effect of having a pocket full of money. He turned to Bill. 'Give 'em a feast,' he whispered.

'Good idea,' said Bill.

'Coot Club meeting in our cabin,' said Pete.

'Come on to the staithe all three,' shouted Joe. 'Supper in the *Death and Glory*.'

'In our cabin,' shouted Pete.

There was hurried talk among the three on the bank.

Something about telling Mrs Barrable was heard aboard the
Death and Glory as she swept by.

'All right,' shouted Tom. 'But they'll have to tell the
Admiral first.'

'Good,' said Bill. 'That just give us time.'

'We'll show 'em,' said Joe. 'What about it?'

'We got all Roy's to choose from ... Mushroom soup ...
That's pretty good ... And what about a steak and kidney. ...
Tom give us that once in the shed ...'

'Christmas pudding,' said Pete.

'Why not?' said Bill. 'Geewhillikins, we'll do it really
proper.'

The *Death and Glory* came foaming up towards the staithe.

'Hullo,' said Joe, who was steering. 'There's *Sir Garnet*
in our place. We'll have to tie up ahead of her. Stand by
to lower sail. No ... Never mind. Lower after we bring up.
Tide's flooding and we'd better swing round and head this
way.'

Sir Garnet was the fastest trading wherry on the river. Her
skipper, Jim Wooddall, was just closing the door of his cabin,
and had a small bag in his hand. Old Simon was coiling down
a brand-new grass rope that they had been towing astern of
them to get the viciousness out of it. Both men lifted hands
in greeting, and the Death and Glories waved back.

They brought the *Death and Glory* up to the staithe and made
fast close by *Sir Garnet*. Jim Wooddall was already walking
off.

'Gone to catch the bus to Wroxham,' said old Simon. 'Not
sailing till the morning.'

'Where are you going?' asked Bill.

'Yarmouth.'

'That's grand rope,' said Joe.

'Wicked when it's new,' said old Simon, coiling down the
last of it on the top of the hatches. 'Well, I'm off, too. You'll
keep an eye on her? Don't want nobody larking about.'

'Nobody shan't touch her,' said Joe, and old Simon strolled off to his cottage.

'Come on, Pete,' said Bill. 'We got to hurry before the shops shut. Come on, Joe.'

Joe took a last look at the *Death and Glory*'s mooring ropes, slackened her stern warp, tightened the one at the bows, and ran after the other two.

They were crossing the road to the shops when George Owdon and his friend rode up on their bicycles and jumped off beside them.

'So you're here again?' said George.

'Any more boats cast off?' asked Bill.

'Nobody to cast them off with you away unless it's young Tom,' said George Owdon.

'Not likely with us watching,' said his friend.

They mounted their bicycles and rode off.

'You didn't ought to have said nothing,' said Joe.

'Oh, it don't matter,' said Bill. 'Come on. George Owdon's nothing. Where do we go first?'

'Roy's,' said Pete. 'We want to get all stocked up before they come.'

They walked, as millionaires, into Roy's shop. Always before, when they had had money to spend, there had been so little of it that they had spent an hour or so outside the window, calculating just how far it would go, and deciding to go without chocolate for the sake of getting bananas, or to do without bananas because it was a long time since they had had tinned fruit. Today there was no need for doubt. They marched in with, first of all, the thought of the Coot Club supper in their heads.

'Mushroom soup,' said Pete. 'Three of them and three of us. Reckon we'll do with three tins.'

'A steak and kidney,' said Joe. 'One of the big ones.'

'And what about tins of beans?' said Bill.

'Christmas pudding,' said Pete, reading aloud from this

label. '"Cover with water and boil for half an hour." That's easy, like the steak and kidney. I say, Bill. Oughtn't we have lit the fire?'

'Burn up in two ticks,' said Bill. 'What about loganberries? And we want plenty of that milk chocolate they give us that time at Acle Bridge.'

They walked round and round the shop, looking at the shelves that were loaded with tinned foods of all kinds to meet the needs of the summer fleets of visitors sailing the hired boats. They read the notice: 'Anything bought and not used will be taken back if returned unopened.' That removed the last faint touch of thrift. 'Go on, Pete,' said Joe. 'You have it if you want it. Shove it on the counter with the rest.'

The pile of tins on the counter grew and grew. Steak and kidney, stewed oxtail, corned beef, peas, beans, pears, peaches, marmalade and strawberry jam, condensed milk, cocoa, chocolate both plain and nutty, a dozen bottles of ginger beer. The shopman, who knew them well, began to think that they were joking with him.

'Who's going to pay for all this?' he said.

'We've got money,' said Joe, pulling out his ten shilling note.

'That's all right,' said the shopman. 'Has your ship come in?'

'We just tie her up,' said Pete, and wondered why the shopman laughed.

Laden with their buyings they staggered back to the *Death and Glory*. Bill lit the stove and put a saucepan of water on to boil. Then, crouching in the fo'c'sle, he lit the Primus and put a kettle on that. They filled the new cupboards with their stores, keeping out only what was wanted for the feast. Pete was sent racing back to the shop to buy new batteries, badly needed for their pocket torches. He came back to find Joe fixing up the table, an old folding table, broken and discarded by one of the hire boats, mended by Joe and now one of the prides of the ship. It almost filled the space between the bunks.

'That look all right, that do,' said Joe. 'Now, when they come, we'll put 'em to sit along this side, two of 'em, and one t'other side, by the door. We'll want to be handy for the stove and things.'

'Coots for ever!' The visitors were standing on the staithe.

'And ever! Come along in.'

'I say,' said Dorothea. 'She's simply lovely. We'd never have known her. Real bunks. And a stove. I don't know how you've done it.'

'That stove was the worst,' said Pete. 'Before we had that chimbley. One minute that'd come roaring up and us in a stew for sparks on deck, and next minute, come a change of wind, and smoke and flame start hunting us out of the cabin. Not bad now that's painted green. Nobody'd know that were a pot chimbley.'

'It looks very nice,' said Dorothea. 'And I do like your orange curtains.'

'My Mum made 'em,' said Pete.

'Come on in,' said Joe. 'You work along that side. What do you think of our cupboards?' He flung open a door and showed the row of stored tins. 'Come on in, Dick. You work in next to Dot. And Tom by the door . . .'

'What's that?' asked Pete.

'Camera,' said Dick, unslinging it.

'Better hang it on that peg,' said Joe. 'How long have you come for? Are you going to have the old *Teasel* again?'

'Not this time,' said Dorothea. 'The Admiral's too busy painting. But we're going sailing with Tom in *Titmouse*.'

'We're all going to Ranworth tomorrow,' said Tom. 'We've just told the Admiral. And Dick and Dot are coming to breakfast at our house so that we can start early.'

'Taking photographs,' said Dick. 'The Admiral's letting me turn the bathroom into a dark room. I say, I'll take a photograph of the *Death and Glory*. We're going to be here till the end of the holidays, and at Easter we're going to be here again and I'll take photographs of all the birds' nests.'

'He's practising all the time,' said Dorothea. 'He can even take photographs in the dark.'

'Flashlight,' explained Dick. 'But I'm not much good at it yet.'

'Did you finish that story?' asked Pete. 'About the Outlaw of the Broads?'

'It's more than half done,' said Dorothea.

'Come on in, Tom, and get sitting down. Bill's ready with the soup.'

Tom, who had been sitting on the floor of the cockpit with his feet inside the cabin, bumped his head getting up, and wriggled into the corner by the door. Bill was having a hard time watching two stoves at once. He poured pea soup into three mugs and three saucers. Joe dealt out six spoons, five in good condition and one that had lost part of its handle. This he kept for himself. Pete was cutting hunks of bread.

Bill burnt his tongue hurrying with his soup, and tackled the tin of steak and kidney pudding, burning his fingers in getting it out of the hot water. It was one of those tins that open with the twisting of a key, but the key twisted off and Bill had to use a tin-opener.

'Ouch!' said Bill, wringing his fingers.

'Dip them in butter,' said Tom.

Joe got out three plates which, with the three saucers, were used for the steak and kidney. Bill, more successfully this time, opened two tins of beans.

'I say,' said Tom, who knew well that the Death and Glories mostly lived on bread and cheese. 'You must have spent an awful lot of money. Somebody had a birthday?'

'Ah!' said Joe.

'We got plenty,' said Pete. 'Earned it.' He caught Joe's eye and said no more.

'There's been a lot more fuss about all those boats that got adrift,' said Tom. 'People were watching the river again last night. Mr Tedder's been bothering Dad about it. All because of that beast George telling everybody he'd caught us casting her off when we were tying up the one we found loose.'

'Well there's been no more,' said Joe.

Bill, who wanted darkness for reasons of his own, was watching the dimming light. The sun had gone down. Dusk was falling, but even in the cabin it was not as dark as he thought it ought to be.

'Don't bolt your grub, Pete,' he said. 'There ain't no hurry.'

Everybody took the hint, and ate in stately slowness, while the saucepan bubbled on the stove. They talked of the wild chase of Tom by the Hullabaloos back in the Easter holidays. They talked of what could be done, with the *Titmouse* and the *Death and Glory* sailing in company. They talked of the foolishness of people tying up boats so that they could go adrift and bring blame on the heads of the innocent. They talked of the twins, Port and Starboard, who had been sent away to school in Paris.

It grew darker and darker.

'What about a lantern?' said Pete.

'In a minute,' said Bill, who was holding a big tin in a damp rag that kept slipping and letting the heat get at his fingers while he was trying to use the tin-opener.

'You can't see what you're doing,' said Tom.

'Joe, you get the grease off of them plates,' said Bill. He had got his tin open and emptied its contents, black and shiny, out on a frying pan.

'Shall I lend you a torch?' said Dick.

'No, thanks,' said Bill and turned his back on the party, taking the frying pan with him into the fo'c'sle.

They heard the striking of a match, which lit up the little fo'c'sle, though Bill's body was in the way and they could not see what he was doing. They heard him strike another, and yet another.

'What's gone wrong, Bill?' said Joe.

'Drat it, there ain't nothing go wrong,' said Bill. 'You wait, can't you.'

Another match flared in the fo'c'sle and went out. Then after a dark pause, they heard the gobble, gobble of liquid pouring from a bottle.

Another match was lit, and the next moment Bill was coming backwards into the cabin, bearing the Christmas pudding in a sea of blue flames.

'What about that?' said Bill.

'I say,' said Dick.

'It's lovely,' said Dorothea. 'Oughtn't you to slop the flames all over it and get some of it burning on each plate?'

Bill hesitated a moment.

'Better not,' he said. 'Wait till that die down.'

He put the frying pan with the flaming pudding on the table and turned to the lighting of the lantern. The lantern, burning brightly, was hanging from its hook under the cabin roof by the time the sea of flame round the pudding had shrunk, died away, flamed up again and gone out. There was a most decided smell of methylated spirits.

Bill carved his pudding and served it out, a helping each on three plates, and a helping each on the three saucers. He watched anxiously the faces of the visitors.

'That want a lot of sugar,' he said.

People helped themselves to sugar again and again and in the end the helpings of pudding disappeared.

'It did burn beautifully,' said Dorothea.

'That's the way to make it,' said Bill, much relieved. 'That don't fare to light without you have a drop of spirit.'

They washed it down with ginger beer, and finished up with oranges, the juice of which took away the last traces of the methylated, which had hung about in people's mouths in spite of all the sugar. Everybody agreed that it had been a first-class feast.

Bill was just passing round a bag of humbugs and everybody was talking at once when there was a sudden bang on the roof of the cabin.

'Who's there?' called Joe.

Tom, sitting close to the door, put his head out into the dark evening.

'No, it's not you I want to see,' said Mr Tedder, the policeman. 'It's that young Joe and the others.'

Not one of the crew of the *Death and Glory* could get out while their visitors were in the way. Dick and Dorothea joined Tom in the cockpit.

'No, it's not you neither,' said Mr Tedder. 'Glad to see you back.'

Joe crawled along one bunk and Bill along the other. Pete was already in the doorway.

'Now, young Joe,' said Mr Tedder, 'you wasn't here last night.'

'No,' said Joe, 'But there hasn't been any more boats cast off. George Owdon say so.'

'Not here there hasn't,' said Mr Tedder. 'Where was you last night?'

'Above the bridge at Potter Heigham.'

'Ar,' said Mr Tedder. 'I heard you was there. And how many boats did you cast off? Word just come through there was half a dozen boats sent adrift below Potter Bridge last night.'

'We never touch no boats,' said Joe.

'You was there,' said Mr Tedder. 'I'll ring through to Potter and see you in the morning.'

He left them and went off along the stage. They heard his slow voice booming in the dusk. 'They was there right enough. Thank you for telling me.'

'Who's that with him?' said Bill.

'Only George Owdon,' said Tom.

'Him again,' said Bill.

'But they can't patch that on us,' said Pete. 'We never go below bridges. We never touch no boats at Potter.'

'Nor anywheres else,' said Joe. 'But if Mr Tedder think we do.'

The cheerful party came to a gloomy end.

'It's just bad luck,' said Tom.

'It's jolly unfair,' said Dick.

'Our Dads'll stop us off the river,' said Bill.

'Oh they can't,' said Dorothea. 'Not for something you didn't do.'

'That makes no difference,' said Tom.

'They'll have to emigrate,' said Dorothea. 'We'll all go to Ranworth and you can lie hid there just like Tom did when he was an outlaw.'

CHAPTER 39

BREAKFAST AT DR DUDGEON'S

Dick and Dorothea came round the corner of the house just as the gong was ringing for breakfast. Tom, coming downstairs eight steps at a time, met them in the hall.

In another minute they were all seated in front of their porridge bowls, and Mrs Dudgeon was pouring out coffee while 'our baby', a good deal bigger and more human than he had been in the spring, lay in a cot in a corner of the room, and smiled and bubbled at his father.

'Where did you say you were going?' asked Mrs Dudgeon.

'Ranworth,' said Tom. 'Coot Club expedition. The *Death and Glory*'s coming too.'

'Keep an eye on those young Coots of yours,' said Dr Dudgeon. 'Tedder looked in last night after you'd gone to bed. He'd been talking on the telephone with Mr Sonning at Potter Heigham.'

'But they hadn't done anything,' said Tom. 'It's all a mistake. They just moored above the bridges, spent the night there and came back yesterday. They never touched another boat.'

'Mr Sonning tells quite another story,' said his father. 'He says they were seen going up through Potter Heigham Bridge. That's all right. But then, after dark, when there was no one about, they came down and cast off half a dozen boats moored by his shed. All his men were busy getting hold of the boats next morning and your three had disappeared. And then, it seems, they came down through Potter astern of a motor-boat and were away before anybody could stop them.'

'I'm dead sure they didn't touch any boats,' said Tom.

'They were as surprised as anything when the policeman came and told them about it,' said Dorothea.

'I don't think they're that kind of lad,' said Mrs Dudgeon.

'No more did I,' said Dr Dudgeon. 'But you must admit it looks rather funny. One coincidence is likely enough ... But three! ... I think you'll find Mr Tedder coming round to take out summonses ...'

'Oh no, Dad,' exclaimed Tom. 'He can't. You mustn't let him. They've not done a single thing. It was just bad luck, their happening to be somewhere about when someone else was casting boats off, or leaving them not properly tied up or something.'

'Mr Tedder won't get his summonses unless he can produce his evidence,' said Dr Dudgeon. 'You can be sure of that. But I am not quite so sure as you are that he won't be able to get it. And it isn't only Tedder who'll be after them. If they've ...'

'They haven't,' said Tom.

'If anyone's been casting off Sonning's boats at Potter, he won't stand it, and you know who his solicitors are.'

'Not Uncle Frank?' said Tom.

'Well, he's in the firm, and if Mr Sonning stirs up Farland, Farland & Farland you'll have Uncle Frank after whoever it is and pretty determined to get them.'

'But he's Port and Starboard's father, and they're Coots. He'd know it wasn't the Death and Glories anyhow,' said Dorothea.

'He may not have quite the opinion of your young friends that his daughters have,' said Dr Dudgeon. 'Well, let's hope they don't get into any more trouble. Where are they now?'

'At the staithe,' said Tom. 'Or on their way here. We're all going to Ranworth together.'

'Any other boats at the staithe?' said Dr Dudgeon.

'No,' said Tom. 'No small ones. Only *Sir Garnet*, and

nobody'd dare to send a wherry adrift ...' Tom stopped suddenly. From where he sat at the breakfast table he could see out of the window across the open lawn to the river. At the side of the lawn there were bushes, and over those bushes he had seen something moving.

'She's coming down now,' he said. 'Bill told me old Simon said they were going down through Yarmouth today. They must be quanting. No sail up. I can just see her vane above the trees. You'll see her in a minute. Here she comes ... I say ... Come on, Dad, QUICK!'

Dr Dudgeon was out of the door almost as soon as Tom. *Sir Garnet* was coming down the river as Tom had said, but she was coming down broadside on and there was nobody aboard her. No one was at the helm. No one was walking her side-decks with a long quant. Her gaff and big black sail were still stowed as they had been the night before. She was coming down the river by herself.

Tom and his father raced across the lawn. Dick and Dorothea raced after them. Mrs Dudgeon watched them from the window.

'She's coming close in,' said Tom. 'She'll touch ... She'll ...'

There was a sudden long scrunch as the stem of the great wherry, pointing rather upstream than down, hit the wooden piling along the edge of the lawn. As she touched, Tom jumped aboard. There was enough spring in the piling to throw her off again, and, as she drifted on, she was further and further away.

'Steady, Tom,' called Dr Dudgeon. 'Don't try to jump back. Make fast lower down if you get a chance.'

But Tom was not listening. His father was a fisherman but Tom was a sailor first of all. He had seen *Sir Garnet*'s mooring rope hanging over her bows and was hauling it in and coiling it on his arm just as fast as he could. Another five yards and he would be too late ... Another three yards ... 'Stand clear, Dick,' he shouted. 'Catch, Dad.' The coil of rope came spinning through the air, uncoiling as it came. Dr Dudgeon caught it.

'Hang on, Dad, hang on . . . Take a turn round that post. . . . Ease her . . . Well done, Dad.'

A wherry drifting with the stream is a heavy thing to stop, and Dr Dudgeon could not have held her without the post to help him. But he had got a turn round it and had only had to ease out a foot or two of rope before the stern of the wherry began to swing in, and her bows came again towards the piling. Tom leapt ashore to fend off. Dick and Dorothea were fending off too. Between the four of them they had stopped her and made her fast. Another minute and it would have been too late. She would have drifted below the Coot Club dyke and they might not have had a second chance.

'Well,' said Dr Dudgeon. 'I'm glad of one thing. I can give evidence myself that you and Dick and Dorothea had no hand in casting her off. But what about those others? I wonder if she'd have gone adrift if I'd had the whole Coot Club to break-fast instead of only you three.'

'I'm sure they didn't touch her,' said Tom. 'Joe was as pleased as Punch because old Simon had told them to keep an eye on her.'

'And here she is,' said Dr Dudgeon.

'Gosh!' said Tom. 'Look here. I'd better take *Titmouse* straight up to the staithe to say we've got her.'

'Quicker to run,' said Dr Dudgeon. 'And the sooner the better. You find out what those Coots of yours were doing. And get word to old Simon or Wooddall if he's about. Put things right as quick as ever you can.'

But as Tom turned to go he glanced up the river. A dinghy with two men in it was coming down and by the way the oars were splashing anybody could see that they were in a hurry.

'It's Jim Wooddall,' he said, and a minute or two later the wherryman, very red, brought his dinghy alongside the lawn and jumped out, followed by his old mate.

'It's them lads,' said the wherryman. 'If their dads don't wallop the hides off 'em I'll ... Simon, ye old gaum, where did you leave that warp?'

'On the hatch-top I coil him,' said old Simon. 'You see me do that, and wicked he were too, for all our towing ...'

They looked this way and that over the wherry. The big coil of new rope had disappeared.

'Pushed over, likely,' said Jim Wooddall. 'And they sons of boatbuilders ... Ought to be in jail they ought ... Forty fathom of new coir rope.'

'It'll float, won't it?' said Tom, looking downstream.

'Not two minutes longer than anyone see it,' said Jim. 'Why, I just bought that rope ...' All the time he was looking round *Sir Garnet*. Old Simon had taken the dinghy's painter aboard and was looking anxiously along the other side of the wherry.

'No damage,' said Dr Dudgeon. 'Bit of tar perhaps, and she may have shifted some of my piling. But it's lucky it's no worse.'

'She ain't hurted herself nowheres,' said old Simon coming ashore again.

'No thanks to them lads,' said Jim Wooddall. 'You ought to teach 'em better, young Tom. Going to the bad they are, straight as the New Cut.'

'And that lie straight as a crow fly,' said old Simon.

The great wherry's bows had swung out and round with the stream. Old Simon was aboard and winding at the winch. Jim Wooddall, who had taken a stern warp to the post on the lawn, now let it slip, hauled it in and took the tiller. The big black sail lifted, the gaff swinging as it went up. *Sir Garnet*, the fastest wherry on the river, was on her way.

The little group at the edge of the lawn watched her go.

'Well, Tom,' said Dr Dudgeon. 'I don't wonder Jim Wooddall was a bit upset. It might have been a serious thing for him. And he's known those lads since they were born, and you see what he thinks about them.'

He walked back to the house, leaving Tom and Dick and Dorothea at the water's edge, watching the *Death and Glory* which was coming down the river, not under sail but rowed by Bill and Joe, who were standing in the cockpit, each working an oar, while Pete sat on the forward end of the cabin top, with his head in his hands.

'They're in an awful stew,' said Dorothea.

Joe and Bill were almost too short of breath to speak and Pete was biting his lips and trying to look as if he didn't care when the *Death and Glory* rounded up by the Doctor's lawn, and Tom and Dick took their ropes.

'What happened?' asked Tom.

'Somebody cast off *Sir Garnet* while we was asleep,' said Pete.

'Pete wake first and we chivvy him out to put his head in a bucket,' said Joe, 'and he sing out she've gone.'

'We come up and look,' said Bill, 'but we didn't think nothing of it, only they'd been quiet getting away. We know she weren't tied up with no slip knots or nothing, because we look at 'em after you was gone, just before we turn in.'

'We didn't think nothing,' said Joe. 'We has our brekfuss, and we was just about finished when we hear old Simon on the staithe, singing out to know if Jim had left a message for him. And then come Jim Wooddall and he were fair out of his mind when he see she gone. And he come ranting at us thinking we done it. And there was somebody fetch Tedder. They was all shouting and saying we ought to be kept off the river. And George Owdon go telling how he catch us casting off the yacht we was tying up. And there was chaps from Jonnatt's telling about that cruiser. And somebody say "Fetch their Dads", and Bill say to me we better get out, and we begin to cast off and get our ropes, and then somebody grab hold of the old ship and won't let go, and Jim Wooddall were shouting to know what time of tide we push her off, and we was telling him we didn't push her off, and there was everybody come across the road from the shops hearing the shouting and yelling, and our Dads wasn't nowhere handy and whatever we say get shouted under, and then that young Phil come from his milk round and say he seen her down river and not so far neither, and Jim and old Simon they grab a dinghy and was off after her, and Jim saying he'd settle with us proper when he come back.

'And then we try to shove off again, but there was half a dozen of 'em grab hold. Somebody sing out to know where we was off to, and we tell 'em we was only going to Ranworth with you. I will say that for George Owdon. He were the only one speak up for us. He say to let us go, we couldn't do no harm in Ranworth being out of the river. And they start arguin', and we see our chance and give a shove off. They was still arguin' when we get away.'

'We'll get stopped off the river,' said Pete bitterly. 'And we ain't done nothing at all.'

'We got to emigrate like you say,' said Bill, looking at Dorothea.

CHAPTER 40

WORSE AND WORSE

Pete woke slowly. Light was coming in through the windows of the cabin, but there was very little in the fo'c'sle where he had his bunk. Pete's was one of those muddled wakings, when yesterday and today seem to have run together. He woke, still half dreaming, into all the noise of yesterday's row on Horning staithe, with Jim Wooddall and Mr Tedder and George Owdon, and everybody else all shouting together. It was a minute or two before he knew that no one was shouting at all, and that the only noise he could hear was the steady breathing of Joe and Bill and the faint creak of the *Death and Glory*'s warps. Why, of course, they were not at Horning staithe but at Ranworth, where there were no wherries to get adrift and bring all kinds of trouble on the heads of honest Coots.

Pete looked across the staithe. The sun was well up. Everything looked extra bright after yesterday's rain. A cat, on its way home, walked slowly across the road by the inn. He heard a man whistling. Why not slip out and be back with the milk before the others woke? He pulled out the milk-can from under the after-deck and scrambled ashore.

Swinging the milk-can, Pete walked to the edge of the dyke beside the staithe and stopped with a jerk. Surely there had been boats in that dyke last night. Why, he remembered looking at them with Tom before going to the other side of the staithe to see the fishing boats pulled up on the green turf. And now the dyke was empty. He ran across the staithe. Half those boats had gone too. There were still a few pulled right up out of the water but all those that had been lying afloat or half afloat with anchors ashore were gone. Pete looked out across the wide Broad. What was that by the reeds away on the further side? The next moment he was haring back to the *Death and Glory*.

He put the milk-can down on the staithe, jumped into the cockpit and charged, stooping, through the cabin to get his telescope.

Bill blinked at him from his bunk. 'What's the hurry?' he said.

'Come out and look,' said Pete, hurrying back into the cockpit with his big telescope. 'Salvage job, I reckon. That must have blowed hard in the night.'

He lifted the telescope and trained it on the distant reeds. Over there was rippled water, and the reeds were waving in the wind, and the water was splashing among them, and . . . one, two, three . . . why, there must have been half a dozen boats or more blown against the reeds. Looking through the telescope he could see the water beating along their sides.

'Come on, Bill,' he cried. 'Quick. Come on, Joe. We got to get them boats.'

Bill was first into the cockpit, Joe close behind him. Pete was already on the staithe, casting off the *Death and Glory*'s warps. He pushed off and jumped aboard.

'Quick. Quick,' he cried. 'We'll get 'em all back before anyone know they've gone.'

But Bill and Joe thought differently.

'They'll take no harm against them reeds,' said Bill.

'Up with that sail,' said Joe.

'But ain't we going to get them?' said Pete. Always before, the mere sight of a boat in difficulties had been enough to bring the *Death and Glory* full speed ahead to the rescue.

'Not going to be had that way twice,' said Joe. 'If anybody see us with them boats they'll say we cast 'em off, same as

George Owdon say when we tie up that cutter that were caught in the trees.'

'Sure as eggs is eggs they'll say it's us,' said Bill, who was hurriedly setting the sail.

Joe steering with one hand and hauling taut the sheet with the other was anxiously looking back towards the village.

'No one stirring yet,' he said.

'What are we going to do?' asked Pete.

'Dig out,' said Joe.

Already they were moving fast. With every yard they got a better wind as they left the shelter of the land and the *Death and Glory* fled from Ranworth staithe as if pursued by ghosts.

'If we can get clear of the Broad before anybody see us,' said Bill coming back into the cockpit.

'But they see us here last night,' said Pete.

'It's the worst that happen yet,' said Joe. 'Who's going to believe us now?'

'Can't we do nothing about them boats?' said Pete. It was dreadful to see them, three or four open rowing-boats, a small motor-cruiser, a half-decked sailing boat and a couple of dinghies, splashed by the waves and tossing, tossing endlessly against the reeds.

'We just got to get out,' said Joe. 'It's the only thing we can do, and that ain't much. Anybody showing yet, Bill?' With the strengthening wind he had to look to his steering.

'No ... At least ... Hullo ... There's chaps on the staithe now.'

A distant shout was blown after them across the water. A man ... Two men and a small boy were standing waving on the staithe.

'That's young Rob, he's a Coot,' said Bill, who had grabbed Pete's telescope and was looking through it. 'He'll tell 'em it weren't us.'

'Put your head in a bucket and boil it,' said Joe angrily. 'He don't know who done it but he know who we are.'

Joe at the tiller, could not look back. The other two saw one of the men take a furious kick at something on the staithe that flew into the air and landed with a splash in the water.

'They're raging mad,' said Pete.

'They're pointing at us,' said Bill.

'Course they are,' said Joe between his teeth. 'And they ask young Rob, what's that boat? and young Rob he chirp up and tell 'em that's the *Death and Glory*. He won't know no better.'

CHAPTER 41

TWO WAYS OF LOOKING AT
THE SAME THING

Tom had already brought the *Titmouse* out of the dyke and round to the edge of the Doctor's lawn when Dorothea arrived on the run to say she was sorry they were late and Dick would be coming in two minutes as soon as he had been able to put his photographs to wash.

'What's that?' asked Dr Dudgeon, looking at the exercise book Dorothea had in her hand. 'Holiday task?'

'It's part of my story,' said Dorothea.

'What's it called?'

'*The Outlaw of the Broads.*'

'Outlaw or Outlaws?' said Dr Dudgeon, rather grimly.

Before she had time to answer someone else came round the corner of the house.

'Hullo, Uncle Frank,' said Tom.

'Hullo to you,' said Mr Farland.

'You've met Dorothea,' said Dr Dudgeon.

'How do you do?' said Dorothea.

'How do you do?' said Mr Farland. 'Well, Tom, I hope we shan't be putting you in gaol.'

'What for?' said Tom.

'You and your young friends. Mr Tedder's got a list of crimes against them that looks pretty bad. That's what I wanted to see you about, Dudgeon. They seem to have been up to something worse at Potter Heigham than casting off other people's boats.'

The Doctor took his pipe out of his mouth.

'By Jove, Tom, I wish you'd never touched that cruiser in the spring, even though I did tell you I didn't see what else you could have done. It's going to be a bit difficult for me if Mr Tedder comes and asks for a summons against those three for casting boats adrift when I know my own son set them an example.'

'Oh well,' said Mr Farland. 'Tom doesn't go in for stealing.'

'Stealing!' exclaimed Dot and Tom together.

'Old Sonning of Potter Heigham's been on the telephone to me again this morning,' said Mr Farland. 'He was pretty well het up about all his boats being set adrift, but he didn't know then that those young rascals had been into his store and cleared out a lot of gear. He says there's a gross and a half of new gunmetal shackles missing.'

'But I'm sure they never did,' said Tom.

'Sonning's sure they did,' said Mr Farland, 'and he's asked us to advertise a reward for evidence leading to conviction. He says they're bound to have sold them to someone else, and the only people who'd buy them would be other boatbuilders. He doesn't think there'll be any difficulty in getting the evidence.'

'But Tom's young friends seem to get along very well without money,' said Dr Dudgeon. 'I don't suppose they've ever had more than a bob or two in their pockets in all their lives.'

Tom looked at Dorothea. She had turned white and for a moment looked as if she were going to be sick. Both of them were remembering the feast in the *Death and Glory* and the crammed cupboards that night when the three small Coots had come back from Potter Heigham.

Mr Farland asked, 'Where are they now, Tom?'

Tom looked up doubtfully. 'You're not going to arrest them?' he said.

'Wish I could,' said Mr Farland. 'At least, I wish we had proof enough against them to get the thing settled. I'd only like to know where they are, in case somebody else finds his boat adrift.'

'They've gone to Ranworth to be out of the way,' said Tom. 'So if any more boats are cast off everybody'll know it isn't them.'

'They may be tired of the game,' said Mr Farland. 'Three times they've done it . . .'

'But they haven't done it at all,' said Dorothea.

'Put it differently,' said Mr Farland. 'Three times boats have been cast adrift when they were somewhere handy to do it if they had had it in mind.'

The *Titmouse* sailed away down river to carry the news to the emigrants at Ranworth. As they turned the bend below No. 7 nest, they saw the *Death and Glory* moored against the reeds.

'They've come to meet us,' said Dorothea.

'Young idiots,' said Tom. 'They ought to have stopped in Ranworth. What's the good of plans if people don't stick to them?'

The next moment he was bringing the *Titmouse* alongside and the three Coots were tumbling out into the cockpit of the *Death and Glory*.

'What's happened?' asked Tom, when he saw their worried faces.

'Someone cast off half a dozen boats,' said Joe. 'They was blown all across the broad against them reeds and Pete see 'em when he turn out.'

'I go and leave our milk-can on the staithe,' said Pete.

'What did you do?' asked Tom. 'Salvage them and take them back?'

'Not likely,' said Joe. 'And have everybody saying they seen us casting 'em off. We up sail and bolt for it.'

'Anybody see you?'

'They come on the staithe just before we make the dyke,'

said Bill. 'And young Rob were there. He know the *Death and Glory*, being a Coot. It's the worst yet . . .'

'We may as well give up,' said Joe.

'Oh, no,' said Dorothea.

'Mother says your people say you can stay on the river, at least at Ranworth, but better keep away from Horning staithe,' said Tom.

'We can't lie at Ranworth,' said Bill. 'Not now.'

'Tell you what,' said Joe. 'We'll lie in the Wilderness above the Ferry.'

'Well, that's off the river and handy for us,' said Tom.

'Emigrating ain't no good,' said Bill.

'I say,' said Tom. 'You know all that money you had the other night . . .'

'We got some still,' said Joe. 'Are you wanting any?'

'Where did you say you got it?'

'Earned it,' said Joe. 'Selling fish . . .' He caught Bill's eye, and winked. 'Thirty bob and a tanner we get and another half-crown for Pete's baits. Coining money we was . . .'

'That's all right,' said Tom with relief. 'I thought it was . . .'

'Why, what about it?' said Joe.

'You know the night those boats were sent adrift at Potter. Someone took a lot of new shackles from Sonning's store.'

'Nobody don't say we was stealing?' burst out Pete indignantly, and Dorothea's heart warmed again.

'They put the two things together,' said Tom, 'and they're advertising to catch the thieves.'

'Papering 'em, same's they did you over that cruiser?'

'Yes,' said Tom a little uncomfortably. 'They think the thieves'll have sold them, and they'll catch them that way.'

'Hope they do and hope they skin 'em,' said Joe. 'Broads ain't Yarmouth.'

'And that'll let us out,' said Bill.

'Not about *Sir Garnet* and those other Horning boats and now this Ranworth lot,' said Tom.

'Someone *must* be doing it on purpose,' said Dorothea. 'But everyone thinks it's the Coots so they aren't looking properly for anyone else.'

'It's getting pretty serious,' said Tom.

'What we want are detectives,' said Dorothea.

'Why shouldn't we find out ourselves?' She went on almost as if talking to herself alone. 'I've never tried writing a detective story.'

'Plenty of detectives in Horning,' said Tom. 'They're all detectives now and every single one of them's trying to prove the Coots have been casting off boats when they haven't touched a single one.'

'Why shouldn't we be detectives too?' said Dorothea.

'We don't need to be detectives to know we ain't done it,' said Joe. 'We know that without.'

'We could use my camera,' said Dick. 'They always have one.'

The Death and Glories looked doubtfully from face to face.

'All the world believed them guilty,' said Dorothea. 'Their fathers' and their mothers' grey hairs went down in sorrow to their graves ... Were going down ...' she corrected herself. 'The evidence was black on every side ... And I say ...' She suddenly changed her tone. 'William'll make a splendid bloodhound.'

'But William ain't a bloodhound,' said Pete. 'Nothing like it.'

'Well, we need one anyway,' said Dorothea, 'and William's the best we've got.'

'What's the camera for?' asked Bill.

'Photographing clues,' said Dick.

'When there's a murder,' said Dorothea, 'they always dash in and photograph everything.'

'But there ain't a murder, not yet,' said Bill.

'There may be,' said Dorothea excitedly. 'The villain fights like a rat once he's cornered.'

Bill, despairing of Dorothea, turned to Tom. 'We ain't none of us villains,' he said. 'You know that.'

'Who said we were?' said Tom. 'But everyone thinks we are and with one thing and another it looks like it. Why, you yourselves thought I'd pushed off that cruiser from the staithe. And I thought you'd done it. The D's are right. If we're going to clear ourselves and save the Coot Club we've go to find out who really did do it. Someone did.'

CHAPTER 42

THE FIRST CLUE

Joe, Bill and Pete brought their old ship round the bend by the Ferry, downed sail and paddled and poled her far into the Wilderness dyke. There they moored her, to the northern side of the dyke, so as to be handy when they wanted to slip along to Tom's.

'Anyone see us come in?' asked Joe.

'Not as I know,' said Bill.

'Anyways,' said Joe, 'there ain't no boats in the Wilderness to *be* cast off.'

They left the *Death and Glory* and went back to the mouth of the dyke to watch for the return of the detectives who had been searching for clues at Ranworth.

At last the *Titmouse* came into sight. Dorothea saw the waiting Coots as soon as they saw her and eagerly waved the exercise book that was Volume Five of *The Outlaw of the Broads*. Tom, who was steering, waved too, and Dick seemed to be trying to show them something, though he was much too far away for them to see what it was.

'All right for them,' said Bill. 'Nobody'll turn Tom Dudgeon off the river.'

'They've found something,' said Joe. 'All of 'em waving like that.'

Pete hurriedly took his fishing rod to pieces. The *Titmouse* came alongside. Joe steadied her, grabbing at her gunwale while Dorothea passed the anchor to Bill.

Dick held out a small bit of rubber tubing.

'That's from a bike pump,' said Bill.

'It's the first clue,' said Dorothea.

'Jolly good thing we went there,' said Tom. 'That young idiot Rob thought you'd been playing the fool with those boats.'

'And he tell the others,' said Joe bitterly. 'I know he tell 'em when I see him there pointing. The young turmot.'

'I told him you hadn't touched them,' said Tom. 'But they'd already sent someone off on a bicycle to tell Tedder, and the chap came back while we were there.'

'He helped like anything without meaning to,' said Dorothea. 'He came and leant his bicycle against the fence above that green place where some of the boats were yesterday. They'd brought the boats back. Well, you know where that green bit ends by the fence and the gate into the wood. There's a bit of bare earth there and yesterday's rain had wetted it. Dick was looking about all over everywhere. He's awfully good at seeing things. Lots of people had been trampling about, pulling the boats up, and I said it wasn't any good looking for footprints when there were such lots of them. And then Dick asked the man to move his bicycle a bit, and he did, and then Dick asked if anybody else had been there with a bicycle, and nobody had. And then Dick made a drawing of the track left by the man's bicycle. I gave him a blank page out of *The Outlaw*.'

'I thought he'd gone dotty,' said Tom. 'But he hadn't.'

Dick had come ashore and was polishing his spectacles. 'I couldn't have done it if it hadn't been for that rain yesterday,' he said.

Dorothea went on. 'Then he grovelled again ... The Admiral won't be awfully pleased ... I say, Dick, don't rub it in now. We must wait till the mud's dry before we try to get it off ... He grovelled again and made another drawing. And we could see it was a different sort of tyre.'

Joe jumped into the air. 'Geewhillykins!' he said. 'Someone come on a bike to cast them boats off.'

'He found out much more than that,' said Dorothea. 'Some of the tracks of that other bicycle were funny and wide with hardly any pattern and a groove each side. And some of them were narrow and the pattern as sharp as anything. And Dick said that someone came there on a bicycle last night and had a puncture and pumped up his tyre before he rode away again. And we hunted along with our noses to the ground and we lost the tracks and found them again on the road to the Ferry, on a damp patch, two lots of them . . .'

'Coming and going,' said Dick. 'And there were the man's tracks as well, quite different.'

'Then we went back to the place by the gate,' said Dorothea. 'We started hunting again and I found the tube from a bicycle pump. It was trodden in the mud and I expect the villain couldn't find it when he dropped it in the dark.'

'I bet he trod on it himself,' said Tom.

'Let's see them tracks,' said Bill, and Dick opened his pocket-book and took out a folded sheet of exercise paper on which were the two drawings.

'Dunlop, that one,' said Bill. 'Same as mine. What's that other?'

'John Bull,' said Dick. 'But that one doesn't matter. That's the track of the Ranworth man. It's the other that had the puncture and was there in the night and lost his pump-tube.'

'There's lots of chaps got Dunlops,' said Joe. 'Bill's got 'em.'

'So have I,' said Tom.

'Ours are Dunlops too,' said Dorothea.

'Don't see as we're much better off,' said Joe.

'Oh yes, we are,' said Dorothea. 'We know it wasn't Tom's bicycle, or Bill's, or one of ours. It was someone else's. We've got to find a man with a bicycle with Dunlop tyres who's lost the tube from his bicycle pump. Now we've got one clue we'll get lots more. And we're going to turn the Coot Club shed into Scotland Yard. And we're going to show Mr Tedder he's wrong and everybody's wrong. Let's go along to the shed now ...'

CHAPTER 43

RIVAL DETECTIVES

The Coot Club shed did not look very much like Scotland Yard when the six detectives trooped in. It was a lean-to against the side of the Doctor's house just above the dyke where Tom kept his boats. There were oars and a spare sail with its spars propped up in one corner of it. A couple of fishing rods hung from nails on the walls. There was a small table with a vice fixed to it that served Tom as a carpenter's bench. There were two chairs, one of which was a safe one. The other needed care. There was also a low bench along the wall under the window, but it was piled with junk of all kinds. There was a big wooden box with a Primus stove on it, partly taken to pieces for cleaning. On the walls were a lot of pictures of birds cut out of newspapers. There was a big map of the Broads that was really in two parts which had been fastened together so as to have it all in one. There was another map on a much larger scale, made by Tom, showing just the reaches of the river near Horning and marking with numbers the nests the Coot Club had found and watched over in the spring.

The map of the Broads caught Dorothea's eye and gave her a new idea. 'Pins,' she said. 'And, I say, Dick, you know those black envelopes your printing out paper comes in . . .'

Dick rummaged in his pocket and pulled one out.

'What for?' he asked, while the others waited to see what was coming next.

'Flags,' said Dorothea. 'We'll make little black flags and

stick them in the map at each of the places where boats have been sent drifting.'

'Good,' said Tom, and rattled one small tin box after another to find the one with the thin noise of pins among all the boxes that made the noise of screws or nails. He found it at last. The pins were rather rusty, but Dorothea said that did not matter.

Joe opened a scout-knife and cut the envelope into small oblong strips of black paper. Dorothea put each pin twice through the edge of a black strip.

'Now,' she said, when a dozen little flags lay in the lid of a tin. 'Let's stick them in.'

'Shall we take the map down?' said Tom.

'Better have it where it is,' said Dick, 'so that we can get a general view.'

A few minutes later they stood back from the wall to look at the half of the big map that showed the northern Broads. A cluster of black flags at Horning Staithe, a few black flags along Horning Reach, black flags at Ranworth and black flags at Potter Heigham showed where the criminals had been at work.

'Them's just the places we've been,' said Bill.

'What do we do now?' asked Pete, looking over Dorothea's shoulder at Dr Dudgeon's prescription forms, on which she was ruling lines with a pencil.

'We want separate notes for each case,' said Dorothea. 'Then they compare them and the truth comes leaping out.'

'Hope it do,' said Bill.

'What was the first?' said Dorothea.

'The cruiser at the staithe,' said Tom.

Dorothea wrote 'Place' at the top of her first column and under it 'Horning Staithe'. 'Where was the *Death and Glory*?'

'Horning Staithe,' said Tom.

'We wasn't the only ones there that night,' said Pete. 'What about the bloke what bung the brick back with my tooth?'

Dorothea wrote busily, in a column marked 'Possible clues'. Then she took another prescription form. 'What was the next?' she said.

'We were at the eelman's,' said Tom, 'and we found that boat with her mast in the trees on our way back in the morning.'

'And there was boats cast off that night all down the Reach,' said Bill.

'Place ...' said Dorothea, 'Horning Staithe and Horning Reach ... *D and G* at eelman's ... Possible clues ... I'll just have to leave that blank.'

'We never saw nobody,' said Pete.

'Next,' said Dorothea.

'That were *Sir Garnet*,' said Bill. 'And there ain't no clues neither.'

'Old Simon ask us to keep an eye on her,' said Joe. 'And last thing I go round her ropes and then in the morning she ain't there.'

'Horning Staithe,' wrote Dorothea. '*Sir Garnet* ...'

'*Sir Garnet* weren't next,' said Pete. 'There was that lot at Potter Heigham.'

'Good thing I'm doing it on separate sheets,' said Dorothea. 'Now, Potter Heigham ... Boats cast off? ...'

'Lot of Sonning's yachts. Half a dozen, that Tedder say.'

Dorothea wrote 'Six yachts'. 'Clues?' she asked.

'We never saw nobody there neither,' said Joe. 'We was up above bridges for the night and next day we come straight through. We see young Bob Curten, but that was when we was coming away being towed and couldn't stop.'

'Bob Curten,' wrote Dorothea.

'What about those shackles?' said Tom. 'Uncle Frank said that whoever took them would probably sell them and get found out that way.'

'Hope he do that quick,' said Bill.

Dorothea wrote 'Shackles ...' 'If we could only find out

who's got them,' she said, 'that would clear the Death and Glories.'

'That wouldn't,' said Bill. 'Not about the boats.'

'It would help an awful lot,' said Dorothea.

'And then there's Ranworth,' said Tom.

'There was Rob,' said Joe. 'But he wouldn't cast off them boats. Couldn't neither.'

'He didn't know anything,' said Tom. 'He thought you'd done it.'

'Silly young turmot,' said Bill.

'But we do know something about Ranworth,' said Dick, looking at the clues hanging on the wall.

'Possible clues,' wrote Dorothea. 'Bicycle with Dunlop tyres. Punctured tyre gone flat and pumped up. Bit of pump missing and held at Scotland Yard.'

'We've got a jolly good lot about Ranworth,' said Tom.

'That's because the detectives were on the spot at once,' said Dorothea. 'If we get plain-clothes men working everywhere so that we all get quickly to the scene of the crime we'll probably be able to grab the villain the next time he tries to do anything.'

She laid the five sheets of paper in a row on the table and pored over them. 'Let's make a list of things to do,' she said.

By the time Mrs Dudgeon's cook had brought them a jug of tea and a large seed-cake, their list was already a long one. Tomorrow was to be a busy day. Messages were to go from Scotland Yard to the Coots all over the district to turn them all into plain-clothes men and to arrange for them to report at once if any boats should be cast adrift anywhere, or if any had been cast adrift already and if so, when and where. Then there was to be a general examination of Horning bicycles and a list made of those which had Dunlop tyres. Further, Scotland Yard was to make inquiries about anybody who had been seen mending a puncture or had taken a bicycle to the shop to have a puncture mended. With all these things to do, the detectives were in high spirits, and even Bill began to think their innocence as good as proved.

But they were not the only detectives who had been at work that day. Heavy steps announced Mr Tedder.

'Now, you listen to me, Joe, and Bill, and you, young Pete,' said Mr Tedder, who had been thinking just how best to surprise a confession out of the criminals. 'What have you done with all them shackles you took that night you was casting off boats at Potter Heigham?'

'We ain't never touched a shackle,' said Joe angrily.

'And we ain't been casting off no boats,' said Bill.

'We got a lot of clues,' said Pete, but shut up quickly on catching Joe's eye.

'I got all the clues I want,' said Mr Tedder solemnly. 'You cast off that cruiser from the staithe and then you was seen casting off that sailing yacht. And then you go off to Potter and play old Harry. You come back and first thing you do, you cast off Jim Wooddall's wherry who ain't done you no harm. And last night ... Do you think I don't know what you was doing at Ranworth?'

'We tie up by the staithe there and in the morning there was a lot of boats blow across the Broad,' said Joe, 'but we ain't touch none of 'em.'

'Why did you clear out instead of helping chaps bring 'em back?' said Mr Tedder. 'And you claiming to be salvagers.'

'Bring 'em back and be told we cast 'em off!' said Joe. 'That's what happen when we find that yacht with her mast in the trees.'

'Listen to me,' said Mr Tedder. 'I know your Dads and got nothing against 'em. I don't want to be harder on you than need be. You own up honest and hand over them shackles and I'll make things as easy as I can.'

'We haven't got no shackles,' said Joe.

'It'll be worse for you in the end,' said Mr Tedder. 'There'll be a notice on the staithe in the morning. Printing it now, they are.'

'Giving a reward?' said Joe.

'Giving a reward they are,' said Mr Tedder. 'You ain't got a dog's chance.'

'Maybe we have,' said Joe. 'We'll have a try for the reward.'

Mr Tedder grunted. He had made up his mind not to lose his temper. 'There's another thing,' he said. 'Maybe you ain't got them shackles, not now, but you know who has. You been spending a lot of money.'

'We earn it,' said Joe.

'Who did you work for?' said Mr Tedder. 'They tell me you was throwing it about. And you didn't get it from your Dads. I know that.'

'We earn it selling fish,' said Pete.

'What fish?'

'Pike,' said Pete. 'We catch a whopper.'

'Pike!' exclaimed Mr Tedder. 'Who'd give you a penny a pound for it to throw it away?'

'Chap fishing,' said Pete.

'Where is he?'

'Gone away to Norwich,' said Joe.

'So he would,' said Mr Tedder. 'Now, don't you tell me lies like that. You've been good lads all of you till you take silly and start acting silly. Just you own up and make it easy for yourselves.'

'We ain't got nothing to own up,' said Joe.

'There's other ways of finding out,' said Mr Tedder, and went off through the bushes.

'How did you know we was in here?' Pete called after him.

'There ain't very little as the police don't know,' said Mr Tedder. 'As you'll find out.'

CHAPTER 44

A SCRAP OF FLANNEL

Dorothea waited a moment at the drawbridge over the Coot Club dyke. There was nothing more that could be done that day and she wanted to get hold of *The Outlaw of the Broads*, which she had left in the *Death and Glory*, and hurry home to be in time for Mrs Barrable's supper. Bother those boys. 'Coming,' Tom had said, but there they were still talking in Scotland Yard. She crossed over into the Farlands's garden, putting William on his leash for fear he might get interested in botany. She went through the garden, round the Farlands's boat-house and through the wooden gate into the Wilderness. Here she unleashed the bloodhound, and the stout William paddled on ahead, sniffing, trotting, scratching among the osiers and then trotting on again. He had formed a high opinion of the Wilderness and the wet autumn mist gave a new flavour to its delightful smells.

She came to the place where the Wilderness dyke opened into the river. Here the path turned to the left along the dyke and Dorothea looked ahead of her through the mist for the first glimpse of the *Death and Glory*. There she was, just beyond the next lot of overhanging willows. Hullo! Dorothea quickened her pace. Tom and the others must have gone round by the road and been quicker than her. There was one of them already at the old boat, standing on the bank, leaning over and patting her enormous chimney-pot.

'Hullo!' called Dorothea. 'You've been jolly quick.'

She got no answer out of the mist.

She called again.

Whoever it was at the green chimney-pot turned suddenly and rushed off into the bushes. The next moment there was a startled squeal from William, a squeal of pain and fright and rage all mixed together, a shout, the crash of someone falling, another squeal from William and the noise of running feet.

'He's trodden on William!' cried Dorothea. 'Hi! William! William!'

Steps sounded behind her.

'What's the matter?' called Tom.

'One of the others went round by the road,' said Dorothea, 'and I startled him and somehow he trod on William . . .'

Tom looked over his shoulder.

'But we're all here,' he said, and she saw Pete, Joe, Bill and Dick coming along behind him.

'What's up?' said Pete.

'There was someone at your boat,' said Dorothea.

'Come on,' cried Joe, and the crew of the *Death and Glory* rushed past Tom and charged along the dyke to get to their ship.

'Where is he?' said Bill.

'Can't see no one,' said Joe.

'But there was a minute ago,' said Dorothea. 'Didn't you hear William squeal? He got trodden on. William! William!'

They had all reached the *Death and Glory*. Joe and his mates were already aboard looking here and there about their ship. Joe was in the cockpit. He had pulled the big key out of his pocket and was opening the cabin door.

'Door's all right,' he said. 'Nobody ain't been here.'

'But I saw him,' said Dorothea. 'I saw him. I thought it was Tom. He was patting the chimney and I called out and then he ran away into the bushes and he must have fallen over William. And where is William? William! William! Come to heel!'

Just then William, breathless and muddy, came out of the bushes, shaking his head as if he were worrying a rat. He came up to Dorothea and plumped, panting, on the ground.

'He's bitten him!' cried Dorothea. 'Good dog, good dog. I knew there was somebody here. And William's a bloodhound after all. Look what he's got.'

William, after a little coaxing, gave it up, a torn and slobbery scrap of grey flannel.

'Somebody's trousies,' said Pete. 'It's like what Tom wear.'

'Well, it wasn't me,' said Tom. 'I was behind her with you.'

''Course it weren't you,' said Pete. 'I only say it's a bit of trousies like what you wear.'

'And anyway,' said Tom. 'Old William wouldn't bite me. He'd be much more likely to bite one of you.'

'He wouldn't bite any of us,' said Dorothea. 'I don't believe he's ever bitten anybody before.'

Dick, when his turn came, looked at the bit of flannel. 'It may be another clue,' he said.

'The villain himself!' said Dorothea.

'Which way did he go?' said Dick.

'He went off into the bushes,' said Dorothea. 'Just there. Then there was a crash and William yelled and he yelled too, not exactly yelling, just short, and then I heard him running.'

'Come on,' said Tom. 'Let's go after him.'

'With William,' said Dorothea. 'Good William. Worry him. Worry him. Come on. You've got to be a bloodhound again.'

But William had had enough of excitement and would take no interest in the search as the others worked their way through the bushes.

'Dick better go first,' said Joe, remembering the detective work that Dick had done at Ranworth.

'Go on, Dick,' said Tom.

It was easy tracking. Anybody could see the place where William's enemy had stumbled and crashed over the unsuspecting bloodhound. Anybody could see where he had charged on towards the road.

'He didn't make for the gate,' said Tom.

'Why should he with that old lock on it?' said Joe. 'Nobody do.'

Dick, stooping low, moved slowly on.

'Oh, go on, Dick,' said Tom. 'We might catch him if we hurry.'

'I didn't think of that,' said Dick simply. 'I was looking for more clues. He might have dropped something.'

They found nothing. They came to the fence that divided the Wilderness from the road. No scraps of grey flannel had caught in splinters or nails. There was nothing to show exactly where their quarry had climbed over. They climbed over themselves and looked up and down the road. No one was in sight.

'Too late,' said Dorothea.

'Dick's found something,' said Pete.

Dick had stopped short close by the fence and was looking at the ground.

'What is it, Dick?' said Tom.

'Bicycle,' said Dick. 'He had a bicycle and stood it here, leaning against the fence. You can see where his handlebar rested and made a mark in the moss. And there's a bit of track. Look out. Don't tread on the marks. They're pretty dim.' He went down on his knees. 'If only it wasn't so dark . . . I do believe it's the same bicycle . . . Dunlop tyre.'

Three torches leapt from the pockets of the Death and Glories and the tracks, such as they were, were lit by a blaze of light.

'Dunlop all right,' said Bill.

'Look same as yours,' said Joe.

'It may not be the same bicycle,' said Tom.

'I'm sure it is,' said Dorothea. 'He went to Ranworth and now he's been here. Oh, if only we hadn't all come along the river. If some of us had come by the road we'd have found the bicycle and we could have looked to see if its pump had lost its tube.'

'We might have caught him proper,' said Pete.

'Wonder which way he went,' said Joe.

But they could find no tracks on the hard road. They searched about but could find no other clues. Dorothea remembered Mrs Barrable.

'Dick,' she said, 'we've simply got to go. But I must just get *The Outlaw*.'

They climbed over the fence again and went back to the *Death and Glory*.

'But what were he doing?' said Joe. 'That's what beat me. If it were the same chap. He come to Ranworth and push them boats off. We know that. But what were he after here? Pushing off the *Death and Glory*? Dorothea and William stop that for him. Good old Puggy!'

'I told you he'd be jolly useful,' said Dorothea over her shoulder. 'The bloodhound leapt on his quarry. With a fearful struggle the villain tore himself free, little knowing that he had left in the jaws of his pursuer the clue that at last would bring him to the gallows.'

'He ain't touched our mooring ropes,' said Joe as they came to the *Death and Glory*. 'I know that. I moor her myself and all's as I leave it.'

Dick was looking again at the scrap of flannel. 'Grey flannel trousers,' he said. 'And rides a bicycle with Dunlop tyres. Probably lives in Horning ... this side of the river anyhow because of his using the Ferry. And he's lost the india-rubber tube from his pump. And one of his tyres has got a puncture.'

'That ain't much good,' said Bill. 'Lots of chaps get punctures. My old back tyre's patches all over.'

'And of course by now he may have got a new tube for his pump,' said Tom.

'We know a good lot about him anyhow,' said Dorothea, climbing into the cockpit on the way to get her book.

'We'll have a look at every bike in the village tomorrow,' said Joe.

'Look here, Dot,' said Dick. 'What, exactly, was he doing when you saw him?'

'Patting the chimney,' said Dorothea. 'At least, that was what it looked like.'

'You come and do it,' said Dick, 'and we'll watch and see if we can guess what he did it for.'

Dorothea obediently hopped ashore again. This, after all was the way detecting should be done. 'I was a long way off,' she said, 'so I couldn't really see. I thought ... I say, Tom had better do it ... (She reached out towards the chimney.) ... I'm not tall enough. He was reaching out at first ... Yes ... Like that and ... No ... much nearer the top. Patting it ... And then his other hand was on the top too ... No ... Much higher ...'

'Oh, look here,' said Tom. 'My arms aren't a mile long.'

'Just stay like that a minute,' said Dorothea and ran back along the edge of the dyke to the place from which she had first seen the *Death and Glory* and her visitor.

'He was a lot bigger than Tom,' she called, and came back. 'And I think he must have had his knee on the roof of the cabin.'

Dick was taking notes.

'I believe I know why he was patting the chimney,' he said, doubtfully. 'But it may have been something else.'

'Go on,' said Tom.

'He's someone who knows they light their stove in the evenings and he wanted to feel the chimney to see if they were at home.'

'Why don't he look through the windows?' asked Bill.

'Somebody might be in the fo'c'sle,' said Dick. 'If the chimney was warm he'd know there was somebody about.'

'If he want to see us why do he run off when Dot call out?' asked Bill.

'He were up to no good,' said Pete.

'Like enough,' said Joe. 'If Dot ain't seen him we'd have come back to find the old ship floating down river like all them others.'

'Perhaps it's a pity he didn't have time to send her adrift,' said Tom. 'If he had, then everybody would have known that it's somebody not us pushing boats off.'

They considered this for a moment, and then Dorothea remembered Mrs Barrable again.

'Come along, Dick,' she said. 'It's nearly dark already.'

'I'll get your book,' said Pete, and a moment later handed it out from the cockpit.

'It'll be quicker going by the road, won't it?' said Dorothea. 'Come on, William ... No exploring. I'm going to put the leash on you.'

'Let's just put the new clue with the others in Scotland Yard,' said Dick.

'What if he comes again?' said Tom. 'Hadn't I better stay?'

'Three of us,' said Joe. 'We'll settle him. All the better if he come again and we see his ugly face.'

Tom, Dick, Dorothea and William went back to Dr Dudgeon's where they hung a scrap of grey flannel beside the other clues, after which Dick and Dorothea took their bicycles and riding slowly, for the sake of the bloodhound, went home for the night.

CHAPTER 45

UNWANTED GIFT

It was Pete's turn to light the fire and he had been looking forward to it. But lighting the fire in the evening is one thing and getting up to light it in the morning is another. Pete lay awake for some time thinking about it until both Joe and Bill, snuggling in their blankets, yelled at him to stir his stumps. Then, making up his mind to it, he threw off his blankets, rubbed his eyes, rolled out of his bunk and, kneeling on the cabin floor, opened the door of the stove. He thrust in a hand to claw out the ashes and bumped his knuckles.

'Who bung up that stove?' he asked indignantly.

First Joe and then Bill answered with a snore.

'It ain't April first,' said Pete. 'I near take the skin off my hand.'

'I'll light the Primus,' said Joe, 'if you don't get that fire lit. We want our brekfuss.'

'Why do you bung up that stove then?' said Pete, and reached in again. 'Whatever have you gone putting in it?'

He felt something rough under his fingers and something hard inside it. There was a muffled clink of metal on metal as he pulled out a small heavy bundle of sacking.

Joe opened an eye and watched him sleepily from his bunk.

'Lot of old iron,' said Pete. 'That's a game to play on a chap!'

'Did you put it in, Bill?' said Joe.

'Put what in?' said Bill, rolling over in his bunk on the other side of the cabin. 'I say, look out for that soot.'

Pete was opening the sacking on the floor by the stove.

'Gosh!' he said. 'Shackles. Beauties!'

'Shackles!' exclaimed Joe and was out of his bunk in a moment, handling the shackles, new gunmetal shackles, shining like gold under a film of grease. 'That's what that chap were doing. Putting 'em down our chimney.'

Pete was counting them. 'Couple o' dozen big 'uns,' he said, 'and eight little 'uns.'

'Wrap 'em up,' said Bill suddenly. 'Wrap 'em up. We don't want to be doing with them shackles. What was that Tedder talking? Saying we had shackles when we didn't have none. Shackles! Ain't you read that paper on the staithe? Wrap 'em up. We got to take them shackles along to Tedder's the first minute we done brekfuss. You get that fire alight, young Pete, and don't you touch nothing else till you get the soot off you.'

The fire was lit. A kettle was put to boil and, meanwhile, there was hurried and worried washing in a bucket dipped from the dyke. They kept looking over their shoulders as they scrubbed themselves, as if an enemy might be lurking behind each osier bush.

'Somebody's patching everything on us,' said Joe. 'Casting off boats *and* stealing. Bill's right. That chap put 'em down the chimney. We got no time to lose. Next thing that Tedder'll be coming and finding 'em. Go on, Pete. That kettle'll be near enough boiling.'

Pete made cocoa from a tin of cocoa and milk powder so that there was nothing to do but pour boiling water on it and stir. They drank it without complaining that he had made it before the water really boiled, so that the powder of the cocoa tickled the roofs of their mouths. At least it wasn't too hot to drink. Their eyes were on the parcel of sacking on the cabin floor.

'Best put 'em out of sight,' said Bill, and put the parcel away in the fo'c'sle.

'Overslept we have too,' said Joe. 'If that chap's put Tedder on, we'll have him here in two twos.'

They ate a thick round of bread apiece and a stout slab of bacon, then another round of bread and marmalade. While they ate, their eyes kept glancing towards the fo'c'sle just because they knew the shackles were there. It was as if they had a keg of gunpowder aboard.

'Come on,' said Joe, almost before they had done. 'Take 'em to Tedder right away.'

'Better take 'em to Tom Dudgeon's first,' said Bill.

'Put 'em in Peter's fish-bag,' said Joe.

They went along the river bank, through Mr Farland's garden, over the drawbridge and so to Scotland Yard. The door of the shed was open. William was asleep on the threshold and Dorothea was busily writing at the table.

'Where's Tom?' asked Joe.

'They've gone on,' said Dorothea. 'They were in a hurry to get to the bicycle shop. You're to go after them. We want a list of all the bicycles with Dunlop tyres. What's the matter? What's happened?'

'Worst that could have,' said Joe.

'I find it in our stove,' said Pete.

'We know what that chap was doing with our chimbley,' said Bill. 'Let her see 'em, Joe.'

Joe emptied Pete's fish-bag on the floor of Scotland Yard and untied the twine that held the parcel of sacking together. Dorothea looked at the shining yellow shackles.

'What are they?' she asked.

'And you gone Able Seaman,' said Joe. 'Don't you know? Them's shackles. New 'uns. Greased from the store. Them's what was took from Sonning's at Potter, and Pete find 'em in our stove. When he go lighting the fire.'

'That chap was putting 'em down our chimbley when you catch him,' said Pete.

'Good, good!' said Dorothea.

'Why good?' said Joe.

'It all fits in,' said Dorothea. 'Don't you see? I *thought* the villain was doing it on purpose ... just casting off boats where you were, trying to make people think you'd done it. Now we know. It'll help a lot. It shows it's all one person. Potter Heigham made it look so funny. Because it's so far away. But with things from Potter Heigham turning up at Horning ... Somebody must have brought them ... It's a Horning person ... We've only to find out who. And he's got a bicycle with Dunlop tyres. And part of his pump is missing. And a bit torn out of his trousers. And ...'

The Death and Glories stared at her.

'What a good thing you found them,' said Dorothea. 'The villain meant to come with a search party and find them himself and then everybody would have thought you had hidden them.'

'Come on,' said Joe. 'Let's get rid of 'em quick.'

'I tell you so, first thing,' said Bill.

'Let's count them,' said Dorothea.

'Two dozen big 'uns,' said Pete. 'And eight little 'uns.'

'Come along,' said Joe, hurriedly wrapping them up again.

'What are you going to do with them?' said Dorothea. 'They'll be safe here. Let's hang them with the rest of the clues.' She pointed to the wall where drawings of tyre-treads, a scrap of grey flannel and a bit of india-rubber tubing hung, each on its nail.

'Tedder's after these shackles,' said Joe. 'We're taking 'em to him just as fast as we can.'

'Perhaps it's safer,' said Dorothea. 'Tom and Dick'll be waiting near the bicycle shop.'

They ran round the house and out of the Doctor's gate and hurried along the road to Mr Tedder's.

Two big boys on bicycles were riding down the road.

'Here come George Owdon and his pal,' said Pete.

The two big boys jumped off their bicycles and waited for the Death and Glories.

'Where are you going?' said George Owdon.

'Police,' said Bill.

'Cast off any more boats?'

'We ain't cast off no boats,' said Joe.

'What have you got in that bag?'

'Tell him,' said Bill.

'Lot of shackles,' said Joe. 'Bet you it's them shackles what was took from Sonning's at Potter.'

'You ought to know,' said George.

'What do you mean ... "You ought to know"?' said Joe angrily.

'Well, don't you?' said George. 'You've seen the notice Taking them to Tedder? Yes. I suppose that's the best thing you could do.'

The other big boy laughed.

'Yes,' said George. 'You take them to Mr Tedder and perhaps he'll let you off easy.'

'We haven't done nothing to be let off,' said Pete.

'Well, if you count casting off other people's boats nothing, and stealing ... nothing,' said George.

'I find 'em in our stove,' said Pete.

'Naturally you knew where to find them if you put them there,' said George.

'Come on,' said Joe. 'Mr Tedder's got more sense than some.'

'Now then,' said George. 'No cheek.'

They heard more laughter behind them as they hurried on their way.

'He's dead sure it's us, because of Tom Dudgeon casting off that *Margoletta*,' said Bill.

'We never look at their tyres,' said Pete a moment later.

'Look at 'em later,' said Bill. 'But it ain't them two. Tell you for why. George Owdon never cast off no boats. He shoot buttles and he take beardies' eggs but he's dead nuts against monkeying with boats. Look how he side with them Hulla-baloos against Tom. And look how he work in with Tedder, watching to see no more get cast off by no one.'

They saw Mr Tedder's bicycle leaning against the railing of his little garden, and knew that he had not yet left his house.

'Dunlop,' said Pete as they passed it and went in through the gate.

'There you are,' said Joe. 'And Mr Tedder ain't cast no boats off neither.'

Mr Tedder, in his shirt-sleeves, opened the door to them.

'See here, Mr Tedder,' said Joe, and took the parcel of sacking out of the fish-bag.

'What's this?' said Mr Tedder.

'Shackles,' said Joe. 'You was asking about shackles and we tell you we ain't got none. No more we hadn't. But Pete find this lot in our stove this morning. We very near catch the chap what put 'em down our chimbley ...'

'Come in,' said Mr Tedder and they followed him into his little parlour.

Mr Tedder opened the parcel and looked at the shackles.

'Where are the rest of 'em?' he asked.

'Them's all we found,' said Joe.

Mr Tedder looked up gravely at the small boys. 'Now,' he said. 'You think again ... No good telling me a yarn like that. And don't you go thinking you can keep the rest of them shackles just because you give up a few you don't want.'

'We don't want none of 'em,' said Joe. 'And we didn't take none.'

'How'd they get into your boat? You tell me that,' said Mr Tedder.

'Down our chimbley,' said Joe. 'I just tell you we near caught a chap putting 'em down.'

'We'd have found 'em last night,' said Pete, 'only we didn't light the fire. It was my turn this morning, and I find 'em soon's I ope the stove.'

'Now look here,' said Mr Tedder. 'You lie here at the staithe and boats get cast off. You go to Ranworth and boats get cast off there. Jim Wooddall lost his new warp off of his wherry what you cast off and we find that in Jonnatt's shed close where you was lying.'

'Oh, they found that,' said Pete eagerly. 'That were a brand new warp and Tom say Jim think it had gone in the river.'

'Course they found it,' said Mr Tedder. 'They found it where you put it.'

'We never touch it,' said Bill.

'And you go to Potter,' went on Mr Tedder, 'and boats get cast off the night you're there, and Sonning's lose a gross and a half of new shackles, and then you come here and bring me some of the shackles . . .' He stopped suddenly, picked up a shackle and looked at it. 'First step,' he said, 'is identification. Ought to have thought of that. You can clear out now, all of you, and I'll see you again, soon's Mr Sonning identify them shackles. Out you go. But don't go thinking we shan't get to the bottom of this. You think it over and tell me the truth next time. Sorry for your Dads, that's what I am. They're all honest chaps.'

'We'd have done better to drop them shackles in the river,' said Joe furiously as they went out.

CHAPTER 46

DUNLOP TYRES

Tom and Dick were in the doorway of Mr Bixby's bicycle shop, where they were asking careful questions. Yes, they had been told, if they were wanting new tyres, there was nothing to beat Dunlops. Not that Palmers were not good too, if they had a fancy for something else. Old Mr Bixby, who had been selling bicycles for nearly fifty years, looked hopefully at Tom.

'What about punctures?' said Tom.

'Any tyre'll puncture if you push a nail in it,' said Mr Bixby, 'but there ain't the punctures nowadays there used to be. Roads better kept maybe. Fewer horses. And hedges not what they was. Thorns are as bad as nails, maybe worse, but you don't get the thorns lying about in the dust same as you used to get before the roads was all tarred.'

Tom looked over his shoulder and saw the three younger Coots, who had come round the corner and were waiting close by. He took no notice of them and they knew they were not wanted, not while Tom was asking questions anyway. He was just working up to something.

'Do you get many punctures to mend?' he asked, and they saw Dick pull his spectacles off. This was the vital point.

'Not so many,' said Mr Bixby.

'Any lately?' asked Tom as if he had no special reason for wanting to know.

'Why yes,' said Mr Bixby, jerking his hand towards a rusty old bicycle leaning up against his work-bench. 'I had that brought in day before yesterday.'

'Dunlop tyre?' said Tom and he could not keep the eagerness out of his voice.

'Yes,' said Mr Bixby. 'They mostly use 'em. Are you wanting a new bike?'

'Not just now,' said Tom. 'I shall some day. But mine's got a lot of wear in it yet.'

'Wanting new tyres for it perhaps?' said Mr Bixby.

'Not just now,' said Tom.

'Oh,' said Mr Bixby. 'You'll excuse me. I'm busy.' And he went off to the back of his shop.

'It hasn't got a pump at all,' said Dick, looking at the old bicycle by the bench. 'I say. I wish we'd asked if anybody's been buying pump-tubes.'

'We'll have to watch to see who comes to take it away,' said Tom. 'Look here, you Coots, we mustn't go about detecting all in a crowd.'

'Something's happened,' said Joe. 'You know that chap what was at our chimbley last night?'

'Yes,' said Tom.

'He put a parcel of shackles down,' said Joe.

'I find 'em this morning in the stove,' said Pete. 'Near took the skin off of my knuckles.'

'Where are they?' said Tom. 'What have you done with them?'

'Took 'em to Mr Tedder,' said Joe.

'And that Tedder say we steal 'em,' said Pete. 'And George Owdon he think the same.'

'Gosh,' said Tom. 'The Potter Heigham shackles.'

'That's what we think,' said Joe. 'And Mr Tedder's taking 'em over to Potter to make sure. Look. There he go.'

Mr Tedder, now in full uniform, came bicycling round the corner on his way to Potter Heigham. The parcel in its bit of sacking was fastened to his handlebars, and as he went by he gave them the sort of look that ought to be given to a gang of criminals by one whose business it is to put a stop to their crimes.

'Anyway,' said Tom, pointing into the shop, 'we've got to see who comes to fetch that bicycle. And if he's got a bit torn out of one leg of his trousers ...'

'We'd better not wait quite so near the shop,' said Dick.

'And not all of us,' said Tom. 'The chap would see us and sheer off and get his bicycle another time.'

They crossed the road and were debating who should stay on watch when someone whom they all knew came round the corner. He seemed in very good spirits. He always was. They saw him take off his black felt hat to the old lady from the sweet-shop. They saw him nod to the boy from the dairy who was collecting milk bottles. They expected a nod themselves and the usual cheerful inquiry as to how all the birds were getting on. But though they saw that he knew them, he neither nodded nor spoke to them, and instead looked suddenly grave.

'That's another what think we done it,' said Bill.

'But it's the old parson,' said Tom. 'He knows we wouldn't.'

'He's going into the bicycle shop,' said Dick.

Two minutes later they saw the old parson come out again. He was wheeling that rusty, ancient bicycle and saying goodbye and thank you to Mr Bixby who had come with him to the door of the shop.

'Well, Reverend,' said Mr Bixby, 'them tyres is a bit worn and you'll expect to get a few punctures in an old tyre. They don't last for ever. Now I got some nice new ones and they'll never be cheaper than what they are now ...'

'I'll have to give myself new ones for a Christmas present,' said the old parson, mounted his bicycle and rode away.

'It weren't him pushing off boats at Ranworth in the middle of the night,' said Bill.

'You don't catch old Reverend poking shackles down our chimbley,' said Joe.

'Was his trousies tore?' asked Pete.

'It wouldn't be him even if they was,' said Joe. 'It just mean we got to look for some other bike.'

They went round to find Dorothea and William looking after Scotland Yard.

'Hullo,' said Dorothea, looking up from her writing. 'What did Mr Tedder say when you showed him those things?'

'He say we steal 'em,' said Pete. 'He've taken 'em to be 'dentified at Potter. And I say, Dot, his bike got Dunlop tyres.'

Dorothea considered for a moment. 'I don't think it was him I saw at your chimney. Besides, William's quite friendly with him. And he never wears grey trousers.'

'You didn't see any fingerprints on the shackles, Dot, did you?' asked Dick.

'I never looked.'

'There's another thing,' said Dick. 'That paper said a gross and a half of shackles were stolen. Why did the villain put only a few down their chimney?'

Dorothea frowned, thinking hard.

'Likely he want the rest himself,' said Bill.

'It's not that,' said Dorothea. 'Why didn't he keep them all? Perhaps he meant to put them all down the chimney, only he heard me and bolted. He may have dropped the others somewhere, only we didn't see them when we were hunting round after William got a bit of his trousers. We weren't looking for them really.'

'It was pretty dark,' said Tom.

'And misty,' said Dorothea.

'Come on,' said Joe, 'let's go and have another look.'

All six detectives and their bloodhound went round to the Wilderness and made a thorough search. Even William did his best, hunting this way and that though, as Dorothea said, it was a pity there was no way of explaining to him what he had to look for.

They found nothing and gathered disheartened beside the *Death and Glory*.

'He must have managed to take them away,' said Tom.

'If he brought them,' said Dorothea.

'He must have all the others somewhere,' said Tom.

Dick was looking closely at the chimney pot. 'They dust things with some kind of powder,' he said, 'and then they photograph them. There ought to be fingerprints . . .'

'Dick,' said Dorothea. 'He's coming again. I know he is. That's his plan.' She turned to the younger Coots. 'Don't you see? If he'd left the whole lot at once, people might think you'd found them. So he left just a few and you took them to Mr Tedder. That's what he thought you'd do. And Mr Tedder thinks you stole them but he isn't sure. Well, if the villain leaves another lot and you take that to Mr Tedder too, it'll look more suspicious than ever . . . As if you were just giving up a little at a time. He'll come again. He'll come again tonight. We must never leave the *Death and Glory* without a guard. Isn't that right, Dick?'

Everybody but Dick was ready to agree. Dick was thinking about something else.

'Feeling the chimney,' he said. 'Feeling to see if it was warm and if anybody was at home. He'll do just the same when he comes again. So the sooner he comes the better . . .'

'We don't want no more of them shackles,' said Bill.

'Go on, Dick,' said Dorothea.

'Fingerprints,' said Dick. 'He'll come and feel the chimney.'

'But it don't take no mark,' said Bill.

'It would if it was wet paint,' said Dick, pulling off his spectacles, polishing them hurriedly and putting them on again.

CHAPTER 47

THE VILLAIN LEAVES HIS MARK

They charged into Dr Dudgeon's gate and round the house. There was a light in the window of Tom's room. Tom was not yet in bed.

'Tom!' called Joe.

'Coots for ever!' shouted Bill.

Pete said nothing but pulled as hard as he could at the string that was hanging from the window.

Tom put his head out.

'Stop pulling,' he whispered. 'You're lugging my bed across the room. And don't make such a row.'

'Tom,' whispered Joe, in the sort of whisper that is meant to carry from the ground to an upper window. 'He's been at our chimbley.'

'All five fingers,' whispered Bill.

'We ain't looked in the stove yet,' said Pete.

'I'll be down in a minute.'

'Coming down the rope?' said Joe hoarsely.

'No,' said Tom.

Two minutes later he joined them in the garden, and they set off at a run back to the Wilderness.

'Dad's not in yet,' said Tom, 'and Mother says I must come straight back. What sort of print is it?'

'Good 'un,' said Joe.

'Might have done it a purpose,' said Bill.

It was a curious thing but, as they hurried through the osier bushes in the dark, Pete found himself wondering if the print were there at all. He had the oddest feeling that when they came to look at the chimney again they would find nothing but smooth green paint. What would Tom say then, dragged out in the night all for nothing?

Tom was first at the chimney, and, in the light of his torch, Pete saw the print again. It was there all right, and what a print! Thumb and all four fingers plain to see, and below them a longer smear made by someone pulling his hand suddenly away.

'Gosh!' said Tom. 'It's a beauty.'

'Look out, don't go clumping,' said Joe as they climbed on the cabin roof. 'You'll have us all through.'

'Look out for the paint,' said Bill, as Pete worked his hand in under the mushroom top to feel if the chimney was full to the brim with shackles.

Joe had jumped down into the cockpit and was unlocking the cabin door.

'Half a jiff while I get that lantern lit,' he said.

The others with lit torches crowded in after him. Joe wrestling with the lantern blocked their way. One match flared and went out and then another. Then the wick of the lantern burned up and Joe hung it from its hook.

'Let Tom open that stove,' he said. 'So it won't be us find 'em.'

There was a tight jam in the cabin in front of the stove. Tom crouched before it, lifted the latch of the door and swung it open.

The stove was empty, except for the ashes of their last fire.

'Stuck in the chimbley,' suggested Pete.

Tom thrust his hand inside the stove and brought it out black with soot.

'Somebody shine a torch down the chimney,' said Tom. 'No good shining it up with that cap on the top.' Bill scrambled for the door and Tom called after him, 'Don't touch the chimney. We'll want to let the paint dry with that print.'

'I ain't a roaring donkey,' said Bill.

They heard his footsteps overhead. There was a pause and then a glimmer of light came down the chimney lighting up the dead ashes in the stove.

'There's nothing there,' said Tom.

'That's a rum 'un,' said Joe.

'We come too soon,' said Pete. 'Reckon that old villain hear us and run for it.'

'Let's have a look round on deck ... All right, Bill. Nothing here,' Tom shouted up the chimney.

But there were no shackles to be seen on deck and few places where shackles could be hidden. There was a bollard on the foredeck, a coil of rope and a small hatch. The sail, neatly stowed along its spar, lay on the roof of the cabin, and the pair of oars that in the *Death and Glory* served as engines. Otherwise the cabin-top was clear but for the mast tabernacle and the green-painted chimney pot. They turned their torches again on that print of the enemy's hand.

'That Dick and Dot ought to see it,' said Joe.

'Too late to yank them out now,' said Tom. 'They'll be in bed. What are you doing, Bill?'

Bill had left the others on the cabin-top and the light of his torch was playing round the cockpit.

'Look ahere. Look ahere!' he suddenly shouted.

'What is it?'

'Them shackles,' shouted Bill.

The others scrambled aft. Right in the stern, under the little bit of an after-deck, in the place where usually was nothing but a bucket and a warp, the light of Bill's torch was playing on a pile of new shackles strung together on a bit of tarred marline.

'Geewhizz,' said Joe. 'We got him. Yank 'em out and let's see.'

'Don't touch them,' said Tom, just as Bill was reaching in to bring them out. 'Scotland Yard'll want a photograph. Don't touch them till we can get Dick.'

'Couple o' score of 'em,' said Joe.

'Can't we pull 'em out and count 'em?' said Pete.

'Better not,' said Tom. 'Let's have a look for any more.'

They shone their torches this way and that under the seats, but found nothing else that did not belong to the boat.

'What are we going to do with 'em?' said Joe. 'Take 'em to Tedder and be told we stole 'em?'

'I'm not going to Tedder with 'em,' said Pete.

'Look here,' said Tom. 'I think I'd better ask Dad. But don't touch them till Dick and Dot have seen them. It was Dick's idea trying to get the fingerprints. Leave them where they are till the morning.'

'What if that Tedder come and find 'em here?' said Pete.

Tom thought for a moment. 'I'll bolt up to Mrs Barrable's before breakfast and get Dick and Dot here first thing. Dick'll get them photographed and then if Dad says we've got to take them to Tedder we'll have to. I'll come too. We'll all go. And if Mr Tedder comes first . . .'

'He may come in the night,' said Pete.

'And if that old villain tell him where to look . . .' said Bill.

'You'll have to get word to me quick,' said Tom. 'And I'll tell Dad what's happened. But we won't touch them now. Not till Dick and Dot have had a sleuth at them. And I've got to bolt. I promised I'd come straight back.'

'What if that chap come again?' said Pete.

'Get a sight of him if you can. But he won't. At least I shouldn't think so. He's probably too busy getting the paint off.'

'That'll be another clue,' said Joe. 'He'll be properly stinking of turps.'

'We can't go round sniffing for him,' said Bill.

'We can't do anything till morning,' said Tom. 'Good night.'

In the morning Bill was the first to wake. He screwed himself round to look up at the old clock thinking he would have time to turn over and go to sleep again. Then he remembered. He tugged the blankets off the others and hurried out.

Yes. There was the pile of shackles well in under the after-deck. He climbed on the roof to look at the hand-print on the chimney. 'Give himself away that time,' he said gleefully as Joe, rubbing his eyes, came out and joined him.

Pete came out too, blinking in the morning sunshine. He looked first at the print on the chimney which, in daylight, did not seem so clear as it had last night in the white gleam of the torches. Still, it was there all right, and proof that some-body had indeed laid his paw on the chimney. Pete turned and crouched in the cockpit to look in under the after-deck.

'Let's get on with it,' said Joe. 'Tom'll be up at the Admiral's by now and they'll be along all three before we had our grub.'

'Hope they come before that Tedder pokes his nose in,' said Bill. 'If he come and find them shackles now . . .'

'Your turn,' said Joe. 'Primus to save time. Boiled eggs. Two apiece and put 'em in the kettle when that start boiling. We got no time to lose.'

Less soap than usual was used in the morning wash and it was a quick breakfast. Everybody was in a desperate hurry to get done and be ready for the rest of the detectives. And everybody was in a desperate stew lest Mr Tedder should come first.

Tom, Dick and Dot arrived together, on the run. Dick and Dot went straight for the chimney. Tom had urgent news for the others.

'I say,' he said. 'I told Dad about the shackles and about your not wanting to take them to Tedder after what happened last time. He says he'll take them for you. He's coming along here just before he goes off on his rounds. You don't mind, do you? Dorothea says it's all right.'

'Good,' said Joe. 'That Tedder'll think twice before he say the Doctor steal 'em.'

Dorothea, looking at the chimney and its print, felt much as she felt when reading over a good bit in one of her own stories. She had been sure the villain would come, and now it was almost as if he were obeying her orders. 'I knew he'd do it,' she said. 'And hasn't Dick's idea worked beautifully . . . the wet paint, I mean.'

'Going to photograph it, Dick?' asked Tom.

'Of course he must,' said Dorothea. 'But where are the shackles? You haven't moved them, have you?'

'Ain't touched 'em,' said Joe.

'That's how I find 'em,' said Bill, and all six detectives peered in under the after-deck.

'I'll get a photograph of the chimney all right,' said Dick. 'But I don't know about the shackles. Nothing'll show much. It's too dark in there, and . . .'

'But it's like the corpse,' said Dorothea. 'Scotland Yard always wants a picture of that to show just where it was found.'

'I'll have a shot,' said Dick.

He fixed the camera on a box on the cockpit floor to get it at the right level, and moved the focusing lever to the spot marked '3 to 10 feet'.

'I'll give it half a minute,' he said, 'just to give the shackles a chance of showing. And then I'll take a photograph from the top of the cabin to show the whole cockpit.'

'And we can mark it with a cross to show the place where the shackles were found,' said Dorothea.

Dick took his three photographs, while the others waited, reminding him in chorus to wind on the film after making each exposure. With pictures as serious as these it would be dreadful if one came out on the top of another.

'Done?' said Joe. 'Shall I get 'em out?'

'Go ahead,' said Tom.

Joe reached in and pulled a heavy bundle of shackles out into the light.

'Green paint,' cried Dorothea.

'Look at that now,' said Bill.

There was no doubt about it. Some of the new gunmetal shackles were smeared with the same green paint that Pete had put on the chimney.

Dick had a close look at the shackles, pulled off his spectacles, polished them with his handkerchief and put them on again.

'What is it, Dick?' asked Dorothea, who knew the signs.

'Clue,' said Dick. 'Let me just try.'

He went ashore and stood on the bank opposite the *Death and Glory*'s chimney and leant out as if to touch it. Then he began searching the ground at his feet.

'Here's where he put them down,' he said. 'You can see there's been something heavy in the grass. He must have put them down while he was feeling the chimney. He wouldn't want them to clink or anything in case there was somebody at home. Then he got his hand all over paint. Then he must have picked up the shackles and got some paint on them. He wouldn't know if it was pretty dark. The next thing he did was to get into your cockpit and push the shackles into that hole.'

'Under our after-deck,' said Joe, who liked things aboard his ship to be given their proper names.

'Let's see if he left any paintmarks on the way,' said Dick.

'Here you are,' shouted Pete. 'On the edge of the coaming. But maybe I do it when I done painting the chimbley.'

'More likely the villain,' said Dorothea. 'Go on, Dick.' She knew his mind was running ahead like a hound with its nose on a fresh scent.

'He went ashore again,' said Dick. 'He'd have to get out of the Wilderness. He wouldn't go our way through the garden.

He'd go the way he went that time Dot and William saw him. We ought to track him.'

'Come on, quick,' said Dorothea.

'You go first, Dick,' said Joe. 'Let's see how you do it.'

'Spread out a bit,' said Dick, 'so as not to miss anything.'

Crouching low and peering at the ground, the six detectives worked their way through the osier bushes to the fence that shut off the Wilderness from the road. On the top bar of the fence was another smear of green. 'Here's where the villain got across,' said Dick.

'And then what?' said Dorothea.

'Don't get over just here,' said Dick. He went a few yards along the fence and climbed over, jumping clear so as to land a foot or two beyond it. Then he worked carefully back looking at every inch of the ground under the fence.

'Here it is,' he said suddenly. 'More bicycle tracks.'

The others crowded round to see.

'Dunlops!' said Pete. 'Same as that Tedder's.'

'We can't know for certain they're his,' said Dick. 'But he had a bicycle the night William got him, and he had a bicycle at Ranworth.' He thought for a moment, pulled off his spectacles, looked at them with eyes that hardly saw them and smiled with the happiness of the successful scientist. 'Yes,' he said. 'He got on his bicycle and rode away. And we know another thing about his bicycle now.'

'What?' asked everybody at once.

'It's got some green paint on the grip of the right handlebar.'

'How d'you know?'

'He'd got a lot of paint on his hand ... That's a big smear on the fence and it wouldn't all come off the first time he touched anything. Of course we don't know how he took hold of his bicycle when it was leaning up against the fence. There may be other smears on it too. But there's sure to be some on his right handlebar.'

'Why the right one?' said Dorothea.

'I know that,' said Pete. 'That were his right hand on our chimbley. Thumb and fingers go so . . .' He put his own right hand on one of the posts of the fence.

'We got him now,' said Joe.

A motor car hooted somewhere up the road.

'That's Dad coming out of our gate,' said Tom.

The Doctor's car passed them, went on to the Ferry Inn to find room to turn round, came back and pulled up beside the detectives.

'We've caught him,' cried Dorothea as the Doctor got out. 'We've got his fingerprints, and there's the green mark where he put his hand on the fence.'

'Look here,' said Dr Dudgeon. 'I'm in an awful hurry. I ought to be on my rounds and instead I'm leaving my patients to die in dozens. So don't waste time. I'll take those shackles to Tedder for you. It doesn't matter how you come to have them, but you are putting yourselves in the wrong by not letting him have them at once. And I want to have a look at those fingerprints. Come along quick and tell me all about it.'

'Look at the paint on the fence first,' said Dorothea.

The Doctor looked at the smear of paint.

'How do you say it got there?' he asked. 'You begin at Ranworth and tell me the whole story. Never mind the things that happened before that.'

They told him everything they could remember, of bicycle tracks, of the figure Dorothea had seen, of William's trophy of grey flannel, of the painting of the chimney. Dr Dudgeon listened carefully. Presently he stepped over the fence. The others scrambled over and took him through the bushes to the *Death and Glory*.

He had a good look at the chimney.

'Who's got the biggest hands?' he said.

'Mine,' said Joe.

'What about Tom's?' said Pete. 'And Tom's ain't big enough.'

'Let's have a look at them,' said Dr Dudgeon. 'And yours, Tom.'

Tom and the Death and Glories showed their hands.

'Green paint on yours, Pete.'

'I paint that old chimbley,' said Pete. 'That stuff don't come off so easy.'

'Um,' said Dr Dudgeon. 'That's a fair sized hand. Bigger than any of yours.'

'That settles it, doesn't it?' said Dorothea hopefully.

'I'm not sure that it does,' said Dr Dudgeon.

'Green paint on the shackles,' said Dick.

Dr Dudgeon looked gravely at the shackles. 'Look here, I may as well tell you. Tedder wants to take out a summons right away.'

'We're sunk,' said Joe bitterly.

Dr Dudgeon looked at him but for a moment said nothing.

'I don't know what to think,' he said at last. 'It isn't only shackles.'

'But they didn't do any of the things,' said Dorothea.

Dr Dudgeon smiled at her. 'I've told Tedder he hasn't got enough evidence.'

'And we've got lots and lots,' said Dorothea.

'Tedder says nobody but you could have got those shackles. He told me yesterday he was sure that you had a lot more, and he thinks that if he had a summons for you the truth would come out. And when I take him this new lot ... And I've got to take them to him. Now look here. You think you've got a lot of evidence. Well, what about consulting a lawyer? Put the whole thing in front of him and see what he says.'

Dorothea's eyes sparkled. 'We'd simply love to,' she said. 'Of course that's what we ought to do.'

'But what lawyer?' asked Tom.

'I'll ring up Uncle Frank and ask if he'll see you.'

'But he's on the other side,' said Tom.

'That's just why I'd like him to see you. Well? Have you any objection to telling him everything you've told me?'

The detectives looked at each other and then, somehow, all five of the boys were looking at Dot.

'We'd love to show him everything,' she said.

'Right,' said Dr Dudgeon. 'I'll telephone to Mr Farland.'

CHAPTER 48

THE LAST CHANCE

Five detectives and a bloodhound were waiting in Scotland
Yard. Three damp photographs were drying on the window.
The one of the whole cockpit had come out very well, and
so had the one of the chimney. You could see the mark left
by the hand of the villain, small though it was in the picture.
The photograph of the shackles in the darkness under the
after-deck was a failure as Dick had thought it would be,
but they had decided that it did not matter so much. Dick
had bought a bottle of red ink on the way back after lunch,
meaning to mark with a cross the place where the shackles
were found as soon as the photographs had dried. Dorothea
was already using the red ink to mark in the photographs
of Ranworth the place where Dick had found the tracks of
the bicycle. William was asleep. The others were watching
the door and wondering why Tom was so long over his lunch.

'Is he going to be all day?' said Joe.

'Bet something's gone wrong,' said Bill.

'Eating and eating,' said Pete.

And then they heard running footsteps and the next
moment Tom came in.

'We've made the most awful mistake,' he said.

'What's happened?' said Dorothea. 'Won't Mr Farland see
us?'

'Go on, Tom,' said Joe.

'No, it's not that,' said Tom. 'We started detecting too late.
We ought to have begun right at the beginning. We ought

to have done what Tedder and the others did and started watching after the very first boat was cast off and then we'd have had a chance of catching the villain in the act.'

'How was we to know there was going to be any more cast off?' said Bill.

'I know. I know,' said Tom. 'But Uncle Frank told Tedder that if only he'd caught you casting a boat off, he'd feel happier.'

'Why?' said Pete. 'He don't WANT boats going adrift.'

'No. But he meant he'd feel there was more proof if only you'd been caught in the act. So of course if only we'd caught the villain in the act everything would have been all right. And we've had chance after chance if only we'd thought of it.'

'Well, it's not too late,' said Joe.

'Yes it is. We've got to take all our evidence to Uncle Frank tomorrow morning. Before he goes into Norwich. And Tedder's going to take his. And if ours isn't good enough it's all up. Dad says Tedder's furious because of Uncle Frank not thinking he's got enough already. And now he thinks that last lot of shackles settles it.'

'But it proves it wasn't us,' said Dorothea.

'Tedder thinks it proves just the opposite.'

'What's the good of anything,' said Pete, 'if that Tedder don't believe a word we say?'

'If only we'd begun detecting at the beginning,' said Tom.

'What else did Dr Dudgeon say?' asked Dorothea. 'Try to remember every single thing.'

In no sort of order, just as it came into his head, Tom told everything he could remember. He told how Mr Tedder thought he had proof enough to take out summonses. He told how his own father was not sure one way or the other. He told how once more Mr Farland had made the policeman furious by saying that all the hard work he had done as a detective was not really enough to prove his case. 'But all

the same Uncle Frank thinks it was the Death and Glories
at the bottom of everything. And if we can't persuade Uncle
Frank tomorrow that it wasn't, Dad thinks he's got to let
Tedder have his summonses. Dad's pretty upset about it
too.'

'We've got a lot of evidence that it wasn't the Death and
Glories,' said Dick.

'But it doesn't show who it was,' said Tom. 'And tomorrow's
the last chance ... What's the matter, Dot?'

Joe, Bill, Pete, Dick, and even the bloodhound, William,
all turned to look at Dorothea, who was sitting at the table,
pulling at one of her own pigtails and scowling most horribly.

'I'm being the villain,' said Dorothea.

'How?'

'I'm just being him and thinking what he thinks.'

'Bet he ain't got no plait to pull,' said Joe, but was instantly
ashamed of himself when he saw the serious way Dick was
looking at his sister.

'Whoever he is,' said Dorothea, 'he knows everything we
do. He knew when you went to Potter Heigham. He knew
when you went to Ranworth. He knew when you hid the *Death
and Glory* in the Wilderness.'

'That's right,' said Joe. 'Look how quick he were coming
with them shackles. And there was that Tedder on to us first
thing.'

'Let her go on,' said Dick. 'That's the way detectives find
things out.'

'He probably knows everything Tom's just told us ... No,
I don't mean he's listening ...' Pete, looking hurriedly round,
had stolen to the door. 'Of course he might be ...'

'Nobody here,' said Pete.

'The villain's in just as much of a stew as we are,' said
Dorothea. 'His deep laid plans have come to nothing. He's
got to do something at once. Time is going on. Tomorrow the
innocent people he had hoped to send in chains to the gallows

are going to see a solicitor and lay the proofs of their innocence before him . . .'

'Do he know what proof we got?' asked Pete.

'If he doesn't he's probably thinking we've got more than we have. You see, he knows he's guilty even if no one else does. So he knows what lots of proofs there must be to find if only we knew where to look for it,' said Dorothea. 'He's probably heard Mr Tedder raging about what Mr Farland said to him. He's wishing there were other boats near the *Death and Glory* so that he could push them off and get the Death and Glories blamed for it. You've been back from Ranworth three whole days and nothing's happened. Nothing new. And Mr Farland saying you ought to have been caught in the act. "Ah," says the villain to himself, "another lot of boats adrift and nothing would save them." He strides up and down, planning furiously, and his friends shrink from him in fear.'

'You don't know who he is, do you?' said Pete hopefully.

'We've got a lot of clues,' said Dick.

'Bad luck everybody using them Dunlop tyres,' said Joe.

'We know a lot about him beside the tyres,' said Dorothea. 'We know he's somebody who's got some reason for wanting people to think it's Tom or the Death and Glories. We're pretty sure he's somebody who lives near here, because if he didn't he couldn't get to know so soon what you and Tom are doing. Then, the thing to ask is, what is going to happen if we can't prove it isn't any of you?'

'We'll be taken off the river,' said Bill.

'Bust up of the Coot Club,' said Tom.

'Well,' said Dorothea, 'who is there who lives near here and has a bicycle with Dunlop tyres and would be glad if the Coot Club got busted?'

'There's only that George Owdon,' said Bill. 'He'd be glad enough if there wasn't no bird watchers on the river.'

'It can't be him,' said Tom. 'He was one of the people

335

keeping watch on the staithe that night when you were all at Potter Heigham.'

'I got an idea,' said Joe. 'Bill, I'm taking your bike.'

'Where are you going?'

'Potter Heigham.'

'They'll grab you sure,' said Pete. 'That Tedder say the chaps at Sonning's was fair mad about them boats, let alone them shackles. They'll half kill you and ask questions after.'

'They'll have to catch me first,' said Joe. 'I got to go. I got to go now. Tomorrow'll be too late.'

Dorothea's eyes sparkled. 'If we could prove George Owdon was there,' she said.

'But everybody knows he wasn't,' said Tom.

'All the better if we could prove he was, and he may have been there even if we can't prove it. But don't get caught, Joe . . .'

Joe had already gone.

Dorothea was scowling again.

'What's he thinking now?' said Tom.

'Shackles,' said Dorothea. 'You see he's still got some. That notice said a gross and a half. How many's that?'

'144 and 72,' said Dick. 'That's 216.'

'He must have about a hundred and fifty left,' said Dorothea, 'and he's wondering what to do with them.'

'I'm going to the ship,' said Pete. 'We don't want any more of them shackles aboard.'

'Come on,' said Bill. 'We'd better keep watch.'

'But we're just getting at something,' said Dorothea. 'And anyway he won't do anything in daylight.'

'Pete's right,' said Tom. 'Nobody could see what he was doing once he's got into the Wilderness. And if he's desperate. . . . Look here. Let's shift her to the river. Nobody would dare to touch her if she's in full view from everywhere. And there's no point in keeping her hid when Tedder and everybody knows where she is.'

'But you'll come back here,' said Dorothea.

'It won't take a minute to shift her,' said Tom. 'And you can go on being the villain. It would be too awful if there's another lot of shackles.'

'I'm coming too,' said Dick.

'All right,' said Dorothea. 'I'll be looking through the evidence.'

Pete ran on ahead and looked all over the *Death and Glory*, but found no shackles. Then, when the others came, they put the anchors aboard, and brought her down the dyke, clear of the osiers, and moored her again just above the place where the dyke joined the river. There she could be seen by anybody on the water or on the banks and no one was likely to risk playing tricks with her, at any rate before dark.

'You'll have to keep a watch on deck all night,' said Tom, as, with easier minds, they went back to Scotland Yard.

They came back to find Dorothea full of a new idea.

'I don't believe he'll bother about the shackles,' she said. 'You see there was the bloodhound the first time and getting his hands all over green paint the second. He may think another try would come off worse. And anyway he's got what he wanted, because everybody thinks you stole them. He's trying to think of something else. He's bothered because of what Mr Farland said to Mr Tedder. He's in an awful hurry because of tomorrow. He's trying to think of something that could happen tonight.'

'Well, there ain't no boats near us,' said Pete.

'I wish there was one,' said Dorothea. 'He'd be absolutely certain to push her off tonight ... If only there was ... The detectives would lurk in the bushes listening and watching. And then, just as the villain creeps up in the dark to push her off, they would leap out and shine their torches on the villain's guilty face.'

Dick jumped. 'I say,' he said. 'We could do something even better. I've got a lot of flashlight powder.'

'Torches are better,' said Tom.

'Not to take a photograph,' said Dick. He pulled his spectacles off at the thought. 'We could wait in hiding with the camera all ready and then, just as the villain was pushing off the boat, we could fire off the flash and get a photograph of him in the very act.'

Dorothea clapped her hands. 'Simply lovely,' she said.

'Gosh!' said Tom. 'That would settle it.'

'But how'd we know which boat he's going to set adrift?' said Bill.

'And there ain't no boats anywhere's near,' said Pete.

'What about Mr Farland's *Flash*?' said Dorothea. 'If we could only borrow her and moor her somewhere.'

'Uncle Frank would never lend her,' said Tom. 'He's laid her up for the winter already, because of Port and Starboard being in Paris. And besides, he thinks the Coots are guilty, so he wouldn't lend her anyhow. He'd think it was some new trick.'

'It's an awful pity,' said Dick. 'We'd have to have a boat in a good place to be cast off from, for one thing. And fairly near the *Death and Glory* for another. And we'd have to get everything ready before dark ... focusing the camera and all that. But if only it worked and we got a photograph of the villain in the very act, it would be as good as all the clues put together.'

'It's no good talking about it,' said Tom. 'It would be a fine idea if there was a likely boat, but there isn't. You came to the Wilderness so as to be away from places where there are boats to be cast off. And if there's no boat the villain can't cast one off. He'll be doing something else.'

'We've got so little time,' said Dorothea.

'Nine o'clock tomorrow morning,' said Tom. 'Nothing much can happen between now and then. We ought to get ready every bit of evidence we've got.'

'I've been going through it,' said Dorothea. 'Let's start at the beginning, and do it in a new way. I'll write down our evidence opposite each case.' She wrote down 'Cruiser at the staithe' and said, 'Evidence?'

'We only know there was someone there that night besides the Death and Glories and me.'

'Evidence?' said Dorothea again.

'Someone was there, to throw that brick back through the window of the sail loft.'

'That's something,' said Dorothea. 'And the next case ...'

'That was the boat we rescued with her mast stuck in the trees.'

'Evidence?'

'We were with the eelman up river when she was cast off. We were on our way back when we found her. Only George Owdon saw us tying her up and thought we were casting her off ...'

'George Owdon,' said Dorothea. 'It isn't exactly evidence, but I'll put it down ... "G.O. was on the staithe".'

'He just come biking on his way to Norwich with that pal of his,' said Pete.

'Never mind,' said Dorothea. 'What about that first case? Wasn't he there in the morning when people thought you had cast off the cruiser?'

'He think we cast her off,' said Pete. 'He say so loud enough. At least he think it were Tom.'

'G.O. in the morning thought it was Tom,' wrote Dorothea. 'Next case.'

'Potter Heigham,' said Tom.

'Potter Heigham,' wrote Dorothea. 'Evidence?'

'Them shackles,' said Bill.

'The shackles are evidence the wrong way,' said Tom. 'Everybody says the Death and Glories couldn't have got the shackles if they didn't steal them.'

'That's what the villain wants them to say,' said Dorothea.

'We know the villain put the shackles in the *Death and Glory* so that they would get the blame.'

'Down the chimbley,' said Pete, looking at his fist. 'I very near skin my knuckles.'

'And there's more than that,' said Dorothea thoughtfully. 'I saw someone at your chimney ... And then there's the bit of flannel torn by our bloodhound from the villain's trousers. If we only knew. I wish Joe would hurry up and get back.'

Pete gently tickled the roll of fat round William's neck.

'That's all the evidence we got with the first lot of shackles,' said Tom. 'But we've got Dick's paint trap with the second lot. There's the print on the chimney ... and then the green paint on the shackles.'

Dorothea wrote busily.

'Will it be an awful job to take the chimney off the boat?' asked Dick.

'Easy,' said Bill. 'It just fits over and there's two chocks to hold it. I can have them screws out in two ticks.'

'We'll have to take it with us,' said Dick.

'Chimney pot,' wrote Dorothea. 'Evidence to be produced in court.' She said the words aloud.

'Court,' exclaimed Bill. 'If they takes us to court we're sunk. It don't matter what happen. If they take us to court there'll be no more Coots.'

Dorothea scribbled 'If necessary' after 'to be produced in court', and said, 'We'll have to show it to the lawyer anyhow.'

'Shall we go and get it off now?' said Dick.

'We'll be lighting the fire tonight,' said Bill. 'I can have them screws out quick in the morning.'

'When Mr Farland sees those fingers on the chimney,' said Dorothea, 'he can't help knowing that there was someone there.'

'That's about all we've got about Potter,' said Tom. 'Unless Joe gets something out of Bob Curten ... But I don't see what he could get. Bob was as certain as the rest of them that the Death and Glories cast those boats off.'

'What came next?' said Dorothea. 'Ranworth ...'

'*Sir Garnet*,' said Pete. 'That night after you come and we was all in the old ship and old Simon tell us to keep an eye on the wherry, and we did and saw her warps was made fast proper, and yet off she go in the night and Jim Wooddall's new warp turn up in Jonnatt's boat-shed.'

'*Sir Garnet*,' wrote Dorothea. 'Evidence?' She waited.

'We ain't got none,' said Bill. 'Everybody go for us and we was lucky getting away. If that George hadn't have spoke up for us ...'

'George Owdon again,' said Dorothea eagerly. 'Go on. What did he say?'

'He tell 'em he didn't see what harm we could do in Ranworth, and we just push off while they was arguing.'

'Dot,' said Tom. 'That ought to go with the Ranworth evidence. Don't you see? George Owdon knew they'd gone to Ranworth.'

'What's the good o' that?' said Bill. 'Everybody on the staithe know where we was going. George only say to let us go. By the time they done shouting I wonder chaps didn't know in Ranworth we was coming before ever we get started.'

'All the same,' said Dorothea. 'That's George Owdon again. He comes in a bit every time except when you were at Potter Heigham.'

'No good,' said Bill. 'What about that Tedder? Tedder come in the first time and every time after. He keep track of us and come knocking on our cabin-top before we'd hardly got into the old Wilderness. But he ain't evidence, no more'n George Owdon.'

'What else at Ranworth?' said Dorothea.

'Tyre prints,' said Dick, 'and bicycle pump.'

'We know somebody come over the Ferry that night,' said Bill.

'We've got a list of the people who use Dunlop tyres,' said Tom digging it out from among the papers on the table. 'Beginning with me and Bill, and Mr Tedder, and the old parson. It's about a mile long. We'd have done better to make a list of the people who don't use Dunlop tyres. It would have been a lot shorter.'

Dorothea was looking through the list. Her finger stopped at a name. 'George Owdon's got Dunlops,' she said.

'Everybody has,' said Tom.

'Don't see how that matter,' said Pete.

'Well, if he had Palmers,' said Dorothea, 'we'd know it wasn't him at Ranworth.'

'Why,' exclaimed Pete. 'You ain't really thinking it's him.'

'In detective stories,' said Dorothea, 'they don't rule out anybody. It's usually the most unlikely person.'

'Gosh,' said Pete. 'I bet it *was* Mr Tedder. Look at the way he try to patch it on us. Policeman too. Nobody'd think it were him. And he use Dunlops. I saw 'em.'

'I'd better make a fair copy,' said Dorothea. 'So as to be sure of not forgetting anything when we're putting our case before the lawyer.'

'Mark at the side where we have a clue to show him,' said Dick. 'We'll take them all with us.'

She set to work, with the others looking over her shoulder and making suggestions from time to time. She had not nearly finished when Joe, hot and dusty from his ride, came into Scotland Yard in triumph.

'How long have I been?' he asked. 'George Owdon could do it quicker.'

'What did you find out?' asked Dorothea, jumping up from the table.

'Real evidence,' said Joe.

'What happened?' said Tom.

'They didn't catch you?' said Pete.

'Nobody see me till I were off again,' said Joe happily. 'They shout after me then but they was too late.'

'Did you find Bob Curten?'

'I find him, and his Dad had tell him never to speak to none of us, but I soon settle that. I say to him, "Young Bob," I say, "Have you seen that George Owdon about?" And what do you think he say? He say, "No, I ain't seen him this ways not since that night you was here casting them boats off." So I clout his head and tell him we don't cast off no boats. And I tell him he got to be here tomorrow morning to go with us to speak up to Mr Farland, but he say he can't do that. So I make him write it down and here it is.' He held out a scrap of paper. Dorothea took it.

'Read it out loud,' said Dick.

Dorothea read, 'I swear I see George Owdon by Potter Bridge that night before you come through. Bob Curten.'

'That's right,' said Pete. 'He see us come through the bridge next morning. He were shouting and signalling, but we was in tow.'

'George Owdon comes in every time,' said Dorothea.

'He'll be putting the rest of them shackles aboard,' said Joe.

'We've shifted her out of the dyke,' said Tom.

Joe turned and made for the door. 'I'll just see she's all right,' he said. If anybody else had been mooring the *Death and Glory*, Joe wanted to have a look at her anchors for himself.

'But we ought to go through the evidence with you,' said Dorothea, too late for him to hear her.

'Let's all go,' said Pete.

Dorothea took her rough copy with her, and they went along the river bank to find Joe, who had had a look at the anchors, feeling the *Death and Glory*'s mooring ropes to make sure they were not stretched too taut.

Sitting in the cockpit and on the cabin roof they went

through the evidence with Joe. He had nothing to add, though, after his ride to Potter Heigham, he tried hard to think that they had proved that George Owdon was the villain. The others saw only too clearly that they had only proved that somebody else could have done the things the Death and Glories were accused of doing. They had no real proof that any particular person had done them. And, worst of all, they had not proved that they had not done them themselves.

'It's a lovely lot of evidence anyhow,' said Dorothea, sitting on the cabin roof beside Joe. 'But it's not enough.' She frowned. 'And somewhere in the village the villain is thinking of the evidence he's piled up against us, and trying to plan something else to make sure before tomorrow. If only we could borrow a boat.'

'The fingerprints are good,' said Dick. 'And the tyre prints. And the bit of bicycle pump. But a photograph of the villain would be better than anything.'

'We simply must get something more,' said Dorothea.

'Do you think he'll come and put those shackles aboard after dark?' said Dick. 'I could wait with the camera in that bush, and somebody else would have to fire off the flashlight just about there ...' He pointed. 'You see we'd have to be careful that the flash isn't in front of the lens. You get nothing but fog if it is.'

'No hope,' said Tom. 'Not unless the Death and Glories were sleeping somewhere else. The villain would never risk being caught like that, with the shackles.'

'I do wish there was a boat we could borrow,' said Dorothea again.

'Most everybody's taking their boats off the water by now,' said Joe. 'Come October and there won't be a boat about except fishermen and us ... and there won't be us if Sonning's take us into court.'

Just then there was a faint drumming somewhere down

the river. Presently a smallish white motor-cruiser came chugging upstream round the bend by the Ferry. Pete, in the cockpit of the *Death and Glory*, looked at her through his big telescope.

'It's the old *Cachalot*,' he said.

CHAPTER 49

A KID FOR THE TIGER

The fisherman at the wheel of his little cruiser saw the *Death and Glory* and recognized her crew. He swung the *Cachalot* towards the bank.

'Hullo you chaps!'

'Hullo ... Hullo!'

'That's the one what bought our fish,' said Pete to Dorothea.

'Got any use for some maggots?'

'RathER,' said Pete.

'You can have what I've got left,' said the fisherman. 'I'll be bringing a fresh lot tomorrow.'

'Maggots beat worrams hollow,' Pete explained to Dorothea.

'Bring her in here,' called Joe as he and Bill jumped ashore.

The *Cachalot* slid up beside the bank and Joe and Bill took her rond-anchors and made her fast.

'You fishermen too?' asked her owner, looking at Dorothea, Dick and Tom.

'Just friends,' said Dorothea.

'I don't know how the cellar is,' said the fisherman. 'But I'll have a look.' He disappeared into his cabin and came out again with half a dozen oranges. 'Catch!' Oranges flew through the air. Tom, Joe, Bill, Pete, and Dorothea caught theirs. Dick was not expecting his, but saved it from going in the river.

'Best I can do today,' said the fisherman. 'Of course, if I'd known I was meeting you ... Never mind, I'll be stocking up tomorrow when I come back.' He looked about him. 'Nice mooring you've got here. How far are we from where the Wroxham bus stops?'

'Not above ten minutes,' said Pete. 'And not hurrying neither.'

'Would you keep an eye on her if I left her here?' asked the fisherman. 'I've got to get back to Norwich for the night and they tell me there's a gang of young toughs about here casting off boats. I don't much like the idea of leaving her at the staithe.'

The Death and Glories looked grimly at each other.

'We never cast no boats off,' said Bill.

'Never thought you did,' said the fisherman.

'Everybody think we do,' said Joe.

'What!' exclaimed the fisherman. 'Are you the toughs they were telling me about? Well, I'd trust you not to cast off the old *Cachalot*. Set a thief to catch a thief, eh? And poachers make the best gamekeepers . . .'

'It's not us at all,' said Tom. 'Only once I did cast off a boat because some people had moored her over a nest we were watching and so now because boats are getting sent adrift everybody thinks it's us . . . The Coot Club . . .' he explained.

'And you know that money you give us for that great old pike,' said Joe. 'They're saying we stole shackles at Potter that day we was there, and sold 'em and that's the money.'

'What's all this?' said the fisherman.

Bit by bit, they told him the whole story. He laughed when he heard about Scotland Yard but, seeing Dorothea's face, he was serious again in a moment.

'It would do most beautifully if he didn't mind,' said Dorothea privately to Dick, with her eyes on the fisherman's cruiser.

They told him about the flying brick that had shown there was someone else about when the first boat had been sent adrift. Pete showed the gap where the tooth had been. They told him of the bicycling visitor to Ranworth, of the shackles in the stove, of the fingerprints on the chimney (which he examined with interest), of the second lot of shackles, of their certainty that someone was doing things on purpose to get the Coot Club blamed for them. They told him that they had only till tomorrow morning to clear themselves, when they had to see a lawyer who believed them guilty and lay their evidence before him. They told him finally of Dorothea's plan.

'We could lay a mud-weight out in the river,' said Joe, 'so she wouldn't go far even if he do push her off.'

'You mean you would be lying hid watching the *Cachalot* being the bleating kid and so you would see who the ravening tiger was if you could catch him in the act of sending her adrift?'

'That's just it,' said Dorothea. 'It's just the one thing that's missing. You see we've got all the evidence we told you about but it isn't enough. If only we could catch him at it people would simply have to believe.'

'And we've only got until tomorrow,' said Tom. 'And if we can't prove it isn't them they're going to get prosecuted for what they didn't do, and the Coot Club'll be smashed up. And it's all just about as unfair as it possibly could be.'

The fisherman was silent for a moment, looking at his ship.

'She can't take much harm,' he said. 'What do you want me to do? Leave her here?'

'No. No,' said Dorothea. 'They'd know we'd be on the look out and the *Death and Glory*'s too near. She ought to be in a more tempting place . . . near but not as near as all that.'

'Put her where you like,' said the fisherman.

For some minutes everybody was talking at once, suggesting possible places. The staithe was rejected at once, because it would be difficult for the detectives to be there without being seen by the villain. Dr Dudgeon's mooring alongside his front lawn was rejected because the villain might think the risk of being seen was too great. Finally Joe had his way.

'That's a good place just beyond that ditch what run to the road below the Ferry. Good bushes there for a hide, and soft banks case she do break away. But she won't take no harm anyways, not if we have a mud-weight down.'

'What if your villain never knows she's there?' asked the fisherman. 'No good putting a bait out for pike if you put it in the weeds where the pike can't see it.'

'Couldn't you say a word to Mr Tedder . . . he's the policeman . . . and tell him where you've left her?' said Tom. 'And if you went into the Swan and just happened to mention it.'

The fisherman laughed again. 'I'll be doing that anyway,' he said. 'They may have a message for me from Norwich . . .'

CHAPTER 50

SETTING THE TRAP

The plan was simple enough. One of the detectives was to lie hid with Dick's camera in a bush close by the *Cachalot*. A little further from the *Cachalot*, so that the flash should not shine into the lens of the camera, a second detective was to lie in the long grass with the flashlight apparatus. When the villain had come and was in the act of casting off the boat, the second detective was to let off the flash and run for his life. The villain would naturally dash in pursuit of him, so that the first detective, sitting tight in the bush, could wait till the coast was clear and then get safely away with the camera.

'Two hour watches,' said Tom. 'Dick and I take the first watch, it's his camera, and I can run faster than any of you. And Dot says he's likeliest of all to come just after dark.'

'Who come next?' said Pete.

'Dot and Joe. Joe to let fly with the flash and bolt and Dot to look after the camera.'

'You and me after them,' said Bill. 'You'll have the camera.'

'You've only got to open the shutter as soon as you hear the villain,' said Dick, 'and close it again after the flash ... And I'll fix the flash all ready so whoever's got it has only to pull the trigger.'

'You'll take awful care of the camera, won't you?' said Dorothea.

'The camera'll be all right,' said Dick. 'If whoever has it keeps quiet.'

'You'd better nip home now and get it,' said Tom.

'I'd better come too,' said Dorothea, 'to explain to the Admiral that we'll have to be late. And we've got to take William home. He'd only bark if we had him in the ambush.'

'What about the shield for the flashlight?' said Dick.

'We'll have that ready by the time you're back,' said Tom.

'Shield?' said Pete.

Dick explained. 'We'll have to let off an awful lot of powder for the flash. The shield's so that it doesn't burn anybody's hair off. It'll be a pretty big explosion. The label says its dangerous to use more than a small lot, and we'll have to use ever so much more because of it being in the open air, and because of not being able to have it near the object. It's going to be like this ...' He pushed a drawing into Pete's hands.

'Come on,' said Dot.

'Tell her, Mother wants you to have grub here,' said Tom.

Dick and Dorothea were gone.

Tom, helped by Joe, set to work with a pair of garden shears on a big square biscuit tin. 'It's all right,' he said. 'They probably won't be doing any more pruning this year.' He cut one side of the tin out altogether, and then cut along the bottom of two of the remaining sides so that they could be bent back. Then, with a chisel, he punched out a square hole in the bottom of the tin, for the handle of the flashlight apparatus. All this took a long time and blistered even Tom's rope-hardened fingers. Meanwhile Pete and Bill took turns to hide by Dr Dudgeon's gate and keep a look out on the road.

Pete was the one who saw Mr Tedder bicycling down the road towards the ferry.

'Tedder's gone down to have a look,' he reported joyfully.

'Good,' said Tom.

Pete stayed to watch the work and Bill took his place among the bushes. He presently reported seeing George Owdon and his friend bicycling the other way. 'Reckon they been down to have a look too. And there's a pack of others gone down. I see three chaps from Jonnatt's. And Jack what work at the butcher's. And that milk-boy. Fine idea stirring 'em up at the inn. He make that kid bleat all right. But if all them chaps don't clear out before dark we can't set our trap.'

Dick and Dorothea came back with the camera and the flashlight apparatus, hidden in a basket under some roses from the Admiral's garden, just in case anybody should guess what they were planning. They came with long faces. The Admiral had put her foot down. Dorothea was not to be allowed out after dark.

'She said ambushes are all right for boys and if there was a row I'd only be in the way. I told her it was my idea in the beginning, but she said I'd have to be content with that.'

'She's right, really,' said Dick, 'but the worst of it is that I've got to be in by ten, and I can't come out again for another watch.'

'We'll have got him by ten,' said Tom. 'But if not, we'll have to fix up different watches. Bill and Pete take second watch and if they haven't got him, I'll come out again down the rope and take third watch with Joe.'

'So long as we get him,' said Joe.

Pete and Bill crept off through the osiers. Behind them, they saw the light in the cockpit go out as Joe, left alone in the *Death and Glory*, closed the cabin door behind him. There was left only the orange glow of the curtained windows.

'Steady on, Bill,' said Pete. 'I can't see a thing.'

'Don't light your torch,' said Bill. 'Hold your hands well out forrard, and keep swimming with 'em, so's you'll touch things before bumping 'em.'

They climbed over the fence into the road and found things easier with every step. Dark it was but after a few minutes the darkness seemed less solid. They could see the shape of houses and trees against the starry patches of the sky.

'Come on,' said Bill. 'They'll be thinking we ain't coming.'

'Don't go so we can't hear things,' whispered Pete.

They came to the Ferry Inn, with its lighted windows, and slunk suddenly off the road, out of the way of a couple of men strolling home.

'Closing time,' whispered Bill.

They hurried on again.

'We'll follow the bank,' whispered Bill. Beyond the garden of the inn they crept along the narrow footpath at the side of the river, startled now and then by the splash of water rats as startled as themselves. They came to the ditch, found the plank and went carefully across it.

'Half a minute,' said Bill. 'I'm going back. You lift this end and I'll lift t'other. So's I can shift it easy if I got to run for it.'

They shifted the plank and went on.

'Pretty near now,' said Bill. 'That your teeth chattering? Pity we ain't outed a few more of 'em.'

'They ain't chattering,' said Pete.

'Better give 'em the password,' said Bill. He stopped and said very quietly, 'Coots for ever!'

'And ever.' Tom's voice came from close to Bill's feet, and at the same moment, Pete saw the dim white bulk of the *Cachalot* moored against the bank.

'No tiger yet,' said Tom. 'Here you are. Get down in my form. Here's the thing. It's wound up already. Got it? I'll put your finger on the trigger. Pull that and off it goes.'

'I got it,' said Bill.

Pete was feeling his way into the bush and Dick, who had been a couple of hours in the dark and could see much better, was pulling him into place.

'Whatever you do don't upset the camera,' he whispered. 'Here's the release.' He pushed the end of it into Pete's hand. 'Press the button to open it. Press it as soon as you hear anybody. And press it again when the flash dies down.'

'We mustn't wait about,' said Tom. 'Or we might put him off.'

'Look out for the plank over the ditch,' whispered Bill. 'Me and Pete leave that loose so's I can drop one end if that old villain come chasing after me.'

Tom chuckled.

'Pete knows he's to stay where he is whatever happens, doesn't he?' said Dick.

'He know,' said Bill. 'He's to lie low till all's clear and then bring the camera along.'

'Come on,' said Tom. 'Give the tiger a chance ... if he's coming. And I've got to show up at home. Ow! I can hardly move. I've got cramp in both legs and five fingers.'

'Dot's dead certain he'll come some time,' said Dick. 'But I say, Pete, you will be careful with that camera? I wish the Admiral would let me stay ...'.

'He'll be all right,' said Tom. 'Come on Dick. Joe and I'll be back at twelve.'

'Joe think that tiger won't be showing up till after then,' Pete's voice came out of his bush.

'He won't show up at all if you chaps don't clear out,' said Bill. 'Pete and me's all set. Good night.'

'Back at twelve,' said Tom.

'Look out you don't meet that old tiger and scare him,' said Bill.

There was silence.

Tired and cramped, Dick and Tom were creeping away to the road and their beds. Two fresh detectives were watching in their lairs.

CHAPTER 51

BLINDING FLASH

Tom and Dick had gone home to their beds. Bill and Pete were waiting in the dark.

Pete, squatting on the ground under the bush, shifted his weight from one foot to the other. In there it was very dark indeed but, looking out through the peep-hole that had been made for the camera, he could dimly see the *Cachalot* where she lay moored beside the bank. He could not really see her, but he could just see that she was there. He fingered the press-button that was to open the shutter when the moment came. He let go of it for fear that he should press too soon.

'Bill,' he whispered.

There was no answer whatever. Just for a moment he thought that Bill had gone. And then he heard voices.

The voices were coming from the direction of the road. Coming nearer. Whoever it was must have come into the meadow from the road and be walking along the near side of that ditch. There was a scrambling noise. They were coming up the bank from the low meadow. Steps came nearer along the bank. Tom and Dick back again, or could it be Tom and Joe? Had time gone on that fast? And then Pete froze. He could not hear what was being said, but he somehow knew that these people who were coming were not the Coots. And not one villain, but two at least. They were talking low and coming quick. Were they going to walk right over Bill?

Looking over his shoulder through the leaves, he saw the faint glimmer of a torch flashed at the ground. There it was again. Whoever these newcomers might be, they would see Bill, lying there in the grass, even if they did not stumble over him.

Nearer the steps came and nearer. Pete watched for that faint glimmer of the torch. He heard no more talking. Suddenly the torch showed only a few yards away. The newcomers were close to him, almost on the top of Bill.

Funny the way they were using that torch. He never saw more than a glimmer of it, as if they were shading it so that it should not be seen by anybody but themselves. Dot must have been right. It could be nobody but the villains. They had fallen into the trap and were on their way to cast loose the *Cachalot* just as she had said they would. But if they were to go and tread on Bill now the game would be up and the trap laid for nothing.

'Close here,' said a voice startling Pete so much that he very nearly gave himself away. They had passed Bill. They were between Pete and the river, going close by his bush. What if Bill had heard them coming and had wriggled down into the meadow so as not to be caught by them? He would never be able to get back to fire that flash. Pete felt the press-button in his hand. Press it or not? No good if there was to be no flash ... Yet ... What had Dick said? Press it if he heard anybody there. He pressed. There was a faint click as the shutter of the camera opened. It sounded to Pete, crouching under his bush in the dark, as if everybody in the world must have heard it. But nothing happened.

Then he saw a glimmer from the torch again, this time on the smooth white-painted sides of the *Cachalot*. It went out. There was nothing but black darkness. People were fumbling along the bank.

'It's them. It's them,' Peter whispered to himself, and kept his finger pressed hard on the button. Why didn't Bill fire that flash and be done with it? If only Bill would give a sign, a whisper ... anything, just to let him know that he was not alone, within a yard or two of the villains and able to do nothing ... nothing. As near as all that and he did not know who they were.

He heard the faint clink of a rond-anchor on the *Cachalot*'s deck. Gosh! In another minute they'd have her adrift and be gone and everything would be too late, and there'd be another boat cast off and everybody believing the Coots had done it.

There was another faint clink.

That would be the other anchor.

And then, suddenly, there was a click in the grass close behind him and a tremendous hissing flare of white light. A tuft of grass glittered silver. Trees across the river showed in the darkness. The *Cachalot* gleamed for a moment. Pete blinked in spite of himself. He had seen a white face that might be anybody's ... figures leaning out from the bank ... pushing ... And then the white light had died away and he was staring into darkness blacker than before.

A voice shouted. 'After him! Quick! Don't let him get away! ...'

The torch flashed close by him. Somebody, stumbling in the dark, brushed against the branches behind which Pete was lurking. Somebody else rushed past.

Behind him there was a noise of running, wild, helter-skelter running. Bill must be bolting for his life.

'We saw you,' somebody shouted.

Suddenly, close one after the other, there was two heavy splashes, followed by curses and more splashing.

'They're in the ditch,' said Pete to himself. 'That give Bill a chance.' He remembered that he was still squeezing the press-button of the camera. He released it. What had Dick said? Press again after the flash die down? He pressed again and heard the shutter click.

He listened. The noise of the chase was already far away.

'Bill'll give 'em a run,' said Pete to himself. 'See in the

dark like a cat Bill can. Better'n Joe. And they can't likely. There's a lot of good mud in that ditch.' He chuckled and found his teeth chattering at the same time.

He began to think of what he ought to do. Sit tight till all's clear, they had said. Well he had done that. First of all there was the camera. He felt for it carefully. Yes, it was all right. Still standing on its tripod. Might easily have got smashed up when that one come blundering by. He felt its legs. He did not know how to make them shut up. He would have to carry the camera just as it was. No matter for that. In the cabin of the *Death and Glory*, with a decent light, perhaps Joe would get the legs off it. Or they could take it to Dick. Pete waited a little longer. All was quiet. He crawled out from under his bush and stood up, getting used to the darkness which had seemed very black after that white flash. Holding the camera in one hand, he felt for his torch with the other, but decided it was not safe to use it for fear of bringing the villains rushing back. He peered out from the bank. Yes, there she was, anchored in the river. They had cast her off, but the mud-weight had held her. The *Cachalot* was all right.

Bother that camera. Worse than a fishing rod it was. Two of the legs closed together and caught his finger. He felt for the third leg, closed it against the other two and held all three together. Then, with his right hand pawing into the dark so as not to run into anything and hurt the camera, he set out for the *Death and Glory*, stopping every few steps to listen. Them villains might be coming back if Bill had given them the slip.

He met no one on the bank, but did not try to cross the ditch. Instead, he slipped along at the side of it till he came to the meadow gate and then hurried along the road at a good pace, glad to have firm ground under his feet. He passed the Ferry Inn, where there was still a light in an upper window, came to the fence along the edge of the Wilderness, climbed over it, and began feeling his way through the osier bushes along the side of the dyke. He stopped suddenly. Someone was talking in the darkness ahead. Lucky he hadn't dared to use his torch. Lucky he hadn't yelled out 'Ahoy, *Death and Glory*!' He very nearly had, just to hear his own voice and not feel so horribly alone.

Someone was talking angrily.

'He's there all right,' said a voice. And then came a noise of loud banging on a door.

Pete crept on. Were they trying to break into the old boat?

The flashing of torches showed him where the *Death and Glory* lay, moored at the mouth of the dyke. But what were those figures in the cockpit?

'You may as well come out now as later,' said a voice.

Pete stopped dead. Was Bill back in the *Death and Glory*, or was Joe there alone? For a moment he thought of charging to the rescue. Then he remembered the camera. It was Dick's camera. More than that, it was at the moment the most important thing in the world. 'Bring it along and we'll take it to Dick,' Bill had said. 'But whatever you do don't get copped with it.'

There was only one thing to do and that was to get the camera with its precious photograph safely into Dick's hands.

He turned and on tiptoe went back to the road, climbed over the fence and made for Mrs Barrable's. How late was it? He did not know. There were still lights behind the blinds in some of the houses, but not in all, and when he came to Mrs Barrable's he found every window dark. They had gone to bed long ago. Wake them? He felt at his feet for a handful of gravel. If only he knew which was Dick's window. Should he bang at the front door and hope Dick would be the first to hear him? That Dick ought to have string hanging down from his window like Tom. Then he thought of taking the camera to Tom. But what if he should meet the villains on the way there and be caught with the camera in his hands? He had a better idea. He would run home, leave the camera at home where no villains would think of looking for it and he could then go back to the *Death and Glory*, tell the others it was safe and get up early and take it to Dick first thing in the morning.

He hurried along, turned the corner and came to his own house. Here he had hoped all would be in darkness, but he found a light still burning in an upstairs window. Well, they didn't lock the door at night, that was one thing. He slipped round into the back yard, opened the scullery door, and, putting the camera on the floor for safety's sake, felt his way across the room. He found the switch and turned on the electric light.

'Who's there?'

'It's only me, Mum.'

'PETE! What in the name of goodness are you doing?' His mother was already coming downstairs. 'Why aren't you asleep hours ago? Something wrong with your boat? Joe and Bill both promise me you go to bed regular.'

'It's all right,' Pete explained. 'I've just got to leave something for Dick. I'll fetch it in the morning.'

'You won't,' said his mother. 'Do you think I'm going to let you go off again, wandering round the village in the middle of the night? You'll go to your bed here this minute and don't let me hear a peep out of you till I wake you.'

'But, Mum, I've got to go back. Chaps trying to break into our boat . . .'

'You won't stop them,' said his mother. 'Do you know what time it is? Now then, into bed with you.'

'But . . .'

'If you're not into bed in two minutes you'll do no more boating this year. I'll begin to think Mr Tedder's right.'

Pete found himself upstairs and beside his bed without knowing how he got there. He wriggled away. 'There's that camera,' he said.

'What camera?' said his mother.

'I left it on the floor,' said Pete.

For one wild moment he thought of slipping out again and

bolting for it. But his mother came down with him into the scullery and herself picked up the camera.

'Where did you get this?' she asked.

'It's not mine. It's that Dick's,' he said, 'and Dick's got to have it first thing.'

'I'll take care of it,' said his mother. 'You can take it to him in the morning. Into bed with you now. Upstairs. Be quick. I'll stay with you till you're under the blankets.'

And Pete, ex-pirate, salvage man, member of the Bird Protection Society, member of the Coot Club, detective and part-owner of the *Death and Glory*, found himself being tucked up and even kissed.

'Not another peep out of you,' said his mother, as she closed the door on him.

For a minute or two he lay, wondering what best to do. And the next thing he knew was the morning sun shining through the window.

CHAPTER 52

SIEGE OF THE *DEATH AND GLORY*

Joe had his orders. He was to keep the lantern lit in the *Death and Glory* and the door closed, so that anybody who came to spy would think that the crew were at home. He stoked up the fire, played a tune or two on his mouth organ and then got old Ratty out for company.

Old Ratty sat on the table and Joe gave him a nut and began eating nuts himself. But Ratty did not eat fast enough for Joe, and presently Joe put the bag away because he was eating a great deal more than his share. Then he and Ratty played an old game of theirs, Joe putting the rat into his sleeve, and the rat working its way up the sleeve and coming out somewhere else. Joe looked up at the old alarm clock. It must be nearly an hour since Bill and Pete had gone off to take their places watching for the tiger.

Suddenly Joe stiffened. What was that, moving on the rond outside? The curtains made it impossible for anybody to see in, though they let plenty of light through. Anybody outside could see that the lantern was burning. Joe waited. There was just the slightest movement of the boat. Someone was touching her, trying to look through the windows, or feeling the chimney.

'Bed-time, Bill,' said Joe loudly. 'Young Pete ought to be asleep.'

He listened, but could hear nothing.

'Hurry up,' he said. 'It don't take half an hour to get a pair of boots off.'

Again he listened. He waited a long time. Then he put old Ratty back in his box, watched the long tail curl out of sight into the cotton wool, and put the box on the shelf over his bunk. Nothing seemed to be stirring outside. Gone, whoever it was. Mighty quiet too. It looked as if the villain had come to make sure first that the Death and Glories were at home, before going on to cast off the *Cachalot*. Cautiously, Joe opened the cabin door, waited a moment and crawled out into the cockpit.

If that had been the villain, he must be getting near the *Cachalot* by now. And Bill and Pete were there waiting for him, ready to spring the trap. Would it work, or would it not? Bill would do his part all right. But Pete? Joe for half a minute thought of trying to join them. But what would be the good of that? Upset the whole plan for nothing.

It was a dark night, and down river there was nothing to be seen but a soft curtain of blackness, with just that dim glow over far-away Yarmouth. Joe tried to make up his mind just where in the darkness the *Cachalot* must be, with the detectives lurking beside her, one ready with the camera, the other with the flashlight outfit in its biscuit-box shield. What if the powder didn't catch? And that Pete! Never taken a photo in all his life. Much better, thought Joe, if we'd all laid for them and dashed out and caught them in the act.

And then, suddenly, a white flare lit up the darkness beyond the Ferry. Trees and the inn showed suddenly black against a silver glow. Then all was dark again.

'They've done it,' said Joe to himself. 'They've done it. Geewhizz! And now what! Was that a shout?'

He jumped ashore and started off along the dyke towards the road. He stopped, listened, and turned back. His orders were clear enough. To stand by the boat. He stood on the bank, with a hand on the gunwale of the *Death and Glory*.

What was happening? Had Bill got away? What if the

villain had caught Pete, camera and all? Again he thought of bolting to their help.

Then he heard running footsteps on the road from the Ferry.

He got aboard. Nearer and nearer the footsteps were coming. They hesitated. They came on again. They stopped. He could hear other footsteps, racing down the road. Then in the Wilderness, close to the *Death and Glory*, someone was crashing through the willow bushes. The next moment, there was Bill clambering aboard, panting fit to burst.

'Two of 'em,' panted Bill. 'Near trod on me, they did. Quick. Quick. Into the cabin. They'll be here in two ticks. Close behind . . .'

'Pete,' said Joe. 'What about Pete?'

'Lying low till they gone,' said Bill. 'He's all right. There was only the two of 'em and they both come after me. Heard 'em splash one after t'other. I drop that plank in the ditch for 'em. Go on. Get the door shut . . . Get the key inside . . .'

Bill lay puffing on his bunk. Joe fumbled desperately with the key. Already he could hear people stumbling through the bushes. He caught a glimpse of a torch. And that old key, which always fell out when he didn't want it to, was sticking in the lock on purpose. It came loose at last. Joe put it into the lock from inside, closed the door, locked it, plumped down on his bunk and waited.

'They're close here,' he said. 'Who are they? Did you see 'em?'

'That thing fair blind me,' said Bill. 'But there was two of 'em. And they cast her off. I see that.'

'But who are they?'

'I don't know.'

Somebody's fist banged on the roof of the cabin above their heads.

'Come out of that,' said a voice.

'That sound like George Owdon,' said Joe.

'You talk,' whispered Bill. 'Gimme time to get breath.'

'Who's there?' asked Joe as sleepily as he could.

'River watchers.'

'All well here,' said Joe.

'We'll give you all well.' The boat lurched as the visitors stepped aboard. Hands pawed over the door. 'They've got the door locked,' said a voice. 'Run him to earth all right. Shine your torch here. You can see the key's in the lock.' There was a sudden angry rattle at the door.

'You clear off and leave us alone,' said Joe. 'We want to get to sleep.'

There was a long silence. Then the noise of muttering in the cockpit. Then someone spoke aloud.

'He's there all right.'

'I bet that's George Owdon,' whispered Joe.

'They'll have the door in in a minute,' whispered Bill, as someone outside started hammering on the door and then kicking at it.

'You may as well come out now as later,' said a voice and there was such banging on the door that Joe, for a moment, looked anxiously at the hinges.

'Stop that,' he shouted angrily.

There was whispering in the cockpit, and then a curse as someone tripped over the bucket which Joe had left there after the last washing up. Some sort of argument went on in low voices. Bill thought he heard the word 'camera'. There was more muttering and they heard someone say, 'I tell you we've got to make sure.'

'Shall I let 'em in now?' whispered Joe.

'No,' said Bill.

'We don't want 'em to go without our seeing 'em,' urged Joe. 'Case that photo don't come off. Pete ain't no expert like that Dick.'

'Keep 'em busy,' whispered Bill. 'Give Pete time to get clear. We don't want 'em to go and catch him with the camera. More row they kick up the better. Warn Pete not to come here.'

'Who are you?' shouted Joe.

'You'll see soon enough. Are you going to open this door?'

'What for?' said Joe. 'We ain't invited anybody.'

'We'll break it in then.'

'You'll have a job,' said Joe.

The answer was a still more violent rattling of the door. Then there was another whispered debate in the cockpit, ending as before with the words, 'I tell you it isn't safe not to make sure.'

The next thing heard in the cabin was the splash of the bucket over the side. Then steps on the cabin roof . . . Then . . . as Bill said afterwards, it was like the end of the world. There was a loud hiss of water on hot coals . . . The door of the stove flew wide open . . . The cabin was full of smoke and scalding steam . . . Bits of coal flew in all directions and lay hissing where they fell. Water poured from the stove.

'You all right?' Joe gasped.

'Beasts!' shouted Bill. 'Beasts!'

Again the bucket splashed over the side, steps sounded on the roof, and another deluge of water poured down the chimney and out over the cabin floor bringing cinders with it.

Bill choked.

Joe, coughing and spluttering, reached for the door.

'We'll open.'

He unlocked the door. It was pulled wide. A hand reached over his head, grabbed him by the collar and hauled him out into the cockpit.

Bill, struggling to escape from all that smoke and steam, was in the doorway. He too was hauled out.

'Any more?' said George Owdon. 'Three of you, aren't there? Where's the third?'

'You can see he ain't here,' said Bill.

'You ain't got no right to make a mess of our boat even if you are river watchers,' said Joe.

'We know now who was casting boats off,' said Bill.

'Shut up.'

'Been swimming?' he asked.

A large hand swung round and caught him on the side of the head.

'Who are you hitting?'

'You ... and you'll get some more if you start any cheek. Come on, George. Better make sure.'

'Wait till the smoke's cleared ... You'd have done better to open the door when we asked you.'

The smoke and steam were drifting out of the cabin and the lamp, burning clearer now, showed the dreadful mess that had been made.

'You might have set the ship afire,' said Bill.

'Ship!' jeered George Owdon. 'A lot you cared what happened to the "ships" you cast adrift.'

'We didn't,' began Joe, but Bill gave him a nudge and he said no more.

'I'm going in now,' said George Owdon. He stooped and went in, hitting his head on a beam as he did so. 'Harder'n ever Tom hit his,' said Joe with some pleasure telling about it afterwards.

'What's he doing?' asked Bill.

'Shut up,' said the other big boy, George Owdon's friend, who was standing guard over them in the cockpit.

In the cabin, George Owdon was looking this way and that. He pushed his way forward, opened the cupboards, pulled everything out on the floor, tore the blankets off Pete's bunk, came back, hitting his head again, and hunted along the cabin shelves, sweeping things off them as he hunted.

'Hullo!'

Joe and Bill, watching the sack of their cabin, heard George Owdon exclaim.

'Got it!'

He had found the square wooden box on the shelf over Joe's bunk.

'Don't you touch that,' shouted Joe. But George Owdon was already feeling in it and pulling out the cotton wool. The next moment there was a yell, and he had flung the box into the forepart of the boat and was sucking a bleeding finger.

Joe broke free from his captor and plunged into the cabin, pushed past George Owdon and picked up the box. It was empty, but he saw something white close under the deck in the very bows of the boat.

'I'll kill that rat for you,' shouted George Owdon.

'You won't,' said Joe. 'All right, old Ratty. It's all right.'

'Leave him alone,' said the big boy in the cockpit, who still had Bill by the collar. 'You're sure it's not there?'

'I thought it was in that box,' said George Owdon, looking at his bitten finger by the light of the hanging lantern.

'Come on then,' said the other boy.

'You wait till morning,' said Joe angrily. 'We'll tell Mr Tedder what you done to our boat.'

'I'll tell him I caught you casting loose that cruiser,' said Bill.

George Owdon laughed. 'Who'll believe you?' he asked. 'We've got something to tell Mr Tedder too. We saw you unmoor that boat and put her adrift. You saw him, didn't you, Ralph?'

'Swear to him any day,' said the other boy.

'Now what about Mr Tedder?' said George. 'This'll settle it. We were watching for you and we saw you take those anchors up and push her off. That was all he said he was waiting for, for someone to catch you in the act.'

'Liars!' gasped Bill.

'We'll tell him first,' said Joe.

'Come on, George,' said the second boy. 'We'll go and tell him now.'

The two of them went ashore and disappeared in the dark.

'Are rat-bites poisonous?' Bill heard George say.

'Hope that one is,' shouted Bill.

There was the sound of a scuffle. 'Let go.' Bill heard George's voice.

'Never mind him,' he heard the other boy say. 'Now you listen to me. What's the name of that kid? We've both got to say we saw the same one.'

They were gone.

Bill joined Joe in the wrecked cabin. Joe was talking to the white rat, persuading it to come back.

'I say, Joe.'

'Yes ... Come on, Ratty, old chap. There ain't nobody to hurt you.'

'I say, Joe. What if that Tedder believe him?'

'Well, you saw him pushing the boat off.'

'Not to swear,' said Bill. 'There was that light right afront of my eyes, and I didn't see nothing not hardly. I didn't know who they was till they come drive us out of our cabin.'

'What about Pete?' said Joe.

'I were frightened all the time he'd come walking in on us,' said Bill. 'If they catch him with that camera, we're sunk. And if he bungled that photo we're sunk too. Pete may have seen 'em, but that's not much good if he did. Our word against theirs, and everybody in the place believing it's us anyhow.'

'If Pete come along, he sheer off when he hear 'em,' said Joe ... 'Good old Ratty ...' He had got the white rat on his knee by now and was stroking it and tickling it behind its ears. 'Pete's got sense. He'll likely be watching for 'em to go. He'll be along, soon as he think the coast's clear. Pete's lucky. His is the only dry bunk in the ship. That water splash over everything. Take us a week of Sundays to put all straight. What was that George looking for, throwing things about?'

'That flashlight make 'em think,' said Bill. 'He were looking to see if we got a camera. That's why they don't say they seen us till they make sure we ain't got a photograph.'

'And if they'd found it?'

'They'd have put it in the river, or spoil the picture somehow.'

'Do you think Pete take that photo?' asked Joe. 'Didn't,
we're no better off than we was.'

'I don't know,' said Bill wearily. 'That light startle me when
I pull that trigger, and if it startle Pete too he'd be too late
maybe.'

For some time they were busy, putting things back into
their places by the light of the lantern, mopping up the mess
on the floor, clearing the bunks.

'It's the end of the old Coot Club,' said Bill in deep gloom.
'We was being a bit too clever. You see, if they asks me I
can't say I weren't there. And it's them being river watchers
and helping Tedder and all that.'

'All right if Pete get that photo,' said Joe. 'Wish he'd show
up. Shall I give him a shout?'

'Better not,' said Bill, but he went out into the cockpit,
turned his torch on and waved it to and fro for a signal, in
case Pete might be lurking somewhere near.

'I'm lighting up that fire again,' said Joe. 'He'll be clem
cold hanging about. Dry things up a bit too.'

They got the fire burning again, boiled a kettle of water
and made cocoa.

'No good going looking for him,' said Bill. 'Pete know
enough not to get caught. Pull the curtains. Leave the door
open. So he'll see all's clear. Gone to Tom's likely. Maybe
Tom'll be coming with him. Well, there's cocoa for all.'

They sat by the fire in the cabin, sipped their hot cocoa,
told each other all the many things they might have done
to George Owdon and his friend if only they had thought
of them in time, and in the end dropped asleep where they
sat.

CHAPTER 53

'ALL THE EVIDENCE WE GOT'

'Wake up, Bill. Where's that Pete?'

Joe was shaking Bill by the arm. Sunlight was slanting through the orange curtains.

'Wake up. That Pete ain't come back.'

'Leave go my arm.' Bill woke slowly. He sat up and stretched out an arm, stiff and cramped after the night. He blinked at Joe and stared sleepily at his own feet, wondering to find them in sea-boots. Suddenly he remembered the battle with the besiegers, the tremendous flash in the darkness, the splashes of the pursuers in the ditch behind him, and Pete, left with the camera in his hiding-place on the bank of the river.

'Ain't he come in?'

'Ain't you heard me tell you?'

'Gone to Tom's. Tom'll have give him a doss down.'

'Come on then.'

Rubbing their eyes, they hurried along the bank, through Mr Farland's garden, over the little drawbridge and so to Dr Dudgeon's. They could hear the clatter of crockery and pans and someone singing in the kitchen.

'Tom! Coots!'

There was no answer as they stood by Scotland Yard looking up at Tom's window.

Bill gave a hard tug at the string. A moment later, Tom, still in pyjamas, looked out.

'You nearly had my hand off that time,' he said sleepily,

and then, waking up ... 'Look here ... Why didn't you fetch me when it was my watch? Why? What? What's happened?'

'They come all right,' said Bill. 'But everything go wrong.'

'Didn't the trap work?'

'I couldn't see a thing after I let go that flash,' said Bill. 'But they was there all right. And I bolt, like you said, and they go in the ditch clopwollop, and the next thing were that George Owdon and that other banging at the *Death and Glory*.'

'Three cheers,' said Tom. 'We've got them.'

'We ain't,' said Joe. 'They say they see Bill pushing off the *Cachalot*. But where's that Pete?'

'Did Pete get the photograph?' asked Tom.

'Ain't Pete with you?' said Joe.

'Of course he isn't.'

'Pete lie low, like you say,' said Bill, 'and we ain't seen him since.'

'Perhaps he went to Dick's.'

'He'd never go to Mrs Barrable's, not in the middle of the night,' said Bill. 'Dick ain't got a string from his window.'

'Why didn't you come here last night?' said Tom.

'We fall asleep. That's why,' said Bill.

Joe was already running for the road. 'Come on, Bill,' he shouted over his shoulder. 'We tell young Pete to lie low and he never dare shift. He's by the *Cachalot* yet. Been there all night.'

Bill pelted after him.

Side by side they ran down the road to the Ferry, round the inn, through the gate and across the meadow to the bank of the river.

There was the *Cachalot*, anchored just out of reach from the bank. Pete or no Pete, Joe was delighted that his idea had worked out so well.

'She lie beautiful,' he said. 'Lucky we put that weight down to hold her. Might have been anywheres by now.'

'Pete,' shouted Bill.

There was no answer.

They came to the apparatus Bill had used to fire off the flashlight powder. It was lying beside the path, with the biscuit-box shield, just where Bill had dropped it before racing off with the villains close behind him. Joe picked it up. It was wet with dew, but Dick would surely want it again. Bill rescued Tom's oilskin.

They pulled aside the branches of the willow bush, where the photographer had lurked in hiding. There was no sign of Pete or of the camera.

'And he ain't come to the *Death and Glory*,' said Bill. 'Nor yet to Tom's. Joe! You don't think they get him? May have been more of 'em than them two. I never think of that.'

'Silly young turmot,' said Joe. 'What if he tumble in the river getting away?' He did not believe it when he said it, but saying it somehow made it seem possible, and both of them looked anxiously along the bank.

'He've been out all night,' said Bill. 'Joe. We got to tell his Mum.'

'If them chaps fright him,' said Joe, 'he'd likely run t'other way.'

They looked down the river and this way and that over the low-lying meadows. There was never a sign of a wandering photographer.

'He'll be all right,' said Joe doubtfully.

'We got to tell his Mum,' said Bill.

'Well, he ain't here,' said Joe.

They had a last look round and hurried back to the village. If Pete's Mum had to be told, the sooner it was done the better.

'Wish that Dot never think of that trap,' said Bill. 'That turn out wrong all ways.'

'What about telling Tedder?' said Joe, as they passed the policeman's house at a good jog trot.

'No use us telling him,' said Bill. 'Pete's Mum'll do that.

You don't really think he tumble in? ... Pete's not one for that ... It were a black dark night ... I couldn't see nothing hardly, after that flash ...'

'Think they'll drag the river?' said Joe.

Bill did not answer and they ran grimly on, round the corner by the inn, and so to the row of cottages, one of which was Pete's home.

Pete's mother was on her knees scrubbing her doorstep. She looked up at them. 'Well,' she began, as if she had a good deal to say.

'We lost Pete,' said Joe.

'Down the river below the Ferry,' said Bill.

'Lost him?' she said. 'You just miss him. But didn't you two promise me that if he come in that old boat you'd see he go regular to bed?'

'Just miss him?' said Joe eagerly. 'Has he been here?'

'He go out just before you two come. Rapscurryhurrying he were too. But what I want to know is what you was doing with him running loose at all hours of the night?'

Pete was all right. There were other things to think of now.

'Have he got a camera with him?' asked Bill.

'He didn't hardly finish his breakfast before he got off with it.'

'He've gone to Dick's,' said Joe. 'Come on.'

'There's going to be no more of that ...' said Pete's mother, but they never heard what there was to be no more of, for they were off again on their way to Mrs Barrable's.

They never got there. Turning the corner of the road they met Dorothea hurrying down to Scotland Yard. She was almost running, carrying a small suitcase.

'Oh good,' she cried. 'Come on, quick. Tell me what happened. Pete said there were people at the *Death and Glory* last night, and he went home with the camera, and his mother put him into bed. But what happened?'

'Did he get a photo?' asked Bill.

'He doesn't know if he did or not,' said Dorothea. 'And Dick and he have rushed back to develop the film. They're coming after us. We can't wait for them. We're going to be late if we don't hurry. We've got to get all the evidence together and take it to Mr Farland. And if we're late he'll be gone to Norwich. But do tell me what happened.'

'Didn't Pete say?'

'About people coming to cast off the *Cachalot*? Yes. Yes. But he didn't know who they were. Did you see them?'

'That flash put me blind,' said Bill. 'But they was there. Two of 'em. I race back to the old ship. And they was after me. George Owdon and that other.'

'Hurrah!' cried Dorothea. 'I knew it was George Owdon. So it's all right after all.'

'Just what it ain't,' said Joe. 'That George he's going to say he see Bill pushing her off.'

'But didn't you see him?'

'Must have been him,' said Bill, keeping up with Dorothea. 'But with that flash I didn't see nothing. I up and run in the dark, and they after me. Into that old ditch they go good and proper. But I didn't see nobody, not till they smoke us out and there they was in our cockpit.'

'What about Tom?'

'Bill's watch and Pete's,' said Joe. 'Wish we'd all have stayed.'

'We're sunk,' said Bill, 'if Pete ain't got that photo.'

'We aren't,' said Dorothea. 'We can't be. Not with all our evidence.'

They were hurrying now along the main street of the village. Shops were opening. People taking down shutters turned to stare at them in an unfriendly way. Outside Mr Tedder's two bicycles were propped against the fence.

'That George Owdon's in there now,' said Bill.

Dorothea stopped, turned and darted to the bicycles. She looked first at one and then at the other.

'Look! Look!' she cried. 'Dick was right.' She pointed at a small smear of green paint on the grip of the right handlebar of one of the bicycles. 'We can prove everything. It's going to be all right. Come on.'

They hurried on to Dr Dudgeon's. Tom was on the look out for them.

'Pete's all right,' Bill called out as soon as he saw Tom.

'Where's Dick?' said Tom.

'Developing with Pete,' said Dorothea. 'They're coming after us. And there's green paint on George Owdon's handlebars.'

'It's close on nine already,' said Tom. 'We can't wait for them. Uncle Frank'll be gone if we don't look out. Look here. What did happen last night?'

Bill and Joe tried to tell all they knew. Dorothea began gathering the clues and packing them into her suitcase. There was the scrap of grey flannel with its label, Dick's drawing of the tyre-treads, the affidavit of Bob Curten, a sheaf of notes and the summary of all the evidence that she had finished before going to bed the night before.

She interrupted the others. 'There's just one thing,' she said. 'I asked the Admiral about lawyer's fees.'

'We got pots of money,' said Joe.

'We can pay,' said Bill.

'I don't see that,' said Dorothea. 'We're all in it.'

It was arranged that the six detectives should contribute equal shares.

'We'll put in for Pete,' said Bill.

'And I've got Dick's as well as mine,' said Dorothea, digging in her purse. 'I don't suppose Mr Farland'll mind a postal order. There isn't time to go and change it now.'

'What about the map?' said Tom.

'Better bring it,' said Dorothea. 'Push the pins well in so that they don't fall out.'

The map, with the black flags showing where boats had been cast off, was taken down and carefully rolled up.

'We haven't put a flag in for the *Cachalot*,' said Dorothea.

'If Pete ain't took that photo right, the *Cachalot*'s going to be worst of all,' said Bill.

The map was unrolled. Another flag was put in its place and the map was rolled up again.

'All the evidence we got,' said Bill. 'It ain't much, not if them two say they saw me cast her off.'

'And there's the chimney,' said Dorothea. 'Have you taken it off the cabin roof?'

Bill and Joe answered never a word but raced for the *Death and Glory*.

Tom with the rolled up map and Dorothea with her suitcase came hurrying after them, to find them both on the roof of the cabin, Bill biting into a huge slice of bread, and Joe working away with a screwdriver in one hand and a hunk of bread in the other.

'Haven't you had breakfast?' said Dorothea.

'That ain't no matter,' said Joe. 'Tip her gently, Bill.'

The chimney left its seating without accident, and a moment later they were on their way.

They came into Mr Farland's garden.

'We'd better just have a look in the road to see if they're in sight,' said Dorothea.

They went to the gate and looked down the road.

'Must have got a photo,' said Joe hopefully. 'Not, they'd be here by now.'

'No good waiting,' said Tom.

Followed by the rest of the detectives, he walked up to the front door of Mr Farland's house and rang the bell.

CHAPTER 54

THE LEGAL MIND

'What's that?' asked Mr Farland as soon as Bill and Joe came into the room carrying the big green chimney pot between them.

'Evidence,' said Tom, unrolling the map and putting it at the end of Mr Farland's long table.

'We've got lots more,' said Dorothea, patting her suitcase.

Bill and Joe, carefully dusting the chimney pot with their hands, stood it upright on the carpet.

Tom looked anxiously out of the window, not that he could see the road or even the gate through which Dick and Pete would come, for the window looked the other way, over the river, but just for peace of mind. From what Joe and Bill had said it was clear enough to him that Dorothea had been right and that they knew now who the villains were. But it was also clear that the trap they had laid was going to work the wrong way, and that if George Owdon and his friend stuck to it that they had seen Bill cast off the *Cachalot* the Coot Club was going to be not better off but worse.

It was going to be Bill's word against George's, and with all that had gone before he did not think Bill's word had much chance of being believed. Tom knew very well that Mr Farland himself had thought from the first that the Coots had been at the bottom of all the mischief that had been going on. And unluckily it had been Pete's turn with the camera. If it had been Dick's there might have been some chance. But Pete had never taken a photograph in his life.

'Won't you sit down?' said Mr Farland to Dorothea.

'I think I'd rather stand,' said Dorothea. She took something from her pocket and laid it on the table in front of Mr Farland. It was a small screwed up bit of paper, one of Dr Dudgeon's prescription forms.

Mr Farland took it. 'More evidence?' he said, unscrewing the paper. 'What on earth's this? They haven't been accused of taking money.'

Out of the paper came a postal order for two shillings, a two-shilling piece, a shilling, three sixpences, and a couple of coppers.

'I think it's the proper fee,' said Dorothea.

Mr Farland had not for nothing been a lawyer all his life. He bowed gravely to Dorothea, but no one could have told what was in his mind as he smoothed out the bit of paper and laid it flat on his table, smoothed out the postal order and laid it on the bit of paper, and piled on it the two pennies, the two-shilling piece, the shilling and the three sixpences, exactly on the top of each other.

'I am not sure that you quite understand the position,' he said at last. 'Sonning's, the boat-builders at Potter Heigham, employ my firm as solicitors. They have been put to considerable trouble by having a number of their boats cast off from their moorings and sent drifting down the river. They have missed a quantity of boat's gear (shackles, to be exact) from one of their sheds. They have appealed to the police and to others to find out who is responsible for all this. On two occasions a small number of the missing shackles have been handed to the police here by one of you two lads ...' He looked straight at Bill and Joe. Until that moment he had seemed to be looking at a picture on the wall behind their heads. 'On the second occasion the shackles were given to a magistrate, Dr Dudgeon, who, on your behalf, took them to the police. Now, we have been having the same sort of trouble here. No stealing, certainly. But I am told that every boat that has been sent adrift was lying somewhere near that boat of yours. And that your boat was at Ranworth when boats were sent adrift there. And that your boat was at Potter Heigham when the same thing happened there and all those shackles were stolen. Stolen is an ugly word, but stolen they were.'

He paused. It certainly sounded terribly as if Mr Farland had already made up his mind.

Bill was just going to say something, when Mr Farland spoke again.

'Now then,' he said. 'I've told you how we stand. I'm ready to listen to what you have to say, but if you have come to me to ask me to get you out of your difficulties, I don't see that I can do anything.'

'But it isn't like that at all,' said Dorothea. 'They simply didn't do any of those things.'

'Miss Callum,' began Mr Farland.

'Oh, look here, Uncle Frank,' said Tom.

'Miss Callum,' said Mr Farland again, and went on, 'If these boys had no hand in all this, somebody else had. Now, have you any idea who?'

Dorothea hesitated.

'We think we know,' she said.

'Think isn't enough,' said Mr Farland.

'We're sure we know,' said Dorothea.

'Take that first occasion,' said Mr Farland. 'When a motor-cruiser was cast off from the staithe. Theirs was the only other boat moored at the staithe that night.'

'There was someone else there,' said Tom.

'That was the night we outed Pete's tooth for him,' said Joe, 'and there was somebody there in the dark and he bung the brick back through the window.'

'Did any of you see this other person?'

'No,' said Tom. 'We couldn't. It was already dark.'

'You can't, on the strength of somebody whom you didn't

see having been there some time before the cruiser was sent adrift, get away from the fact that all that night their boat lay there, and was still there in the morning, when the other boat was drifting down the river.'

'But don't you see?' said Dorothea. 'It was done by an enemy.'

'Why then did the enemy cast off the other boat instead of theirs? He must have known the difference.'

'He did it because he hated the Coot Club,' said Dorothea, 'and he wanted Tom and the others to get blamed for it.'

'It's that George Owdon,' said Bill. 'We always think it were and now we know for dead certain sure.'

'But look here,' said Mr Farland. 'George Owdon was watching the staithe here, when you lads were casting off the boats at Potter.'

'We ain't cast off no boats,' said Joe doggedly.

'We've got evidence,' said Dorothea. She put her case on the floor, opened it, rummaged in it for a moment, and laid young Bob's affidavit on the table.

Mr Farland read it. 'I swear I see George Owdon by Potter Bridge the night before you come through. Bob Curten.'

'Was he in two places at once?'

'Bike,' said Joe.

'And what about Ranworth?'

'Bike again.'

Dorothea took Dick's drawing of the bicycle tracks out of her case. 'We found bicycle tracks on the soft ground by the staithe at Ranworth,' she said. 'This is the place.' She put the drawing and a photograph on the table. 'It's a Dunlop tyre. And we know someone crossed the Ferry that night. And we know George Owdon's got Dunlop tyres ...'

Mr Farland looked at drawing and photograph. 'Almost all bicycles have Dunlop tyres,' he said. 'What make of tyres does Tom use? ... But never mind that. They tell me you lads were actually seen casting off a yacht from the staithe.'

'We salvage her,' said Joe. 'We was tying her up when we was seen ... not casting her off. It's only that George Owdon say we was.'

'There's another thing,' said Mr Farland, looking at some notes on the table before him. 'George Owdon and his friend have been giving up a lot of their nights to watching just to prevent this sort of thing happening. I have to ask myself, "Isn't it likely that you have a grudge against him on that account?"'

'Not half the grudge he got against the Coot Club,' said Bill.

'That birds'-nesting affair?' said Mr Farland thoughtfully.

'When he try to get them bitterns,' said Joe, 'and we fetch keeper just in time.'

Mr Farland stroked his chin. 'Yes,' he said. 'You don't like George Owdon and George Owdon doesn't like you. But that doesn't prove anything much. Now, what about those shackles?'

'We never steal 'em,' said Joe. 'Pete find that first lot in our stove and Bill find that second lot in our cockpit, and the one what put that second lot in our boat is that one what print his hand on our chimbley like Dick say he would.'

'What's that?'

Dorothea explained. 'You see that first time we knew someone had been there. I saw someone feeling the chimney, and then he heard me and ran away in the fog and fell over our bloodhound. And William got a bit of his trousers.' She laid the scrap of flannel on Mr Farland's table. 'And the next morning they found some shackles in the stove and took them to Mr Tedder. And then Dick thought that if we kept the chimney covered with wet paint we'd get a fingerprint if whoever it was did it again. And we did get a fingerprint. There it is. And there was some of the green paint on the second lot of shackles.'

'Not quite good enough,' said Mr Farland. 'If Bill or Joe

or Pete had been messing about with green paint they'd be likely to get some on the shackles themselves.'

'Ask George Owdon to fit his hand to that print,' said Joe. 'It's a sight too big for us.'

'It's no good, Uncle Frank,' burst out Tom. 'If you don't want to believe them. If only Port and Starboard were here, they'd tell you.'

'There's green paint on George Owdon's bicycle,' said Dorothea.

A bell jangled somewhere in the house. A moment later the door opened, and Mrs McGinty, Mr Farland's house-keeper, came in and said, 'Mr Tedder to see you, Sir. Urgent.'

Mr Tedder came in, but he did not come alone. With him came George Owdon and his friend.

'We ought to have gone to him right away,' said Bill. 'Didn't I tell you?'

'Shut up, Bill,' whispered Tom.

George Owdon and his friend had just for one second looked taken aback when they saw Tom and Dorothea and Bill and Joe standing in the room. But only for a second. Then they stood quite at their ease, listening to Mr Tedder.

Mr Tedder had the air of the detective who has run his criminal to earth. 'Open and shut,' he said. 'We know who done it now. Got all the proof we was needing. From information received Mr Owdon and' (he looked in his note-book) 'Mr Strakey kept watch on the cruiser *Cachalot* last night where she were moored below the Ferry. At ten forty-three p.m. they hear footsteps approaching. At ten forty-seven ...'

The door opened again and Pete and Dick, very much out of breath, slipped into the room.

'I'm very sorry we're late,' said Dick, and dodged past the others to the window, where he stood in the sunlight with both hands behind his back.

Pete looked from face to face, and stood by Bill and Joe.

They looked at him, but could make nothing of the violent nodding of his head.

'At ten forty-seven,' went on Mr Tedder, 'the witnesses, Mr Owdon and Mr Strakey, hear anchors bein' put on deck. At ten forty-eight they jump up out of their place of conceal-ment and catch the guilty party apushing of the *Cachalot* off of the bank. He dodge 'em and they give chase and run him till he lock himself into his own boat. Not being official they couldn't take his name and address, but they catch him proper, and report to me, and sorry I am, young Bill, for your Dad's as decent a man as there is about this place.'

Mr Farland looked at Bill.

Bill spluttered. 'But it was t'other way about. It was Pete and me catch them two pushing of her off.'

'He said he was going to say that,' said George Owdon.

'One minute,' said Mr Farland. 'You see that chimney pot, Owdon. Would you mind just fitting your hand to that mark?'

'Certainly,' said George Owdon. 'It'll be a perfect fit, too, for I made it myself.'

'How was that?' asked Mr Farland.

'Ralph and I knew pretty well all along that it was these boys who had been playing the mischief with the boats, and one evening when there was a bit of a fog, we expected they'd be up to something, so I went to their boat and felt the chimney to see if they were at home, or if we had to go to see what they were doing elsewhere.'

'And you found them not at home?' said Mr Farland.

Dorothea almost groaned. Here was one of their best bits of evidence and it did not seem to be evidence at all. She looked at Dick, but Dick had his back to her. He was looking at something in his hands.

Mr Farland turned to Bill. 'About this affair last night. Did I hear you say you saw these two boys pushing off the *Cachalot*?'

Bill waited a moment. 'Not what you call see 'em,' he said, 'not till they chase me to the *Death and Glory* and we had to ope our door along with their emping buckets down our chimbley.'

'So you admit that you were near the *Cachalot* at the time they say. Why did you run away if you were doing no harm?'

'Didn't want 'em to catch Pete,' said Bill.

George Owdon looked at his friend. Mr Farland looked at George.

'How was it you didn't see Pete if he was pushing off the *Cachalot* with Bill?'

'He wasn't,' said George.

Mr Farland turned to Pete. 'Were you there?' he asked.

'Yes,' said Pete.

'What did you do when Bill ran away?'

'Sit tight,' said Pete. 'That's what they tell me to do.'

'Did you see those two pushing off the *Cachalot*?'

'Not to know 'em,' said Pete. 'But someone push her off. We do know that. We . . .'

Mr Farland turned again to George. 'Dark night wasn't it?' he said. 'You had torches, I suppose.'

It was George's friend, Ralph, who answered. 'With that great flare they made we couldn't help seeing him.'

George, for the first time, stopped smiling and gave his friend an angry look.

'Flare?' said Mr Farland. 'They lit a flare just when they were pushing the boat off?'

'Not exactly,' said George. 'If Pete was there too, that perhaps explains it. We didn't understand it at the time. There was a white flare, and we saw Bill pushing the boat off. He must have seen us at the same moment, for he bolted and we ran him to earth in their old boat.'

'What was the flare like?' asked Mr Farland.

'Like a photographic flashlight,' said George.

'Did you light a flare?' Mr Farland asked Pete.

'I did,' said Bill.

'But how could you light a flare when you were pushing off the *Cachalot*?' asked Mr Farland.

'I tell you I weren't pushing of her off.'

'We saw you,' said George Owdon.

'Why did you light the flare?' asked Mr Farland in the same quiet, even tone that he had used all the time.

'We was taking a photograph,' said Bill. 'To catch whoever it was pushing the *Cachalot* adrift.'

'They hadn't got a camera,' said George.

Mr Farland swung round.

'How do you know?'

Neither George nor his friend answered that question. There was a stir by the window. Dick was fumbling with something in his hands. 'It's done,' he said. 'It'll go black if you keep it in the light. But I can print another.'

'Come on,' said George's friend.

'Not just yet,' said Mr Farland, without lifting his eyes from the photograph. 'Just shut the door, will you, Tedder? This is very interesting.'

Tom, Bill, Joe, Pete, and Dorothea strained their eyes to see what there was on that small piece of shiny paper lying on Mr Farland's blotting pad. George and his friend were also doing their best to see from where they stood.

'A very remarkable likeness,' said Mr Farland. 'What do you think, constable?'

Mr Tedder looked at the photograph.

'Well, I'll be danged!' he said.

Mr Farland thought for some minutes.

'The value of evidence,' he said, 'fluctuates with its context.' The six detectives heard the words but had not the smallest idea what he meant. He went on. 'This photograph will in any court of law (here he looked gravely at George and his friend) serve as proof that the boat that was cast off last night was cast off by George Owdon and ...'

'Strakey,' said Mr Tedder.

'Strakey,' said Mr Farland. 'But that is not all. It gives an entirely new value to a great deal of other evidence that, without it, I should have been justified in dismissing as unconvincing. Owdon, am I right in thinking that you ride a bicycle?'

George nodded.

'And it has Dunlop tyres.' He laid Dick's drawing on the table in front of him. 'This,' he said, 'concerns the Ranworth affair. It also has reference to the theft at Potter Heigham. One of our witnesses is prepared to swear that George Owdon was at Potter Heigham on the night that theft was committed. Again the fact that Owdon and, er, Strakey did in fact cast off the boat last night and informed the constable that they had seen the boat cast off by someone else, who in fact was in the public interest recording by means of photography the truth of that case, suggests with other evidence that might otherwise be unmeaning that Owdon and Strakey were deliberately trying to manufacture evidence to bring innocent persons into disrepute and even into danger of punishment by law. Have you anything to say, Owdon?'

'It was his idea,' said George Owdon.

'I knew nothing about it except what you told me,' said Ralph Strakey.

Mr Farland looked from one to the other of them and back again.

'Apart from the first lot of shackles,' said Mr Farland, 'which you dropped down the chimney of these boys' boat on the day when you suffered, I think, some damage to your trousers . . .' (George stared at the scrap of grey flannel at which Mr Farland's finger was pointing.) 'Apart, I say from the first lot of shackles, and the second lot on which you left some green paint that had covered your hand when you felt their chimney to make sure that your victims were away, there are more than a gross that have not yet been recovered. Where are they?'

'Box in the tool-shed,' said George. 'Look here. I'm not going to stand any more of this. I'm going.'

'I shall not keep you,' said Mr Farland. 'But, before you go, let me tell you that I shall be calling on your uncle when I return from my office tonight. Between now and then I shall expect you to write an exact confession of all that you have done in this damnable, yes, damnable, plot to bring discredit on the innocent. As solicitor to the firm you robbed I shall have to decide whether or not I advise them to prosecute. My decision will depend on the completeness of the document that you will have ready for me before I see your uncle. It had better be signed by your accomplice as well as by yourself. You can go.'

George Owdon and Ralph Strakey left the room without a word. As Joe said afterwards, 'If they'd have had tails they'd have tripped on 'em.'

Dorothea gasped. It was as if she had not breathed for the last five minutes. Tom had turned very red. Dick was again blindly rubbing at his spectacles. Bill and Joe were staring at Mr Farland as if they saw him for the first time. Pete found he had tears in his eyes. He blinked angrily. 'Might have been us,' he said. 'Only we didn't do it.'

Police Constable Tedder cleared his throat.

'I'm sorry I ever thought it,' he said. 'Ought to have knowed different I ought. If anybody say a word against you young chaps again I'll know what to say to 'em. My garden's open to you day or night, for worrams, so you leave they chrysanthemums alone.'

Mr Farland was smiling now. He said, 'They'll forgive you, Tedder. It was a wicked plot and a clever plot, and many people have been taken in by it beside you. It wouldn't be a bad thing if the truth got about, though as a solicitor I suppose I ought not to say so.'

'I'll tell 'em at the post office,' said Mr Tedder. 'I'll tell 'em at the store. I'll be up the village, come opening time. Chaps'll be rare pleased to hear that bit of news.'

'And I'm late for my office,' said Mr Farland. 'Well, I know some others who'll be pleased. I'll be writing to my daughters tonight. And, if I may, J should like to congratulate the detectives . . .' He looked to see that Mr Tedder had already gone. 'I'm ashamed to think that if you had left it to the law things might have gone badly with you.'

The door opened, and Mrs McGinty came in and said, 'There's a gentleman to see you, Sir, urgent . . .' but she had not got more than three words out of her mouth before the owner of the *Cachalot* was in the room beside her.

'They tell me these boys are accused of casting off my boat,' he said. 'I've come to say I lent her to them and they're free to cast her off if they want and not get into trouble about it.'

'They're not in trouble,' said Mr Farland.

'It's all right,' said Dorothea. 'Everything worked beautifully. They fell into the trap, but if the photograph hadn't come out we might have been done at the last minute. Scotland Yard's won in the end. I knew it would.'

Mr Farland picked up the photograph and passed it to his latest visitor. Then he saw the little pile of money on the table.

'Six and eightpence,' he said, 'is a solicitor's fee. You are quite right.' He bowed to Dorothea. 'But, in this case, as I told you, I could hardly be solicitor for the accused. I seem, indeed, to have been acting as judge. And the one thing you mustn't do in a court of law is to try to bribe the judge. You had better put this money away before I see it . . .'

'Your boat's all right,' said Joe to the owner of the *Cachalot*. 'They push her off but they never see she were anchored. She lie there beautiful, just off the bank. We'll put you aboard if you'll come along to the *Death and Glory*.'

'I shall be getting the sack from my partners if I don't leave you,' said Mr Farland.

'Thanks a million times,' said Dorothea.

There was a chorus of thanks from the others.

Dorothea collected the clues and put them back in her suitcase.

'What are you going to do with them?' asked Mr Farland.

'Taking them back to Scotland Yard.'

'I may have to ask you for them again,' said Mr Farland. 'But I think not. I fancy they won't be needed.'

'Wake up, Bill,' said Joe. 'You take t'other end of our chimbley.'

'Gosh, young Pete,' said Bill. 'You give us a fright.'

They all went out together into sunshine that seemed extraordinarily friendly. A light breeze was stirring the river and they could see the water sparkling through the trees.

'Come on,' said Tom. 'Let's all go sailing.'

THE END

WHAT HAPPENED TO THE FISH

Months later, when the worst of the winter was over, the Death and Glories, once more at peace with all the world, were lying at Horning staithe. It was a Saturday morning. They had come aboard after school the night before. Smoke was drifting from their chimney in the crisp air of late February, when Pete, on the look out, saw the *Cachalot* coming up the river, and called the others to come out.

'That fare to be a coffin he got on deck,' said Pete.

'Never,' said Bill.

It certainly looked like it, a long, narrow packing-case, roped down between the rails along the *Cachalot*'s cabin-top.

The *Cachalot* came close alongside.

'Ahoy, you,' called her owner. 'Busy?'

'Not all that,' said Joe.

'Hop aboard. I'll bring you back in the afternoon. I'm just taking your fish to the Roaring Donkey, and you chaps ought to be there.'

'Tell you that were a coffin,' said Pete.

In two minutes they were aboard and the *Cachalot* had swung round and was on her way.

'Lay at Thurne Mouth last night,' said the fisherman of the *Cachalot*, 'but I didn't want to hand over without you.'

'What about Tom?' said Joe.

'Take him, too, if you like,' said the fisherman, 'and that girl and the other boy, the one with the glasses.'

'They ain't here,' said Bill. 'Won't be till Easter. But we can get Tom.'

They were unlucky. The *Cachalot* stopped by Dr Dudgeon's lawn only for them to learn that Tom was out. 'Never mind,' said the fisherman. 'He can bicycle over any time. The fish'll still be there . . . By the way,' he asked, as they started off again, 'what happened to the tiger who was taken in by the bleating of the kid?'

The Death and Glories looked gravely at each other.

'Them two,' said Joe. 'George Owdon and that other. They go away next morning and we never seen 'em since.'

There is no need to describe their run down the Bure and up the Thurne. On that cold February morning, they took turns in steering the *Cachalot* and in going into her cabin to sit by the stove and get the tingle out of their ears and noses.

They passed under the bridges at Potter Heigham, getting friendly waves from a couple of Sonning's workmen as they passed. Bob Curten, once again a full member of the Coot Club, waved from the road-bridge and they waved back. They tied up at the mouth of the dyke leading to the Roaring Donkey.

The long packing-case was taken off the top of the cabin and the great fish, once again, was carried to the little inn.

A small crowd was waiting.

'Here you are,' said the landlord, coming out to meet them. 'I tell a few chaps you was coming. I got that mantelshelf all ready.'

The landlord's wife called the Death and Glories to come into her kitchen and have a cup of hot tea. Perishing they must be, she thought. They went in with her, leaving the landlord and half a dozen eager fishermen busy round the packing-case. Ten minutes later they heard the voice of the owner of the *Cachalot* calling them. They ran out of the kitchen into the inn parlour. At the door they pulled up short.

The room was full of people. Just opposite the door was a

wide brick fireplace and over this on the wide mantelshelf was a glass case, the biggest they had ever seen. In the case was the world's whopper, swimming against a pale blue background among green weeds that looked as if they were alive.

'Geewhizz!' said Joe.

'I've been fishing sixty-seven years,' said an old man with a white beard, 'and I've never caught a fish like that.'

'Talk about heathen worshippers,' said the landlord cheerfully, looking at the admiring crowd. 'No, I don't care who caught it, nor yet what I pay. They'll come from all over England to the Roaring Donkey to take a look at that there old fish.'

'Go on,' said the owner of the *Cachalot*. 'Go on and read what's on the case.'

The three boys went nearer. Men, staring at the fish, made room for them. On the glass front of the case, in gold letters, they read the weight of the pike, the date when it was caught and ... Pete was reading aloud and suddenly choked ... 'Pike ... $30\frac{1}{2}$ pounds ... Caught by ... why, it's us.' There in gold letters were their own three names.

The old fisherman with the white beard turned from looking at the pike to look at the Death and Glories.

'Are you the boys who caught that fish?' he asked.

'We didn't exactly ...' began Joe.

'Poor lads,' said the old man. 'Poor lads ... So young and with nothing left to live for.'

'Let's go and catch another,' said Pete.

*Other Books by Arthur Ransome
published in Puffins*

SWALLOWS AND AMAZONS

SWALLOWDALE

PETER DUCK

COOT CLUB

WINTER HOLIDAY

PIGEON POST

WE DIDN'T MEAN TO GO TO SEA

SECRET WATER

THE BIG SIX

THE PICTS AND THE MARTYRS

GREAT NORTHERN?

NINNY'S BOAT

CLIVE KING

With his black hair and funny name, Ninny has always been treated as an outcast by the blond, superstitious people he lives with. It's typical that no one thinks to tell him of the impending flood, so he is left to fend for himself. Displaying courage and resilience that surprises everyone, Ninny survives the gruelling journey to safety in the Isles of the Ocean and makes some interesting discoveries.

THE HOLLOW LAND

JANE GARDAM

An unforgettable collection of stories set around the Cumbrian fells – a 'hollow land' of abandoned underground mines, sudden tumbling rivers . . . and vivid, larger-than-life people. (Winner of the Whitbread Award).

THE MIDDLE OF THE SANDWICH

TIM KENNEMORE

It's too bad that Helen's mother has to go into hospital just now. It means that Helen has to stay with her aunt and attend the village school for a term instead of going straight from her private London school to the local comprehensive. At first it's all pretty difficult. But then Helen starts to find her feet, and does some much-needed growing up.

THE ISLANDERS

JOHN ROWE TOWNSEND

One spring day two exhausted strangers are washed up in a canoe on the remote and lonely island of Halcyon – with a shattering effect on the small, self-sufficient community that lives there. Because their arrival leads to the heart of a great mystery: what were the origins of the islanders and how did they come by their peculiar customs and laws?

Heard about the Puffin Club?

... it's a way of finding out more about Puffin books and authors, of winning prizes (in competitions), sharing jokes, a secret code, and perhaps seeing your name in print! When you join you get a copy of our magazine, *Puffin Post*, sent to you four times a year, a badge and a membership book.
For details of subscription and an application form, send a stamped addressed envelope to:

The Puffin Club Dept A
Penguin Books Limited
Bath Road
Harmondsworth
Middlesex UB7 0DA

and if you live in Australia, please write to:

The Australian Puffin Club
Penguin Books Australia Limited
P.O. Box 257
Ringwood
Victoria 3134